CN00925163

BABY DID A BAD
BAD THING

BABY DID A BAD BAD THING

GABRIELLE LORD

HODDER

A Hodder Book

First published in Australia and New Zealand in 2002
by Hodder Headline Australia Pty Limited
(A member of the Hodder Headline Group)
Level 22/201 Kent Street, Sydney NSW 2000
Website: www.hha.com.au

This edition published in 2003

National Library of Australia
Cataloguing-in-Publication data

Lord, Gabrielle, 1946- .
  Baby did a bad bad thing

  Reformatted ed.
  ISBN 0 7336 1592 9 (pbk.).

  1. Women private investigators - Fiction. 2. Murder -
Investigation - Fiction. I. Title.

A823.2

Text design and typesetting by Bookhouse, Sydney
Printed in Australia by Griffin Press, Adelaide

To Margie

ONE

It was unusual to see a mug kerb-crawling this early. But as the silver Ford neared the gutter, the few huddled street workers, risking a drenching in the driving rain, ventured out from under the shelter of the Ferrari building. Business was always slow at the beginning of the week and, lately, it hadn't improved that much even on Friday and Saturday nights. Although more lucrative than working in a brothel, where the workers split the fee with the house, street work was the hardest and most dangerous. Only the desperate were out now in this weather. The tiny stilettoed ballerina with an artificial blue rose in one hand tottered towards the kerb.

Behind the dark windscreen, the driver studied her. It had been dark since just after five although the winter made the hour seem later and the hairs on the back of his hand glinted in the dash light as he glanced at his watch. He turned up the volume of his sound system. The singer wailed, bouncing the syncopated words against the driving down-beat, then his voice fell to a whisper: 'Baby did a bad bad thing' he sang. 'Baby did a bad bad thing.' The driver liked the look of the little ballerina very much. But something put him off. Maybe she was too old. He wanted a young one. The young ones reminded him of someone.

A few turns around the circuit and he noted a thin, pretty girl smoking nervously, her other arm surreptitiously clutching a small leather bag over her shoulder. He slowed the car to get a better look. She didn't look too out of it. Maybe she was new to the game. She was finely made, her short yellow skirt revealing legs that seemed too slender to carry the weight of the long black boots at the end of them. A white scooped top showed her breasts and he imagined he could see her shivering. He knew the girls didn't carry money with them for obvious reasons and robbery wasn't normally his thing. But she might have some sort of concealed weapon, mace, for example. The newspapers had run a piece last weekend after the second attack and he'd smiled when he read it. But there was no doubt the girls were warier this week. He'd cruised the circuit the last couple of nights just watching what was available and he'd seen how the girls in the back streets seemed to be watching out for each other. That's why the brunette appealed to him. She was the right type and she was alone. She kept glancing back towards the terrace house behind her, and that concerned him. Perhaps she was just keeping an eye out for a resident who might yell at her to move away. But there was always the possibility that her minder was in there somewhere, keeping an eye on her business, jotting down the time and the rego numbers of her customers. The driver had made his numberplate appear ambiguous by deliberately bending the black frame around it. An alert bystander could probably make it out. But they'd need good eyesight and good weather.

This girl was definitely just what he was looking for. Neat, slight build, an oval face, only a little make-up as far as he could see. The rage built steadily through his body. The bitch. She will come to see, he thought, that she's brought this on herself, that *she* is the cause of it. I am simply an agent. And it's payback time.

There was no need to rush. He had plenty of time. No one knew where he was and he loved the feeling of power that anonymity gave him. He was almost at the point of leaning over towards the passenger window to get her attention when, at the last moment, something made him pull back. He took his foot off the brakes and increased his speed, turning the corner and almost running down a six foot tranny from the group who usually worked the other side of the road later in the night. He braked suddenly, cursing with rage.

'Stupid pervert! Watch where you're fucking going!'

The tall figure froze in the headlights, leather fringes and spangles shivering, the whites of her eyes under the black make-up like a spooked horse.

'Fuck you!' she screamed. 'You nearly killed me!' A white cowgirl boot kicked his duco hard. 'You could've killed me!'

Despite his anger, the driver laughed. 'Not *you*! No way! Frigging freak!'

He accelerated away, leaning on the horn as she scrambled to the footpath. He wanted a real woman, not some man who wanted to be a woman. He drove the length of the street and noticed three girls spread some distance apart, waiting, all of them engaging his glance, eyes asking 'are you looking for me?'.

The singer was still sobbing through the speakers as the driver slowed the car and the group of girls turned to look at him. One in particular interested him, very young, a bit stoned but not totally out of it, dark hair damp from the rain and twisted up in a looped plait. She was wearing a casual shirt and sneakers. She looked very fresh and he liked that. She kept her eyes engaged with him, hurrying over.

He rolled down his window.

'Want a girl?' she asked, heavy-lidded eyes blinking slowly.

'How much?'

Suddenly, an exotic-looking Polynesian girl, large breasts in a tightly laced bodice, materialised beside the young girl he fancied.

'Not you,' he said, and pointed at the slight young girl beside her. 'You,' he repeated. 'How much?' He had to lean right across the front seat because they stood well back from his car. Wary.

'French and sex, eighty,' said the young girl. 'Straight sex, seventy. Plus twelve dollars for the room.'

'I'm not going to one of your filthy brothels.'

'Use one of the safe houses,' said the Polynesian, ignoring the driver, talking to her companion. He could see the indecision on the young girl's face as she looked up at her friend, then down at him. He flung the passenger door open and patted the front seat in what he hoped was a friendly manner.

'Come on,' he said. 'I just want some fast French.' He patted his wallet. 'I'll give you the eighty anyway. I know a good place to park. You'll be back here in ten minutes. Max.'

The girl stepped closer. The Polynesian grabbed her companion. 'Robyn,' she whispered, 'don't get in the car. It's not worth it.'

Robyn looked from her friend to the mug. He looked all right to her. She checked her instincts, but they were asleep under the narcotic. Just another mug, she thought. Like they all are. The rain squall suddenly intensified in slanting sheets.

'Come on,' he said, 'I won't bite.' As soon as he'd said it, he wished he hadn't. It might make her think of recent events in her line of business. But Robyn didn't seem to make any connection. 'Look, Robyn,' he said, pretending concern, 'you're getting drenched. Hop in.' He pulled out his wallet and took out two fifties, shoving them towards the window. 'Look,' he said, 'I'll give you a hundred. Just for some head.'

'Don't, Rob,' he heard the Polynesian girl say. 'He's too keen. This doesn't feel good.'

Robyn shivered and water dripped off her hair down her face.

'But no brothel,' he was saying. 'I've got a thing about going to brothels.'

'What thing?' asked the Polynesian.

'They've all got video cameras,' he said. 'I don't like the idea of that.'

The Polynesian looked at him in disbelief. 'You don't know what you're talking about.'

Robyn blinked and smiled. He was hooked she reckoned and she played her line. 'Another fifty for car work,' she said. 'There've been girls attacked in cars the last few weeks.'

'Don't!' the dark girl begged, but Robyn was already stepping into the car, grateful for the relative shelter. 'I'm watching you, pal,' said the Polynesian. 'You ring me, Rob, the minute you're finished.'

'Don't worry, darling,' said the driver to her, 'I'll make sure she does.' His teeth gleamed as he moved his hairy forearm to pat his companion's bare knee. 'I'll look after her,' he said. 'Look,' he added, 'I'll meet you after this and you can join us in a double. We'll go to the house. Okay?'

The Polynesian girl studied him. He smiled again.

'I'll pay double for a double.'

'What did you do?' asked Robyn. 'Rob a bank?'

'You ring me, Rob.' The Polynesian girl frowned as the driver pulled away from the kerb. He checked the rear-vision mirror. She continued to stare after them until he made the turn. His companion was unsteadily fishing tissues out of her bag; she was more stoned than he'd realised. Then she looked around.

'Where do you think you're going?' she asked.

'Hey, Rob,' he said, smiling and patting her knee. 'Just down here,' he said. 'Just a little way along here.'

'No,' she said. She couldn't let him take her to his turf. It gave him too much power. 'You go where I tell you,' she said. 'Take a right up this one-way.'

'Sure.' He smiled, driving straight past the street she'd indicated and turning left.

'I said *right*!'

'It's just down here,' He flashed his teeth at her, his tone reasoning and placatory. But he turned into a dark laneway where 'no standing' signs and piles of compressed cardboard cartons filled the narrow footpath of the desolate corridor. 'We can park just up here,' he said.

'I don't like this,' she said. 'Get back onto the main drag.'

The lights and life of Oxford Street were only a little distance away, Robyn reasoned. No real harm could come to her. She was simply pissed off at being disregarded. As usual, she thought.

He'd slowed the car and it was almost completely dark now because the lights over the deserted buildings were not on. The car stopped. Rain slanted past the beam of the headlights until he switched them off. Now the lane was suddenly black.

Robyn hesitated. If he tried anything on, she thought, she could bolt for it and run the short distance up the hill. She could even hear raised voices and bursts of laughter from the pub, it was so close.

'Give me the money now,' she said, fear breaking through the drug haze.

He was hardly listening. An expensive headjob in this back lane was not on his agenda. He felt the girl tense up beside him so he fiddled with his belt as if he were about to undo it. 'You better make that phone call,' he said sweetly, 'or your friend will be worried.'

'Pay me now,' she said. 'Or I'm out of here fast.'

He shrugged. 'Sure,' he said. She didn't want to let him see that she was frightened so she felt around for the door handle with her left hand under cover of her bag. Although Robyn failed to notice the spanner just next to his right hand in the door pocket, some atavistic sense warned her. *This feels all wrong. Get out and run*, it said. She could feel panic travel up to her heart as her groping fingers found the door handle and it fell off in her hand.

'Oh, by the way,' he said, 'I should have mentioned earlier'—his big hand closed around the heavy shifting spanner—'that handle on your door keeps falling off.' She noticed his toothy smile in the dim interior as he started to sing. Too late she recalled the ugly mugs' listing: '*Drives a car, passenger door handle disengaged. Middle-aged, dark complexion, well presented. Sings just before the attack and sometimes during it.*'

'Been meaning to fix it for ages,' he grunted as he raised his arm.

Neither did she have time to notice that his jacket was slashed into ribbons, swinging like vertical blinds as his arm came down. Robyn didn't even have time to scream.

TWO

Gemma stayed up late watching television, lying the full length of the pale blue Italian leather sofa she'd bought when she redecorated. Two fat club-style armchairs completed the suite, a couple of manila folders on one, and on the other, curled up like a plump striped cushion, her cat, Taxi. He raised his head and winked at her.

'Come over here, you big fat thing,' she commanded. Taxi didn't even bother opening his eyes so Gemma grabbed him, collapsing back onto the sofa, the warm heavy cat draped across her stomach like a poultice.

The rain was heavier now, scudding and lashing across the timber deck outside the sliding doors beyond the dining table, the wind flailing it across the glass. The sense that all that separated her cosy nest from the seething, opaque darkness outside was a thin layer of fragile glass made her feel very vulnerable. In the last few months, Gemma had been aware of a heaviness in her, a feeling of oppression. When first aware of it, she'd put it down to the blues of autumn and now the cold of winter. Now, she wasn't sure what it was about and wrapped a friendly old grey cardigan, one of Steve's, more closely around her. She shoved Taxi aside, and hurried over to pull the curtains across, so that the blankness of the glass and the driving rain were hidden by brilliant blue, yellow, white and extremely expensive fabric. She shivered, but it was only a reflex. Nothing and no one could get in here, she thought, considering her sophisticated security system. Unless they knew the code, they'd have to dig a tunnel to get in.

But her sanctuary *had* been breached, at the speed of light, shooting through the optic fibre. And although words on a screen were nowhere near as menacing as a physical presence, each morning now for several days, she'd dreaded checking her email. She flopped back onto the sofa wishing the cyber-stalker to hell. And wishing she'd never entered a chat room. Wasting time pretending to be someone she was not because she was bored one night. Silly, silly girl, she scolded herself. She'd talked to her friend, Detective Sergeant Angie McDonald, about it.

'He'll get bored after a while,' Angie had told her. 'And there's not much we can do. He's really only a digital address. I'll talk to some of the whizz kids in Technical Services and see if they can come up with something.' She'd shrugged. 'Sorry, Gems.'

But the cyberstalker hadn't got bored; instead, he'd upped the ante considerably.

Outside, the wind howled over the scrubby coastal vegetation and, somewhere, distant lightning jerked the picture on the television screen. The late news repeated the item that had been headlines earlier. Idly watching footage of a fire, Gemma suddenly sat up, her attention captured when she heard the name.

'Philanthropist Benjamin Glass,' said the reader, 'whose house was completely destroyed in the blaze, has not been seen since the fire. Police suspect arson.'

Benjamin Glass, billionaire philanthropist, was hardly the sort of person who'd be setting fire to his property for the insurance money, Gemma thought. The reporter went on to say that Mr Glass's good works were legendary. 'The man is practically a saint,' said a friend in a three-second grab.

The news finished, she switched off the television and picked up the manila folders on the armchair. These contained information on two new cases for Mercator Security and Business Advisers, Gemma's company. Although mainly dealing with insurance fraud, the company also had a little sideline developed by Gemma in response to a need where, for a very reasonable price, suspicious spouses or lovers could check up on their partners. Or busy career women could check out a new man they were dating. For less than two hundred dollars, Gemma could get back to a client with basic information about the person of interest, that he was in fact who he said he was, that he lived and worked at the places he said, and that he was single and without a major criminal record. Or not as the case might be. No need even for a potentially embarrassing personal meeting, just credit details over the phone. All she needed was a name and a birthday. All this information was quite freely available, but the legal searches might take an inexperienced person the best part of a week; Gemma could ring back in twenty-four hours.

Already entered onto her PC files, the new folders would soon house any photographs, surveillance reports or other physical evidence that might be gathered. She read the clients' names again. One was a woman, Minkie Montreau—Minkie—the funny name was vaguely familiar. Gemma pulled a face at the nickname, conjuring a spoilt brat-woman with a fur and a simper. The other was a Peter Greengate. She picked up Peter Greengate's folder, opened it and shut it again. She recalled his voice on the phone. He'd sounded in a bad way, she thought. Quiet and desperate. She knew nothing about Minkie Montreau because Spinner had taken the call and made the initial entry. Spinner, her ace operative, was one of a staff of four, counting herself. From time to time Gemma still liked to get out on the road herself. She saw that Spinner had written a note under the woman's name—'*fatal fire*' followed by a question mark. She frowned, wondering what that meant. And suddenly remembered Minkie Montreau. Fifteen years ago that name had been a well-known label and Minkie Montreau was *the* designer of expensive underwear and negligees in brilliant floral satins. Gemma remembered a magazine interview with the erstwhile university medallist who'd turned her engineering brilliance to the design of uplift bras and almost magical figure-trimming torsolettes for the less-than-perfect figure, which meant about ninety-five per cent of the market. But then she'd dropped out of sight. Now, Gemma thought, she's probably just another hard-working Sydney businesswoman. Like me.

The big injection of money which had come to her from her father's life insurance she'd put into state-of-the-art software, not to mention a complete refurbishment of her apartment, office and wardrobe, and it was beginning to pay off. Gemma's security business, started seven years ago after she'd left the police service, was growing all the time and she had her fingers crossed, knowing she was one of only two left on the shortlist to pick up a huge contract with the Department of Social Security which would get her out of debt and guarantee her future expansion. A girlfriend, ex-detective Jenny Porter, now a risk analyst with Social Security, had as good as promised Gemma as much work as she could handle. 'We're outsourcing many of our departments,' Jenny had told her, 'including fraud investigations. We've narrowed the list down to you or Solidere Security.

Forget I told you any of this.' Gemma promised
and then did some discreet investigating herself.
She checked them out and the word so far was that
Solidere was a well run business with good professional standards and a lot of money behind it.
Gemma was confident, however, that she'd have
the edge, given that she'd been in the business
longer than her rival and because of her connection with Jenny. When I get that contract with
Social Security, she thought dreamily, I can expand
even further and Mike or Spinner can take over
and manage it for me. Then I can please myself.
Her thoughts turned to lazy *caffé latte* mornings at
Tamarama and late nights with Steve, dancing in
a dive, not having to worry about being up at
6 a.m., having to fill in for an operative who'd suddenly rung in sick. Thanks, Dad, she said despite
herself, for the money—now almost all gone—that
allowed me to build this business up. And all the
time she was thinking of her father, she was trying
not to think of the way she'd nearly died on
another wet, windy night like this. Shifting her
thoughts away from this, she made a mental note
to ring Jenny in the next few days to see how things
were shaping up and jumped when her mobile
rang.

'Yes?'

'Gemma? I thought you'd be in bed.'

Her heart lifted. 'Stevie. Where are you?' Behind
him, she could hear sounds consistent with a nightclub, low voices and music playing.

'Not far away,' he said. 'Is it too late for a visitor?' Taxi was looking over at her with narrowed green eyes, as if he knew that his rival for bed rights was on the other end of the line. Gemma smiled.

'Depends on who the visitor is,' she teased. 'I need more information. Where've you been?'

'You know that matter we talked about a few weeks ago?'

Gemma remembered dropping in on Steve unexpectedly one afternoon to find him studying black-and-white police photos. He'd whisked them into an envelope immediately when she walked in and quickly pushed it aside.

'You'll have to do better than that,' she said now.

'What if I said a randy undercover cop found himself in your area with a few hours to spare and a story to tell?'

'I'd say he might get lucky.' Gemma felt her body surge with excitement. 'You drive carefully in this weather,' she added, as the storm increased outside her haven.

'You bet,' he said. 'I'm on my way.'

Gemma put the phone down, recalling how she'd sneaked a look at the photographs in the envelope when Steve was in the shower. The faces were familiar to her: stolid Mrs Lorraine Litchfield and her glamorous daughter at the funeral of their late husband and father, Sydney crime boss Terry Litchfield, gunned down some time ago outside his home—a daring drive-by shooting—and left to die in the gutter.

Now she danced Taxi round the room, holding one of his front legs stiffly up in the air, like a dancing partner, noticing as she did the dryness of the skin on her fingers and terracotta clay still under her nails. Despite scrubbing and lashings of hand cream, her skin felt tight and parched. She'd spent most of the afternoon down at Phoenix Bay, at the boatshed she was renting, working on her sculpture. The boatshed, on the southern side of the hidden beach south of Tamarama, was a magical place to work. When a full moon pulled the water right up to the stone seawall, Gemma could hear the water lapping under her floorboards. She thought with pleasure of the stylised lion she'd been modelling, copying from the picture of an archaic statue in a book on the isles of Greece. It had required a large amount of clay and a lot of work with tools and hands. Now the almost completed lion leaned out from the bench that ran down the northern wall of the boatshed, slowly drying. She was very proud of the way she'd captured the vigour and thrust of the original so that it faithfully reflected the proud tension of the beast, the way it pressed forward into some timeless place, yearning into eternity. She threw Taxi back down on his chair where he stood, tail lashing, looking away from her while she danced on into the bathroom and showered. When she came out, he was sitting neatly on the client folders in his snail position, tail wrapped tightly around himself, paws under-tucked, eyes almost closed, probably planning revenge, she thought. Gemma put on a cream silk negligee and its matching robe, puffed her new Annick Goutal perfume near her neck, ran a touch of pencil round her eyes, fluffed up her hair and was in the kitchen putting on coffee when she heard a car pull up outside. The powerful motor cut out and in a moment she heard Steve's gentle tap at the door. It was a measure of Gemma's trust that she had given Steve a key to the strong grille door at the front of her apartment. During working hours, she let people in and out.

Gemma opened the door and there he was, wearing the black Armani birthday shirt she'd given him, and a gold Scorpio zodiac chain that she hadn't. With the light shining on the raindrops on his shirt and hair he was like a dark angel and he looked so good that she wanted to laugh out loud. Instead, she stepped back, as much to take him all in as to let him walk by her into the hallway. She could see the tension and strain in his tanned face, the tired sadness in his eyes, the way the furrows running from nose to mouth had deepened. Oh Stevie, she thought to herself, you work too hard and too long. And you work in bad, bad worlds. So do you, whispered a little voice. So do you. She hugged him.

'You bloody gold-chained lair,' she whispered, drawing back for him to kiss her and they stayed there, swaying together until she gently disentangled herself.

'I've got fresh coffee on,' she said eventually.

'Anything stronger?'

'Sure.' She went to the sideboard where the

crystal decanters stood with their silver labels on chains around their necks.

'I came via the boatshed,' said Steve, 'and shone my torch through the window.'

Gemma poured Scotch into a glass, smiling to herself.

'I couldn't see much of him under his drapes. But he's got great front feet,' said Steve. 'You could put him out there in the garden.'

Gemma nodded, pleased that Steve had bothered to look in on the lion. Then she remembered that Steve noticed everything, it was what made him so effective.

'He's not actually finished yet,' she said. 'And I'm going to do another one so I'll have a pair.'

Gemma passed Steve's drink to him. He tossed it down and threw himself on one of the armchairs. Taxi had vanished. She was dying to ask about the zodiac charm and could barely wait till he put his glass out for another drink. She fetched some ice from the fridge, went back to the decanter and turned around, keeping her voice as casual as she could.

'Where did you get that Scorpio charm?'

Steve squinted down at it, pulling a face. 'A woman gave it to me.' He swung it into his hand and jiggled it up and down. 'It's what she thinks is appropriate for a boyfriend.'

Gemma felt her heart give a throb of jealousy as she reached out and touched it. At the same time, she wanted to gather more intelligence about Steve's undercover job.

'It looks expensive,' she said. But then, money would be no object to Terry Litchfield's widow, Gemma knew.

Steve shrugged. 'I suppose it is,' he said. 'I don't really take much notice of it, except when it hits me sometimes at the gym.' He stood up. 'That email you've been getting—I want to see it.'

Gemma shook her head, wishing she'd never mentioned it to him. 'No, you don't,' she said. 'It's horrible.'

Steve came closer. 'How did you get involved in something like that?'

His question caused her body to tighten defensively. She didn't want to talk about it, not now, and certainly not with Steve. She picked up her empty cup and his glass and walked out to the kitchen. 'I'll tell you tomorrow,' she said. 'It's too late now. Do you want another drink?'

He nodded and she made him another one, then brought her coffee mug out and curled up on the floor, leaning against his legs. He smoothed her hair and sipped his drink.

'How's it all going?' she finally asked, knowing that he wouldn't say much.

'I think it's going to be okay,' he said. 'I got through the first meeting with the person we're targeting.'

'Stevie, I hope you're being really careful,' she said, looking up at him, suspecting already whom he meant. Steve squeezed her shoulder. Still looking at him, she put her hand over his. 'Is that squeeze supposed to be reassuring?' she asked.

'It is,' he said.

'You might have to do better than that,' she said. 'I know you can't say much but I happen to know already that you're working with Terry Litchfield's widow—'

'How do you know that?' Steve asked too quickly, and she realised she'd caught him off-guard.

She looked at him more closely. 'You're rattled,' she teased. 'Have I touched on a sensitive issue?' He was looking hard at her, obviously not pleased that she knew so much. 'Steve,' she said, 'you must have known I'd guess. I'm an investigator too, remember.'

He grunted noncommittally.

Gemma laughed at his discomfort. 'Oh come on,' she said. 'What's the worry? I'm discreet. And I can't imagine you'd be doing anything you shouldn't with that woman.' She paused. 'Unless the widow's a cradle-snatcher or you're looking for a mother figure.'

Steve frowned, taking his hand away from her shoulder. 'What do you mean?'

'Oh Steve.' She was irritated by his unusual denseness. Normally, Steve was right there with her. 'Lorraine Litchfield must be old enough to be your mother! And *you're* forty-five.'

Steve said nothing, leaving an odd silence. 'You know I can't say much, Gems,' he said, after drinking more of his Scotch.

'But *I* can,' she said, taking his hand back again. 'I can put two and two together.'

'Yes, but does it add up to four?' He put his glass down. 'Hey'—he took her hands in his—'come to bed.'

She loved Steve's solid body, strong from his daily work, and the way he fitted into and around her. 'Listen, you,' she said as they snuggled together, 'I'm not kissing you with that bloody charm around your neck.' She took it off, flinging it and the other woman with it over the edge of the bed. She melted into his kisses, aware that he smelled different somehow. He was wearing a sultry aftershave she didn't recognise and when she closed her eyes, she could have been lying with a stranger. It was as if the miasmas of the dens and dives he'd been in over the last few months had seeped into his skin.

Later, she snuggled up to his back and stroked his arm, wondering where he'd spent last night. On the lounge or in the spare bedroom of another woman's house?

'What is it?' he asked, feeling the silence.

'I was wondering,' she said, not wanting to own up to where her thoughts really were, and using the acronym for deep undercover work, 'why you wanted to be a DUC. It's not everybody's cup of tea.'

Steve settled himself on his back and she resettled her head on his chest. 'I suppose it's because I'm an action man,' he said. 'I was never much of a scholar. I knew I'd be hopeless inside, stuck at a desk all day, always wanting to be outside doing something.'

'You could have been a gardener,' she joked.

He gave her a soft slap. 'I need to keep on the go,' he said. This sort of life suits me.'

'But the danger—' she started to say.

'Greatly overrated,' he said, 'by guys who want to look like heroes. And television drama. Like most investigative work, it's slow and boring. Mixing with dickheads all day.' He laughed. 'Just like working at the Police Centre.'

'No, but—' Gemma started to argue.

'Do the job properly,' Steve interrupted, 'follow procedures, keep alert and it's okay. Safer than going to work in the traffic every day.' He stroked her hair. 'What about you?' he asked. 'What did you want to be when you were growing up?'

Gemma considered. 'I wanted to be safe,' she said, remembering a household filled with menace. 'And I wanted to have an ordinary mother and father like I thought other people had.'

'No mothers or fathers are ever ordinary,' said Steve, and she kissed his chest, loving how he just knew things.

'I didn't want any of the usual things that my girlfriends wanted. I wasn't attracted to further study. And I certainly didn't want to ever have children.'

'That's not what I meant,' he said. 'I'm talking career. Why you ended up in the game you're in. You know what I mean. First the cops, now this. Stalking people.'

She pounced and pulled his pillow out from under his head. 'I'll stalk you!' she said, beating him with it. She resettled and considered. 'Law and order,' she said. 'The order part of it appealed to me. After a crazy childhood, the thought of order is quite appealing.'

'You never talk about what you liked doing when you were a kid,' he said.

Gemma pulled the covers up over them; it was cold in here, she thought. 'Not much to tell,' she said. 'Aunt Merle, who practically brought us up, had a couple of art books. I used to love looking through those with Kit. She used to make up stories about the people in the paintings and sculptures. I wanted to make things too—people, animals. I liked the idea of making something beautiful out of a lump of clay or stone.'

'I used to make things out of tins,' said Steve, 'and then pot them with my air rifle.'

Gemma laughed and snuggled closer. 'You're such a *bloke*, Steve.'

'Yes,' he said, grabbing her, 'and you wouldn't have it any other way.'

'I used to make things with plasticine,' said Gemma. 'I felt I could somehow make something mine, really own it—if I could get its essence down in something solid.'

'You've ended up doing that,' Steve pointed out. 'Getting the essence of people. On video, in your reports. Some of their essence, anyway.'

They lay together in silence a while, and Gemma wondered if making copies of another artist's work would ever really satisfy her.

The scent of the foreign aftershave brought her

attention to the present and she leaned up on an elbow and looked down at him. 'What's Lorraine Litchfield like?' she asked.

Steve turned towards her, gathering her in.

'She's tough,' he said. 'But you'd have to be, to be married to a crim like Terry Litchfield. If she'd had a few decent breaks, she might have really made something of herself.'

Gemma settled down to sleep, aware that Steve had turned and was now lying on his back where she could sense his eyes open in the darkness. She rolled back to him.

'What is it?' she asked.

'I can't sleep,' he said. 'You know what it's like.' Gemma did know. The life of an undercover operative was adrenaline-charged day and night, the agent always being fearful of making the one tiny slip that would give him away. The silence of late night was filled with the crashing of the sea on the rocks below her place. 'Your target,' she said. 'It's George Fayed, isn't it?'

It hadn't taken Gemma long to work out that Steve must have been targeting the new 'king' of Kings Cross. Why else would he be working with Lorraine Litchfield, widow of the deposed and murdered ex-king? The personal introduction of Steve, Gemma knew, coming via Lorraine Litchfield to this criminal, would help Steve make contact with George Fayed, and then, if all went well, effect penetration of the drug lord's empire.

'Ssshh,' he said, kissing her. 'Go to sleep.'

'He'd be toey as hell,' she said. 'And paranoid

about security. Angie told me he's got his own counter-surveillance team.'

She thought about the bodies of two dealers, rumoured to have tried to brass Fayed, who'd been found in abandoned scrubland recently, dead from heroin overdoses. She took his hands and held them tightly. 'I wish you weren't doing this job,' she said. 'Why didn't they get one of the young cowboys to do it?'

'Listen here, woman. I know how to handle myself,' he said. 'I don't need you to be worrying about me.'

She considered further. 'If I knew where you were going to be each day,' she said, 'I could get Spinner or Mike to hang around where you are. That way, you've always got some sort of back-up if something goes wrong.'

'Gems, it's a crazy idea. And it wouldn't work. I'm all over the place. I have to move fast sometimes and the people I'm dealing with don't give much warning of a meeting. And I certainly don't want you hanging around. You know how that could compromise things for me.'

'Well,' she said a moment later, 'maybe I could keep an eye on Fayed for you. Keep you posted.'

Steve squeezed her hands gently. 'Gemma, get real. Physical surveillance is useless with someone like him anyway.' He kissed her again. 'After those Royal Commission tapes men like Fayed are paranoid.' This was the first time he'd mentioned Fayed's name, Gemma noted. He put one of her hands to his lips and kissed it. 'Now go to sleep,' he said. 'Stop asking questions.'

'I've got a bad feeling about this job,' she said. 'Something's been hanging over me for the last few weeks. A premonition or something . . .'

'You're sounding like a copper's wife,' he said. 'Don't.'

'And I get the feeling,' she said, 'that you don't want me anywhere near you.'

'Too right I don't,' he said. 'You know my rule.'

'Yes, I do. The less I know, the safer you are,' she quoted like a good girl.

'And the safer *you* are,' he said, leaning up on his elbow, looking down at her sternly.

•

Steve's side of the bed was empty when she woke an hour later than usual. She lay there, sure she'd been woken by someone who had just that second left the room.

'Steve?' she called. There was no answer. She was alone in the apartment. An awful sense of dread immobilised her; the smoky aftershock of a nightmare still fogged her mind. She pulled the blankets tighter around her naked body, remembering the tail end of the dream. A huge meteorite, its jewel-like facets gleaming in the anti-light of deep space, was rushing at her. Then she was standing in some windy place, an avenue of lions stretching behind her, looking to the heavens through the immensity of light years of distance, sensing the meteorite's presence as it raced through time and space in her direction. Ahead lay a dark lake in which the moon swam. She recalled the lions from the dream, their bleached features blunted by aeons of erosion.

Finally, she got up and as she made coffee, she pulled out her book on the isles of Greece and flicked through it until she found the subject of her dream, Delos and the Avenue of Lions, beside the Sacred Lake. A series of lions like the one sitting on the bench in the boatshed, stretched away into the distance. I must have seen this picture and forgotten it, she thought to herself. She recalled another lake somewhere, renowned for the huge meteor that had plunged into it. Feeling she'd explained the dream to herself, she closed the book.

When she was making the bed, she trod on something. Bending down, she saw the heavy gold zodiac charm on the floor. In the bright light of day, the curled stylised scorpion merely looked gaudy. Lions and a scorpion, she thought, all before breakfast. She picked it up and put it away in a drawer. I'd better let Steve know it's here, she thought. His 'girlfriend' will be cranky that he's lost her gift to him. And, despite herself, she couldn't help smiling in satisfaction.

She had breakfast inside because, although the rain had stopped, the wind had swung into a gusty south-easter, churning the ocean into white tips. Out to sea, she could see several rain showers and a long container ship sliding along the murky horizon. She put the gas heater on, loving to see the red-gold filigree it formed on its ceramic grid, and munched on Kit's cumquat marmalade with her toast and coffee. She looked around her living area: a large, open space with lounge, dining table and chairs, the cedar sideboard—the only piece of furniture from her childhood home—polished floorboards partly covered in a Persian rug and, opening out from that, the long timber deck where she often sat in good weather with her laptop under a striped beach umbrella, overlooking the sea. Her bedroom, once the formal dining room of the original house, from the days when people had family dinners, was tucked away with the bathroom, behind another door to the right of the long blue lounge. She had everything necessary for contentment, she told herself in an effort to dislodge the last of the nightmare's influence, but she jumped as Spinner's voice crackled on the two-way down the hall, past the door that signalled her private domain.

She took the last of her toast into her office.

'Tracker Three,' Spinner's voice filled her office. 'Tracker Three,' he repeated. 'Copy please, Base.' From time to time Gemma still liked to get out on the road herself. She unhoused the radio. 'Good morning, Spinner. What's happening?'

'The target is still with his girlfriend,' said Spinner. 'I've been sitting off her place now for two hours. He arrived here a couple of hours ago, she came out to greet him, he pulled her into the car and they couldn't wait. I can wrap this one up. You should see what I got on video!'

Gemma thought of the target's wife who would also receive a copy of the action tomorrow.

'I won't bother taking it to her workplace today,' said Spinner. 'I'll drop in on the Rock Breaker instead and see what's cooking there. Then maybe the Big Limp this arvo.'

These were insurance company jobs. Both the Rock Breaker and the Big Limp were collecting compo payments because, according to their medical reports, they couldn't get out of bed without help. Over the last two days, Spinner had obtained excellent footage of the Rock Breaker building an elaborate fishpond and waterfall in his backyard. Spinner had also followed him up to the Blue Mountains—despite the fact that the Rock Breaker maintained that driving a car was impossible—where he'd obtained clear evidence on video of the Rock Breaker pilfering large slabs of bush rock as well. National Parks and Wildlife might have something to say about that, Gemma thought. They had him cold, lifting and arranging rocks that must have weighed nearly as much as he did. Spinner also by now had good film of the Big Limp doing endless laps of his swimming pool and bench presses in his timber and glass living room. But when anyone knocked, the Big Limp could only hobble painfully to open the door, limping and lurching as if one leg was inches shorter than the other. Insurance work was the bread and butter of her business.

'Spinner, you're a legend,' she said.

'I know,' was his modest reply. 'Are you coming

to Mike's party tonight?' he asked. 'I'd like to introduce Rose to you.' Spinner had been cautiously dating a woman whose Greek Orthodox practice was a challenge to his fundamentalist position. For Spinner, coffee with full cream milk was decadent.

'I doubt it,' she said. 'I want an early night tonight. I'll be late up tomorrow.' There was a silence and Gemma could feel Spinner's disapproval over the ether.

'Look, Boss,' he said, his voice revealing concern. 'It's not my business, but you should tell Steve about that job you're doing for Shelly. He'd hit the roof if he knew. You can't have a relationship that's based in dishonesty.' Spinner had a righteous edge to him, honed, Gemma felt sure, by his adherence to the charismatic church he attended far too often in her estimation. She wished now she hadn't told him about her friend Shelly's approach to her on behalf of the street girls to investigate the recent spate of violent attacks.

'It's not dishonesty,' she said, feeling defensive. 'It's discretion. I don't have to tell him everything I do. He doesn't tell me everything.'

'No,' Spinner agreed. 'But what you're planning tomorrow night is dangerous, ma'am.' Spinner only called her 'ma'am' when he was pissed off with her.

'I've spent years working with dangerous,' she said. 'It's my job.'

'*Was* your job. You turned in your badge and your gun years ago. What if he attacks you?'

'We want him to do that,' she said. 'Then we've got him. We'll match him to the physical evidence—'

'What physical evidence?'

'The Analytical Laboratory's got a nice little amp of seminal protein and a DNA profile of this particular brute. All they need is something to match it against and snap! We take another nasty piece of work off the streets for a while.'

'And just who's this "we"?' said Spinner in a lofty tone. '*I'm* not licensed to take on an armed man and neither are you.' Spinner was barely five feet tall. 'You could be dead before I get to you. I could lose you in traffic. Anything could go wrong. That's why you really shouldn't do this. What if you get in the car and he pulls a knife?'

'He's a basher, not a slicer,' she said, trying to laugh over the chill she felt. 'He doesn't use a knife.'

'*Yet*,' said Spinner. 'But like you say, it's not my business.'

Gemma was trying not to remember a time on the street years back when a man struck out at her with a knife and how terrifying it was despite her uniform and handy service pistol.

'Once you get in a car with a stranger,' Spinner was saying 'you've lost control of the situation. I don't have to tell you that. It's crazy.'

'I'll have Mike,' she said.

'What's he supposed to do? Wave goodbye? Once you get into that vehicle you could have the

SAS surrounding the area and *still* get into trouble.'

'Speaking of Mike,' she asked, wanting to change the subject 'What do you think of him?'

'I'll call you,' he said, signing off, not wanting to say too much over the radio. Gemma rehoused her receiver.

Mike Moody, the new operative she'd hired not long ago, until recently an agent with the Australian Federal Police and broodily good-looking, seemed to be shaping up well. His reports, although never a match for Spinner's clear and succinct contemporaneous notes, were intelligent and well observed. Mike had worked on computer crime and was up to date with the latest in electronic surveillance and counter-surveillance. As a rule, Gemma was very wary about employing expolice, knowing from her own experience of eleven years in the job how slack they could be, golfing instead of sitting in hot cars all day, watching some small-time fraudster's house. But Mike had been personally recommended. Just like the crims, Gemma thought with a smile. Everyone wants personal introductions these days. It's the only way in anywhere—and that goes for any milieu, she knew. Her phone rang.

'Mike's good.' Spinner's voice brought her back to the present, picking up where their radio conversation had left off. And alerted her. After working with him for years, Gemma had a sixth sense for what Spinner was thinking.

'I can hear a qualification in your voice,' she said. 'Spit it out.'

'Maybe I'm too suspicious,' said Spinner, 'but I can't help wondering why an ex-federal cop with his experience would want to do this sort of work.'

Spinner's words mirrored her own thoughts exactly. She'd asked Mike Moody this very question during the initial interview.

'Why did he leave the job?' Spinner asked.

'Personal reasons. His marriage was in trouble.'

'So it helps a marriage to leave your job?' Spinner's voice was dry with disbelief.

'Apparently,' said Gemma, 'the missus wasn't happy about being married to a mere federal agent. She felt he should be grander by now—at least an inspector or a chief.'

'She's going to be even less happy married to a sneaky private eye. Did you check him out good?' said Spinner whose grasp of grammar had been curtailed by becoming apprenticed as a jockey when he was under fifteen.

'Of course I did,' returned Gemma, a trifle peeved. 'I checked him out real good. I know his ex-boss in Canberra.'

Working on the road as a surveillance operative is a very special calling, she knew, and although Spinner was a natural and she was blessed to have him, she was realistic enough to know that only a few people were really suited to it. Mike Moody, despite his good references and solid work so far, still had to prove himself. He'd done some routine jobs with insurance frauds for her but Spinner was still the man for anything delicate. Or difficult. Or Gemma did it herself. She was hoping both Mike and her other new operative, Louise Chapple would train up to be as good as the little ex-jock. It was the sort of work that required affability, ease with people of every sort, an understanding of human nature, a sharp flexibility for when things went arse-up, as well as the capacity to remain unseen day after day if need be, while the target is tracked.

'Okay, okay,' said Spinner. 'We'll see how he goes with the Wicked Black Swan.'

Fourteen-year-old Belinda Swann was neither wicked nor black, but Spinner's penchant for interesting nicknames for his targets overrode the facts of the matter. In this case the girl's ex-boyfriend, now an ex-police officer as well, was facing charges of sexual intercourse with an underage person. He had requested Gemma's aid.

'She told me she was twenty,' he'd said. 'And I believed her. Why the hell wouldn't I? She told me she worked for Qantas. She's nearly as tall as me and takes a C cup. Now I find out she's fucking *fourteen*! Her father's a superintendent and he wants my balls. You know what they'll do in court. Dress her in short socks and pigtails. And I'll look like a bloody child molester.'

Gemma had given Mike Moody the Belinda Swann brief to see what he could find and Mike had sat off the Swann household every night for the last week, waiting to get something—anything—on Belinda that might help the defence. But either the girl had found renewed interest in schoolwork or, as was more likely, she'd been 'gated' by her overbearing father, because all he'd got so far was Belinda doing her homework, watching television and throwing leaves, sticks and dirt into her father's swimming pool.

'Mike Moody's references are the best,' she told Spinner.

'Okay, okay,' he said again. 'I'm only wondering. Now tell me. What's on your mind lately?'

'Lions and scorpions and outer space calamities,' she joked. 'I dreamed of a black meteorite heading my way.'

'That's one way of putting it.'

'What are you talking about, Spinner?' She was sometimes irritated by his tendency towards the gnomic or scriptural or both.

'Something's troubling you. Something's going on.'

'You know I've got a lot on my mind at the moment,' she said, as if he was merely stating the obvious.

'That's not what I mean.'

'What *do* you mean?'

'How long have I been working for you now?'

'Spinner. I don't need this discovery learning crap. Tell me straight.'

'You can't hide it from me. Something's haunting you.'

A long time later, she remembered those words and wondered if things might have gone differently if she'd told Spinner and investigated earlier.

'*You* are,' she said, 'with your fundo bullshit.' That phrase usually stopped him in his tracks. 'We were discussing Mike Moody.'

'Like I said,' he said after a pause, 'maybe I'm too suspicious.'

'Stay too suspicious, Spinner,' she said, smiling. 'It's what makes you a great operative.' She was about to ring off but thought of something else. 'What about Louise? How's she shaping up?' Louise had joined the business a few months before Mike.

'She's good,' he said. 'She's persistent. And she doesn't stick out in a crowd. That's a good quality to have in our game. Only time will tell if she's suited in the long term.'

Spinner rang off and Gemma put more coffee to perk, setting up the cups, the milk and sugar, and poured herself a big mug before switching on the computer. For a while, she couldn't shake Spinner's words about haunting out of her mind. It was good, she thought, to have work to take her mind off nightmares and electronic pests.

She rang Minkie Montreau and made an appointment to visit her at her house next morning. Then she walked into her office and logged on. She typed in her password. Her heart sank— she had eighty-nine new emails. 'Shit!' she said out loud. No wonder Spinner reckons I'm haunted. He's right on the money there. This hostile electronic assault, combined with her concern for Steve, was too much. She needed to work off the resulting unease with a good sweat.

Back in her bedroom, she put on her joggers, deciding on a quick run around the cliffs to work off the emotions she could feel tightening her body. She trotted outside, stretching her arms and doing lateral bends to each side, warming up, then started jogging up the steps to the roadway. Something moved at the very edges of her peripheral vision and she thought she heard a faint sound, making her stop and frown. Mid-step she'd turned, looking back down to the front garden. It was damply innocent. Just the trees dripping and the lawn sodden after the rain, a long rose cane that needed pruning moving slightly against the window of her office. Maybe it had only been that. The suspect cane grew in front of the dense, polished greenery of the coprosma or looking-glass bush that covered the lower half of the window in her office. She waited a few moments more, but the garden remained exactly as it had been, cold and still. She turned back to the steps and continued on her way, looking up at a grey and featureless sky. The nightmare was still haunting her.

A thin drizzle started as she left the footpath and ran down to the cliff walk. Because of the damp and the relative lateness of the hour—most people were at or on their way to work—there were only a few other joggers. Beneath her, the gunmetal sea exploded on the rocks, pushed by strong southerly gusts and a rolling swell. The horizon itself was invisible, hidden by curtains of squalls and showers.

Gemma glanced behind her, thinking she heard footsteps. But there was no one on the track and now the drizzle turned to real rain. She puffed up the rise through the old tram cutting, reflecting on her general level of fitness and her ability to defend herself. Although the unarmed combat she'd learned in her time in the police had been very basic, like many women these days she'd taken it further, enrolling in a martial arts course, building up her strength and stamina with gym work and circuit weights. Great for preventing osteoporosis, and for general wellbeing, but when it comes to self-defence, Gemma discovered, nothing beats dirty old-fashioned street tactics.

At the top of the hill, she paused, catching her breath and taking in the spectacular southern headlands, the misty shrouds, part ocean spray, part rain, that veiled them. She quickly made the descent to the boatshed in Phoenix Bay she'd been renting since the beginning of the year. Although many people had heard of the Phoenix Bay rip, notorious for taking swimmers on long detours, and responsible for several deaths over the decades, the beach itself was not well known, tucked away as it was between Tamarama and Bronte. The rip normally ran off the northern end of the beach, just past the old surf club building, and went out to sea for a mile or more. Today, she could see its curve—a denser, darker texture on the surface of the sea. Dinghies in rows bleached on the boat racks built on the sloping rise to the coastal path and at the southern end of the bay lay a large launch, beached some weeks ago after an accident. Gemma went over to it, noticing the large, padlocked outboard motor. It's a wonder someone hasn't tried to knock that off, she thought, as she headed back to the boatshed.

Although she kept nothing of value down here, the double doors that faced away from the sea were secured with a small padlock. Gemma unlocked and went inside, shivering in the cold, still air, pleased all over again when she pulled the damp cloths off her lion. His poised presence seemed to charge the atmosphere of the boatshed, and because his position on the bench made him a little taller than her, she had to look up at him. She wasn't quite sure what to do about his open-jawed head. The blunted face of the original had no features save this ancient, silent roar. Beside him, also under damp fabric drapings on a square of timber, crouched the unformed lump of his potential brother. She pulled the sheets off and picked up a clay tool, cutting it through the embryonic lump. When she had time, she'd start modelling his back legs and haunches, the place she'd started with the other one. Then the forequarters and head. She put the tool down and re-covered the clay.

Her surroundings were very simple—a tiny fold-up bed she'd stowed under the bench on the southern side of the shed, the 'kitchen' area, a cold water sink and a power point for a jug. Next to it was the 'bathroom'—merely a shower head on a rubber hose that attached as required to the tap—and an old-fashioned toilet, a rope replacing the original chain flush. Her dream was to buy this place, renovate it into a beautiful space and spend a lot more time here. She glanced at her watch. Time to go.

Running back home Gemma enjoyed the downhill slope, gearing up for the next rise. A nankeen kestrel hung suspended above the cemetery, reminding her of the boy, Hugo, whom she privately called the Ratbag, who used to live in the next-door flat. She wondered where he was now and how he was getting on with his corporate mother whose new boyfriend had caused her to sell up and move to Melbourne, taking her nine-year-old son with them. Gemma realised she still missed him and his frowning, anxious face, his unswerving and loving allegiance to the father who completely neglected him. He'd be nearly thirteen now, she thought.

She was running between Bronte and Tamarama when a bedraggled rat staggered across the path, almost stumbling into her feet. Revulsion turned to pity when she realised both its eyes were coated with a grey film. The wretched thing was blind. She waited while it blundered into the bushes on the side of the path before continuing. Gemma shivered. It felt like a bad omen.

A short time later, she ran down the stone steps into her front garden where the heavy sky was reflected in pools on the pathway. The new owner of the flat where the Ratbag and his mother had lived had created an elaborate terrace garden on the southern side, complete with fountain, urns,

tiles and statues so that it looked a bit like a
Disney-style Pompeii. The once grand old house
in Phoenix Crescent had been divided into four
asymmetrical apartments in the '60s, Gemma
owning the downstairs northern section that
looked east out to sea. On summer mornings she
had to keep the blinds down because the sun
shone in before 5 a.m. and bleached the fabrics of
her lounge room. Thus Taxi had the run of the
little patch of grassy lawn and Gemma's spasmodic
gardening attempts, battered by southerly winds
and currently little more than weedy turf and
scrub. Below that, the land fell away to a steep
drop and the rocks lashed by the sea.

She let herself into her apartment and collapsed
on the lounge where Taxi had embedded himself
in the corner. He barely looked up from his sleep
as her weight jolted the blue leather cushions.
Then, remembering the odd moment she'd experienced halfway up the steps on her way out, she
went back outside again. The peripheral movement
had come from the environs of the coprosma bush.
Beside it, one of her neglected roses wintered away,
one tiny mummified bud all that remained of the
last autumn flush. She carefully lifted the thorny
cane aside to check the bush. Cold drops showered her when she moved its branches, peering
through. When she looked closely she could see
definite signs of disturbance in the soil under her
window, as if someone or something had trodden
down some of the bottom leaves and smaller
branches of the bush and left indentations in the

damp earth. She stared hard at the marks but they were too inconclusive to make out. It could have been a blackbird, she thought. She'd seen one recently on a run to Kit's place near Gordons Bay, the floundering, surreptitious movements of those birds as they hopped around the lowest reaches of bushes and shrubs, or ran low across the ground were well known to her from trips to Melbourne and the Police Academy at Goulburn, but not so common in Sydney.

Back inside she had a quick shower, dressed and was pulling up her skirt zip as she entered her office. She nudged the mouse and there they were again across her screen, line after line of new emails. She deleted the first, then the next and the next, not opening any of them, knowing from the past few days how ugly they'd be. Gemma could feel the blood of anger and fear pumping through her body as she dealt with one after the other. It was going to take her a while. She couldn't just lean on the 'Delete' button because, interspersed between the repetitive lines of *'Please Hurt Me. Make My Violent Rape Fantasies Real'* were what looked like genuine messages concerning her business and even a couple from friends. She avoided those, saving them till later, working her way through the deletes. This was crazy. She'd have to contact her server and have something done, even if it meant closing down her email for a while and getting a new electronic address.

She was halfway through the vicious infestation when her buzzer rang. Sidling up to the window, she glanced over the bushes outside. A well-dressed man, her 10 o'clock appointment, stood on her doorstep, looking around him as people often do when they're waiting for a door to be opened, nervously adjusting his tie.

She hurried back to her desk to delete the last message. She didn't want anyone, particularly Steve, ever to see this horrible stuff. Even having deleted all these, she wondered how many there would be by tomorrow morning. She logged off, leaving the genuine correspondence for later.

From the lounge room Gemma picked up the manila folder with Peter Greengate's name on it. Determinedly putting the cyberstalker out of her mind, she hurried into the second office opposite her own, used by the operatives when they came in from the road, and placed a cassette in the player, switching it on. The others were only very rarely in the office so she was alone a lot of the time. Their job was to be out on the road, tailing, trailing, sitting off houses, watching targets through their high-powered binoculars or the automatic zoom focus on their digital video cameras, punching out their reports on laptops from where they sat in their cars, only dropping by the office to file information or to be briefed on new cases.

She answered the intercom on the next buzz. 'Yes? Who is it?'

'Peter Greengate,' he said. 'To see Gemma Lincoln.' The voice was hesitant, fading away at the end.

She pressed the switch and the front door

unlocked. 'Please come in, Mr Greengate,' she said, going to the door to let him in, standing back as he entered, taking her time to appraise his tall, stooped figure, his passive handshake, the caved-in look of his face, especially under the cheekbones. Late forties, she guessed, and looks like he needs a good feed.

'In here,' she said, standing back to let him go ahead into her office on the left of the front door. Across the hall from the other office issued the sounds of male voices and laughter.

'Excuse me for one moment,' she said to her visitor with a smile. 'I'll just ask my colleagues to make less noise.'

The tall man stood watching her while she went into the opposite room. Behind the door she turned down the cassette player recording of Spinner and Mike's office chatter, a tip she'd learned from Shelly. 'I never let the mugs know I'm working alone,' Shelly had once said. She came back, closed the door of her office and indicated that Peter Greengate should sit down in one of the comfortable chairs near her desk.

He began to talk in a dull monotone and Gemma wished, as she always did at times like this, that she could have something printed and hand it out as people came in.

'I've never done anything like this before,' he said.

Gemma nodded. They all had variations of these same themes. Now, she thought, he will go on to tell me he's not the sort of person who usually does this sort of thing.

'I'm not the sort of person who usually does this sort of thing,' he said.

Gemma chimed in with her stock response. 'I'm sure you're not the sort of person who goes around spying on people,' she assured him, 'let alone your wife.'

'But in this case . . .' he started.

'In this case, you've made a wise decision,' she said. 'So what can I help you with?' she asked, opening the folder and picking up her pen.

Peter Greengate looked away and his light grey eyes seemed to stare at the leaves of the bush outside the window.

'I think she's seeing someone else.'

'Involved with a man?' said Gemma because the expressionless way he spoke made it sound like his wife might be interviewing the plumber, or electrician.

Greengate nodded. Gemma made brief notes for the record of the interview.

'What makes you think this?'

He was silent a long while. Gemma mentally listed some of the indicators of adultery: the sudden interest in looking fit and tanned, glamorous new underwear, visits to the gym, a new diet, a change of perfume or aftershave, a new hobby that took the person away from the marital home once or twice a week, absences from work, changed routine, 'taking the dog for a walk' or 'going out for some fresh air' after dinner, evening classes, unexplained expenses on the credit cards, vagueness, telephone calls where the caller hung up—the list of clues left by adulterers was depressingly familiar.

'What have you noticed,' prompted Gemma, 'to make you suspect this to be the case?'

He turned back to her and his answer was unexpected. 'I found her washing some clothes,' he said. 'She was really embarrassed when I walked in.' He leaned forward. 'Men's clothes,' he said. 'I asked her whose they were and she could hardly talk to me. Said something about someone at work and a broken-down washing machine. And then there was the other thing.' He paused and Gemma waited, pen poised. 'Something she said to a friend on the phone when she didn't know I was in the house.'

'What was that?' she asked.

'I heard her ask her friend to say that if I ever asked her—the friend, I mean—' Gemma nodded— 'if Patricia was with her, she was to always say yes she was, even if she wasn't.'

'Any other things?' said Gemma. 'Does she go out a lot?'

He shook his head. 'Her mother sometimes. Outings with a girlfriend.'

Patricia, he told Gemma, was a teacher librarian in a high school. He passed over the picture of his wife that Gemma had asked him to bring with him and she studied the pretty face of a woman with an uncertain smile, wearing an exotic silky outfit and a necklace of what looked like dead snakes around her neck. Smaller snakes dangled from her ears. Interesting-looking woman, Gemma thought. Pity about the snakes. On the back of the print was Mrs Greengate's birthday and her home and work addresses.

Although Gemma had developed what she called 'Sunday School' language for many of her clients, she still liked to give them a little warning that she was going to get personal. 'I have to ask questions that concern delicate matters,' she said and Peter Greengate's pale eyes stared her. 'Have you noticed any changes in your intimate life?' she asked.

For a moment, she thought he hadn't understood her and was about to rephrase her question in a more direct fashion when he spoke.

'We don't *have* an intimate life,' he said. 'I presume you're talking about marital relations? All that business stopped a long time ago.'

Gemma decided to wind up the interview. '*Reports no sex,*' she jotted in her notes before looking up. 'Mr Greengate—'

'Call me Peter,' he said in the same flat voice.

'—Peter,' she said, 'we can certainly help you. But are you aware that it's a costly undertaking? The base rate is fifty-five dollars an hour. That doesn't cover extras like meal allowances or extra travel expenses. Or any other contingency that might arise.'

'I knew it wouldn't be cheap,' he said. Then he became oddly animated, new colour in his face, lowering his voice to a whisper. 'You must be very discreet.'

'We *are* extremely discreet,' she said. 'I use only very experienced operatives on these matters. In fact, Peter, I'm going to handle this case personally.' Every now and then Gemma liked to get back on the road, sharpen up instincts made dull by too much desk driving. Pick a new brief and see it through.

'When do you think she's meeting the other party?'

'She and her friend Sandra always go to art classes on Tuesday nights,' he said. 'Then they have supper. So she says. She leaves the house at about four and doesn't get in till sometimes nearly ten. She's always'—he searched for the word and his face tightened into contempt—'*happy* when she comes home.'

Gemma could see how this aspect of his wife's behaviour alone might well affront a man like Peter Greengate.

'We'll start next Tuesday,' she said. A few hours might be all it takes, she thought, to establish whether she plays up. 'May I suggest a deposit of two hundred and twenty dollars?'

He nodded.

'We'll pick Mrs Greengate up as she leaves the house,' she said to him, 'and take it from there. Is there anything else you think might be important that I should know?' she added.

He sat there, unmoving, then briefly shook his head. She finished writing, closed the manila folder and waited. He didn't seem to notice her cue, but remained seated in some dream of his own. Finally, Gemma stood up and so did he. Because of his stoop, his eyes were on the same level as her own. If he'd stood straight, she realised, he'd be much taller.

'It all started a few years ago,' he said suddenly. 'Some of her work was exhibited at a fancy art gallery. Since then she's been different.' He paused and Gemma saw something shift in him. 'If she's being unfaithful to me . . .' His eyes darkened and the sunken cheeks flushed. She waited for him to finish his statement but abruptly he turned away. 'Really,' he said, 'she leaves me no option.' Greengate pulled out his wallet and made the deposit in cash.

As she showed him out, he turned on the front doorstep. 'I want proof,' he said. 'I want it on video or photographs.'

'Peter, we always provide video evidence for our clients. It's part of the service.'

'I want to see with my own eyes,' he said, suddenly savage. 'What she's capable of doing.'

There was a pause and Gemma had the distinct impression that Peter Greengate was deep in some dark sexual fantasy concerning his wife and a stranger. She didn't want to shake his hand so she started closing the door, a bright smile on her face.

'We'll be in touch,' she said, 'as soon as we have something to show you. It won't be long, I'm sure.'

She was pleased to close the door on him. As she put the money away she remembered how once, not long after she'd started her business, she had decided *not* to hand on evidence of adultery gathered on another man's wife, instead telling the client she'd found nothing incriminating. She knew it was unethical, illegal and that she'd defrauded him of his fees. But something about that man had chilled her, making it impossible for her to hand over the video evidence and report. She'd talked it over with Kit.

'I really thought he would do something terrible to her,' she told her sister. 'I could sense his hatred. I felt he was *hoping* she'd been unfaithful to him. He didn't want a divorce. He wanted vengeance.' In fact, Gemma thought, most people really *don't* want to know the truth. She recalled the silly rationalisations some clients engaged in when confronted with incontrovertible evidence of adultery.

'In the end,' Kit had said, 'you've just got to trust your own judgment. Write a cheque for the amount he paid you and give it to the Sallies or someone, and then you won't feel so bad about defrauding him.' Now, years after that case, Gemma had a similar feeling. She glanced sideways out the window. Peter Greengate was still there.

He'd continued to stand outside, staring at the door, until finally he turned away. Gemma shuddered. Sometimes people were *spooky*.

Her radio crackled again. 'Tracker Two, Base. Copy please?' Louise's voice was as slight as her build. But slightness and transparency, two of the qualities Gemma associated with Louise, had certain advantages in this business.

'Base, Tracker Two. Go ahead.'

'I don't feel well, Gemma. I won't come in today.'

'Sorry to hear that, Louise. What's up?'

'I took Mum out for her birthday last night and we must have eaten something that upset us. We were both up all night.'

Louise's cases involved several insurance claimants, none of whom had yet been sprung doing anything they shouldn't have, and an assistant manager at a retail food chain, suspected of pilfering goods. This job needed the cooperation of the police to intercept the car with the goods in the target's possession. So far, they'd had no success. The loss of a day's work wasn't too drastic at this stage of Louise's operations.

'Okay,' said Gemma, feeling irritated nevertheless. 'Take it easy and let me know if you'll be in tomorrow.' She signed off.

THREE

Two hours later, Gemma sat in the passenger seat of Detective Sergeant Angela McDonald's car, that being the only way she could get some time with her friend and erstwhile colleague whose day was as heavily booked as Gemma's own.

'Another sex worker was attacked last night and we finally got hold of her clothes,' said Angie, indicating a rape kit on the back seat. 'I'm taking this to the lab.' She glanced across at her friend. 'Hey, Gemfish. What's up with you?' she asked, shrewd green eyes assessing her under a frown. Angie had always been able to sense her moods.

'Just a nightmare I had last night,' she said, recalling the black meteor racing through space towards its collision point. 'It's hanging around a bit.'

Gemma fixed her attention on the police radio calls and staring at the students mounting the steps to the university. Youngsters crossed the footbridge to and fro, moving from lectures to the bus stops and Gemma momentarily envied their simple life.

Angie turned the police radio right down and zipped through the traffic along Parramatta Road.

'Actually,' she confessed, 'I'm certain Steve is working in some sort of operation involving George Fayed. Have you heard any goss?'

'A little,' she said. 'There was something going on last year. The Feds were doing a big intelligence-gathering operation on Fayed and Oradoro.'

'Sounds like El Dorado,' said Gemma, 'and fabled treasures.'

Angie laughed. 'Oradoro is the name of Fayed's import and export company, his so-called legit business. The fabled treasure is the usual white powder. We'd love to get him off the streets.'

'He'd only be replaced by someone else when you pull him in,' said Gemma. 'There are people like him coming up the ranks all the time. He's replaced Litchfield. That's how it goes.'

'That doesn't sound like the Gemster I know and love,' said Angie, glancing at her friend with concern. 'Where's your "Let's get the bastards" muscle?'

'I don't know,' said Gemma. 'Maybe I'm running out of steam.'

Angie didn't pursue the matter any further. 'Some crims I don't mind,' she said after a few minutes. 'They do their job. We do ours. But George Fayed's a real smartarse. He knows how to operate right under our noses and he loves doing that. He and his executives use their mobile phones to move his gear around, and set up the deals. It's so damn frustrating. Our intelligence tells us he buys direct from the Chinese. But you'll never see him anywhere near the importers. Except for the times he's supervising unloading of his imported arte-facts and antiquities. Fancies himself as a collector of art. We've gone over his consignments and never found anything that shouldn't be there and all the time he's laughing at us. He's got people every-where. He's even got a couple of nephews in the job,' she added, 'trying to get into the Drug Squad. Now I wonder why they'd want to work there?' Her cheeky grin lifted Gemma's spirits. 'We got one of them suspended, we're working on the other one. The Drug Squad guys would give their cute little chrome-plated .38s to get Fayed.' She corrected herself. 'Don't know how you'd go about chrome-plating a Glock.'

Gemma smiled. Tough little Angie who liked to beat the boys on both sides of the crime coin at their own games. Like any successful woman offi-cer, she'd learned the hard way how to survive in the brotherhood, but she'd never lost her own indi-viduality, or capitulated to becoming 'one of the boys' and, Gemma knew, some of the senior offi-cers would never forgive her for that. Like any military organisation, the police service was hier-archical, power-dominated, favour-driven and on too many occasions, unbelievably inefficient and downright stupid.

Angie's face suddenly became serious. 'I've heard on the grapevine that Steve's involved in a joint operation with the Drug Squad and the Plas-tics,' said Angie, referring to the nickname of the

Federal Police. 'You tell that gorgeous boyfriend of yours,' she said, 'to be *real* careful. He's got the cutest bum in the job. I'd hate anything to happen to it.'

'I've tried,' said Gemma, 'but you know what Steve's like.' She swung around to face her friend. 'And don't you dare look at his bum!'

'Calm down, girl. Only teasing. And you always bite. Fayed's place is on the way to the lab. Want a look?'

Angie took a right-hand turn and drove up a residential street. 'I don't want to park too close,' she said, 'but you can see the place from here. It's that charcoal monster on the corner over there. The whole family lives there now, George and his wife, their sons, George's old mother and a couple of other male relatives.'

Gemma pulled her binoculars out of her briefcase and studied the Fayed fortress.

'He's a real family man,' Angie was saying. 'He had the whole building renovated and rebuilt so that the first floor could accommodate his oldest daughter's wedding—over a thousand people, three priests including an interstate bishop— Fayed's a good Catholic family man. We heard he spent a million on the reception. Can you believe it?'

What would it be like to be the son or daughter of a drug boss, Gemma wondered, feeling a flash of empathy for Fayed's children. What do they tell their friends? She studied the building. Three-storeys high, it had been converted from a warehouse or factory and had a sloping driveway that ended in a huge metal roller door suggesting an underground level. The large wedge-shaped building squatted blindly on the corner block, no windows except for narrow incisions of smoky glass, and then only on the upper level, reminding Gemma of an old Martello tower. The only other distinctive feature was a black and white sign embellished with a stylised golden lizard and the words '*Oradoro Export Imports*' on the northern wall. Access from the street appeared to be only by way of the huge roller door.

'I've had a chat to some of the guys who were involved in the surveillance last year,' Angie said. 'Fayed's paranoid about security. Never leaves the place empty. Which makes it impossible for our technicians to get in and do their sneaky little fit-out.' Gemma remembered that the technical people needed a clear stretch of time to get their electronic gimmicks into position. 'The guys created a fault to the power in the street,' Angie was saying, 'and then tried to get inside posing as Energy Australia to test for a fault, but it didn't make a scrap of difference to Fayed. He's got his own generator in there so he wouldn't let them in.' Angie settled back in her seat, looking at the corner building. 'Hell, we've heard he's even got a zoo in there! Can you believe it? What sort of weirdo wants to keep animals locked up in a prison?'

'What does he keep?'

'He's licensed to keep reptiles.'

'That'd be right,' said Gemma. 'Like attracts like.'

'Hey, I *like* snakes,' Angie said. 'I don't like George Fayed.'

'That explains the logo,' said Gemma, passing the glasses. 'Take a look.'

Angie took the binoculars. 'That's some big goanna,' she said, responding to the stylised reptile behind the sign's lettering.

Gemma shrugged as she took the binoculars back. 'Why would you want a goanna as your logo?'

'They don't talk,' said Angie, 'and that flickering tongue is always gathering intelligence about the environment. That's Fayed to a T. He's got closed circuit cameras on the street so he knows what's going on outside. And he's got them on the inside as well. Can you imagine closed circuit TV in all your rooms? Keeping tabs on what's going on in your own house?'

'Must be a sultan thing,' said Gemma. 'Back in the old days, they had to murder all their brothers when they took the throne. That way, they got rid of any rivals.'

Angie laughed. 'Fayed has much the same ambition. Always looking to expand his markets and eliminate the competition. Like any corporate CEO.'

Gemma picked up the binoculars again. 'I can't see any cameras,' she said.

'You wouldn't—they're microscopic—pinhole lenses. They're probably watching this car right

now. We should have gone in yours,' she said.
'They'd recognise this as a police car.'

Gemma peered around the street. There were
several cars and a tradesman's van parked across
and down the road from the huge building. A few
pedestrians went about their business. It looked
just like any ordinary, inner west suburban Sydney
street, she thought, with neat little Victorian ter-
races, geraniums in pots, a cat curled in view in
one window. Fayed's castle was not even a particularly discordant note; there were several old
converted warehouses in the district. She moved
the binoculars back to one of the narrow windows
on the third floor of Fayed's fortress and then
almost dropped them. From the dark corner building someone was looking straight down the lenses
of her binoculars with his own. Their eyes connected. It was a nasty shock.

•

On the way to the Lidcombe laboratory, Angie
filled Gemma in further on Fayed's form. Despite
a history of standover violence, drug distribution
and suspected gun running, the police had failed
to make anything major stick. Fayed's own legal
team, augmented by the best counsel money could
buy, ensured that. And apart from three months
in prison on an assault charge years ago, Fayed had
lived the luxurious life of a Sydney drug lord. 'He's
got a real nasty streak in him,' said Angie. 'He grew
up in refugee camps, violent war zones.' She threw
Gemma a quick glance, then concentrated on

changing lanes for a right-hand turn before continuing. 'Have you heard of the "French Connection"?' she asked.

'The movie?'

Angie shook her head. 'No. But I suppose it's based on that. One of Fayed's preferred punishments. He abducts people who've offended him and injects them until they're addicted. Then he chucks them back onto the street when they're hopeless addicts and no further threat to him.'

'Sounds like an urban myth to me,' said Gemma.

'I'm just passing on street talk,' said Angie. 'Otherwise he uses a lethal dose.'

Gemma thought of Steve and her blood ran cold. 'What do you think he would do to someone like Steve?' she asked, 'if he discovered his real identity?'

Angie threw her a glance. She didn't answer. She didn't have to. But then she leaned over and patted Gemma's knee. 'C'mon, Gemster. Steve'll be fine. He's a good cop. He knows how to survive. Hell, girl, he's survived for years!'

It's true, Gemma thought, but it's time he stopped and came home. Came in from the madness. She rooted through her briefcase looking for a tissue and finally found one hiding right at the bottom, under her Filofax, notebooks, diary and Swiss Army knife.

Angie noticed it and laughed. 'You're such a boy scout,' she said. With one hand she lifted the console between them and brought out a silver pen. 'Look at this,' she said, pressing the side of the pen. A wicked narrow blade sprang out. Angie laughed. 'Now *that's* what I call a knife.'

Gemma waited in the car park of the laboratory while Angie took the package up. She took the switch-blade pen out of the console and examined it, finding its pressure point, wondering what had become of the hoodlum Angie must have downed to acquire it. By the time she'd put it back again, her friend was striding across the parking area, trim and athletic in her navy suit, jacket blowing back to reveal the white polo neck jumper sleek around her upper body, red hair clipped back into a chignon.

'They're flat out in there,' Angie said, jumping back in and slamming the door. 'Never enough staff, always too much work. Just like us. Whinge, whinge.' She belted up and drove out of the grounds, and was back onto the highway within minutes. 'What do you think Steve's doing with Fayed?' she asked, keeping her eyes on the road.

'I'm still working it out,' Gemma said hesitantly. 'I had to ask myself how come the widow of an old crim like Terry Litchfield would agree to work with the cops. So I thought Lorraine Litchfield must *believe* . . .' She paused, to refine her interpretation. 'No,' she said, 'it's got to be stronger than that. I reckon the police have shown her *proof* that George Fayed was responsible for her husband's death.'

'That makes sense,' said Angie. 'Terry Litchfield was the Man around Sydney for years. He'd be an obstacle for someone like Fayed. They hated each other's guts. You should have a talk to the Major Crime people.'

As they drove, the messages on the police radio, almost incomprehensible unless the listener was conversant with police codes and acronyms, provided a constant reminder of Sydney's simmering underside. The business of crime was just another part of the city's activities—break and enters, assaults, motor vehicle accidents, reported shootings. The passionless voice allocated work, accepted bids to attend, updated the record and occasionally cracked a joke so deadpan as to make the listener wonder whether it had been intentional or not.

'So if Fayed killed Lorraine's husband so that he can be Sultan, that makes him *her* enemy now. Just like the police always have been, and—' Gemma paused and Angie flashed her a look—'do you know that old Arab proverb?'

'"The enemy of my enemy is my friend?"' Angie quoted.

'Right,' said Gemma. 'So she agrees to team up with Steve and together they cook up a way to get at Fayed.'

'That's good,' said Angie. 'That's how I'd do it if I were working in with Lorraine. I'd suggest that she put the word out to Fayed that she's interested in doing a deal with him because she's just a lone, lorn widder woman. She could either be looking for a partner or she might say she wants to get out of the business altogether but she could offer him the Litchfield infrastructure, the distribution and services built up over many years as her part of the deal, and then introduce Steve as some big inter-state buyer and business mate of her late lamented husband. That would give Steve the bona fides he'd need to meet Fayed.' She paused. 'And then, set up a meeting where Fayed is busted holding. Or get evidence on video like they did during the Royal Commission.'

'That's not going to be easy,' said Gemma. 'Men like him never hold now. The crims are getting better educated every day. That's only for the lieu-tenants and the mules.'

'Steve's got a job ahead of him,' said Angie. 'But if anyone can do it, he can.'

I hope so, thought Gemma. And I want this to be his last job. She corrected herself—his last job *undercover*, she added silently. Otherwise the phrase sounded too ominous.

Angie dropped her back at her car in Riley Street a couple of blocks from the Police Centre. Gemma resisted the impulse to go back to Fayed's fortress once more, despite the man with the binoculars. His minders wouldn't know her car. Another time, she thought. Instead, she bought a meat pie and ate it in the car, *'You shook me all night long'* belting out on the radio. She regretted that pie for the rest of the day.

•

Several times in the afternoon she found herself in her office starting to do the same job twice, or leaving something half-finished, only to pick it up again a little later. Her work was constantly being interrupted by thoughts of Steve and Fayed. Finally, she stopped, made a brew of strong coffee and took it to the dining table, where she sat, staring through the glass doors out to sea. For a moment, she was tempted to take the rest of the day off and go down to the boatshed, but she rejected the idea. I've got to get my head back together again, she told herself, and do my job properly. First things first. Gemma knew she was good at switching off any worrying thoughts by taking practical action. So she spent the late afternoon busying herself with productive paper work, making sure the records were up to date with the many jobs the operatives on the road covered, entering any final results into her computer files. She made a note of the jobs that needed finalising, frowned when she saw that Louise hadn't got much in the way of results over the last three weeks and then checked her voice mail. There was a message from Kit suggesting she come over for dinner tonight because she was cooking Gemma's favourite lasagna, this message followed by a hurried but lecherous thank-you-for-last-night call from Steve that made her smile. This made her want to hear Steve's voice, even if only for a moment. She dialled his mobile.

'Hullo?' A woman's voice.

Gemma felt her hackles rise. Who was this woman answering her man's mobile? 'Steve, please,' said Gemma, her voice curt. 'I want to speak to him.'

There was a silence, then Gemma heard the woman's voice. 'Steve? It's for you.' The voice was dismissive. 'Some woman.'

Too right, honey, Gemma thought.

'It's me,' she said to Steve's formal and distant voice.

'I'll call you later,' he said, still in the same impersonal tone.

She rang off, regretting her impulse. She checked the third message.

'Gemma? It's me. Shelly. Please ring me. It's really urgent. He's done it again and he's nearly killed her. *Ring me.*'

Shelly Glover, now retired from active service, as she put it, owned and managed one of the better brothels in Sydney. Gemma had met her years ago at a Neighbourhood Watch meeting. Despite the enormous financial liability of her on-again off-again boyfriend, Kosta, Shelly had paid off the house, Baroque Occasions, not to mention the elaborate nymphs in fountains in the courtyard and florid mirrors in the bedrooms, and her daughter Naomi went to one of the better Eastern suburbs private schools. Apart from some financial assistance from her stepfather, Shelly had done all this 'lying on my back', as she liked to say. Very few sex workers had got things together like Shelly had, Gemma thought. She played the piano beautifully and embroidered gorgeous cushion covers with silk and gold that sold for a small fortune in an exclusive homewares shop in Double Bay. Gemma remembered Kosta as being a spoilt Greek boy whom Shelly sometimes doted on and at other times abused, as he did her.

She wanted to eat before she returned Shelly's call. Taxi nearly tripped her as she went to the kitchen to make some late lunch then nagged at her while she chomped her way through peanut butter on two thick slabs of bread washed down with orange juice, before dialling Shelly at Baroque Occasions. They spoke only briefly, arranging to meet at St Vincent's Hospital later in the afternoon.

Nothing prepares you for the terrible damage caused by a violent assault, Gemma thought, until you see it for yourself. The only reason she knew that the grossly swollen face lying on the pillow belonged to a young woman and not some monstrous alien was because she could read the name 'Robyn Warburton' above the bed in the four bed ward.

Gemma winced as she saw the tight red-purple skin of the bashed woman's face where it showed through gaps in the bandages. She noted inflamed ligature marks on the girl's narrow wrists, bruised fingers and broken nails. She felt a sense of kinship with her already, knowing that it was her clothing that had been in Angie's car for delivery to the laboratory for examination. Another woman, older, with a gaunt, handsome face, sat nearby holding Robyn's hand. Gemma hadn't noticed

Shelly's presence at the long window until she walked over to join them.

'Thanks for coming,' Shelly said as Gemma kissed her. Just by looking at her, Gemma thought, no one would ever guess how this slender woman in tweed slacks and a blue jumper made a living. She wore little make-up, apart from pale lipstick. Even the fabulous long gold fingernails that flashed with every move she made could have belonged to any successful business woman, and her dark hair was simply brushed back and tied behind with a ribbon. Gemma recalled a time she'd seen Shelly floating down the staircase of the brothel in a dress like a stream of molten gold, hair piled up, golden bracelets and stilettos, matching fingernails—a golden-goddess illusion for the mugs.

'This is Brenda, Robyn's mum,' Shelly said, introducing her to the older woman. Brenda raised her tanned face to Gemma, her mouth set in a narrow line that looked like it hadn't smiled in years. Gemma noticed the powerful muscles rippling in the woman's upper arms and shoulders under the loosely draped jacket as she automatically put out her hand.

'Look what he's done to my little girl,' Brenda said, clamping her lips even more tightly. She gently put her daughter's hand back down on the bed and lifted the light coverings up.

Gemma saw the heavy dressings that covered both breasts, and angry red stripes fanned over her ribs and belly.

'Why would anyone want to do something like this?'

Because he can, Gemma thought. Purple-red weals were embossed on the delicate skin, some of them punctuated with bloody wounds.

'You wouldn't believe what he's done to her between her legs,' said Brenda, smoothing the nightdress back over her daughter's body. 'You just couldn't imagine it.'

I don't have to imagine it, Gemma thought, recalling the victims of other sexual attacks she'd seen over the years. Too many people imagine rape victims as merely having tousled hair, a torn skirt and perhaps a scratch or two. They don't think what a powerful right hook with a man's rage behind it does to a woman's face. They can't imagine what it's like for a lightly framed human body to be bashed with a crowbar, or a hammer. Repeatedly. They don't think of what it's like to be almost choked to death.

The girl stirred and moaned through the heavy sedation.

'It's okay, sweetie,' her mother said, stroking the bruised hand, distress contracting her face.

Robyn opened her eyes. Then closed them again.

'I wanted you to see first-hand what he did,' Shelly whispered. Gemma couldn't take her eyes from the restless young girl. 'The bastard disengages the handle on the inside passenger door,' she added.

Gemma had a sudden memory. Ten years ago,

when she was still in the job, she remembered a series of attacks on street girls where the attacker used exactly this technique. Then, suddenly, the attacks had stopped.

'She's probably going to lose the sight in one eye. I'd give a lot to get this bastard alone,' Brenda said, her voice choking.

Me too, Gemma was thinking. She felt nothing but contempt for this cowardly attacker who preyed on the vulnerable.

'If I get my hands on him . . .' Brenda whispered.

'The cops are doing as much as they can,' Shelly said, 'but they never get the resources they need.' She paused. 'And really,' she continued, 'until he strikes again, there's not much they can do. They've pretty well told us to look out for him. That reminds me.' She fished into her snakeskin purse and pulled out a dirty business card. 'The girl that was beaten up last month,' she said, 'found this next to her when she came round.'

Gemma took the business card. '*Oradoro Imports Exports*,' she read, superimposed over the dinosaur-like reptile she'd already seen once before. 'That's George Fayed's business,' Gemma said.

Shelly grimaced. 'That doesn't surprise me.'

Was it a message? A warning? Or just a business card dropped on the footpath? It certainly didn't constitute evidence of any sort. Gemma put it in her briefcase.

Shelly noticed something and leaned forward. 'I think Rob's trying to say something.'

Both Brenda and Shelly moved closer.

'What is it, darling?' said her mother. 'I'm here.'

Robyn opened her eyes again. They were panicky and unfocused.

Brenda smoothed the hair on her daughter's forehead. 'You're safe,' she said. 'It's okay.'

Robyn shook her head. 'He kept singing. All the time he was hurting me. He just kept on singing.' Her eyes were wide as she relived the terror and pain, thrashing from side to side in the bed and Gemma feared she'd hurt herself more.

'I'm getting a nurse,' said her mother, but as she reached for the red panic button, her daughter suddenly lapsed back into unconsciousness.

Shelly looked at Gemma and picked up her purse. 'I need a smoke,' she said. 'There's a balcony down the end of the corridor.'

They left Robyn and her mother and walked the length of the corridor, stepping out onto a little balcony where an unhappy rubber tree languished in a pot that smokers had used as an ashtray, and a couple of plastic chairs were propped against a wall. Shelly teased a cigarette out of the packet with her impossibly long golden nails and lit it.

'He hit her with something heavy, maybe a shifter or something like that, as well as his fists,' she said, exhaling. 'And whatever it is that leaves that odd-shaped bruising just for good measure.' She leaned against the parapet of the balcony, staring through the bare plane trees at the street below.

'What was she saying about singing?' Gemma asked.

'He sings. He turns up the music on his car radio and sings along while he's doing that to them. Whistle while you work.' Shelly's voice was bitter. 'I've had about enough of this life. Maybe I should sell out to the Lebanese drug lord.'

'What Lebanese drug lord?'

'Ex-client of mine's been putting a lot of pressure on me to sell. So's Kosta. He wants the money. But I don't want to sell. That house is my life. God knows I've worked my arse off for it.' She became aware of Gemma's face. 'I know you don't have a very high opinion of Kosta. But lately he's been really sweet to me.'

'Because he wants something,' Gemma warned.

Shelly ignored this. 'The ex-client won't say who the buyer is,' she said, 'but I know George Fayed has already bought up some of the houses in Kellett Street and Bourke Street.'

'Fayed?' Gemma was all ears.

'You'd never know it. It's all done with front men. The word is that he's buying the brothels, stocking them with his own addicted girls and then just chucking them out without any pay when they're too sick to work.' She sighed. 'One girl objected and ended up dead from an overdose. Then a girl gets bashed and that card is found beside her. Makes me think.' She looked out over the balcony in the direction of the Cross. 'Once this place had some sort of class. People would come here for a bit of Paris.'

Gemma remembered the elegant clothing shops and shoe shops that had once enticed shoppers from the suburbs, now long gone.

'They'd come to the Cross for a bit of glamour and wickedness,' Shelly continued. 'Now it's just addicts and dealers and dirty little hangers-on.'

These days, the main drag was filled with fast-food outlets, garish tourist junk shops selling plastic koala key rings, and strip joints with overweight spruikers bothering pedestrians. The back lanes were filled with rubbish, needles log-jammed the drains and barely conscious teenagers staggered against walls trying to sell themselves. And the only people from the suburbs here were the folk who'd come to gawk at or buy the services offered. Or their children, on the run from difficult parents.

Her thoughts were interrupted by Shelly.

'Naomi does her School Certificate this year.' She plonked herself down on one of the chairs. 'She wants to go to university. That's when I'll sell my house, so my daughter can go to university. I'll get a nice little unit near the city. But not a moment before I'm ready, and certainly not to the likes of George Fayed.' She paused a moment, reflecting. 'That poor little kid lying in there is only a few years older than Naomi. What sort of life has she had? What sort of future?'

'How well do you know her?' Gemma asked.

Shelly shrugged. 'I've sort of kept an eye on Rob for a couple of years. She's a good kid. She worked at Classique until she got busted for drugs. Once a girl's using, no one wants them in a house.' She blew out a jetstream of smoke. 'She was stoned when she got in the car with him. Staying alive on the streets depends on a girl's instincts. Once they start doing drugs, they've lost their best defence.'

'I'll want to talk to the other girls he attacked,' Gemma said.

'If you can find them,' said Shelly. 'I've heard they left town.'

'Robyn's very slight,' said Gemma. 'What did the other ones look like?'

'You're asking me if he goes after a type?'

Gemma nodded. 'Because if I'm going to be attractive to him, I need to look like his style.'

'I can tell you now what his type is. He'd probably go for me if I was still on the street. I lost five kilos with Hep B at the beginning of the year. He likes that wasted Ally McBeal look.'

He would, thought Gemma grimly. What sort of fight could an Ally McBeal put up against even a man of even average strength? Gemma looked down at herself with a critical eye.

'I can lend you a dark wig and a hairpiece,' Shelly said. 'And if you wear black, and dark stockings and heels you'll look a lot thinner.'

Gemma made a face.

'I'm not saying you're fat,' said Shelly with her rare smile. 'It's just that you haven't really got that frail look. But if you want to give it a go we can meet at the safe house and I'll lend you the right stuff.'

She dropped her cigarette over the balcony coping and Gemma stepped back inside with her.

'I'd better shake a leg,' said Shelly. 'I've got a client in less than an hour.'

'But you're retired!'

'I have. This is legit. I'm working as a sex surrogate.'

'Shelly, be serious.'

'I am, sweetie. It's all legit. This guy could claim it on his health insurance if he had the right cover. He was referred to me by these two counsellors who do couples' therapy,' Shelly continued as they headed towards the lift. 'It's the truth,' she said, noticing the look on Gemma's face. 'Cross my heart and hope to die. Two of us work for them. They trained us. Stop looking like that,' she protested. 'They brief us on what should and shouldn't happen each session, depending on the client. As us girls know,' she said after some reflection, 'there's a a lot more to sex than just sticking it in.'

They waited for the lift, watching the little red light slowly make its way towards their level.

'The counsellors taught us these breathing techniques and we don't have sex with the client until we're instructed. It's just work to me, but'—here Shelly raised her neat eyebrows—'sweetie, this guy sure needed help. I suppose I always thought men were just lousy lovers when they bought it and didn't have to bother. The first time we had sex I asked him what he did with his wife, to demonstrate to me. I just wanted to know, you know?'

'And?' Gemma asked.

Shelly shook her head. 'Sweetie. It was woeful. Pitiful.'

The lift arrived and the doors opened. Shelly continued, quite unfazed by the other passengers.

'His idea of good lovemaking was to stick it in, wiggle it around a bit, come in thirty seconds and dribble on my neck.'

They stepped into the lift and turned round to face the closing doors.

'I said to him: Is that *it*? Is that how you make love to your wife?'

The silence in the lift was palpable.

'After that,' Shelly said, 'I was very happy to follow the program the counsellors had given me, the breathing and the massage and such. He needed a lot of education, I can tell you. A lot of feedback. But do you know what he said? His wife never tells him anything. About sex, what she likes, I mean. Not once. She just lies there in silence. Can you believe that?'

Gemma stared down a particularly shocked woman who'd deliberately engaged her eyes in a power struggle.

'It's good money,' said Shelly, 'and it's nice to pass on what I've learned. I feel I'm actually doing something even more beneficial than my old trade. He's only going to need a few more sessions.'

'Shelly, you are an amazing woman. What does Kosta think of your professional work?'

Shelly shrugged. 'He's out of town just now. He never knows what I'm doing.'

Gemma became aware that a woman was quietly

weeping into a tissue in one corner. Everyone pretended not to notice, including Gemma, and by the time they'd reached the foyer level, her focus was back to her line of inquiry. The lift doors opened.

'What about the car used in the attack on Robyn?' she asked, pulling out her notebook as they stepped out and walked over to where two chairs and a pot plant made a quiet corner in the large reception area.

'Robyn's friend took down the rego number and the police went and talked to the bloke. Reckons the car was stolen yesterday.'

'He would,' said Gemma. 'Did you get his name?'

'You bet I did,' said Shelly grimly. 'I've still got a friend or two in the cops. But he doesn't match the descriptions from the other two attacks.'

Gemma knew that sex workers circulated their own information about 'ugly mug' customers who'd frightened or endangered them. Girls in the safe houses and the well-run legal parlours were reasonably safe, unless the man was a psychopath who didn't care if he got caught red-handed. And that had certainly happened once or twice.

'Maybe this attack is unrelated to the other two?' Gemma suggested.

Shelly shook her head. 'No. It's him all right. The other two girls talked about that singing he does. No one knows about that except us.'

'What does he sing?' asked Gemma.

'I don't know.'

'So what *is* the description?' Gemma asked. They got up and started walking towards the foyer and the exit doors.

Shelly sighed. 'Not very good. It could fit about half the male population. Average height, dark. A weird, whispery voice. Although that could be an act. Deep-set eyes. Strong, well built.' She thought a moment. 'I think it's amazing that the girls remember anything about any of them. All the mugs look the same to me.'

'Give me the car owner's name,' said Gemma, 'and I'll have a chat with him. Maybe watch him for a while.' Shelly pulled out a business card with something scribbled on the back of it.

'Peter Fenster,' she said, passing the card to Gemma.

Outside the main doors, they were about to go their separate ways when Brenda ran out to them.

'I remember you now,' she said to Gemma. 'I knew I'd seen you before. You used to be a copper.'

Gemma nodded.

'You busted me,' said Brenda. 'For possession. About ten years ago. I got six months.'

Ten years ago, Gemma was thinking, Robyn would have been about ten or eleven then. She shook her head. 'I don't remember, Brenda. I busted a lot of people. It was my job. I hope there are no hard feelings,' she said, wanting to go home.

'You did me a favour,' said Brenda. 'I've been clean ever since. I do weights. I take care of myself.' She started crying again, pulling out a handkerchief and wiping her eyes. 'But I couldn't help my little girl.' She put the handkerchief back in her pocket. 'If you're going to go after the animal that did that to my Robyn, you're my hero.' She pushed her hair away from her face and Gemma could see that she was a good-looking woman under the exhaustion and distress. 'I'd do anything,' Brenda was saying, 'to help you. Anything to get that mongrel.'

'Thanks,' said Gemma.

'I mean that,' said Brenda.

FOUR

First thing next morning, Gemma stood on the balcony of Minkie Montreau's waterfront house at Vaucluse looking across at the Harbour Bridge. She followed the movement of a small ferry riding the slight chop of the water. Even with the grey wash of the rain over the skyline and mist veiling the tops of the tallest buildings it was still a breathtaking panorama of the most beautiful harbour in the world. Gemma shivered, remembering another night two years ago in an apartment not far from here when the harbour had been dark with rain and she'd thought she was going to die. She stepped back inside the splendid room, reassured that there was nothing sinister here. Rich fabrics at the windows and a carpet thick as a fleece created cosy opulence in the overcast light, and Minkie Montreau, an elegant woman in her late forties, Gemma guessed, hovered near an oversized damask sofa, finally settling on its edge like a nervous moth on a magnolia. Around her neck was a string of huge South Sea pearls, so pure, so luminous that they seemed to cast light and the woman bloomed with nervous energy, her neck and face lit up with pearl light. Gemma wondered if she was wearing her famous floral satin underwear beneath the classic black trouser suit.

'The insurance company is saying it was arson,' Minkie Montreau said, a crooked grimace twisting her brilliant red lipstick. 'And I was shocked to hear the police have been informed.'

'That's quite usual,' said Gemma. 'Standard procedure with suspicious fires, Mrs Montreau.'

'Miss, actually.' Minkie Montreau lowered her head and studied a huge ruby on her left hand.

'I'm sorry,' said Gemma. 'I thought you said your husband—'

'I kept my maiden name, long before it became the usual thing to do. I was a successful professional woman for many years before I married.'

'Yes,' said Gemma. 'I remember.'

Minkie Montreau lifted her head, although the fingers of her right hand still fiddled with the ruby ring. 'So, I now find myself the subject of a police investigation.' She stood up, unable to contain her distress, hands flashing diamonds and rubies as she moved around the room, touching things blindly as she passed them, as if to reassure herself that what was happening was real, and not some nightmare. She walked to the apple-green silk-covered wall between the french windows and leaned against it as if she needed a support. 'And I'm getting the distinct impression that I'm their prime suspect.'

You would be, Gemma thought. The closest person to the victim usually has the strongest motive. Add in whatever sort of money goes with this lifestyle and the motive for murder becomes even stronger. Gemma's eyes took in a Picasso hanging next to a Chagall in which a garlanded blue donkey floated in a purple sky near a pair of drifting lovers. Then she noticed a framed portrait of a man in his sixties, whose eastern European features were partly hidden by a single red rose in a crystal vase, standing on a table next to a porphyry cigarette case. She recalled the 'Fatal fire' note and Spinner's added question mark.

'That's why I need you,' Minkie Montreau said. 'I adored Benjamin.' She turned to look at the portrait. 'You don't know what it's costing me, talking business like this with him dead.'

Of course, this is Benjamin Glass's wife, Gemma realised as Minkie spoke. Bad sign, lady, using the past tense and already wearing widow's weeds.

Minkie was still standing against the wall, eyes half-closed, as if awaiting the action of a firing squad. Gemma leaned back in her seat, looking straight into her client's eyes.

'How do you know your husband is dead?' she asked, remembering the ambiguous police report on television. 'He's listed only as missing.'

Minkie Montreau pushed herself away from the wall, frowning. 'Of course he's dead,' she snapped. 'He's been completely'—she searched for the right word—"*vaporised*".

Gemma was astonished at the woman's sudden display of ire.

'The fire at the house was extraordinary. You can't imagine what it was like. Someone up there took some video footage.'

She collapsed back onto the white damask, hunched over her knees, her body shaking. Gemma waited, not untouched by this visible distress, but knowing that her business was to stay separate from it. Human beings don't vaporise in fires, Gemma was thinking. Even in the crematorium ovens at well over 1000 degrees Celsius natural teeth are not destroyed and certain dense bone fragments have to be pulverised before they can be fitted into the polystyrene boxes with the chrome plate on the lid and handed back to the relatives.

'That's why you must help me,' said Minkie Montreau, now blowing her nose and wiping copper-shadowed eyes that Gemma could see were alive with intelligence.

'Miss Montreau—' she started to say.

'Please. Call me Minkie.'

Gemma nodded. She took a breath. 'The first thing to remember, Minkie, is not to take this investigation personally. It's completely normal procedure whenever arson is suspected. Any suspicious fire may become a criminal matter. Both the fire brigade and the police have teams that will examine this issue. No one's pointing a finger at you.'

'Yet,' concluded Minkie, rummaging for a cigarette. She found one, and then searched around for a light, finally picking up a huge gold cylinder from a cedar side table. 'God knows how long Benjamin's had these,' she said grimacing as she inhaled. 'I haven't smoked in ages.'

'Tell me,' said Gemma, 'when did you last see Benjamin?'

Gemma watched the woman's face closely at this mention of her missing husband, but could see only disgust as she squashed out the long stub immediately.

'In the morning,' she said. 'He went to work yesterday just as usual. Then he drove to Nelson Bay in the late afternoon. That's where we have our holiday house. I was intending to join him on the weekend.'

'And—' Gemma started to say.

'And he was his usual self, if that's what you're about to ask me. We had breakfast in my sitting room as we always do. I saw him off. He was wearing his new winter coat.' Her lips compressed as if she were trying not to cry. 'There was a tiny thread near the collar. I picked it off for him when I kissed him goodbye.'

It was very convincing, Gemma thought. That little wifely detail of the thread. The projected scene of domestic contentment was perfect. But was it the truth? Gemma was about to ask another question when Minkie Montreau answered it herself.

'I've called you in because I want you to do a parallel investigation—on my behalf. I don't want to be left in the position of passively waiting for the police to tell me what's going on. I need someone who's completely disinterested.' She raised her coppery eyelids to Gemma. 'I must know exactly what happened,' she said. 'How that fire started. What caused it. What happened to Benjamin and why.'

Gemma clearly saw that here was a woman who was used to power and very uncomfortable with delegating or indeed trusting any agent other than herself. How, she wondered, did such a woman give up a lucrative career and become someone's nice little wifey?

'I'd do it myself,' Minkie continued, 'but I simply don't have the expertise. Or the contacts.' She flashed a glance at Gemma who saw again her sharp intelligence at work. 'How will you conduct this?' she asked.

'I'll talk to the relevant people,' said Gemma, impressed by the woman's question. 'I'll go over the witness statements, re-interview anyone who might have seen or heard anything. People some-times remember details after they've completed their witness statement. I'll have a look at the fire site. I'll find out all I can about the fire itself. I'll do everything the police or the fire investigation people might do.' And then some, she thought to herself. 'Firstly, tell me what you told the police,' Gemma asked, 'regarding your movements on the day of the fire.'

Minkie looked away for a second, fingers clasp-ing the huge pearls. 'I didn't do much that day,' she said. 'Benjamin left about 8.30. I pottered around here the rest of the morning. In the after-noon I went shopping and then'—Gemma was alerted by the pause and waited in silence until the woman continued—'and after that I came home. It was later that night when the police came round and told me about the fire. She shrugged. 'It was awful.'

Gemma wondered at what might have been omitted from the narrative. The best way to lie, she knew, was to tell the truth—just not all of it.

'And that's all you did that day?' she asked, giving Minkie a chance to add anything, knowing from her experience as an interrogator that anything originally left out, then later admitted, is often extremely sensitive.

Minkie Montreau paused for a second, then nodded, reaching under a tapestry cushion for a crocodile-skin bag. She pulled out a wallet and began counting five hundred dollar notes. 'Will this be sufficient to get things started?' she asked. 'Of course, I'll want a full inventory of every expense and time spent.'

'And you shall have it,' said Gemma, taking out a card, writing her rates on the back and handing it over. 'Now I'll need to ask you a few more things.' She knew she wouldn't have to use her Sunday School language here. She came right out with it. 'Minkie,' she said, 'did you have anything to do with your husband's disappearance?'

There was a fraction of a second's pause before Minkie shook her head. 'I did not,' she said emphatically. 'I'm not going to pretend to you that marriage to Benjamin Glass was always a garden party. But I owed him a lot. In many ways he was my best friend.' Again, Gemma noted her use of the past tense.

'Did you have an insurance policy on the house?'

Minkie shrugged. 'I'm not even sure of the amount,' she said. 'But yes, and it would be large— several million. And yes,' she said, shooting a glance at Gemma, 'I would stand to collect it all. He has no other living relatives. There were two maiden sisters, much older than him, but they died years ago. And yes, it would be helpful to me.'

'I'd like the name of the insurance company, please,' Gemma asked.

'It's with Australasian Magister.'

'Do you have a copy of the policy?'

Minkie shook her head. 'There's probably one somewhere with Benjamin's things. At the office. In his study. I don't know.'

'So you haven't seen it recently?'

'No.'

'This may sound like something out of a gangster movie,' said Gemma, 'but if you know of anyone who might want to hurt your husband, this is the time to tell me. Strictly in confidence. Is there anyone you can think of?'

Minkie Montreau considered. Gemma watched a range of emotions move across her features.

'Gemma,' she finally said, 'Benjamin was a big man. I mean that in many ways. He was imaginative and generous. But it stands to reason that a man of his stature and influence will have offended other people. Little people are always offended by big ones. It's the world we live in.' She took a deep breath. 'He was widely known as an entrepreneur and a philanthropist and he favoured a couple of charitable organisations.' She paused. 'But I don't personally know of anyone who would wish him ill.'

Gemma was alerted by the words Minkie had used. 'You say,' she said, 'you don't *personally* know of anyone who would wish him harm, but maybe you've heard something? A rumour perhaps? A suspicion?'

Minkie went to the french windows and watched as a couple of tug boats shoved a container ship under the Harbour Bridge. Then she turned back to Gemma and shook her head. 'No,' she said. 'I can't bring anything to mind.' She turned her attention back to the rain-swept harbour.

'If I'm going to do my job properly,' Gemma said to Minkie's back, 'I'm going to have to go everywhere, speak to everyone. If you've got any secrets now, you might as well tell me. Because it'll all come out one way or another. Either to the police, or the insurance people or me. Better it's me and we can discuss damage control. If necessary.'

Minkie turned away from the french windows, walked back over to the table and opened the cigarette case. She upturned its contents into the dainty Japanese-style wastepaper basket near the grand fireplace and then closed the lid with a snap.

'I myself have no secrets,' she said, putting the glassy box back on the table. 'I live a quiet life, I have a couple of women friends, I go out to the theatre, galleries, lunch, things like that. I make the occasional foray into the antique buying world. I used to make time for Benjamin. That's it.'

'Are you sure?' Gemma asked, hovering over her note pad. 'I *myself* have no secrets,' she'd said, implying that she knew someone else who did, thought Gemma, making a note of it.

More hesitation. Minkie Montreau shrugged. 'Yes,' she repeated. 'That's it.'

'What is your financial position?' Gemma asked.

'Fine, thank you.' Was her response, Gemma wondered, just a little too fast?

'Just two last questions,' she said, closing her note book and standing.

'First, was there an outstanding loan on the property?'

Minkie shook her head. 'No,' she said. 'It was fully paid for. Why?'

Gemma pressed on with the next query. 'Did your husband have a pet on the premises on the night of the fire?'

The woman's face hardened. 'Why on earth do you want to know that?' she said.

Gemma gave a half-smile, shaking her head as if her question was merely a whim. 'Did he?' she repeated.

'Well . . . yes, now that you mention it,' Minkie said with reluctance. 'He had a cat. I can't bear them.' She wrinkled her nose as if smelling something unpleasant. 'A dreadful black and white thing. Benjamin was very fond of it. It lived at the factory. But he'd take it up to the Bay if he was going to be there for a few days.'

Gemma nodded and reopened her notebook, noting it down.

'So where is the cat now?' Gemma asked.

Minkie Montreau's shadowed eyes widened. 'I have no idea,' she said. 'It's not a matter I take an interest in.'

'Do you have a photograph of it?'

'Why all this interest in a damn cat?'

'*Do* you have a photograph?'

'No. Of course not. Like I said, I couldn't stand the animal.'

'Could you describe it to me?'

Minkie Montreau's bronze-shadowed eyes blazed and Gemma wondered what it would be like to really cross this woman.

'What is this, Miss Lincoln?'

'Miss Montreau,' she said, mirroring her companion's return to the more formal address, 'I have to ask myself why you are so defensive about this matter. Please accept that I wouldn't be asking you these questions if they weren't of vital importance to an arson investigation.'

'How?'

Gemma didn't answer and waited until the fire went out of the woman's eyes. Minkie lowered her shimmering lids. Now her voice was soft and compliant.

'It's a black cat with a very distinctive white ear

and white cheek. On opposite sides. A bit like large houndstooth check. Benjamin called it Harlequin.'

Gemma made relevant notes. 'You mentioned the video footage of the fire,' she asked. 'Where can I find that?'

'I think the police have it now,' said Minkie. 'And once you've seen it, you'll understand how I know that Benjamin is dead. No one could have survived a fire like that.'

As Minkie was showing her out, Gemma turned back to her near the front door and the two of them paused.

'I remember your famous lingerie business. I bought a Hawaiian-print satin bra of yours once.'

Minkie almost smiled. 'I put my business into the hands of managers,' she said. 'Benjamin was very old-fashioned. He liked me to be at home for him.' She sighed. 'And at one stage, that's all I wanted to do.' She shrugged. 'But now,' she said, 'Who knows what might happen? I might go back to work.'

'Back into lingerie again?' Gemma asked, But Minkie shook her head.

'No,' she said. 'No more of that world for me.'

'I'll be in touch,' said Gemma, stepping outside, noticing the beautiful wooden double doors of the house.

'How long will it take?' Minkie said.

Gemma turned back to her. 'How long is a fire investigation?' The words sounded like a riddle.

Minkie remained standing at the door, fiddling with the bronze monster with its tail in its mouth that formed the handle. She looked up at Gemma. At these close quarters, her strange green eyes reminded Gemma of a cat. So Minkie's next question caught her off-guard.

'Why did you want to know all that stuff about the cat?'

'Oh,' said Gemma, with a dismissive hand wave, 'Just a general interest question. I've got a cat myself.' She smiled, trying to put Minkie at ease, aware of the other woman's intense scrutiny, wondering if she'd fall for the lie.

In the moment before Gemma turned away and the security door closed between the two women, Gemma realised she'd seen something else in the woman's light green eyes.

Minkie Montreau was scared stiff.

Sitting in her car parked opposite Minkie Montreau's house, Gemma made two necessary phone calls. '*Thunderstruck!*' screamed the singer on the car radio, '*Thunderstruck!*' She had to turn down the volume of one of her all-time favourite rock hits when Detective Sergeant Sean Wright from Physical Evidence answered. She made a date to see him, and in the second call she organised a meeting in an hour's time with Nick Yabsley from the Fire Investigation Unit. She was about to pull out for the drive to Chullora when she saw Minkie Montreau's slender figure get into a canary-yellow BMW parked nearby and pull out. On an impulse, Gemma turned her car around and settled down to follow. It'd been ages since she'd done a vehicle follow. At the first corner, she let another car come between her and her target. It was the sort of wind-whipped day that she hated, with the cold and the damp permeating everything and the rain only a nuisance, never a decent soaking shower. Thin drizzle meant her windscreen wipers were needed every few minutes.

She followed the car down the hill to Bondi Junction where it turned into a parking station. Keeping two other cars between them for cover, Gemma followed the unmistakable yellow BMW up two levels before the Beamer found a space. Gemma drove past, finding a spot further along and swung in, keeping her eyes on the slim figure that had just got out of her car and now hurried towards the exit. Gemma had to jump out of her own car and sprint so as to keep up with the woman on the stairs. She raced down after her and saw Minkie hurrying along the first floor level. Gemma followed, pulling her damp hair back into a short ponytail with a rubber band found fortuitously in her jacket pocket. She knew this altered her general appearance quite a bit, but she hung well back, just in case Minkie's intuition was working. But the other was intent on moving as quickly as possible, hurrying through the crowds of the retail centre, making her way to a dark little coffee shop near one end of the level. This made things awkward for Gemma who had to pass by the glassed-off wall of the little café and the empty tables outside. She tucked her head down and quickly walked straight past, checking the interior with a brief glance. Minkie seemed to be staring, eyes fixed on the entrance. She's waiting for someone, Gemma knew as she hurried past, searching for a place she could safely watch the coffee shop. The minute I left her house, she thought, Minkie organised to meet someone.

A large, open plan newsagency across the way offered her a vantage point from where she pretended to browse among magazines and journals, while watching the coffee shop unnoticed. It didn't seem to be very long before a short, dark man hurried past the newsagent's window. Gemma smiled to herself as she saw him turn into the coffee shop, walk straight to the back table where Minkie Montreau waited and sit opposite her. Gemma dawdled towards the shop's exit, finding a good observation position from where she could look straight into the café opposite while remaining safely hidden behind a tall rack of cards. Now the two heads at the back table were huddled together. Gemma saw Minkie's hand reach out and lift a packet of cigarettes from the man's shirt pocket and that one intimate action revealed to Gemma the nature of their relationship. Minkie took a cigarette out, lit it and tossed her head back. She was taking to smoking again, Gemma thought, with enthusiasm. No sign now of her earlier disgust.

The conversation was animated, Gemma would have written if she were making a report, *with frequent touching of hands, indicating a great degree of intimacy*. 'No other living relatives,' Minkie had told her, so it couldn't be a son. At least, not a Glass son, Gemma thought. Perhaps it was a Montreau son. Or a nephew. But it didn't feel that way, she reflected, watching them as they drank their coffees.

Gemma followed them down the stairs again, back to the Beamer. She got in her car, noted the time in her notebook and wrote a quick description of the man: '*Medium build, about 5' 9", dark, longish hair, dressed in leather jacket and jeans. Looks years younger than subject.*' She considered and added the word '*arty*' to her description. He was a gallant man too, she thought as she studied him opening the driver's door with an exaggerated flounce for Minkie and closing it after her deliberately before walking round to the passenger side. So, they're going off somewhere together, Gemma thought. If I didn't have the appointment with Nick Yabsley I'd definitely follow them.

Gemma started her car and sneaked a look back at the BMW. It was still stationary. She drove past it, worrying that she might be seen. But there was no way the two people in the front seat could have noticed anything. Unless Minkie Montreau was guilty of incest, the man was no relative. Locked in a tight embrace, straining together, the two were kissing passionately. You should have told me, Gemma thought as she turned out of the parking station. Naughty, naughty girl.

FIVE

By the time she got to the Fire Investigation Unit in Chullora the light rain had almost stopped. She turned into the driveway, parked where the security officer told her and made her way inside, past the cluttered ad hoc waiting area, and into the warren of offices, some partitioned, some open with narrow walkways lined by filing cabinets. Nick Yabsley came out of his office almost the moment she walked past it.

'Traffic must have been terrible this morning,' he said, shaking her hand, his good-humoured face beaming. 'I was expecting you earlier. Would you like a tea or coffee?'

'Coffee, thanks,' said Gemma, following him into the small room, where a large table took up almost all the available space. 'Sorry I'm late,' she said. 'Something developed and I had to follow it up.'

Nick nodded.

'How are things here?' she asked, looking around the squashed premises.

'Busy,' he said. 'Always busy. I'd ask you to sit

down, but I'm about to leave. Something's come up. Sorry.'

He saw her face. 'Look,' he said, shrugging, 'you know how it is in this job.'

'Sure,' she said, thinking quickly. 'I'll come with you. I'm a good navigator and I know some really bad jokes.' She hurried on, leaving him no time to refuse her. 'So what'll Sean Wright tell when I see him?'

'I shouldn't do this, you know,' he said.

But she followed him outside to where Fire Brigades' vehicles were parked in a line.

'Hell, Nick, you're the boss. You know from the old days I won't faint. I've got my camera.'

'I wouldn't do this for just anyone,' said Nick, throwing gear into the back of a powerful station wagon—boots, overalls, a small black case.

'Where are we going?' Gemma asked, climbing into the passenger side

'The very fire scene you're interested in, as a matter of fact.'

'Nick, you're a doll,' she said, patting his arm as he reversed too fast and turned the car around, prior to leaving the narrow yard.

'A voodoo doll, maybe,' he said, a smile creasing his amiable face.

The station wagon shot up onto the roadway, signalling a right turn, Nick's hands on the wheel seeming about two sizes too big for the rest of him, Gemma thought.

'Tell me what Sean said,' Gemma persisted, her curiosity growing.

'That it's arson,' Nick said, 'and that it's the same as the other two.'

'What other two?' asked Gemma, very interested now.

'What do you remember about arson from your studies?' he asked, swinging the car back onto the main road, heading north.

'Nick, this is my first arson job since I left the Kremlin,' she said, referring to the concrete fastness that was the Police Centre, its Russian nickname reflecting its culture as well as its architecture. 'And it's a long time since my lectures at the Academy. That's why I need your help.'

She settled down in her seat, finding a comfortable place to put her feet among all the folders and containers that lay on the front passenger floor area. She cast around her memory.

'I certainly remember the tip about the family pet,' she said. 'I remember the lecturer saying that it's almost always for insurance purposes, and the only deviations from that are the vengeful men who burn down the house after the divorce so the wife can't have it. And something about fire bugs. And they're not very common.'

'Good girl,' said Nick, with the easy, politically incorrect manner of men of his kind. Once Gemma would have snapped, but these days she was more tolerant, making the same allowances for them as she did for the aged, the frail and the ignorant. 'And because you're an ex-copper,' he continued, 'you'll appreciate the fact that police investigations are based on a different premise from ours. Police treat all fires as suspicious. We don't. We presume innocence until guilt can be proven.'

'That's why everybody loves a firey,' said Gemma. 'You're all such nice, good, decent blokes.'

'Give it a rest,' he said. 'Compared to coppers, *anyone*'s nice.' He groped around on the back seat. 'See that plastic container over there?' he asked her and Gemma retrieved it for him.

'Hungry?' he asked, pulling its lid off to reveal a packet of sweet biscuits. She shook her head.

'The Fire Investigation Unit is only called in two per cent of the time,' said Nick, taking a biscuit. 'In ninety-eight per cent of cases, the cause of the fire can be determined by the local officers in the field. They can see pretty clearly whether or not an accelerant's been used, and when they get an inventory, the insurers can determine whether or not personal property has been removed prior to the fire.'

Gemma nodded, remembering her training.

Nick continued. 'So what's weird about *these* fires—'

Gemma interrupted. 'Tell me about these fires,' she said.

'The fire that destroyed Benjamin Glass's holiday house shared almost identical characteristics with two others that we've been working on. One was a derelict factory building at Botany. The other was a pharmaceutical warehouse out at Engadine.'

Gemma was intrigued. 'What characteristics?'

'We've never seen anything like it before,' Nick was saying. 'Not in this country, although the Yanks had a few in the seventies and eighties.'

'A few what?' she asked, increasingly piqued.

'I've got a video cassette back at work that'll show you better than I can tell.'

'You mean you've got a video of the fire itself?'

'Sometimes an old firey gets lucky,' said Nick.

'*Lucky*?' said Gemma. 'Who the hell took that video? I'd be wanting to talk to him.'

'A neighbour.'

'I find that very odd,' said Gemma. 'How come this neighbour was all set up to film the fire?'

'He wasn't,' answered Nick. 'He was filming his grandson's birthday party but when he saw what was happening in the background, he forgot about the fairy bread.' He pulled something out of his pocket. 'Take a look at these,' he said, passing her some photographs.

She studied them. Benjamin Glass's house, painted in grey-green leaf and sea tones, had been a grand cement and glass edifice, big enough to serve as a small hotel. She could clearly see the three levels. Wrap-around balconies at each level surrounded three sides of the house.

'It was through those glass doors downstairs— you can see them in the pictures—that the video shows what looks like a series of small, bright white flashes. Inside and behind the lower balcony.'

Gemma found the area he was talking about— tall folding glass doors that would have opened out onto the bottom balcony area.

'Bright white flashes?' said Gemma. 'MIPs?'

'That's right,' said Nick with a grin at her use of the acronym. 'Multiple ignition points. A sure sign of arson. Then the accelerant goes up— columns of white-hot flame explode through the doors and start shooting up the sides of the building.'

Nick changed lanes to join a queue in a turning lane, indicator ticking. 'It was only a matter of seconds,' he said, 'before all three levels were going up. White flame. Then it was no time at all before the roof was penetrated. It looked like some crazy pyrotechnic display. Huge white gouts of flame. Roof flaps bursting through in a matter of minutes. Then, less than a minute later, there's a total collapse of the building as it caves in on itself.'

'God almighty, that's fast,' exclaimed Gemma. 'What on earth gets a fire going like that?'

'That's what we'd like to know.'

Gemma sat silent a few moments, considering. 'So,' she said. 'What do you reckon you've got?'

'We know we've got a case of arson,' said Nick. 'Identical to two others in the last couple of weeks and probably committed by the same person. And that's about it at this stage.'

'What is it that arsonists want?' Gemma asked. 'Is it always the money?'

'Nine times out of ten it is. They want the insurance, but they want the full amount. No point in just a bit of damage and a couple of grand for a repaint. It must be total destruction if they're to collect the full amount. And that's hard to get.' He shrugged. 'That's the reason for using an accelerant in the first place.'

'But surely that's counterproductive,' she said. 'Because then you blokes will know it was arson. Arsonists must know that.'

Nick shook his head. 'You'd be surprised,' he said, 'how many people commit serious crimes without doing any research into what the outcome might be.' Gemma thought about that for a moment. 'But if they're a little bit smart,' Nick continued, 'they'll try and introduce the accelerant in some sort of plausible way. That's difficult, too, because a lot of insurers won't pay up if people have stored highly flammable material in their houses. There are regulations covering this sort of thing. So the arsonist tries to make it look natural in some way, by shaving electrical wiring to make it seem worn, and making sure there's a lot of fluff and dust or wood shavings lying around near the short circuit. And making sure everyone's away on the day of the fire so that no one can put it out prematurely.'

'What do *you* think the accelerant was?' she asked. 'At a guess.'

Nick shook his head. 'I can't guess,' he said. 'We've never seen anything like it before these fires. And I've been looking at fires now for over thirty years.'

'What next then?' Gemma asked.

Nick swung the wheel with his too-big hands and they settled down to follow the highway north.

'We're waiting to hear back from the experts,'

he said. He leaned forward and shoved a cassette into the tape deck. A jazz singer's cool voice floated above a husky piano and whispering percussion: 'The very thought of you, and I begin to . . .'

'If these three fires are the work of the same person,' Nick said, 'then there's someone out there using the accelerant from hell. And that by itself is some sort of lead. If they were three insurance jobs, then the police will need to find if there're any connections between the three fire sites. Like who owns them, or leases them. That sort of thing.'

'Like if they all belonged to Benjamin Glass, for instance?'

Nick nodded.

'And if there's no connection and the three are just random burns?' Gemma asked.

'Then we're dealing with someone very sick. And very dangerous.'

Gemma thought of Minkie Montreau. The woman was an enigma.

'We could have one death already,' Nick said.

'Benjamin Glass?'

He nodded.

Because she'd known Nick for years and knew him to be a man of discretion, she almost told him what she'd seen Minkie Montreau doing in the car in the car park. But instead, she changed tack. 'Did you know Benjamin Glass had a cat?'

'I did not,' said Nick. 'I wonder what happened to it. We're always very interested in the pet.'

Gemma smiled. 'You see?' she said. 'I remember more from those lectures than I thought.'

Nick gave her an appraising glance.

'I've made an appointment with Sean Wright,' she said. 'See if Physical Evidence come up with anything interesting.'

'Sean Wright and his mob will be going back to Nelson Bay,' said Nick, glancing at his watch, 'working away with their little sieves. If Benjamin Glass or his cat was in that house,' Nick continued, 'and there's anything left of either of them, they'll find it. If not, well'—he paused—'that's a whole new story.'

'What if he's there, but the cat's not?' Gemma asked.

'Then that's a different story again, isn't it?'

'Indeed it is,' said Gemma. In the silence, Gemma found her thoughts drifting with the jazz singer's words, wondering where Steve was and what he was doing so that when Nick's mobile phone rang, it startled her.

'Yabsley,' said Nick in his calm and pleasant voice, putting the ear phone in. 'What do they mean, they don't know?' he said sharply.

Gemma glanced sideways at her companion, now frowning deeply. 'They're *supposed* to know. It's their job to know.'

Gemma's curiosity index rose several points.

'Yeah, I've got that,' said Nick. 'Only traces of the fire load itself.' There was a pause. 'No accelerant?' His voice rose. 'That's impossible. I've been in this game a long time. I know when an accelerant's been used. I could see it!'

Gemma saw Nick's frown deepen.

'That can't be right.' He listened without responding to the caller, then rang off and tucked the ear phone back in his pocket.

'What's the story?' she asked.

'I can't believe it,' he said. 'They can't find any traces of an accelerant!'

'But you saw it! Nothing burns like that without one,' she said.

'So far, there's no indication of the use of any of the usual highly flammable materials. That's the analyst's first report.'

'But there must be some indication!' said Gemma.

'They're not exactly saying an accelerant hasn't been used,' Nick said. 'But they simply can't find any traces. They're going to have to run more tests. I'd hoped they might give us something useful. Never mind. It's all part of the job.'

'Benjamin Glass's wife is part of my job,' Gemma said. 'Yours is more straightforward.'

'What's she like?' Nick asked.

Gemma considered the question, looking out at the tall trees they were passing and the shadows they made. A university degree in engineering turned to a successful business in lingerie was unusual enough in itself; then to marry a millionaire later in life and become a lady who lunches and frequents the art world pointed to someone with an extremely wide range of interests, even if of late they had narrowed somewhat. 'The word that comes to my mind,' said Gemma, 'is "complicated". I get the feeling she's very intelligent and not the sort of woman who'd show her hand easily. And there's something'—she searched for the right word—'hidden, or secretive about her.' We recognise each other, she thought to herself, we are both people with secrets.

'The police have already talked to her,' he said. 'Sean told me.'

'Yes, and she didn't like it one bit,' Gemma said. 'She's not used to dealing with situations like this, where she's not running the show.'

'I wonder if we'll hear anything about that cat.'

'If I do, Nick, you'll be the first to know,' she promised.

•

Gemma woke suddenly to realise she'd fallen asleep, head leaning against her window. She blinked and looked around. The car was humming along steadily, passing the trucks and road-trains taking up the slow lanes, settling down behind the traffic that moved along the Pacific Highway. She felt a little more rested, but she could still feel the leaden quality that seemed to come and go like a mist through her moods lately.

The rest of the trip passed pleasantly enough, the jazz singer spiking the atmosphere in the car until Gemma realised that it was over two hours since they'd set out and she was hungry. After a pit stop for an iced doughnut and a bad coffee, they soon found themselves turning off to the iso- lated headland where Benjamin Glass's luxury holiday house had once sprawled.

She pulled out the photographs again and looked at them, concentrating on the squat tower that formed the north-east corner of the third level.

Nick tapped the picture without looking at it, keeping his eyes on the road. 'See that tower area? That's where he was supposed to have been working at the time of the fire,' he said. 'He had a separate apartment in that block. His wife's quarters were along the eastern side of the top level, and the lower levels were for business conferences and guests. The Crime Scene people will be looking through all the rubble, of course, but they'll concentrate their efforts in that corner.'

It would have been a beautiful place to live, Gemma thought, and for a moment, she felt envious of the wealth that had enabled Benjamin Glass to enjoy it. From up there, Gemma thought, looking at the squared-off tower, there'd be 360-degree views of the coast. Then she remembered the reason for her journey. They were on their way to look at the ruins of this house. Any envy vanished.

•

Gemma could smell the fire on the light breeze a long time before they pulled up near fluttering blue and white Crime Scene tape. Her breath steamed in the sunlight as she climbed out of the station wagon and looked around. A pair of kookaburras laughed at them before taking flight over the tree-tops while Nick went round the back of his vehicle and fitted her out with a small overall and together they crunched through the scorched grass towards what remained of the house. The whole area looked, Gemma thought, like a scene from a Steven Spielberg film after an intergalactic strike. It had been divided into grids by the investigators for systematic searching. Gemma stared at the molten, twisted mass that seemed to have bubbled up through the earth and then spread like treacle into igneous lava channels that charred through the surrounding soil and heat-blasted vegetation.

'Holy smoke,' she said. 'What did *that*?'

They stood together in silence, staring at the black demolition job. Gemma looked around, remembering the video. Someone must live nearby. 'Neighbours?' she said. 'Where are they?'

Nick took her arm and drew her to the beach side of the scorched headland. Across the gully that separated this outcrop from the next was a modest timber house, nestled into the side of the hill. 'Over there,' he said.

Gemma went closer to the tangled mess. The structure had all burned away but she could still see something that might have been the floor downstairs, some fancy turquoise-coloured stone. In what would have been the double garage, an ashen frame delineated Benjamin Glass's car.

'The first guys on the scene found that parts of the steel girders had vaporised,' Nick was saying. 'They'd never seen anything like that in their lives.'

'What would happen to a human body in such temperatures?' Gemma asked.

'That's what we really don't know,' he said. 'Normally, in even the hottest fires, natural teeth and bits of the large bones remain. But this isn't normal. In house fires, steel rarely melts, let alone *vaporises*.'

If steel was vaporised, Gemma thought, even human teeth might be destroyed.

'Maybe Benjamin Glass was in the place when it went up,' said Nick. 'But because of the nature of the fire and the lack of physical evidence, the Crime Scene people aren't jumping to any conclusions just yet. Nor am I.'

Gemma turned the possibilities around in her mind. If it turns out that he *was* in the fire, she thought, did he start it himself? She knew arsonists sometimes perish in their own fires, or turned up at the nearest hospital with burns. Or was he murdered? If so, who started the fire? Could it have been Minkie? But then, why on earth would she call in yet another investigator? Gemma thought of the man she'd briefly seen in Minkie's BMW. Who was he? Where did he fit in? It was quite possible that he had reasons to want his girlfriend's husband dead. Or what if Benjamin Glass himself set the fire to make it look like he'd died, and then scarpered? Gemma remembered not to let these questions overwhelm her. She would work through each one until only one possibility became clear. It would take time. And if an experienced fire investigator like Nick Yabsley wasn't sure yet what had happened, Gemma knew she would have to be patient.

Nick took a last batch of photographs and the two of them were about to leave when they saw another station wagon approaching them, sides emblazoned with the NSW Police Forensic Services logo. It pulled over under a large orange angophora tree and two people got out. One was Detective Sergeant Sean Wright and the sleek young woman with him must have been from Photographic, Gemma thought, if the cameras she was unloading were anything to go by. Sean ambled over to where Gemma and Nick waited. Gemma remembered him as a smart, ambitious man whose shadowed eyes seemed far too old for the rest of his boyish face. While in the police service, Gemma had often collided with his competitiveness. Now that she was out of the job and no threat to him, he seemed more relaxed.

'Long time no see,' he said, shaking her hand first and then Nick's. 'What's it like out of the job?' he asked.

Gemma laughed. 'Some things stay the same,' she said. 'The paperwork, the reports, running sheets, that sort of thing. But there's no one breathing down my neck. And I get to choose the work I do.'

Sean walked back to the station wagon and started pulling on overalls.

'Find anything yesterday?' Nick asked him. Behind them, the young photographer's gleaming head bent over her work as she uncapped film and loaded cameras using the front seat as a work bench.

Sean shook his head. 'Nothing in the way of

human remains,' he said. 'No trace of anything. Yet,' he added.

'Would you mind introducing us?' Gemma asked, indicating the young photographer.

'This is Melissa,' he said.

'Detective Senior Constable Melissa Grey,' said the young woman, and the two women nodded to each other.

'Sean,' Gemma said, keeping her voice relaxed, 'did you hear anything about a cat?'

Sean shook his head as he fastened the overalls. 'Nup. So far, we've found nothing. We moved in as soon as it had cooled enough. And that took ages. We had a big team. Kids from the Academy. We examined a lot of debris. Found zilch so far. It's been too hot to get right to the centre. Such as it is.' He turned to Nick. 'In fact, we found almost no debris. It's almost like the whole joint just melted. All we got left is that.' He indicated the smooth, swirled remnants of the house, spreading out, Gemma thought, like dark spaghetti on a big black plate. She found herself staring at it and as the four of them surveyed the charred ruins she wondered when would be the right time to tell Sean about Minkie Montreau and her young man.

'What's your take on this?' Nick asked Sean.

'Hard to say,' said Sean. 'With everything gone, it's not like I can look for the usual fraud indicators.'

Gemma was pleased to find that memories from her student days and several training sessions with the Fraud Squad were starting to kick in again.

Would the land be more valuable without the house on it? The answer here was definitely not. Was the area declining in value? Again, the answer to this was a definite no. The entire Nelson Bay area was booming, with prices rising every year. Had the place been for sale for a long time with no takers? Again, a negative answer. As far as they knew, the place wasn't listed with any of the local real estate agents, and even if it were, a beautiful mansion like this would be snapped up fast. It was only bad houses in undesirable areas that failed to attract buyers, month after month, year after year. These were the sort of places mysteriously burnt down, not an elegant and desirable residence such as this one. She knew that the police would check whether the insurance had been recently upgraded, and whether a copy of the policy had recently been sent out to Benjamin Glass. They would also check if there was an outstanding loan on the property and if it was in arrears. And they'd ask further questions about that cat.

'It's not going to be an easy investigation,' Sean was saying. 'You get a feeling about these sorts of things. It's arson all right, but why? And who? And is it murder as well? People are funny animals,' he said. 'They set things up in weird ways. They make mistakes, or they do things that don't make sense. You know why?'

This was the Sean Gemma had known and not loved in the old days, the man who always knew just that little bit more than the next person and took great pains to make sure everyone knew it.

'I'll tell you why,' he said. 'It's not what actually *is* the case that's important,' he said, 'it's what people *believe* to be the case and they are often two very different stories.'

Something about these words arrested Gemma's attention. It sounded like a riddle to her. 'What do you mean?' she asked.

Sean raised an eyebrow.

'Have you seen a copy of the analysts' report?' Nick asked.

Sean nodded. 'Yeah,' he said. 'When the experts don't know, it makes it a bit hard for the likes of us. That's why I came back today. To keep looking through the guts of the place. I don't want to miss anything. And I'll keep coming back to make sure I don't.'

'You won't miss anything,' Gemma joked.

Sean turned his elderly eyes on her and he wasn't smiling. 'No,' he said, 'You can be sure of that.'

And in that moment, Gemma decided she'd keep Minkie Montreau's secret to herself just a little longer. In fact, Mr Right, she said to herself, you can sort the whole thing out on your own.

•

She and Nick had a late lunch in Nelson Bay, the only people eating in the spacious café with its honey-coloured flagstones and the rain falling in a soft straight curtain outside in the street. Gemma ate fish and chips and Nick had a hamburger and most of her chips while she stole his salad.

'What is it,' she asked, 'with men and salad? They just don't get salad, do they?'

Nick grinned and stole another chip from her plate. 'Salad's all right if you're a rabbit,' he said.

Their hot chocolates arrived, with marshmallows melting on top. Gemma sipped hers, looking around at her surroundings.

'Nice floor,' she said to Nick, pointing to the Italian tiles with the toe of her shoe. It brought to mind the pretty blue-green floor back at the Benjamin Glass fire scene. 'Strange,' she said, 'that the flooring back at the Glass holiday house survived so well. The colour wasn't touched.'

Nick looked up at her while pinching the last of her chips. 'Are you referring to that glassy stuff on the ground floor?' he said.

'Yes. That turquoise surface. I would have thought it would've been blackened or charred by the fire.'

Nick wiped his mouth and put his knife and fork neatly together. 'That floor was more than blackened or charred by the fire,' he said to her. 'It completely changed its molecular structure. Like metamorphic rocks.'

'What do you mean?' Gemma asked.

Nick took a sip from his hot chocolate. 'We worked out from the architect's plans,' he said, 'that the turquoise area was the concrete slab of the entire ground floor.'

Gemma stared at him, trying to imagine the heat that could transform grey concrete into blue-green glass. All she could think of was the furnace of a pottery, where oxides became enamelled glass. Or the immense fire at the centre of the earth, smelting sedimentary rock into molten streams, to cool as hard, igneous basalts or granites.

'Concrete turned into glass,' she said. 'That's hot.'

'Same thing happened at the factory fire at Botany. The fire at Engadine wasn't quite so severe.'

'I hope the cops find out what links these three properties. Apart from the fires, I mean,' she added.

Nick shrugged. 'You might have to do that,' he said. 'Non-fatal fires aren't high on their priority lists and I don't think much would have been done about those first two fires.'

Just like bashed street workers aren't high on their priority lists, Gemma thought. You've got to be dead to get the right attention. Now, with Benjamin Glass missing, maybe dead, priorities would change. She made a mental note to sniff around the Securities Commission to see if there were any links between the fires.

She had looked up to see that Nick had pinched almost all her chips.

'Take them all,' she said. 'They'll only make me fat.'

'Look at you,' he said. 'A stiff wind and you'd blow over.'

'I can still put up a fight,' she said, smiling at him.

'That Sean Wright's a bit of a prick,' he said, taking the last chip.

Gemma grunted. Over the years, she'd learned discretion, even with someone like Nick. 'He's a copper, Nick,' was all she said.

They sorted out the bill at the counter and walked outside into the drizzle.

'I'd really like to know,' she said, 'where that cat is.'

•

Back in Sydney, Nick gave her the video of the fire at Benjamin Glass's mansion, and Fire Brigades' footage of the Botany factory fire as well as an archived tape used for educational purposes of an American hotel fire. She watched, replaying the Glass fire several times, noting the three brilliant flashes Nick had mentioned, clearly visible through the trees in the background. At first the fore-ground was taken up with a birthday cake and the noisy appreciation of little boys. Then the video operator lost interest in the party and the camera focused in on the lower glass doors through the trees as it zoomed to show the tall jet of white-hot flame spearing up through the roof and the mag-nesium brilliance of the explosions in the lower parts of the house. She then played the video of the factory fire. Even to her untrained eye, it was the same sort of fire as that recorded by the neigh-bour as Benjamin Glass's holiday mansion went up. Finally, Gemma watched the American hotel footage, complete with on-the-spot witness reports.

On the drive home from the Fire Investigation Unit, she passed Centennial Park where she and

Steve had thrown bread to the ducks last summer. Where are you now, Steve? she whispered to him across the city. Please keep safe.

•

It was almost dark by the time Mike dropped in to the office. Louise was still away and Spinner had gone home. Gemma swivelled on her chair as she heard him go into the room opposite hers.

'Hullo, Mike,' she called out.

'You're still here,' he said. 'I wasn't sure. I've got a couple of reports to wrap up.' He put his head round her door. 'Is there anything new you want me to do?'

She liked the way he offered, unlike Louise who, although a good enough worker, somehow gave the impression that she was doing Gemma a favour when she took on a job, instead of earning her salary. Spinner and Mike always took their laptops home with them, ready to plug into the world at any time, always ready for a job. But Louise never took hers, leaving it in a drawer in the operatives' office. Gemma thought it was a telling detail.

'Do you want a coffee?' she asked, coming over to the door.

'Black and one, please.'

He held her gaze a moment longer than was completely necessary before going back to his office and Gemma felt a little awkward. She glanced down at herself. As far as she could see, everything was in order: her navy slacks were clean, her cream blouse and red and cream striped

jumper seemed innocent of any blemish. She went
to the little mirror behind the door and checked
that she didn't have spinach wrapped around a
front tooth. Reassured, she went out to the kitchen
for something to eat and started the coffee-making.
Taxi was sulking, hiding under the lounge.
He didn't even bother batting at her fingers when
she crouched down to tease him. Nor did he come
running when she opened the fridge, usually a
sure-fire cue to get him up and going. 'What's
wrong with you?' she asked him, irritated that the
shelves were almost bare apart from a little smoked
salmon and some salad. I wish there was someone
who'd just do the marketing every week, she
thought. Someone who'd make sure there were
always plenty of goodies in the fridge. She realised
she felt like something more substantial—and hot.
She found some bread and a lump of good
Gloucester and made toasted cheese, with an extra
slice in case Mike wanted some too. She carried
the coffee and the toasted cheese on a tray, knocking with the toe of her shoe and pushing the door
open in the same way.

The second office was smaller than her own, but
warmer in winter because the windows were free
of climbing vegetation so the low sunshine filled
it during the afternoons. Mike was printing out as
she put the tray on the low table next to the
printer, noticing the expensive automobile magazines in a pile. Men, she thought. They don't get
salad but they do get the internal combustion
engine. She failed to interpret this in any satisfac-

tory way as she passed his coffee to him and offered him the toasted cheese. He took a slice and she perched on the edge of the desk used by Louise and, to a lesser degree, Spinner. Spinner pretty well lived in his vehicle, making his office in the white Rodeo utility, where a change of tarpaulins or the addition of metal frame fixtures on the back created a new disguise when necessary. He himself could do wizard-like transformations, using old beanies, headbands, leather jackets and football jerseys, turning himself from a wizened old man to a sturdy flyweight contender and back again in minutes.

'Mike,' she started as he bit into his toast, embarrassed by what she had to say, 'I've been getting nuisance email.'

'That's no good,' he said, between chews.

'No,' she agreed. 'I want to talk to you about what I can do.'

He finished the toast, picked up a pen and started doodling a series of overlapping triangles.

'What sort of nuisance email? Spam?'

She shook her head. 'Pornographic,' she said. 'It's horrible.'

Mike looked at her with surprise and she felt a blush start at the base of her neck. She looked away and cleared her throat.

'What's the best thing to do?' she asked. Part of her reasons for employing someone with Mike's capabilities had been to keep computer technology in-house, and save a small fortune in services and fees.

'I can install a program for you,' Mike said, 'that will block the addresses of any known nuisance.'

Gemma shook her head. 'That's just it,' she said. 'It's not just one or two addresses. They're all different. Lots of them from all over the place. Somehow my address has become available to any perv in cyberspace.'

Mike looked even more surprised.

'Somehow, someone who knows my email address is encouraging people to write to me. I'm getting dozens every time I log on. It's diabolical.'

Gemma thought of the ugly threats and sexual hatred conveyed by strangers at the speed of light. The net is the greatest producer, distributor and retail outlet for pornography than any other system, she'd read somewhere.

'My sister says if a traveller from another galaxy wanted to know what human beings are like,' she said, 'they should just check our reflection on the Internet.'

She noticed Mike looking at her closely, penetrating grey eyes very direct.

'I can install a selective firewall,' he said, 'that searches for certain key words, so any email containing any of those words would be automatically blocked.'

'That would be great,' said Gemma, feeling the heavy burden of the last few days easing. 'Please do that.'

'Just give me the list of words.'

'I can do better than that,' she said, picking up

her now empty plate and cup. 'Come to my office and you can see for yourself.'

She went to her computer and logged on, entered her password and waited. Her heart sank. There were dozens more already. She could feel the warmth of Mike's body as he stood behind her, watching while she opened one of the emails at random.

'*Hi Dirtygirl*,' she read, '*I really enjoyed your fantasy. I came in my pants just reading it. You must really like it rough. This is what I'd do to you. First I'd handcuff you, one hand on each side of the bed then I'd gag you . . .*'

Gemma turned away, sickened, and Mike stepped back to let her get up.

'Look,' he said, 'you don't have to read the rest of it. I can do that and make a list of the words that crop up all the time. That should get rid of the majority of them quickly. Any that slip through, we'll just add to the prohibited list.'

'But what about genuine messages?' she said. 'My friends might use some of those words in their emails.'

'Nice friends,' he said.

It was the sort of remark that Spinner might make, but at least Spinner was predictable and Gemma was never offended by his narrow-mindedness. It was part of his charm. Now, Gemma felt both defensive and angry at Mike's words. She didn't want this response from him.

'That's very self-righteous,' she said, trying to laugh it off.

'You can email them that they'd better clean up their language or they'll be purged,' he said and the moment passed. 'As a general rule with email,' he went on, 'presume that anyone can read anything you've written. That way, you'll take more care with it. It might feel the same as writing a letter, but it's a letter that can be accessed by a lot of people. A letter in a drawer in your house doesn't have that potential.' He considered a moment. 'And shut your PC down for a while,' he said.

'But I need it,' she said.

He shrugged. 'Suit yourself. You're the boss.'

SIX

Gemma cleaned up the last of her lasagna, picked up her glass of red wine and looked around Kit's freshly painted dining area, a section of the cosy living room, with old-fashioned picture rails and heavy red curtains closing the window against the sea beneath the cliff walk. Kit was looking terrific these days, Gemma thought, glossy and alive. Since her divorce some years ago, Kit had blossomed.

'You look great, Kittycat,' she said.

Kit smiled to acknowledge the compliment, then looked more closely at her younger sister. 'I can't say the same for you, Gems,' she said. 'You're working too hard.'

'It's not really work,' said Gemma. 'It's life in general.'

Kit took the empty plates away and Gemma followed her out into the kitchen.

'I've been getting awful email,' Gemma said. 'Horrible stuff. I was even feeling guilty that somehow I must have caused all these pathetic dirty-minded sickos to come after me. It's been horrendous.' She scraped the dishes and put them on the counter.

'Gems, I don't understand,' said Kit, turning round from the sink. 'How does something like that sort of harassment start?'

Gemma knew exactly how it had started, but there was no way she could admit that to her sister. 'I'm not a hundred per cent sure,' she said vaguely. 'But I imagine it's not difficult to get to someone's email address and post it somewhere in cyberspace and invite the weirdos to respond. It's a high-tech version of writing your enemy's name and phone number in the public toilets.'

•

Later they finished their wine with coffee in front of the open fire. Outside, the Pacific roared like a train, driven by a strong south easterly that had risen only in the last few minutes.

'Don't you think it's odd,' she persisted, 'that a complete stranger got hold of your email address in the first place?'

Gemma shook her head. 'I just don't know,' she said. 'But it's not that hard. No one regards email addresses as particularly private.' That at least was true. She felt the relief of answering honestly.

'Any interesting clients?' she asked, tossing back the last of her wine, changing the subject.

Kit flashed her a look.

'I know you can't talk about them, but you could sort of give me a general idea.' Gemma said.

'You know, along the lines of whether you've got anyone who's in love with their poodle or something a bit different.'

Her sister just laughed.

'I had this dream,' Gemma said, changing back again. 'A huge meteor was coming towards me. I was on Earth but I knew it was up there, light years away. I was standing near the lions. On Delos, I think.'

Kit got up and walked over to the bookshelves, pulling out a large illustrated art book.

'I looked up Delos,' said Kit, 'when you first told me about the lions you were making. Delos is where Leto gave birth to Apollo and Artemis. And, according to the legend, no one else was allowed to be born or to die there.'

'Sounds like fairyland,' said Gemma. She phrased her next question carefully, worried about giving too much away. 'If a person came to you,' she said, 'saying they'd always felt something was missing from their lives, what would you say?'

Kit laughed and shook her head. 'I don't have a particular formula that I use when people say things to me, Gems. It all depends on who they are and what their lives are all about.' She paused. 'But it's a very common feeling,' she added. 'Many people feel an emptiness in their lives they can't account for. Sometimes whatever or whoever they've been using to fill it up suddenly isn't there anymore. Or it doesn't work any more. Or they reach a certain age and look back and feel they've missed something along the way. I see a lot of people who say that to me in their different ways.'

Gemma thought of the violent man stalking Sydney's sex workers. 'You don't happen to be seeing someone who picks up women who look a bit like Ally McBeal and bashes and rapes them?'

'I hope not,' said Kit. 'But he probably wouldn't tell me if he was.'

'I thought clients told their therapists everything.'

'Whatever made you think that?'

'But wouldn't you know? If they were withholding secrets from you?'

Kit laughed. 'Gems, I think you attribute powers to me that I don't have.'

'Yes,' said Gemma impatiently, 'but I know you can read people, read their energy. That must tell you things.'

'It might tell me that they're withdrawn and secretive in their way of being, but it doesn't necessarily tell me what their secrets are.' She paused. 'Anyway,' she added, 'someone like that doesn't *do* therapy unless he's had some huge insight into the fact that he's using violence against women as an outlet for old rage. I doubt if that happens very often.'

'I visited one of those people's victims in hospital,' said Gemma. 'She's in an awful state. How would someone like that be if you just met him on the street?'

'Hard to say,' said Kit. 'Alienated. He might be the kind of loner the profilers talk about. But not necessarily. Some violent men can be quite charming as long as everything's going according to their script. If charm was part of the family training. But if this fellow targets street girls it might be because he can't face women socially. Or he might have a grudge against sex workers in general.'

Gemma immediately thought of her client Peter Greengate, whose hatred had for an instant hardened his eyes and how he'd remained standing, watching her closed door instead of walking away.

'I'm going to visit the man who owns the car used in the last attack. He claims it was stolen.'

'He would,' said Kit. 'You be careful. Why not send a man instead? He could do some of that "all women are asking for it" routine and see what the guy's reaction is.'

Gemma considered. 'I want to get the feel of him myself.' She saw Kit flash her a look, then look away.

'Will's coming over for dinner tomorrow night. Can you handle my cooking two nights in a row?'

Gemma hadn't seen her nephew for ages. 'How is Will?'

Kit smiled. 'He's very well. He's studying Law part time. He's got a job with the Registrar General's department. It's hard to believe he's been straight now for over two years. He says he can't believe it either sometimes.'

'It's good, Kit.' She thought of something. 'And thanks. I'd like to come over but I'm undercover tomorrow night. I'm on the streets as a sex worker. And I'm hoping to pull a special client.'

Kit's face drained of colour. 'Not that man we've just been talking about? The one who's attacking street girls?' She looked sick and Gemma wished she could take the words back. I should never have told Kit about this, she realised too late.

'What is it?' Gemma asked. 'I can see you don't approve.'

Kit shook her head. 'Of course I don't. It's crazy. Don't do it.'

'It's okay,' she said in a calm voice. 'Kit, I know what I'm doing.'

'Do you?'

Gemma felt provoked and she could feel her face getting hot. 'Yes,' she said. 'As a matter of fact I do.'

Kit stood up and walked to the mantelpiece where two photographs stood in oval frames. She picked one of them up and Gemma, straining to see, recognised an early portrait of their mother.

'I don't think you do,' Kit said. 'It's not only a foolish idea, it's also very dangerous. Surely I don't have to remind you of what happened a couple of years ago when I was almost murdered as a direct result of your acting out.'

Gemma sat, open-mouthed. '*What*?' she said. 'What acting out?'

'I'm referring to your habit of picking up men.'

'Oh, for heavens sake,' Gemma began, feeling anger and irritation together. 'That was just unlucky. I don't have a habit of picking up men!'

'Gemma, stop deluding yourself. You're still

doing it! Except now you've got hundreds of men harassing you by email. How did that happen?'

Gemma felt guilty and defensive. But she couldn't—wouldn't—admit to her sister that she had indeed been silly and flirtatious, pretending to be someone she wasn't on an Internet chat line.

'I didn't think it was your habit to blame the victim,' she retorted, going on the attack.

'It's not a question of blaming anyone. It's a matter of living responsibly,' said her sister. 'We express who we are in everything we do. Have a look at what your behaviour says. I think you're behaving in a very foolish way. You seem compelled to keep putting yourself into dangerous situations.' She put the photograph of their mother down. 'But what makes it even *more* dangerous is that you seem to be completely unconscious of this.'

'I'm not unconscious about it. It's my job for God's sake,' Gemma said. 'I don't do it for fun. It's my work!'

'Exactly,' said Kit. 'You just rationalise it away. Don't you ever ask yourself why you're drawn to the sort of work you do? Why do you want to do these sorts of things? Like dressing up as a hooker to attract a potential killer?'

'Because I'm suited to it,' Gemma snapped. 'Because I've got the training for it.'

'So have heaps of others. Someone else could do it.'

'Oh, I see,' Gemma said caustically. 'So it's okay for someone else to do dangerous work, but not little Gemma? You talk about my childhood as if you weren't there too. It was *our* childhood and if I was affected, so must you have been!'

Kit's voice didn't change and the very mildness of it irritated Gemma even more. 'The police are properly equipped for this sort of thing,' Kit was saying. 'It's not your job to be running some pro-active operation to catch such a dangerous man.'

'The police *aren't* doing it. That's just the point. And it *is* my business. That's why Shelly asked me and that's why I've taken it on. I make my living investigating people and their lives and their problems. Just like you do but in a different way. You take on dangerous clients. Don't try and tell me otherwise. I don't criticise you for that.' She was surprised at her own vehemence and realised she wasn't quite finished with Kit yet. 'You reckon *I'm* compelled, as you put it,' she said. 'But what about you? Maybe you're the one with unconscious motives here. Still protecting little Gems at all times! In a couple of years I'll be forty, Kit. I don't need protection from my big sister anymore.' She stood up, grabbed her jacket and her purse, wanting to go home, feeling unaccountably sad. 'And I've got enough on my mind just now,' she added, 'without having to deal with your criticism.'

She strode out of the room and up the hall, aware of her sister following. Outside, the sea crashed against the shore as the wind strengthened, rattling the windows and whining under the doors. Kit moved in front of her, opening the front door and standing back to let her pass. Gemma stood there a moment, unwilling for them to part like this.

'Kit, I know what I'm doing.'

'Please, Gemma. Reconsider.'

Gemma strode out into the night, aware of her sister's shadow, as she stood silhouetted against the light in the hallway. Gemma walked back to her car. She didn't look back.

SEVEN

Next morning, Gemma was back at Minkie Montreau's mansion, still feeling unhappy about her conflict with Kit, and the angry parting of last night, but she was soon immersed in the case at hand. She looked hard at her hostess, whose pale face and cat-like eyes now seemed untouched by grief. I'm not going to say anything about your young man just yet, Gemma thought to herself as she followed Minkie up the magnificent staircase on the way to Benjamin Glass's study, noticing the sphere of diamonds at the back of her neck, like a miniature mirror ball, that formed the clasp to the South Sea pearls. I might need something over you, Miss Minkie M, she thought. Better at this stage to gather more intelligence, and not warn you that I know one of your secrets. Minkie had stopped on the wide landing outside a set of handsome timber panelled double doors, her hand on an amber crystal knob. Very fancy, thought Gemma, thinking of her own humble office and the cassette recorder across the hall chattering away when she was alone with a client.

'I never go in here,' said Minkie, opening one of the doors. 'It was his territory.'

For a second, Gemma thought she saw a chink in the woman's cool façade. But it was back to business within a second.

'Please excuse me,' she said. 'As you can imagine, I have a lot to attend to.' She drew back, almost as if something in there might jump out and bite her. Then she hurried away, leaving Gemma at the threshold of the room.

She stepped in, looking around at the green velvet curtains draped across the tall windows, the large antique map over the marble fireplace, the rows of books in the leadlight bookcases, and the deep pile of the luxurious rug on the parquetry floor. With the harbour visible in slices through the cedar blinds, soft grey light fell gently on row after row of more beautifully bound books on the left-hand side of the room. On the right towered a full-length portrait of Minkie in a cream evening dress, her right hand holding a book, almost obscured by the billowing folds of the dress. Gemma walked up to the mantelpiece, checking out the photographs. They were mostly shots of the wealthy pair at various functions and Gemma couldn't help but notice that in every picture, the couple faced away from each other, or one was deep in conversation with a third party, while the other stared out at the photographer, or smiled tightly to no one in particular. Benjamin Glass was an angular man with irregular, squinting features. In one photo his thick white hair was all that could be seen of him, taking up much of the foreground, his wife elegant and poised with a small group of equally well-dressed people to the right. In this photo she had her hand on the arm of a young man in the sort of gesture that said, 'Listen, I just *have* to tell you this,' while the young man's beautiful companion smiled up at him. Gemma picked up the photo, studying it but it was impossible to tell if it was the same man she'd seen with Minkie in the coffee shop and the BMW. All she'd really been able to get was an impression, certainly not enough for her to identify him in a photograph.

She put the picture down and looked around. Dominating the room was the huge desk, or rather, table of highly polished cedar, wide and low, clear of anything except a ritzy crystal and gold desk set and a carved, delicately painted babushka doll. Gemma sat down in Benjamin Glass's heavy leather chair and leaned back, studying the room from this perspective. The room had the hush of a cathedral sacristy, or vacant, panelled court room; the skittle-shaped wooden doll, with its intricate high gloss features, wide eyes and flowery robes seemed very out of place in such a masculine shrine. Minkie's face looked dreamily out of the framed portrait, the cat-green eyes staring out at Gemma.

Gemma turned her attention away from her hostess's painted face and, using the keys Minkie had given her, tried the first drawer under the desk top. It opened easily and she looked through its contents. Insurance policies, business papers, a list of the charities and institutions that Benjamin Glass supported with his philanthropy, clippings and photos of him opening hospitals he'd endowed. *The man's practically a saint,* Gemma remembered. The second drawer held accounts books and bank statements. And two large rolls of cash held together with rubber bands. Gemma picked one up and tried to estimate the amount. They were bundles of hundred dollar bills. She put the roll down and flicked through the accounts books, noticing the huge amounts of money that passed through the Glass's several accounts. It's another world, she thought to herself, the world of the wealthy. She made a mental note to ask Minkie's permission for an independent audit, in case the figures revealed something unseemly. She felt overwhelmed by all this useless information. The third drawer seemed to have collected odds and ends, loose photographs and a set of jade or azurite worry beads. She sat there staring at them for a moment, then got up and went over to the mantelpiece, collecting the framed photographs and returning with them to the desk. She seated herself back in the boss's seat. With great care, she prised each from its frame to check that there was nothing hiding behind them. There wasn't. She refitted them and replaced them, returning them to their positions under the antique map.

She knew from past experience that books often held secrets and her heart sank when she consid-

ered how many books there were in the room and
how many potential hiding places in every volume.
She would need Spinner, Mike and Louise to come
in with her and go through them. To find what,
she asked herself? She opened the drawers in an
elegant sideboard, finding only more rare books
and liquor. She pulled up the rug under the desk
and patted it down underneath where she could-
n't lift it, also tapping the parquetry underneath it.
It all sounded solid. There didn't seem to be any
hidey-holes in the flooring. It's hard searching for
something unknown, she thought. Maybe I'm
looking straight at it, and not recognising it. She
got under the desk and lay on her back, her eyes
adjusting to the dimness. She felt around the
underside. From her experience she knew that
men sometimes taped things there but there was
nothing here, nor the housing for any secret
drawer. She crawled back out. I'm looking for
something, she thought, that will put a dent into
the pure-as-the-driven-snow image of Benjamin
Glass, philanthropist and all-round thoroughly
decent man.

She gathered up the loose photos that still lay
on the desk and was putting them back in the
drawer when she noticed something right at
the back, almost out of sight. She reached in and
pulled out a boxed deck of cards. She picked them
up, opened the pack and tipped them out. Just
common blue-etched playing cards, the sort that
are handed out by cabin crew during long flights.
She took the deck out and started shuffling the

cards, remembering the games of solitaire she'd played by torchlight in lonely stake-outs when it was too risky to watch a portable television. Gemma was handy with cards and slapped them and halved them, splicing the two halves together like a fancy gambler in a western. She imagined the missing man had sat here like her, doing this. Cards were soothing to play with, she thought, a bit like Middle Eastern worry beads. Is that what he did with them? Were they just an old-fashioned executive toy? Where are you, Benjamin Glass? she asked. *Who* are you?

Gemma put the cards down and pulled the babushka doll over, admiring the delicate silver and gold filigree paint of its body, the refinement of its pretty face. She opened it and found, not unsurprisingly, the next one. She opened the second one and there was the third, not quite so detailed in its decoration. There were still more to go, she knew, but she turned her attention back to the cards. She halved the deck, turned one half, then holding each half with her thumbs on the top, bent them a little to get the right tension then let them go, watching the blur as the two halves whizzed, straightened and interleafed with each other, splicing back into one deck again. She idly repeated the motion, enjoying the purr and snap of the cards as they combined. She was repeating this again when something odd caught her eye. This time, she slowed the action and repeated it with much more attention. As the cards whizzed past, it seemed that the etched back design was moving and changing in a manner that reminded her of primitive animation. Little dots of white danced in front of her eyes. Gemma frowned. This was very peculiar. Puzzled, she cut and spliced the cards again. She repeated the trick three times and each time, tiny white spots danced, in exactly the same sequence as before. Very interested now, Gemma slowed down the action, and one by one, let each card go. She brought the cards right up close and studied each one. I don't believe it, she thought as she realised why the white spots danced. She'd seen this once a long time ago. She repeated the action, stopping the whizz at a white spot. She pulled the card out and studied it.

Suddenly Gemma stood up, experiencing the rush that she always felt when she was on the point of discovery. Her mind raced through the possibilities. Perhaps they were just a novelty, a party trick. Or did they indicate something more? Like the babushka doll, the cards pointed to something unusual, something unexpected in the man's study and in his life, although Gemma could hardly imagine anything less sinister than a nest of painted wooden dolls. She reached over and unscrewed the third rosy-cheeked figure. And the fourth, and the fifth. But when she came to the last one, instead of the little solid doll who lives in the middle of her hollow sisters, she found a tiny security key. Aha, she thought, here's something. She put all the dolls back inside each other again, and placed the key in an envelope. Then she picked up the deck of cards and the envelope, closed the drawers and walked out of the room.

Gemma descended the grand, curving staircase, wondering where Minkie might be.

'Minkie?' she called, feeling a little silly as the nickname echoed in the empty space of the atrium. From somewhere, the sound of a chair scraping indicated that her call had been heard and in a second or two Gemma heard the tip-tap of her Italian shoes on marble floors.

'I need to speak to you,' Gemma called. She heard the sound of a door opening and her hostess suddenly looked out from one of the rooms opening off a corridor that led from the atrium.

'Down here, Gemma.'

Gemma walked past paintings on the walls and treasures in glass cases.

'Come in,' said Minkie, stepping back as Gemma followed her into a private sitting room. This space was feminine and soft, quite different from the formal elegance of the downstairs living room they'd first spoken in and the strongly masculine study of timber and baize green. On a dainty table, creamy pink camellias swam in a glass bowl, the water and the glass magnifying the impossibly perfect blooms. Gemma remembered the meaning of camellias from a book she read long ago on the language of flowers—beautiful, but cold. Are they an omen, she wondered?

'I need to ask you about these,' Gemma started to say, holding up the deck of cards. I found them in your husband's desk.'

Minkie Montreau looked away as if busy finding a suitable place for the folder she was holding, but not before Gemma noticed the sudden blanching of her face, closely followed by an angry red blush. Gemma waited, letting the pressure of silence build between them. Minkie turned back to face her, her colour almost normal again, and licked her painted magenta lips.

'Ah, those,' she said, as if for a moment she hadn't understood to what Gemma was referring. 'Yes. Benjamin enjoyed card games very much.'

'I'm sure he did,' Gemma said. 'Especially with this deck.'

'What do you mean?' Minkie frowned.

'Are there any other decks around?'

'Quite possibly,' said Minkie. 'Benjamin enjoyed a weekly card night with friends. I never attended them. They were only social games anyway.'

'I'd like to see the other decks,' said Gemma, alerted by the woman's defensiveness. 'May I look around?'

'But of course,' said Minkie. 'It's why you're here.'

Gemma searched drawers and cabinets in the formal living room and soon found four more decks. She cut and checked each deck, whizzing them past her eyes. Minkie stood watching her until the phone rang. She picked up in a corner of the room, turning away from Gemma, speaking softly and in monosyllables. Gemma was hardly surprised to find that all four decks provided her with the dancing white spot show. In the corner, Minkie was replacing the handset.

'Minkie,' Gemma said. 'I think you'd better tell me about Benjamin and his interest in playing cards.'

Minkie Montreau came over and sank into the upholstery of the grand lounge. The normal pallor of her face had become ghostly.

'Benjamin had this weakness for card games,' she said. 'I didn't mention it because I really didn't think it would have any bearing on what's happened.'

'Tell me.'

'He loved *winning*. Whether it was the share market or a race horse—not that he went to the track often. But when he did, he absolutely had to win. He became very, very upset if he lost.' She looked up at Gemma. Today, the cat eyes were shaded with a deep charcoal, making them look larger and darker, if somewhat bruised. 'It was his only character defect really. I found it rather amusing at first. But I'm pleased to say he hardly ever lost. He has—he had—the most unbelievable luck. Incredible luck. He was a legend among his friends. Benjamin always won.'

'I'm sure he did,' said Gemma, 'with these.' She pushed the five packs of cards into the centre of a little alabaster and bronze table. Minkie looked at them and then back at Gemma.

'Why do you say that?' she said.

Gemma laid half a dozen cards face down on the table. She held the first one up to Minkie, with the face pointing away from her. 'Do you want me to tell you what that is?' said Gemma. 'It's a three of clubs.' She picked up another one, also with its back to her. 'And that's a four of hearts.'

Minkie stared.

'That's the queen of hearts,' Gemma said, lifting another card face up towards the other woman. 'And I can tell you the others if you want me to.'

There was a stunned silence.

'Show me,' Minkie finally said. 'How is it done?'

Gemma showed her. In the top left-hand corner, in the intricate etched floral pattern, tiny changes had been made. One of the filigree flowers had its fourth petal missing.

'Four petals, four suites,' she said. 'Now look here.' She pointed to the design of the border that ran around the edge of the cards, enclosing the floral design. It was a symmetrical Greek key pattern. 'See how the seventh sequence of the pattern has been doctored?' she said, pointing to the missing etched line. It was these doctored bits, she realised, that created the effect of the dancing white spots in the fast moving cards. 'He's used some sharp pointed object to lift off the surface of the printed pattern,' she said. 'This one has the second petal of the four-petalled flower missing. And the ninth castellation of the Greek key border missing. It will be a nine.' The nine of clubs lay on the table in front of them. 'And those with the first and third petal removed from the flowers in the corner are hearts and spades respectively.' She pointed to the tiny white spots.

'But I don't understand,' Minkie said, examining the cards. 'Why would Benjamin have marked cards?'

Gemma let the silence lie around them for a long moment before holding up the key. 'What about this?' she said.

Minkie stared at it. 'Where did you find that?' she asked. Gemma waited, watching her. Her bewilderment seemed genuine. 'Benjamin kept all his keys on a large keyring I gave him,' she said. 'I don't know what that key is for. Or from.'

'It looks like the key to a safe to me,' said Gemma. 'It was hidden inside the babushka dolls.'

Minkie looked shocked. 'The dolls?'

'Does your husband have a safe?'

Minkie's expression brightened visibly. 'That's it,' she said. 'Yes, he does. It must be the key to the safe.'

'Where is it?'

Minkie swivelled her head on its sinewy neck. 'I really have no idea.' She saw Gemma's look and her face hardened. 'Look,' she said, 'I can see you don't believe me. But we didn't live in each other's pockets. We were not a conventional couple. Sometimes that's hard for people to understand. Especially people like—'

'People like me?' Gemma asked, angered by the presumption and standing up. Her hostess stood up, too. Gemma took a step closer to Minkie. 'You don't know anything about me,' she said. 'If you did, you'd know that there's nothing conventional about me.' She thought of her parents and their tragic, fatal union. Was there something similar about the union of Minkie Montreau and Benjamin Glass? Is that why the alarm bells were starting to ring in her mind? Is my unconscious presenting me with a big fat clue that I can't see? she wondered.

'I didn't mean to say it like that.' Minkie tried another tack. 'I meant, about our marriage—it was different from the usual suburban arrangement of domestic togetherness. Benjamin's affairs were none of my business,' she said. 'I know he kept a safe somewhere. I imagine it's hidden somewhere in his study. It was his private domain.' Her face softened. 'He used to call it his "cubby house". As I've already told you, I never went in there.' Yet she was a presence in the cubby house, Gemma realised, thinking of the large portrait which dominated the room.

'Let's go and check it, shall we?' she asked.

Minkie followed her back into the study.

'People often hide their safe behind a painting,' she said to Minkie and together they struggled with the heavy portrait. It took all Gemma's strength to lower it from the wall, even with Minkie's help.

But, apart from a few opportunistic spiders, there was nothing but wall behind. In a few minutes, they'd checked behind the other paintings in the room. Nothing.

'Okay,' she said, looking at the rows and rows

of books that lined the walls almost up to the roof.
'They've all got to come out.'

In spite of the coolness of the day, Gemma soon
worked up a sweat lifting and piling books. Stacks
of them now stood around in piles on the floor, and
on every available surface. They checked the walls
behind the now empty shelves, Gemma running
her fingers carefully over the surfaces, but there
were not even any joins, just the smooth, cold,
painted render. She found nothing. They stood in
among the piles of books, making their way around
them.

'Is there anywhere else you can think of,'
Gemma asked, 'where your husband might have
kept a safe?'

While Minkie considered, Gemma frowned.
What am I hoping to find, she asked herself. Something that will explain why one of Australia's
richest men was a card cheat?

'Perhaps the safe was at the Bay?' Minkie suggested, cutting into her thoughts.

Gemma thought of the spread-out twisted
molten metal she'd visited, a whole house melted
across the earth like a huge pancake. And even
though most safes claim to be fireproof, she had
little hope that any safe could have survived an
inferno in which steel girders vaporised. Gemma
thought about the likelihood of the safe being at
Nelson Bay. That would put its contents, whatever
they were, too far away. As a rule, people want

access to their valuables without an intervening two- or three-hour drive. She shook her head. 'I don't think so,' she said.

'Your jewellery,' she said to Minkie. 'Where's that kept?'

'Here,' said the other. 'I keep it in my bedroom because I wear my pieces all the time. I know it's not satisfactory, but the security is very good here.'

Gemma glanced at the pearls, worth a hundred thousand at least, she thought, just for them. She tried another tack. 'Do you have any idea where he kept important documents?'

Minkie shook her head. 'Things like his Will are with his solicitors. His practice was to keep all his other papers here. You would have seen these when you looked through his study.'

Gemma nodded.

'Will you be telling the police about these things,' Minkie said, 'the key and the cards?' There was a little-girl lostness in her voice, which surprised Gemma.

'I'm not obliged to tell them anything unless it involves a serious offence.'

'They're not really important, are they?' asked Minkie.

'I can't say that at this stage,' said Gemma. 'My feeling is that these cards could be very important indeed.'

Minkie looked as if she were about to burst into tears but she rallied quickly and shoved her hands in the pockets of her jacket, shivering.

'I'll need a letter from you,' Gemma said,

'authorising me to look around your husband's office.'

Minkie pulled open a drawer, took out some stationery, and scribbled and signed a short letter on the heavy paper. She put it in an envelope and passed it to Gemma.

'Give that to Rosalie, his assistant,' she said. 'She'll look after you.'

'And I'd like to take these with me, too,' Gemma said, picking up a deck of cards from the pile. 'I'll return them when I've finished with them.' She slipped them in her pocket with the letter and the key. Now that she had what she needed, Gemma decided it was time to show some of her own hand. 'Minkie,' she said, 'I'm puzzled by you.' She paused: she had the woman's complete attention. 'You hired me to investigate the mysterious fire at your holiday house. You say you believe your husband died in that fire. Yet you withhold vital information from me.' The indignation in Gemma's voice was genuine, she realised, as she felt irritation at Minkie's duplicity. 'I know that you're keeping things from me,' she said. 'And this is just another instance. You first told me that the games he played here once a week were only social games. Now I discover he used marked cards. And he played for money. That's a very different picture.'

Minkie looked away. 'I don't think you understand,' she snapped, anger showing in her own eyes. 'Money meant nothing to Benjamin. It was winning that was important.'

'Money might have meant a great deal to the people he was playing with.' Gemma put the decks of cards down in a small tower, one on top of the other. 'Tell me the truth. How much money was involved?'

'In the card games?'

Yes, Gemma was about to say, did you think I meant something else? She filed that away with what she'd seen in the BMW.

Minkie shook her head. 'I really have no idea,' she said. 'I loathe card games myself. I never joined them. It was Benjamin's thing.'

She paused. 'I suppose,' she conceded, 'that the card games could have some bearing on the matter.'

'It's quite possible that your husband took large amounts of money from people in crooked games. It's quite possible that someone is very angry about this. Being cheated of money is quite different from losing it gambling. It provides a definite motive and if I'm to work with you in an investigation into your husband's disappearance, I should have known about it. You should have told me. I'll need the names and numbers of all his card-playing friends. I'll have to talk with them.'

Minkie sat in silence under Gemma's relentless onslaught.

'Now,' she said, giving the woman one last chance, 'is there anything else I should know? About either your husband or yourself that might have a bearing on my investigation? Any relationship perhaps, that might be problematic?'

There was a long silence during which the unknown dark man from the café loomed in Gemma's mind. The cat eyes looked across at her, long and cool, and Minkie Montreau shook her head.

'No,' she whispered. 'There's nothing else. Nothing at all.'

EIGHT

At the Police Centre it seemed to take ages before the stout young woman calling Angie from the security desk finally located her. Eventually, Angie, trim and neat in her dark blue suit, auburn hair neatly tied back, a pale pink blouse giving a lift to the navy blue, appeared on the stairs to the foyer. She and Gemma greeted each other and walked to the lift.

'Sorry to keep you waiting,' she said. 'I couldn't get away from a meeting. I've just been given a new title. Sex Industry Liaison Officer.'

'Congratulations. Any money in it?'

'Of course not. But it gets me out of the house.'

On the fifth floor, Angie swiped them both in through the security door of her section and ushered Gemma through, past littered desks and filing cabinets covered with photos of pets and postcards and into Angie's glassed-off office.

'Want a coffee?' Angie offered. Gemma nodded and her friend vanished for a few moments, returning with two steaming white polystyrene cups.

'Take a look at these,' Gemma said, putting the marked cards in their box down on the desk next to her coffee.

Angie frowned, opened the box and took them out, looking closely at the backs of the cards, then studying the business sides, cutting and splicing them in a fast blur, just as Gemma had done, from halves to the full deck again. She smiled broadly. 'Pick a card, any card. And I'll tell you what it is.'

'Ah-ha,' said Gemma. 'You worked it out.'

'I learned more than just how to drink the boys under the table when I was with Fraud. Where did you get them?'

'They belong—or belonged—to Benjamin Glass.'

'The missing billionaire. Sean Wright's on that job.' Angie made the cards into a fan then, with a deft wrist movement, expertly opened them into a 360-degree circle. 'Does Mr Right know about these?' she asked.

'Not yet. I'll tell him about them if he tells *me* anything useful.'

'You know our friend Mr Right isn't known for his generous spirit when it comes to sharing information about an investigation.'

'I'm hardly competition anymore, surely. I'm out of the job.'

'There was a rumour going round a while ago that he liked you.'

'What? Mr Right? He doesn't like anyone.'

'I'm just passing information. How's Kit?'

Gemma sighed. 'I don't think I'm talking to her at the moment.'

'But you can't have an argument with Kit. I know what she's like,' said Angie.

Gemma came straight out with it. 'Do *you* think I'm doing something dangerous by going on the street? To get a lead on that guy who's been bashing the street girls?'

Angie sat down in her chair and leaned back, looking at Gemma with her clear eyes. She shook her head. 'No more dangerous than what we do all the time. In fact, because of your background, probably less dangerous than most. Why?'

'Kit reckons I'm living out some sort of compulsion. Putting myself at risk.'

'She would. That's how she sees life.' Angie laughed. 'You know I like your sister. And I admire the work she does, Gems. But these bleeding heart social workers . . . from a police perspective . . .'

Angie's opinion of tertiary qualifications had always been dismissive and Gemma was stung. 'She's not a bleeding heart. And she's not a social worker, either.' said Gemma, defending her sister. She stood and walked over to the fabric screen partition which gave Angie's office some privacy and stared at the photographs of Angie's two dogs, Flo the German shepherd and Gig the Samoyed. Around them on the partition were stuck pictures from several hideous crime scenes treasured by Angie for reasons known only to herself. Gemma turned away from the photograph of a headless man sitting upright, his shotgun at an improbable angle nearby. She focused on her friend.

Angie was eyeing her curiously. 'You're really letting this get to you, aren't you,' she said. 'That's not like you.'

'I don't know what I am like anymore, Ange. I've had these strange feelings . . . premonitions. I don't know. I had this dream. About a meteorite.' She went over to a filing cabinet and fiddled with an empty vase on top of it. 'It's spooked me. I keep feeling I should be looking out for something, but I don't know what.'

'Stop dreaming, girl. I'll knock off early and we'll get our good clothes on. Go out for a night on the town. How long since you've been to Indigo Ice?'

'I'm not so crazy about nightclubs anymore,' said Gemma. 'I haven't been out for ages. Things are difficult at the moment. Psychos are tormenting me with obscene email. Steve's out there doing something dangerous. I feel there's something missing from my life. Something important.'

Angie picked up the deck of cards and let them fall through her fingers. Then she slowly swivelled in her chair from side to side. 'You want to hear what I think?' she said. 'I think we're sold that line, us single women, by a whole lot of people. For a whole lot of reasons. And eventually we come to believe it—that because we're not doing the family thing, there's got to be something missing. Then everyone loads us up with *their* stuff. Like, you have to have babies, or you have to have a man to look after, or you have to meditate, or you have to listen to your inner whatsit, or have whatever they think you have to have. It's crap, girl. It's a beat-up. No way *I'm* going to end up cooking dinner every night and folding socks and ironing some dickhead's can't-see-me-suits,' said Angie, referring to the dark police overalls. 'I've got my job, the dogs, the gym, training with the SPG, volunteer work. Occasionally, I even get sex. Hell, I haven't got *time* for anything to be missing. And neither have you.'

Gemma collected up the marked deck. It was time to go. Angie saw her to the lifts.

'Come on, honey. Let's kick up our heels. We'll have a drink and stir a few men.'

'I think I've done that already,' said Gemma, pulling out a card. She grimaced. It was the queen of hearts.

It was late by the time she arrived back at the office. She pulled up outside, switched the ignition off and sang along to the loud radio music. '*Will I ever get to see your face again?*' she sang, thinking of Steve. Then she noticed Mike's car still parked on the street. Once inside, Gemma knocked on the door of the operatives' office and went in. She plonked the cards on the desk beside him. Mike picked them up, turned them over a few times then looked up at her.

'Where did you get these?' he asked. 'They're crooked.'

'Minkie Montreau's husband has five decks, all like these.'

'So the great, possibly late philanthropist is a dirty rotten cheat,' said Mike. 'You just never know about people, do you?' He chuckled. 'I've got that program,' he went on. 'To block those emails.'

A short while later, she watched while Mike started entering the forbidden words as she read them from her list.

'*Fuck*,' she read, leaving a pause while he typed it in.

'Okay,' he said. 'Next.'

'*Cock*,'

She heard a sound behind her and Louise suddenly materialised, standing by the door, blinking in a startled way.

'Oh, I'm sorry,' she said. 'I'll come back later. I just wanted to get my laptop.' She stood awkwardly by the door.

'Come in and get it,' said Gemma, jumping up, feeling unreasonably irritated by the pale, quiet woman. This would be the first time Louise had wanted to take her laptop home with her. 'It's quite all right.'

Louise stared first at Gemma then at Mike. 'I thought I was interrupting something personal,' she said.

'I didn't know you were coming in today.' Gemma frowned. 'You didn't ring.'

'I'm sorry if I've come at an inconvenient time,' said Louise. 'I was in the area and I wanted to see what new jobs had come in as well.' She paused.

'Mike told me he was going out with you on some street job tonight. I don't want to miss out on jobs just because I'm not here.'

'You're not missing out on anything,' said Gemma in a matter-of-fact voice.

'But I could've worked with you tonight, Gemma,' said Louise, and there was no mistaking the resentment in her voice.

Mike swung round on the swivel chair, interrupting. 'Gemma, speaking of tonight, I need to get some footage on Belinda Swann. I know she's going out with a girlfriend this evening. It's a chance to see her out of school uniform. I can do that early, then afterwards, I'm yours.'

Gemma saw Louise's expression as Mike ignored her and it wasn't pretty.

'Louise,' she said, determined to keep the irritation out of her voice, 'I need a man for the job we're talking about. It's nothing to do with your competence, or you being away sick.' Then she turned her attention back to Mike. 'Okay. Back to business.'

'Are these all the words you want listed?' he asked.

'So far,' she said. 'I'll check my email today and see what's there. It's so damn depressing.'

'I'll deal with them for you if you like,' he offered. 'I can go through them and make a list. See what words and addresses we need to block.' Gemma felt immensely grateful. 'Thanks,' she said to him.

'I still don't see why you couldn't have asked

me,' Louise persisted. 'You know I'm available at nights if Mum's okay.' Now she sounded forlorn as well as resentful.

'You were *sick*,' said Gemma, starting to lose patience with her. 'And I didn't know you were coming in right this minute. And anyway, that's not the point with this job. Louise,' she tried again, choosing her words carefully, 'first, I need a male on this particular job, because of its nature. And secondly, Mike's living arrangements leave him completely free at night.' Mike batched with another separated man whom Gemma had only spoken to on the phone. 'It's no reflection on your capabilities. Okay?'

Louise remained staring at her, face tight and angry. Gemma had been aware of underground rumblings between Louise and Mike for some months now. Hostility wasn't uncommon between operatives in a business such as hers where there is always an unspoken rivalry—different contracted rates of pay, different success rates 'scoring' solid evidence—and these differences can create jealousies if not handled with sensitivity and discretion, Gemma knew. Sometimes, she had to admit, she wasn't the most practised manager of other human beings.

Gemma smiled, attempting to soften the situation. 'I'm going to be a sex worker for the night. And like the other girls, I'll need a minder.'

Louise looked from one to the other. 'You mean a pimp,' she said.

'No,' said Gemma with deliberate patience, 'I

mean a minder. "Pimp" is no longer a reflection of what the job entails.'

Louise glared at both of them, picked up her laptop, put it in its bag and left the room without another word.

'Right,' said Gemma briskly as soon as she'd gone, 'I'll ring when I start work, Mike, and tell you where to meet me.' She went into her own office and gathered up her things. Maybe Louise wasn't going to work out after all, she thought. I've got enough on my plate at the moment without having to deal with sulky women.

Mike crossed the corridor, knocked on her door and came into her office.

'Let's get this program into your system now,' he said.

She started up her computer and gave him her seat. She liked seeing his broad, strong body sitting at her desk, scrolling through the email. It was good, she thought, to be taking action and to have his support. For a moment, she wished it was Steve sitting there. Then was glad it wasn't. She didn't want Steve ever to see the stuff that was coming through to her just lately. She left Mike to it, and went through the door at the end of the hall into her personal domain, where she made a snack, took a shower and changed her clothes.

On her way out, she called goodbye to Mike who was still sitting at her computer. 'I'm going out now,' she added, popping her head round the door, 'so will you just close the front door when you leave? And slam the security gate? It'll lock automatically.'

'Sure,' he said. 'I'll see you later. With a bit of luck, when you turn this on next, the only email you get will be email you want.'

She waved goodbye, leaving him at her computer making his list of nasty words, while she checked her notebook for Peter Fenster's address and left.

Gemma pulled up in the narrow street. This was it. She got out of her car, noticing a plastic gilt icon of Agios Yiorgos dangling from the rear-vision mirror of a bronze Mitsubishi Scorpion parked outside the address, a one-storey terrace house. She walked in through the rusted open gate. Weeds grew among the pavers of the front path, rows of cacti in rusting tins decorated the length of the verandah and two wintering rose bushes struggled to survive in the cemented front yard. She stepped up onto the verandah, past the cacti and pressed the bell. Nothing happened. She tried again and waited. She was about to press the bell yet again, thinking that she might have to come back another time, when a man opened the door.

'Peter Fenster?' Gemma asked, flashing her private investigator's ID. His heavy gold watch glinted and his mouth twisted into a smile as he took and read Gemma's licence, molten brown eyes narrowing in a tanned face.

'So?' he said in a deep voice that matched his

solid body. 'Who wants to know?' He looked at her card again. '"*Gemma Lincoln*"' he read, '"*Mercator Security and Business Advisers*".' He handed the card back. 'Not interested,' he said. Gemma couldn't help noticing the way his eyes travelled over her body. Some men are offensive from the moment they open their eyes in the morning, she thought, and Peter Fenster was one of them.

'I'm a private investigator,' she said. 'May I come in?' She had to roar her request because next door had suddenly started a chainsaw.

'No way, lady,' said Peter Fenster. 'What's this all about?' He scowled. 'If it's anything to do with that bitch I divorced—'

'It's about a vehicle registered in your name reported as being involved in a vicious attack on a young woman,' Gemma interrupted, watching his face closely.

'I reported my car stolen,' he said quickly. 'It's been missing for days. Nothing to do with me.'

'So you say,' said Gemma, noticing the way he'd immediately excused himself. But then, to be fair, he'd already been through this with the police. 'Must be inconvenient,' she said.

'Very,' he said. 'I don't know nothing about an attack.'

'What were you doing on Monday night?'

'Like I said. No car, no transport. I was here.' He drew back. 'I don't have to answer your questions anyway.' He started to close the door but couldn't resist a parting shot. 'Those women ask for it, you want my opinion.'

'I don't want your opinion,' said Gemma. 'For your information, this girl weighs about forty-five kilos. She may lose the sight of one eye.' She could feel the anger boiling up in her. 'Do you think she asked for that?' Calm down, she told herself. Don't bite. The man's just a prick. It's not worth losing your cool, girl.

'Those sluts do anything. Go with anyone. Just for money.' He paused, warming to the topic.

Gemma changed it fast. 'That Mitsubishi parked down there,' she said, pointing to the parked car. 'Whose is it?'

He didn't answer.

'Why don't you answer my question, Mr Fenster?'

'Why should I? I don't have to talk to you. Women like you—'

'Yes?' she snapped. 'Women like me *what*?'

Stop it, she told herself. You're losing control of this. This is the second time recently you've been riled by this phrase. She took a breath and deliberately kept her voice quiet and calm. 'The person responsible for these attacks,' said Gemma, 'just can't help himself. He has to go out and hurt someone, because he's a sick, ugly, bastard.' She said the last three words slowly and pointedly before continuing. 'The girl who was attacked has given us a very good description of the offender. Tall, dark, deep tanned skin. Brown eyes.' She kept her own eyes, hard and unblinking, on his, noting the film that seemed to overlay their surface like an oil slick. She was aware of his scent, a mixture of strong aftershave and his own slightly acidic notes.

Peter Fenster almost smiled then sniffed. 'She's doing pretty good for only one eye,' he sneered.

Gemma kept her voice calm and steady. 'We're building up a picture of the wanted man,' she said. 'It's only a matter of time before he gets put away for a nice long stretch.' She was aware of a sudden shocking silence as the neighbour stopped the chainsaw next door and her last few words filled the void.

'You can piss off,' Fenster said, stepping back. 'I don't have to answer any of your questions. I've already had the bloody cops trying to push me around.' He slammed the door shut.

Gemma stood there, heart racing with fury. I shouldn't let men like him get to me, she was thinking as she turned to walk past the dead garden and festering cacti plants. But I got to him, she realised. I rattled his cage.

She went back to her car and sat there, about to drive away when she heard the door of Peter Fenster's house. Quick as a flash, she pulled out her video camera and waited, lining him up in the viewfinder, zooming in, getting a good shot of his upper body as he stamped down the path and out onto the street. He didn't notice her.

When Gemma got home, Mike had left, locking up after him. She wanted to switch on her computer and see if there was an improvement, but she decided to wait till the morning. She made herself two grilled cutlets, a grilled tomato and some leftover fried rice for tea, munching it in solitary grandeur at the dining table with a glass of chardonnay, looking at her reflection in the sliding glass doors opposite, backed by the impenetrable darkness of the winter night.

Peter Fenster's words stayed in her mind. A man with those attitudes could do anything to a woman, Gemma thought, especially one whom he believed he had the right to dispose of in any way he wished. And the world was full of men like that. The ugliness of his words faded as Taxi smoodged around her feet, rubbing his cheeks against her ankles, rolling and turning almost inside-out around the legs of the chair, purring like mad. Then he stood up on his hind legs, digging his claws into her knees. She pushed him down, then lifted him up, draping him over her leg. 'No,' she told him, 'you're not getting any cutlet. There's some perfectly good hard tack for you, mister.' She set him down and he stalked away, to sit on the arm of one of the lounge chairs, a plump ginger delta-shaped cushion with his back to her, tail twitching.

Although she didn't like admitting it to herself, Kit's words of the night before were still troubling her. Am I really a driven victim, helpless in the face of unconscious urges? she asked herself. And if so, how can I ever discover what they are? She picked at the rice, barely tasting it. It was troubling to think that in some deep way she was not the person she thought herself to be; a person who made decisions based on reason. Our whole society rests on the assumption that we are logical creatures. Although, she had to concede, she'd seen precious little evidence of the truth of that premise in her own family life. She remembered the vivid nightmare, the meteorite hurtling through space towards her as she stood near an ancient lake. Some strange power in us drives our dreams, she thought. I don't make them up. It was worrying to think that inchoate inner forces might drive her waking life as well as her dreams.

She cleared away, tossing out the last of the wine because it had gone bitter in the few days since it had been opened. I must be improving in some ways, she thought. I don't do the whole bottle in one sitting anymore like I used to. Angie's invitation reminded her that it had been a long time since she'd gone out for fun. She remembered the heady nights of hot rock'n'roll and strangers in her bed. She stowed plates and cutlery in the dishwasher, wiped down the benchtop and poured dried food into Taxi's bowl. Then she went outside into the night. It was cold. She looked up at the sky. Hard to tell what it might do, she thought, leaning against the railing. Suddenly, she wished she were an ordinary married woman with a nice, safe husband sitting in a chair reading the newspaper while she oversaw baths and homework, a casserole in the oven, the kids' lunches already cut and waiting in the freezer for the morning, tennis and shopping during the day till three o'clock, a nice normal life, without cyberstalkers, bashers and fire investigations. A simple world where her parents hadn't died in dramatic and dreadful circumstances, where balancing the household budget and making lucky dips for the school fête were the most taxing chores of the day. Get real, she told herself, thinking of her married girlfriends who spent all day at work then had to push heavy shopping trolleys to the car on the way home, pick up kids, lug the shopping in, put it away, prepare dinner, put the washing on, bath the kids, serve up, wash up, hang washing out, make sure everyone's got clean, ironed clothes for the morning and then go to bed with a man who can't understand why his wife isn't very interested in sex anymore.

It was too cold to stay outside any longer. Gemma walked back into the apartment, closed the sliding doors and pulled the curtains against the darkness. You've got a good life, she told herself. An interesting life. Some interesting challenges.

NINE

Gemma was aware that the circuit for legal street soliciting, agreed on by the workers and Kings Cross police, takes in a large part of William Street, apart from the corners which are forbidden because of traffic safety. Other areas in Forbes, Bourke and down to Yurong Streets are tolerated unless the police decide to be tough, and several narrow dark lanes closer to Taylor Square are used by girls who don't want to share their takings with a house. Girls like Robyn Warburton. At least, Gemma thought, it's not raining tonight.

She found the address of the safe house, a narrow terrace on a corner, and walked straight inside, wondering why there was no security. Then she felt a presence behind her and spun around. It was the doorman, a stooped, burly fellow in his fifties, jeans hanging under his gut, following her down the hall.

'Is Shelly here?' Gemma asked. 'I'm supposed to be meeting her.'

'She's coming in later tonight,' he said, 'but she

left something for you if you're Gemma. She told me to be sure you get it.' He walked ahead of her and hunted around on the floor behind a chair, passing her a plastic shopping bag.

Gemma took the bag from him and glanced into it. Carefully wrapped in a silk scarf was a long, dark wig as well as a long hairpiece and an envelope filled with hairpins. Underneath the hairpiece was a poster. *'Have you seen this man?'* was printed on a sheet of A4 paper above an identikit-style drawing of a man with deep-set eyes and a very firm jaw. Did he look familiar to her in any way? Gemma scrutinised the sketch. Could it be Peter Fenster? Probably not.

'Is there somewhere I can go and change?' Gemma asked the doorman who was now busy with a form guide for the trots.

'Use one of the rooms,' he said, jerking a finger down the hall. 'No one's here yet.' He grinned. 'Hey,' he added, attempting a joke, 'I won't even charge you.'

Gemma walked into the nearest room and closed the door. It was serviceable, with a bed, a table with a dim lamp and a box of tissues, long curtains and a rug on the floor. She took off her clothes, self-conscious and wary. She'd heard that some of these places had video cameras running all the time and peepholes. She looked around. There were so many places for a covert camera to be hidden in the fittings of the room that she decided just to get on with what she was here for. She pulled off her jumper, blouse and slacks, took her mobile out of her pocket, and laid out the clothes she'd carefully chosen—a tight dark skirt, a black voile blouse, suspender belt, her black satin Special Blessings bra, sheer black stockings and a pair of black ankle-strapped sandals that she'd only worn once because they had such high heels. She dressed, wriggling into the skirt, cursing because it was tighter than it had been last winter, sucking in her tummy to do up the zip, tucking in the blouse, leaving the two top buttons undone so that her cleavage showed, and pulled on the stockings, attaching them to the belt. 'We express who we are in everything we do,' she heard Kit saying as she fastened the second suspender. She straightened up. Is it true, she asked her dim reflection in the mirror on the wall at the end of the bed, that something in my psyche has led me here, to this room in a brothel, dressing like a sex worker, making myself the bait on a hook to catch a man who hates women? She dismissed the idea. Her sister saw things that weren't there, she decided. I'm just doing my job.

She scrunched her tawny hair up into a short ponytail and pulled on the wig, tugging it down each side, adjusting the forehead section. It fitted her head well, she thought as she looked in the mirror, surprised at the way the dark hair completely changed her appearance. Perhaps not Ally McBeal, but now she definitely looked Mediterranean. She tried adding the hairpiece for extra bulk, but got into such a mess that she decided against it, rewrapping it carefully up again in the silk scarf and putting it away. She opened the tiny, almost never-used beaded evening bag she'd brought along for the night and fished out her make-up container from where it nestled up against the capsicum spray on top of her wallet. She'd removed the credit cards and the only cash was a twenty-dollar bill for a cab. She added more smoky black around her eyes, and a darker, deeper colour than she usually wore on her lips. By the soft light from the bedside lamp she studied herself. The black clothing diminished her physical presence, but she wasn't sure that she looked thin, let alone wasted, so she used the eye shadow to make dark contours under her cheekbones.

Then she rang Mike. 'Where are you?' she said.

'Outside the Hellfire Club, about to get some amazing footage on the innocent little Belinda Swann. Boss, you should see her! Half-naked with leather all over the bits that don't matter. I should be with you in an hour, depending on traffic.'

Gemma was ringing off when she heard Shelly's voice in the hallway.

She slipped her mobile into the beaded bag and packed up her other clothes in the shopping bag she'd brought along with her. She was about to step out of the room when she nearly bumped into Shelly, who was coming in.

'Wow!' said Shelly. 'What a transformation. Is that really you?'

She walked around, checking Gemma from every angle.

'You don't look too bad yourself,' said Gemma, self-conscious under Shelly's professional scrutiny.

Her companion stepped back, frowning. 'I think you could button that blouse up, though. It's bold enough as it is.' She did up the buttons Gemma had left undone, and Gemma had a sudden memory of her mother doing the same with a little pink knitted cardigan. The memory vanished as soon as Shelly stood back, cocked her head and then nodded.

'That's it. Looks more classy. That's what you're offering them. Class. There're plenty of girls offering tits. You're projecting another image. Come on and I'll show you your beat.'

'What can I do with these things?' she asked, holding out her bag of clothes.

'Leave them here,' said Shelly, 'with Cyril. You'll need to change here before you go home. Unless you want to go home in your work gear?'

'I don't think so,' said Gemma nearly tripping in the unaccustomed high heels, forgetting how to balance herself. She tottered outside following Shelly into the chilly evening, shivering in her transparent blouse. So this is what it's like, Gemma thought, as she looked up and down the street, stepping out in absurd clothes to catch a mug. Car headlights made streams of freakish reflected light on the roadway, mixing with the glowing flashes of coloured neon. Two young girls leaning against a building down the road looked her way. Shelly noticed her glancing in their direction.

'It's okay,' she said. 'I've told the others that

you're not competition, even though you'll be looking like you're working near them.' She threw another appraising glance at her companion. 'Although the way you look, I don't think they'll believe me.'

'Stop it,' said Gemma. 'I feel weird enough as it is.' Then she realised something. 'Shelly,' she said, uneasy, 'what do I actually do? What do I say when a man approaches me? I've got to seem like the real thing.'

'We're all the real thing, my dear,' said Shelly drily. She gave a little laugh. Already, men in cars were slowing down, seeing the four women on the corner. 'Develop a line that you're comfortable with,' said Shelly. 'Like, "Looking for a girl tonight, luv?"'

'*Luv?*' Gemma was incredulous.

'You're creating a fantasy,' said Shelly, 'of sweetness and light. You're like a girlfriend, except you never bleed and you never have a headache.'

'I can feel one developing already,' said Gemma. 'These bloody shoes.'

'Then you establish the price.'

'Which is?'

Shelly started to recite the rates agreed on by the William Street workers but Gemma interrupted in horror. 'Fifty dollars for oral? You're joking!'

'Get the money first,' said Shelly in her practical way, although Gemma hardly heard her. Although she didn't plan to fulfil her part of the bargain, the thought of wrapping her mouth around some strange man's penis was horrible. 'Put the money somewhere safe,' Shelly continued. 'Have you organised a minder?' She glanced at her watch.

'Yes,' said Gemma. 'He's on his way.'

'Okay, then. Have you got all that?' Shelly fussed round like a mother hen. 'Especially about keeping the money safe?'

'But I'm not going to do the work,' Gemma protested. 'I can't take their money.'

'You'll have to if you want to get into his car.' Shelly laughed.

'I'm not getting into a car until Mike's here to follow,' Gemma said.

'Then just say you suddenly feel sick, hand back the money and move on. Keep smiling. Make sure he doesn't think that he's the reason for your change of mind. He might get ugly.'

Gemma looked at a car with four noisy young men in it. One of them leaned right out the window and spat at the women on the corner.

'Or you could ask for too much,' Shelly suggested, ignoring them. 'Robyn said he kept talking up the payment. So ask for double the usual fee. That way, the honest punters will tell you to piss off. The only one who'll agree is the one who already knows he's not going to pay anything because he has other services in mind.'

Gemma shivered, looking round again, hoping to see Mike's bulky figure striding towards her. She was already feeling scared, alone and unsure.

I don't like this, a little voice was saying in her mind.

'And if he starts singing,' Shelly added, 'move fast.'

By midnight, Gemma's feet were numb and she was furious with Mike Moody who hadn't turned up. It was clear something had happened to him. But what if she'd been on a stake-out depending on back-up? She could be dead by now. She'd already left three messages on his voice mail and checked her own. There was nothing from him. She even wondered briefly if she should ring Spinner. But the thought of his moralising was too much. Fortunately, business was quiet with most of the kerb crawlers just looking. Occasionally, a girl would get into a car and be away half an hour or so, then return and wait again. Several men had approached her on foot, but her outrageous price list had sent them on their way. 'In your dreams, darling,' one of them had said, and her blood had suddenly boiled. She wondered how a woman could stand to do this, night after night, month after month, year after year, dealing with the insults, the abuse, the constant threat of danger. She heard the contempt in the men's voices, the unctuous pet names. The false smiles, the lying, the dishonesty, the hatred. She saw it reflected back at the mugs by the girls in a bitter cycle of suspicion and distaste. She came to see the service these women do as one for all women: taking the heat off, providing a safety valve for the rage of men. Deflecting hatred and sexual poison from us, she thought, from women like me. She saw Shelly once at about eleven-forty talking to a small group of workers and tottered over to join them.

'No one's heard anything tonight,' Shelly said. 'I've checked with the other girls. It's a quiet night. Looks like he's lying low for the time being.'

'Too quiet,' said one of the others, a gorgeous, fake-tanned brunette in mauve shorts and thigh-high black boots. 'How's a girl to live?' It was in that question that Gemma realised the beautiful brunette was a tranny.

'Where's your security?' Shelly asked. 'You didn't introduce me.'

'He was a no-show,' said Gemma.

'Typical man,' said the tranny. 'Never there when you want them. Darling, they're all the same.'

'How long are you staying around?' Shelly asked.

Gemma looked at her watch. She was cold, uncomfortable and her feet were killing her. 'I'll give it another hour,' she said with resignation. 'Then I'm going home.'

An hour later, she'd had more than enough of deflecting the mugs and she was hurrying down Oxford Lane, taking a short cut back to the safe house when the headlights of a car behind her lit the walls of the buildings ahead. She turned but had to flinch away again because the lights were on high beam. Ahead, her shadow loomed. She kept walking, aware that the car had stopped, lights still on, and that the door had slammed shut. Now she quickened her pace. The lane seemed very isolated and the man's footsteps were coming fast behind her. Another huge shadow merged with her own, turning it into a monstrous two-headed creature. No point in turning around because he had the advantage of the blinding light behind him. Gemma tried to run and nearly went over on her ankle, hobbled by her high heels.

Now she was starting to feel really afraid. The footsteps were getting closer and she couldn't run, nor could she afford the time it would take her to remove the crippling shoes. She kept walking as fast as she could, aiming for the corner of the L-shaped lane where the lights would no longer be a problem and there would be at least a view of the busy street at the lane's other end. But she went over on her ankle again, this time painfully. She wasted precious moments ridding herself of the interfering shoes. She started to run, not caring that the road surface cut into her feet. She opened her little beaded bag and fished around for the capsicum spray, grasping it tight. I'm ready for you, you bastard, she told herself. The road was hard and cold to her feet. Now she had turned the corner and could look back because the harsh lights no longer blinded her. The shadow, huge on the walls, was following fast. In a split second she made a decision and started running again, wanting to lead him nearer the more populated Francis

Street. She increased her pace, aided by the slight downhill slope. Then a voice behind her made her skin crawl. 'Hey, *you*,' his raspy whisper, jerked out in time with his thudding feet, echoed in the dark. 'What's your hurry, bitch?'

She heard him turn the corner. Gemma barely had time to think *this is it!* and brace herself. She heard him closing in behind her, stopped suddenly, turned and swung round with the spray can hissing. She was about to give him a good faceful when something came at her, partly deflecting the spray— *thunk*—and hit her. It couldn't have been a fist. It felt like a long metal tentacle whipping around her body, burning and smashing her to the ground. For a second, she thought she'd been hit by a car. Time and her mind seemed to slow right down. The capsicum spray, the little beaded bag and her mobile lay next to her on the ground. Get up, she ordered herself. In order to live, you must be upright. If he gets you down here, you're gone. In the tiny dazed space of time before autonomic shock shut her systems down, Gemma forced herself to stand. She couldn't see properly: some of the spray had found its way to her eyes. But she could hear the voice of her trainer from the Academy: this person means you ill—don't underestimate him—you don't know what his plans for you are— presume they are not pleasant—fight for your life.

So that when she felt the arm grapple her from behind and apply a choke hold, she reacted as if her life depended on it, instinctively elbowing down and hard with all her strength, targeting his soft lower belly. She heard his shocked grunt, felt his clutch loosen enough for her to swing out and around. He fought to maintain his hold on her, head down as he sought to regain balance and wind. Gemma seized the opportunity with more instinct than training and, bending her right leg, she raised her knee as fast and hard as she could. She felt the sharp impact of his jaw and teeth against the bones of her knee as his own momentum collided with all the upward force concentrated in her knee. The impact threw her off-balance but in the dim light, as she stumbled to regain her footing, ignoring the pain in her knee, she saw him falling backwards, his clothes swirling around him in strips.

Then her knee buckled and she went over again, this time on her ankle. She struggled to her feet but found she could barely use her left foot. Half-hopping, half-falling, bumping along a wall, she stumbled towards the lights and people of Francis Street. She made it to the corner and tried to call out, but she had no wind. She propped herself against the wall, her breath screaming through her throat, trying to recover. It wasn't until she could breathe again that her brain kicked in. She looked behind her. She couldn't see anyone in the dimness. Leaning against the wall, she realised that her legs could barely hold her up right.

It took several minutes for her to retrace her footsteps, hoping she'd find him on the ground, hoping she'd knocked the stuffing out of the bastard. She knew that a good knee to the head could do this, and she wished she'd been able to follow that up with another kick to the windpipe. With a blow like that, there'd be no way he'd get up quickly. She hobbled back to where the lane turned, where the headlights had shone on the walls. It only seemed a few seconds since she'd stumbled out of there. But there were no head-lights, no car. The lane was empty. The bastard had got away.

•

'I didn't get a look at him,' she told Tim Conway at Kings Cross police station. She'd hobbled into a restaurant where a superior maître d' had looked her up and down but had let her ring the police. A nearby squad car had picked her up.

'All my attention was on survival. I didn't think or feel anything in the moment except to get him off me and get out of there.'

Gemma had worked with Tim years ago and remembered him as a decent man. She felt her bruised side with a tentative hand, wincing at any pressure. She realised her whole left side was hurt-ing painfully where he'd whacked her in the first few seconds of impact.

'You know what it's like in a blue. All mixed up and crazy. I only saw the top of his head, really. When I kneed him. I don't remember getting this,' she said, wincing as she touched a nasty cut that ran across the backs of her left fingers. 'He uses a horrible aftershave.' She suddenly remembered

Steve and how he'd smelled like a stranger the last time he'd been in her bed.

'You might need a stitch or two,' said Tim, peering at the deepest cut. Sitting in the almost deserted office of the police station, drinking the coffee made for her by Tim's workmate, Debbie, Gemma became aware of a deep cellular trembling. Her whole body was shaking from the bones out. She saw Tim staring at her short skirt, the transparent blouse.

'And don't say a bloody word. I *was* asking for trouble.'

She told Tim about working for Shelly and the street girls.

Tim looked away, keeping his thoughts to himself. 'Are you sure you can't remember anything else about him?' he asked.

'All I can say,' she said, while Tim recorded the details, 'is that he was about five eleven. I think he was dark but that might have just been the night, and he had a nasty, whispery voice. Oh, and awesomely bad aftershave.' The trembling in her legs increased and her knee and left ankle, twisted as she stumbled after the knee-butt, throbbed a warning. 'And,' she added with satisfaction, 'he'd have a very sore face right now.' Now her knee was swelling up, and a deep graze oozed blood. 'There was something else. Something odd.'

Tim waited.

'When he went flying, I had the impression that he was wearing ribbons all over his jacket.' She noticed the look on Tim's face and leaned forward, searching her memory. But it was all so distorted and weird that she couldn't refine it further. 'What time was it that I rang you from the restaurant?' she asked.

Tim checked the report. 'Your call was logged 1.28 a.m.'

'He grabbed me only a few minutes before that,' she said. 'It didn't take me all that long to get back into Francis Street, although it felt like an eternity at the time. In spite of this,' she added, indicating her left leg. 'Have you got a rape kit here?' she asked. 'I want to get these clothes bagged as soon as possible. If he's a shedder, there might be something on my blouse.' She remembered how his grip round her neck had loosened when she'd elbowed him. Now she was glad that Shelly had buttoned her up to the neck, going for the 'classy' look. But she had a sudden realisation. 'How could he have got away so quickly?' Gemma wondered. 'Maybe there were two of them?'

Tim made a note. 'We've only been told about a lone attacker.'

'Yes, but you know how sometimes there's a second man hiding in the back seat,' said Gemma. 'Big thrill to trick a sex worker out of her money. Two men against one little girl.'

'Deb?' Tim called out. 'Get a rape kit for us. And have you got anything Gemma could wear home?' He looked down at her leg. 'You'd better go straight up to Casualty,' he said. 'Get someone look at your cut and that bit of two-by-four you've got for a leg.' Gemma saw that now the ankle joint had began to puff up too, matching her knee, so that her leg was starting to look very swollen.

'Here,' said Debbie. 'One rape kit and you can borrow my tracksuit top.' She handed Gemma both items.

In a couple of minutes, Gemma had bagged and labelled the transparent black blouse, donned the grey tracksuit top and was making her way painfully towards the main counter.

'Send this off to the Lidcombe Analytical Laboratory, will you?' she asked. 'Ask Ric Loader to check it against the DNA sample they took from the Robyn Warburton assault. I want to nail this bastard.'

'We've got to catch him first,' said Debbie. 'We need his name and address.'

'You might just have it,' said Gemma. 'Have a look through the records. Ten years ago, I remember an offender who used to tamper with the inside passenger door handle when he picked up sex workers.'

Debbie looked blank.

'It was before your time,' said Gemma, feeling a hundred and ten and aching all over. 'If you find him, and there's any physical evidence associated with his file, will you send it over to Ric?'

'Of course,' said Debbie. 'It just might be our lucky day.'

'I need to get to Casualty,' said Gemma.

'I can't really leave here,' Tim said, 'or I'd run you up to St Vincent's myself. Maybe Debbie might?'

Shortly afterwards Gemma and Debbie were driving down Victoria Street, past the cafés and the restaurants. They were almost at the intersection of Burton Street, and the entrance to St Vincents when the call came over the radio. Gemma listened, imagining the scene sketched in by the terse police call. Some poor bloody woman had been found dead. Debbie turned to Gemma as she grabbed the handset.

'I'm sorry,' she said, 'I'll have to go. I'm the closest.'

'Be my guest,' said Gemma with a generosity she didn't feel. Her left ankle was hurting like hell now. 'I'll grab a cab.'

'Car 141,' Debbie called. 'I'm one minute away from the scene.'

She turned left, only a street away from the hospital. Gemma saw an empty cab drive by and tried yelling out the window. It was only a couple of hundred metres from Cas, but she didn't want to try walking. Maybe the cab driver had a guilty conscience or maybe he was on his way home at this late hour. Either way, he didn't stop for the woman yelling out of the passenger window of the squad car.

Debbie turned into Womerah Avenue, and they drove past the dark shape of the school. Gemma could see a small group of people further along the narrow road, and an ambulance parked halfway on the footpath. Debbie parked the car behind it and climbed out, leaving the lights on.

'Step back, please,' she said to the gathering.

'There's nothing you can do so I suggest you all go home and let us get on with our work.' The onlookers moved further away and Gemma managed to wriggle out of the passenger side door. She tried putting some weight on her left leg and nearly screamed out loud in pain. Using the police car as a support, she stumbled round the back of the car, glancing behind her, aware that the crowd was moving away, revealing a dark green plastic council recycle bin. The lid wasn't completely closed. The bastard had just shoved her in the bin, Gemma was thinking, and then she recognised with horror to whom the matted dark hair at the top of the bin and the graceful arm that hung down one side belonged, her delicate fingertips already starting to darken and her broken golden fingernails shining in the lights.

Debbie and Gemma waited, fending off the curious, till the Crime Scene people arrived and taped off the street.

'I know who she is,' Gemma told them as they set up their cameras. But then she realised she'd forgotten Shelly's second name. Finally it came to her. 'Glover,' she said, 'Michelle Glover.' She gave what details she could, including the fact that Shelly had a daughter, Naomi, a stepfather and a boyfriend, Kosta.

Debbie dropped her off at the hospital. It was a typically busy Saturday night and seemed a long time before she was seen. She waited in a timeless limbo with strangers with bloody noses, a little girl who whimpered constantly and a man who'd lost most of his last three toes riding barefoot on a motorcycle. Images of Shelly in the wheelie bin kept her mind going round and round. Did the same man who attacked me, she wondered, also attack Shelly? Would he have had time to recover if the capsicum had reached his eyes?

Finally, her knee and ankle were cleaned, bandaged and strapped, and the bruising on her flank checked. Her left side was red and swollen in odd-shaped, plait-like weals.

'Good heavens,' the young resident doctor exclaimed. 'What did he hit you with?'

She winced at his touch. 'I don't know. Some bloody thing. Whatever it was knocked me for six,' she said, straightening up from trying to see the marks.

It was nearly six in the morning before she rang Steve's mobile and left a message. Then she ordered a cab. Her head was spinning with exhaustion, anger and grief. She needed to sleep and the painkillers the doctor had prescribed, picked up by the cab driver, made everything seem a long way away.

She limped up the steps to her apartment as the sun was rising behind a bank of opalescent cloud, fell onto her bed, and slept for five hours without stirring.

·

She woke with what felt like a hangover, thankful it was Sunday. Her injured knee and foot felt heavy and dead this morning, the pain now only a dull ache. She hobbled out to the kitchen, trying to put no weight on the leg, pleased that the sun was shining brightly now. At least she didn't have a murky day closing around her, worsening her mood.

Taxi whinged around her, demanding food. She found the last chicken wing, thawed it under hot water and hoped it wouldn't give him a tummy ache. Then the full awfulness of the previous night overwhelmed her—Shelly dead and jammed into a rubbish bin, the violence she herself had suffered, and her sense of betrayal that one of her operatives had let her down. Mike Moody, she thought to herself, you're dead. You'll never work in this town again. She leaned against the counter, staring through the sliding glass doors with sightless eyes. Hot tears took her by surprise and she quickly pushed them away. Shelly was one of those friends who didn't quite fit in anywhere else, but with whom Gemma liked to catch up a couple of times a year, hear the word from the street. Now there would be no catching up ever again. She felt a surge of anger through her tears. No one should die like that, she thought. Dumped contemptuously in a rubbish bin.

Part of her longed to ring Kit for tea and sympathy, but that seemed impossible just now. Kit wouldn't say anything unkind, Gemma knew, but the unspoken words would still make Gemma feel bad. You seem compelled, Kit *wouldn't* say, to deliberately put yourself in situations where your very life is threatened. Now look what's happened.

Is it true? she asked herself. Is that really what I do? She looked at her bandaged fingers and her strapped-up leg. She had a vague working idea, mainly culled from reading and some of Kit's more interesting cases, about the 'repetition compulsion', the way people continue to re-create the relationships of their childhood in their marriages, their careers and their relations with their children, repeating dangerous patterns of neglect or hostility. But when she looked back to her childhood she couldn't see anything remotely similar to the way she lived now. She was certainly not a depressed woman, medicated by and living with a psychiatrist husband as her mother had been. Her life and her mother's life seemed light years apart. But it was true that she had been involved in a serious assault last night and it was also true that her father used to assault her mother. She remembered hiding with Kit in the big wicker clothes basket while her father raged and her mother wept.

Gemma took her tea and some vegemite toast out onto the timber deck. It was a perfect winter's day, and a calm blue sea lay under a soft sky. Taxi, leaving bits of chewed chicken wing strewed around the floors, came outside to harass her, trying to climb up on her lap. She kept pushing him away, wincing as she unwittingly twisted her damaged foot. Steve and the world of George Fayed seemed light years away from her now. She sat there, staring out to sea, wondering how she was going to deal with an injured leg and damaged fingers as well as everything else.

She poured another tea and hobbled with it back to the lounge room, where she collapsed onto the blue leather sofa beside the phone. Had the black meteorite struck last night? Or was it still spinning soundlessly through unthinkable distances in her direction? She looked out to sea again, to the blue horizon, the perfect sky. Out of the blue, she thought. That's the expression we use for something completely unexpected. This sort of thinking will do you no good, she scolded herself. Time to get back into your life, girl.

With an effort, she tuned back into the present moment, and checked her voice mail. The first one was from Mike Moody's flatmate, Roger Hollis. It had arrived around midnight.

'Mike asked me to ring on his behalf,' the vaguely familiar voice said, 'but I mislaid your mobile number. I do hope I haven't inconvenienced you too much by not ringing earlier.'

He sounded quite jolly about this, Gemma thought, and she felt like ringing him straight back and saying, Oh not at all, old cock. No inconvenience whatsoever. Nothing I enjoy more on a Saturday night than being bashed by a stranger in a lane. She smoothed Taxi's ears to calm herself down.

'Mike's had to take a few days off,' the message continued. 'Doctor's orders. He was involved in a brawl last night and got injured. He'll ring when he can. Goodbye, Gemma.'

She was surprised and incredulous together. A brawl? Mike had been watching Belinda Swann. How could a fourteen-year-old schoolgirl give him a problem? She rang back, angry and determined to find out. No one was there to take her call, the recorded message told her, so she left instructions for Mike Moody to ring her, asap.

The next communication was from Nick Yabsley at the Fire Investigation Unit. He had a result from the Government lab that might interest her. She realised she'd barely thought of Minkie Montreau and the fire investigation in the last twenty-four hours. Would Gemma please ring him back Monday morning? Gemma made a note to do so although it felt as if the mystery of the fire and the missing philanthropist belonged to another time and another place. The next message lifted her spirits. Twisted ankle, aching flank, swollen knee and all, she smiled at Steve's voice.

'I hope to get away for some stolen hours with you. I'll ring again as soon as I can.'

Behind his words, she could hear the sound of a crowded room—a café perhaps, or a bar. She played it again, then listened to the next message.

'Sean Wright here, Gemma. We found that silver Ford. We've given it a good going over. We found a lot of different fibres. And a lot of what might be animal hair. And we're hoping we might have picked up some traces of the driver. It's all gone off to the scientists. You owe me one now.'

Animal hair? she thought. This reminded her she

still hadn't found the whereabouts of Benjamin Glass's cat.

The next message seemed to be nothing but music, a few bars of something that sounded like it came from her favourite repertoire, bluesy rock and roll, and was teasingly familiar. It wasn't 'Bad to the bone', she thought, but something like that. Then came the *beep beep beep* of a hang-up. She ran it back again and this time listened more carefully. She wasn't sure, but in front of the music, closer to the handpiece, she thought she could hear the sound of heavy breathing. The message tape clicked off. Great, she thought. Just what I need now, a breather. She couldn't help thinking what Kit might say. I wonder what part of my unconscious *you* are, she thought, putting the phone down.

TEN

Gemma drove into the city through the early peak hour traffic and parked in the Police Centre car park, courtesy of Angie whom she'd arranged to meet first thing Monday morning. The limping walk down to Oxford Street was painful and she was aware of stares. But she finally made it and now she waited for her friend at the Galleon, a café in an arcade off Oxford Street. She ordered an orange drink to help clear the mean taste in her mouth, a result of the analgesics she was taking. She'd almost finished it when her friend walked in, looking fresh and elegant in a crisp white blouse and navy trouser suit, her red hair pinned in a french roll. Somehow she'd managed to avoid the commissioner's insistence on uniform at all times and could have been mistaken for a successful corporate executive. Angie sat down, pulled her chair into the table and looked Gemma up and down.

'I heard what happened,' she said. 'How's your leg?'

'I'm managing.'

'Do you think it was the man we're after?' Angie asked. 'What's your gut feeling?'

'I can't say,' Gemma said. 'I sent the blouse I was wearing to the lab at Lidcombe. Maybe they can get something that will match up with Robyn Warburton and the Ford and then we'll know for sure that it's the same person.'

The waitress hovered by their table and they ordered cheese and bacon toasted melts and coffee, the same as they always used to have in the old days when they escaped here for lunch.

'What's the latest on Shelly?' she asked Angie as the waitress departed.

'Still down at the morgue,' said Angie. 'Her clothing's been sent to Lidcombe.'

More clothing, more DNA extraction, more information, but still they were no closer to whoever it was who bashed and killed women. If indeed basher and killer were one and the same person.

'I feel I owe Shelly something,' said Gemma. 'I'll ask around. See if anyone saw anything. Heard anything.'

'It could be our man,' said Angie, 'or any one of a large selection of ugly mugs.'

Gemma nodded. 'Sean actually rang me and told me they'd found the car,' she said, 'the Ford. Lots of fibres and possible animal hairs.'

Angie's eyebrows rose and she reorganised the serviette on her lap. 'That surprises me,' she said. 'Sean passing on information. He must be after something.'

'He's always after something,' said Gemma. 'He'll be looking for a trade-off of some kind. He told me I owed him one.'

'Well, you know he fancies you,' her friend teased. 'He wants your body, Gemster.'

'Then he's going to have to try a whole lot harder.'

Angie laughed, swallowed the last of her coffee and put her cup down. 'Now,' she said, 'will you please tell me the whole story of what happened to you?'

Even telling Angie about the ordeal made Gemma's heart race faster and she could feel her temperature rising as she described the attack and its aftermath.

'Same lane where the other young girl was attacked,' said Angie when Gemma had finished. 'Could be the same offender again.' She looked at her friend closely. 'What do you think?'

Gemma glanced away at two suited men, plain clothes police officers, hunched over their table.

'I thought so at first,' she said. 'But then I looked at the differences. The man we're looking for is a kerb-crawler. The man who attacked me didn't pick me up. In fact he got out of his car.'

'But he did have a car.'

'Yes. But he came after me on foot. Why didn't he pick me up in the car like he'd done with the others? That way he'd be sure to get me. At least he'd think so. I'm not sure it's the same person.'

'What does he look like?'

'Angelface, I wish I knew. He had the lights on high beam. I couldn't see him.'

'Any singing?'

Gemma shook her head. 'And don't ask me what sort of car it was either. It was impossible to see around the headlights.'

'How the hell did he get away? You'd kneed in him in the face and sprayed him with capsicum.'

'I think I missed with the spray. But he seemed to get away so fast. Maybe he had an offsider.'

'Maybe they work as a team,' Angie said. 'The girls are networking already. Looking out for the prick.'

'Or pricks. Did I tell you about the ribbons?'

Their meal arrived and Gemma bit into hers, hungrier than she'd realised. She told Angie the impression she'd had, of flying streamers.

'Might've been an effect of concussion,' said Angie. 'It's unusual attire for a violent criminal.'

Gemma kicked her under the table, then immediately regretted doing so, because she'd hurt herself. 'I can only tell you my honest impressions,' she said. 'He seemed to be wearing something ribbon-like.'

They decided against another coffee and called for the bill, having the usual argument about who was paying until Angie capitulated.

'I want to see if Sean's around,' said Gemma. 'I'll walk back with you. Although "walk" probably isn't the correct word.'

'You do what you can, honey,' said Angie. 'We're here to help.'

Leaning on her friend's arm, Gemma limped slowly back to the Police Centre. By the time they got to the fifth floor, her knee and ankle were very painful.

Angie cleared some papers off her chair and indicated to Gemma she should sit there. She stood, hands on hips, as Gemma hobbled over and sat at her friend's desk.

'Just look at you,' she said, leaning against the partition, arms folded. Gemma remembered the days when she herself used to sit in partitioned offices such as this one. She missed the fun with Angie, but they could keep the rest, she thought. The call-outs, the rivalries, the bitching. The closed male upper ranks.

'Are you still carting that quaint little antique .38 around?' Angie asked.

'Why?' said Gemma, spinning round to face her friend.

'Because if you are, you're stupid. Especially if you're going to act like that—'

'Like what?'

'Pro-active, Gemster honey. And I'm not punning on pro. You're going to have to upgrade. You need a decent piece. Something that'll deliver a one-shot party stopper.'

Gemma laughed. 'You've been hanging out with too many ex-SASies, Ange.'

Angie pushed back a loose strand of dark red hair, leaning closer. 'You listen to me,' she said. 'The world is changing, Gems. If you hadn't noticed. We get drive-bys now. We get schoolkids

shooting and knifing each other. We get crims with
M16s. If you're going to be on the streets and anywhere *near* the likes of George Fayed, you get
yourself properly tooled up.'

'I don't plan to get too close to him,' said
Gemma. 'And what's the matter with the antique?
It's foolproof and I feel safe with it.'

'Yeah? How would you carry it?'

'In my briefcase, like a lady,' said Gemma.

'Gun in bag with zipper gets you dead, lady,' said
Angie. 'You listen to your girlfriend. Come down
to Georges Hall with me on the weekend. Get some
hard training with a Glock 27. It's more compact
than the 19 issue. We'll shoot the balls off some
B-12s.'

Gemma remembered the man-shaped target
templates from the police range, then looked down
at herself and her bandages.

'Don't you think I should wait until I can walk
first?'

Angie shrugged. 'Okay,' she conceded, 'but
don't you forget what I said.'

'Yes, but I—'

'Don't give me whatever bullshit you're starting,' said Angie. 'You've got to be equipped
properly these days. Okay?'

Gemma picked up a pen and put it down again.

'Someone like George Fayed would have you
dead without thinking twice. There's Terry Litchfield shot down, two dealers and two other people
who have simply vanished over the last couple of

years. Last seen in the company of that reptile lover.' Angie walked out to make more coffee.

What brought all *that* on, Gemma wondered. It was probably Angie's practical way of showing affection, Gemma thought to herself. She weighed up the pros and cons of upgrading her personal defence but Sean Wright's staccato laugh interrupted her. He appeared around the door, holding a large envelope, smirking at her. He was in top form, she could see.

'I heard you copped a belting, Gemma.'

'Thanks for the sympathy, Sean.'

'Nothing to it. All part of the new sharing and caring police service.'

'I heard you were down at the morgue,' said Gemma, 'and they let you out.'

Sean smirked again. 'That's right. And no doubt you want to know how the autopsy went on Michelle Anne Glover.'

It took Gemma a second to recognise Shelly's full name. 'I do,' she agreed.

Angie's phone rang and her friend returned as if on cue, and leaned across the desk to pick up the receiver, turning into the corner with it.

'The doc is finalising his reports now,' said Sean. 'You could ask him. Or I might tell you if you ask me nicely.'

'I'm asking you nicely,' said Gemma sweetly.

'Okay, then,' he said. 'But first, what do you know about HTAs?'

HT *whats*? Gemma's mind raced, trying to make sense of the acronym. She'd heard it somewhere before. 'I've heard of them,' she bluffed. 'But what've they got to do with Shelly?'

Sean reached into the envelope he was carrying.

'Nothing to do with Shelly at all,' he said, waving the contents at her. ' HTAs were used in the fire that destroyed Benjamin Glass's holiday house. And the other two earlier fires.'

Damn, thought Gemma, remembering, too late, Nick Yabsley's message to ring him. If I hadn't forgotten to do that, she realised, I wouldn't have to listen to Mr Right crowing on about it now.

'HTA stands for high temperature accelerant,' said Sean. 'I went back to the fire site the day after we met you and Nick up there. Things had cooled down a lot. I took some more samples and I want to go back and take some more.' He tapped his finger on the reports. 'Everything's so brittle because of the heat. It's taking longer than I anticipated to get to where the lowest levels of the house stood.'

'Yes, but what *are* these accelerants?' Gemma asked. 'What do they actually mean?'

Sean cleared his throat. '"*Test results from infra-red spectroscopy and x-ray fluorescence spectroscopy*,"' he read, '"*indicate the presence of ammonium perchlorate, iron-oxide, and a polymer binder*"—'

'Give it a rest, Sean,' said Angie who'd finished her phone call. 'Let's hear it in plain English.'

Sean stopped reading and slid the report back into its envelope. 'You did ask,' he said. 'The reason why it took them this long to find out what was used is because the mix was so potent it completely destroyed itself. Or almost. Usually there's enough unreacted material for the scientists to collect and identify.'

'So what the hell are we looking at?' Gemma repeated.

'Rocket fuel,' Sean said, after a pause.

Gemma was astonished. 'How on earth would someone get hold of that? What sort of person would have access to it?'

'A rocket scientist, silly,' said Angie. 'This building's full of them.'

'I've made a few preliminary inquiries,' Sean said. 'It's only available from a few very secure sources, mostly defence installations in the US.'

'You're talking about legally available?' Gemma asked and Sean nodded.

'I had a chat to Ric Loader at Lidcombe. He reckons it wouldn't be difficult to make,' he said. 'Although getting the balance so finely tuned as this stuff would require professional expertise and sophisticated equipment. It can be set off with a remote control. Electronically.'

Gemma considered this information. Arsonists as a rule are not particularly professional or sophisticated. A tin of kero or petrol and some sort of wick device was usually as complicated as they got. Some of the clever dicks, she remembered, often tried out some sort of delaying technique, a candle, or a mosquito coil in a bucket of primed kindling, so that they could be safe at home miles away in bed when the fire broke out. But quite a few of them were easily scooped up at the local Casualty section, where they were being treated for the burns they'd received setting their own fires. This was in a different league. Sophisticated electronic detonation. Rocket fuel. This was classy.

'Have you checked with the Securities Commission?' Gemma asked, 'in case there's a relationship between the companies who own the other buildings? After all, there were two other identical fires.'

'Of course I checked,' said Sean irritably. 'That was the first thing I did.'

'And?' Gemma asked.

But he saw it coming and shook his head. 'Not telling,' he said. '*You* do the leg work if you want to know whether there's a connection.'

Gemma felt her anger rising at this blatant power game, but then she caught sight of Angie, signalling her from behind Sean, shaking her head and mouthing '*There weren't any*'. Gemma smiled. In that moment, she loved Angie with all her heart.

'I already know, Sean,' she lied. 'And there isn't. Just checking up on you.' She spoke in exactly the same superior tone Sean had used to her and saw with satisfaction that she'd scored.

'Okay, you two,' said Angie. 'That call I just had was from the morgue. The doc's finished with Shelly. He'll be faxing up his report. It's probably coming through to your office right now, Sean.'

Gemma brought her imagination back from the blue-white heat of the fire and concrete slabs melted into igneous turquoise and applied it to a body stuffed into a rubbish bin. Shelly. She imagined her friend's body stitched up again on the table, a tag hanging off her toe, all her physical secrets laid bare by the scalpel and the unflinching eye of the medical examiner.

'The Kings Cross police are trying to get in touch with her last client,' said Angie.

'But she told me she hasn't been working for years,' Gemma said.

Sean snorted in derision. 'That's what she tells you. You know what the girls are like,' he said. 'They say they always use condoms and they don't. They say it's really quiet when they're making a big quid. They live in another world.'

'Hang on,' said Gemma, coming to her dead friend's defence. 'Shelly had no reason to lie to me. She told me last time I saw her that she was working as a sex surrogate on behalf of some local therapists. Working with a man to improve his basic performance skills which, according to her were pretty woeful.' She glared at Sean, raising an eyebrow, and he turned to leave.

'What's up, Sean?' Angie couldn't resist calling after him. 'Wasn't you, was it?' Then she pulled out her notebook and leaned her neat backside against the desk. 'Okay,' she said. 'Our girl Shelly turned to good works in her later years.' She flicked through her notes. 'You don't happen to have the name of these counsellors, do you?'

Gemma shook her head. 'No, but Shelly said their office was down the street from where she lived.'

Angie rolled her eyes. 'Bourke Street has a few houses in it, Gemster. If you do find out the names of the sex therapists, please let me know. And in the meantime, if you come across—forgive the expression in this context—the man who was her last booking, tell me or Kings Cross police. We're still looking for Shelly's diary.'

'If she kept one,' said Gemma.

'According to that fat Greek she hangs out with, she did,' said Angie. 'She liked things nice and orderly.'

Gemma felt tears fill her eyes at the thought of her friend. This will never do. Pull yourself together, girl, she told herself. I'll find that diary, she promised Shelly. I'll find out who did this to you.

Gemma drove to the Vaucluse mansion again, using the handbrake as much as possible to spare her leg, an awkward movement with bandaged fingers. It was a relief to be back on the fire investigation. This was impersonal business, just doing her job, gathering and recording information, assessing the characters of the people she interviewed, forming conclusions as to what made these people tick. This wasn't like the work she'd undertaken for Shelly. She had a very clear sense that last night she'd crossed over a boundary and into no-man's land where she'd left her detachment behind. Last night she'd exposed herself as a target. The next attack could maim her, or worse.

Her mobile rang. It was Angie. 'I'm passing this info on to you,' she said, 'because us girls have to stick together. Guess what I've just heard about the Nelson Bay fire?'

Gemma listened and her mouth set in an angry line. Right, Minkie bloody Montreau, she thought, as she rang off. You're in big trouble.

She parked her car and hobbled up to the door, composed herself and pressed the intercom.

'Who is it?' Minkie's voice, breathless, hurried.

'Gemma Lincoln.'

'Come in, please.' Gemma heard the faint electronic hum as the outer gate released and she opened it and stepped onto the tiled front door area. In a moment or two, the large doors opened, and Minkie, glamorous in a dark red woollen sheath, the pearls shining like moons around her neck, stepped aside to let her in.

'I hope you have some good news for me?' she asked, ushering Gemma into the large drawing room with the french windows. 'I've just heard from the insurance company. They're refusing to pay up. God knows what will happen when I try and wind up the estate without a body.' She swung around, waiting for Gemma's response.

Gemma let her stew for a moment, noticing that the red rose in front of Benjamin Glass's framed portrait was already dead in its vase. She kept her voice soft and low. 'Miss Montreau, you've been lying to me. You've lied to me right from the start. I'm giving you one more chance to tell me what's really going on, or I'm walking out the door.'

Minkie's face went ashen. 'I don't know what you mean!' The cat eyes flickered away and back. 'What on earth are you saying?'

'Who is he?' Gemma went on. 'What's his name? Before you make a fool of yourself any further, I have to tell you I saw you together in the coffee lounge in the mall at Double Bay and then necking in your car.'

For a second, Minkie Montreau stood straight, but then all the stuffing suddenly seemed to leave her. She backed against the lounge and almost fell on it, covering her face with her hands. 'Please,' she begged, 'don't bring'—she paused before saying the name—'my darling Anthony into it. Please. He's got nothing to do with anything in my life except me.' She took her hands away and Gemma could see the tears in her eyes.

'That's not just naive,' Gemma said. 'It's a completely stupid thing to say.' Minkie stood up, walked to the cigarette box and stood uncertainly next to the table. Then she took the lid off and Gemma saw it had been filled with fresh cigarettes. Minkie took one and lit it. Standards are falling all over the place, Gemma thought, looking past the puff of smoke to the dead rose. This woman is under a lot of pressure.

'I also had a call on the way here from a colleague,' she continued in the same quiet manner. 'A Nelson Bay security firm has a record of a back-to-base burglar alarm going off at the house only minutes before the fire. Then it stopped because whoever went inside the house disarmed it. Someone had to know the security code to do that.'

'But that's impossible!'

'Not if that person knew the code.' Gemma used the standard non-leading question: 'What can you tell me about that?'

'I don't understand,' Minkie said, the edge in her voice betraying her stress. 'Who is doing this? Why is this happening?' She looked at the cigarette in her hand and frowned, as if wondering how it had got there.

'How many people know the code at the house?'

Gemma waited.

Minkie put the cigarette down in an ashtray that looked as if it had been hewn from solid amethyst. 'I can't give you an answer to that because I simply don't know. Of course, it would have been kept strictly private. But Benjamin might have given it to Rosalie.'

'Rosalie?'

'His secretary. Sometimes staff members used the house,' said Minkie and her voice was edged with anger. 'They're like family to him. Some of them have been with him for years.' Gemma remembered the letter of introduction she had in her briefcase.

'You're thinking,' said Minkie, 'I can tell, that Benjamin might have had a thing with Rosalie? No?' She had picked up that little European habit, Gemma thought, of adding the negative to the end of a question.

'I'm not thinking that,' Gemma echoed, 'no.'

'When you meet her, you'll realise how impossibile that would be!' Minkie sniffed.

Gemma lowered her voice, keeping the annoyance out of it as best she could, readying herself to leave. 'I've learned that nothing's impossible in my game, Miss Montreau. But I doubt very much if I'll ever meet her now.' She saw the puzzled frown shaping between Minkie's manicured eyebrows. 'I'm taking myself off this case. I can't deal with someone who withholds information and misleads me. It's a waste of my time. And yours too, although that's your business.'

'But you can't just walk out on me like this!' Minkie Montreau said, hands clawing at the pearls.

Indeed I can, lady, Gemma thought. I've got enough problems of my own. A hostile cyber dickhead, my boyfriend in a dangerous operation, a fight with my sister, an old friend murdered, not to mention an injured body. I don't need your crap as well. She turned to go and in doing so, twisted her left leg so that pain shot through from thigh to instep, making her wince in shock. She came to a sudden halt. She recovered quickly, but tears of pain jumped to her eyes. There was no way she could take another step. Her dramatic exit was completely undermined.

Minkie was suddenly beside her, helping her to a seat. 'You poor thing. You've really hurt your-

self,' she said. 'Sit here for a minute. Let me make
you a cup of tea.'

•

So now they were sitting together, Gemma's left
leg propped up on a beautiful hand-embroidered
cushion, having tea from exquisite bone china.

'My friend's name is Anthony Love,' confided
Minkie, looking away, stirring in sugar with a silver
apostle spoon.

Was the woman laughing at her? Gemma wondered. But her face seemed composed enough
when she turned back to Gemma, placing the
spoon on the saucer. 'I met him'—again, a tiny
smile around Minkie's glossy lips irritated Gemma
afresh, with its implications of a lover's secret memories—'when he helped me choose the paintings
for the beach house.' She gave a little shrug. 'He's
an artist and a very gifted one. He does installations, wonderful things, hangings, tapestries,
huge, fabulous paintings. He's trembling on the
brink of success. One of his hangings sold last
week for the same price as a Sisley sketch.' Her
voice had the unmistakable awestruck tones of one
in love with both the art and the artist.

Gemma thought of her lions of Delos stretching away in the distance, spotless against Aegean
skies, roaring an eternal silence, an offering for the
gods, not objects with a price.

'We started seeing each other about a year ago,'
Minkie was saying, talkative now on the subject of
her lover, 'when I went to the gallery where his

work was showing.' She paused, stubbing out the cigarette, again with that puzzled look, as if she couldn't believe she was doing this again. ' Look,' she said, 'I know what you're thinking. I'm a woman of a certain age and Anthony's'—again that infuriating smile—'younger. You're probably thinking I'm fooling myself. But you see, Gemma, it's not like that. I have influential friends. I can help him further his career. I want to do that so much.'

'What does he do for you?' Gemma couldn't help asking.

'He makes me feel alive again,' she said, with a half-smile. 'You're young. You don't know about that yet. I thought that part of my life had finished. We do all those crazy things young lovers do. Run through rain together. We kick autumn leaves in the gutters. We wash each others' back. He cooks for me. He gives me massages. We book into funny old hotels under silly names. We stay in bed till late and order room service banquets.'

Gemma interrupted the rhapsody. 'Did your husband know about your lover?'

Minkie shook her head. 'If Benjamin knew— which I doubt very much because I've been very careful not to embarrass him in any way—I doubt if he'd have cared anyway.'

Gemma looked sceptical and Minkie noticed. She made a little dismissive wave and a fortune in diamonds and rubies flashed. 'He was past all that business. He was impotent,' said Minkie, looking her straight in the eye. 'He couldn't get it up. For a while he tried those dreadful injections and then

Viagra came on the scene. But he developed the most terrible headaches.' She laughed. 'It was a change for the man to have the headache. I must say I found that quite amusing.' Her green eyes half-closed in laughter.

But that doesn't mean that he was impotent with everyone, Gemma thought. He might have been quite active with another partner. This interview was going quite well, she realised. She was gaining a lot of information, despite the ruination of her dramatic, sweeping exit. Now she was getting to play good cop, bad cop all by herself. She nodded encouragingly, but Minkie was fiddling with her pearls, lost in her thoughts.

'I'll have to talk to Anthony Love,' Gemma told her. 'If I know about him, you can be pretty sure other investigators will.'

'But he's got nothing to do with the fire. Or Benjamin's disappearance,' said Minkie. 'He's as gentle as a lamb. Anthony's an *artist.*'

As if, Gemma thought, that immediately puts him above the affairs of the world.

'Listen to me, Miss Montreau,' she said severely, 'if you are the subject of an insurance investigation—and if they've decided not to pay you yet, you can be absolutely sure that you *are*'—she paused to let that sink in—'you have no idea of the degree of surveillance you're probably under already. That's why,' she continued, 'it's essential that you tell me the truth. Insurance companies have cameras with infra-red capabilities that can catch you in your house here. In this room if you've got the curtains open like this. Or his. Or anyone's. They can pick up conversations hundreds of metres away. And be filming you all the while. You wouldn't know if the kid sitting a few tables away in a café with a Walkman and the newspapers in front of him was actually taking photographs of you and your boyfriend and recording every word you say because you'd never see a camera or a recording device. These insurers have a big pay-out to protect and they don't mind investing money to avoid it if they can. Don't you realise that there's already someone like me out there doing all this already for the other side, watching every move you make?'

Minkie Montreau clearly hadn't. She went ashen at the words. 'You don't think that they know already? About Anthony?'

'I most certainly do, ma'am,' she said, relishing the moment. But Gemma's own words had affected her, too. She hadn't actually given the subject of her shadow self, the insurer's investigator, much thought up to now. She tried to dismiss it, but for some reason this doppelgänger grew larger in her mind. She experienced a deeper level of the dread that had lately chilled her, as if she'd walked through a deadly mist of toxic spores or the cold air of an ancient tomb. She found herself thinking of the freezing barren atmosphere of outer space where the meteorite hurtled. And then just as suddenly, the dread was gone.

She struggled to get back on track, giving herself a cue she could easily follow. 'So if you didn't start that fire—'

'I didn't. I swear I had nothing to do with it! Why would I want to destroy my own beautiful house, burn the paintings that Anthony and I had chosen together? Why would I want to harm Benjamin?'

'Try this for size,' said Gemma drily, setting her cup down and struggling to sit up straighter. 'It's an old one but it's a good one. You stand to gain a fortune from the insurance and from the estate. Kill your impotent husband and you can marry your lover and live in luxury for the rest of your lives.'

Minkie looked shocked. And then burst out laughing. '*Marry* him? Oh, I don't think so.'

It wasn't quite the response Gemma had been expecting. Minkie's green eyes were soft now with good humour.

'What you said sounds bad, I agree,' she continued, trying to cover her amusement, 'but I truly didn't want anything to change.' She cocked her head to one side. 'I need you to believe in me, to continue to work for me. To find out the truth. Even more so now that it's probably going to look worse and worse.' She took out a lace handkerchief and dabbed the corner of each green eye. 'The insurers and the police will never understand that things were just perfect the way they were. Most people are so dull. So *conventional*.' She fiddled with the handkerchief. 'And,' she said, rather too tartly, 'you said yourself there were other possible motives. You're forgetting the card games.'

'Hardly,' said Gemma. 'Have you listed the names I asked for?'

'I can do better than that.'

Minkie went to an ornate gilt and marble table, picked up a book and handed it to Gemma. 'That's the gamblers' club book. All the members. You can keep it.'

Gemma flicked it open. Names and phone numbers. She put the book in her bag. She'd chase them all up, find out what went on at these card parties, how much was won and lost. Find out if there was a loser, a card-playing rocket scientist angry enough to kill the man who'd cheated him.

'They were all business friends of Benjamin's,' Minkie was saying. 'I barely knew any of them except to say hullo. I'd welcome them, offer them drinks, then they'd go into my husband's inner sanctum'—she indicated the study upstairs—'and I'd either go out, or go to my sitting room. They were stag nights, boys' nights. You know what I mean.' Minkie rolled her green eyes heavenwards. 'Gambling with cards is so vulgar,' she said.

Gemma was on the verge of saying something about stocks and shares but she controlled herself.

'If your husband always won, and he would have done, given the advantage he had,' she said, 'he must have made a lot of money over the years. Were you aware of any angry losers?'

Minkie shook her head.

'You told me you needed money,' Gemma

reminded her, 'so money *is* a motive.' She wriggled up from her sitting position, testing her leg on the ground. It held up to some weight. She applied a little more and stood, feeling a bit like a resting horse, with one fetlock bent. Minkie rose with her and they stood a moment together, eyes on the same level. 'The insurers and the police,' she went on more gently, 'know enough about human nature to know that sex and money are two very powerful motives for just about every crime. And when you get the two together like you do in this case'— she saw that register on her companion's face, saw the green eyes flinch—'it's not realistic to expect them *not* to be very, very suspicious about you.' And you can't expect me not to be, either, she thought to herself. 'And it's a fact that someone who knows the code at the beach house deactivated the alarm. Have you and Mr Love spent time at Nelson Bay?' She felt absurd saying the name of Minkie's boyfriend.

Minkie nodded. 'But Anthony didn't know the code,' she said.

'How do you know that?' Gemma said. 'He could easily have watched the numbers you pressed.'

Her crestfallen hostess helped Gemma towards the grand front entrance. 'Please,' she said. 'Stay on my side. You must discover what really happened. I can't possibly be suspected of murder and arson. It's not possible for me to go to prison.' Gemma watched the pale face closely. This dialogue, at least, was genuine. 'I'm used to having a *lot* of money,' Minkie was saying. 'Just having enough will not do.'

Gemma raised an eyebrow. Poor baby, she thought. Just having enough is most people's dream. 'I'll need Anthony Love's address and details,' she said firmly.

'He's between flats at the moment,' was Minkie's response. 'It's best to contact him through the gallery that shows his work.'

Gemma looked hard at the woman standing opposite her. Again, she had the strongest feeling Minkie was lying through her little white teeth. 'Are you trying to tell me you don't have your lover's home address?'

'Look,' said Minkie plaintively. 'It's better not to go there. Please. It's a very delicate situation. Anthony's tipped to win the Stanford Macquarie Prize and any scandal might affect that.'

'Miss Montreau,' said Gemma, irritated by her duplicity, 'we're living in the twenty-first century, not the nineteenth. Scandal can only make an artist's prices higher. Especially in the art world.'

'You don't understand,' said Minkie.

Gemma decided to leave this line for the moment. 'You'd better give me the gallery's address, then,' she said.

•

As Gemma drove to Gallery Europa, she thought over the interview. She wasn't so sure now of Minkie Montreau's involvement in the death of her husband. The woman had seemed guileless, even naive, and her manner and revelations about her lover were convincing. But, Gemma reminded herself, *she's very smart and there's something she's not telling me.* She could be playing both sides against the middle: hiring me as a sort of devil's advocate to find the weak links in her story, so as to develop the necessary alibis and defences. *She's married to a cheat.* Like attracts like, she thought to herself. Was this the biggest cheat of his life? Had he staged his own disappearance? She knew there'd be close scrutiny of Benjamin Glass's financial affairs and if large sums of money had vanished it would certainly look as if the missing man had gone underground. Or it could also imply that his affairs were going bad. Maybe it was suicide. There were many possibilities. *Because if Minkie had a secret life, why not her husband?* But someone had set off the alarm at Nelson Bay. It was possible Benjamin Glass himself might have done it inadvertently. *Though, if I were Minkie,* she thought to herself, *and I wanted to set things up so that it looked as if an outsider had broken in, the best way to do that would be to deliberately engage the alarm and leave it that way. And not then switch it off.* Her mind was going round in circles. This investigation had too many possibilities. *Give me a simple case like the Rock Breaker or the Big Limp anytime,* she thought. But her mind drew her back to the Nelson Bay puzzle. If the house *had* been empty and the alarm on when the fire started, where was Benjamin Glass? She turned ideas over and over in her mind, trying to fit the facts of the case with various criminal scenarios. If he hadn't staged his death, then maybe Minkie and Benjamin were in this together, with him disappearing until the insurance was paid out. And that's why the HTA was used, so that a case could be made for the *absence* of human remains. Someone with his sort of money could access rocket fuel and smart electronic circuitry.

She found Gallery Europa in a small Paddington side street. The stern concierge who sat in the reception area of the gallery raised bored, pencilled eyebrows under lacquered hair as Gemma limped in.

'How may I help you?' she asked with a tone that implied she found someone of Gemma's appearance beyond any help. She looked her up and down with her enamelled eyes.

'An artist,' Gemma said, 'called Anthony Love. I want to talk to him.'

'Oh,' said the woman. 'And how do you suppose I can help you with that?' She raised her perfect arched eyebrows to the ceiling.

Gemma pulled out her ID and pushed it at the woman. 'I need to ask him a few questions. About a homicide. The police will be asking, too,' she added for emphasis.

That had some effect. 'How very colourful,' said the receptionist, finding a card with a number scribbled on it. 'I believe he can be found on this number,' she said, copying it onto a gallery business card and handing it to Gemma. 'But a person like that could be anywhere. Doing anything. Being anything. Creating anything.'

'What's the Stanford Macquarie?' Gemma asked.

The woman looked at Gemma as if she were a knuckle walker. 'It is *the* art prize,' she said, 'for amateur artists.' She sniffed. 'Which Monsieur Love most certainly is. Winning the Stanford is the difference between eating pasta in a Darlinghurst flatette and entertaining politicians in a waterfront at Birchgrove.'

Gemma was getting the picture.

'If he should drop in,' she said, 'please tell him to ring this number.' She passed her card over. The woman's interest level rose a little, she put the card somewhere in a drawer and Gemma turned and walked out, steeling herself against the pain in her leg.

•

By the time she got home, she had to almost hop because the ache in her leg was starting to throb again. She checked in the operatives' office and saw that Spinner had been in and that Louise's laptop was sitting on a shelf near the large desk. They'd been and gone, she surmised. She went into her room and sat at her desk. She rang the artist first and, while waiting, noticed that Spinner had dropped in his reports, neatly printed out and filed, in the 'completed' basket on her desk, together with the diskette to go into her records.

The phone was answered. 'Hullo?' a woman's voice said.

'Is Anthony Love there?' Gemma asked.

There was a long pause. Finally, the woman spoke. 'He's not here just now,' she replied. 'Who are you?'

'My name is Gemma Lincoln. Please ask Mr Love to ring me as soon as possible. It's an important matter in connection with a fire investigation.'

The woman made an odd noise.

'I beg your pardon?' Gemma said, frowning.

'Yes, yes,' the woman said, still sounding peculiar. 'I'll ask him to do that.' Then she rang off.

Gemma sat there, fiddling with Spinner's diskette. Was that Mrs Love? His mother? His wife? His girlfriend? She turned her attention to the diskette she was absentmindedly flicking: the final report on the Big Limp and next to that, old Rock Breaker, both badly sprung, she thought, as she scanned Spinner's results. Each report to the insurance companies included the indisputable video footage, timed and dated and destined to end up in a serious fraud charge for two dishonest citizens.

She was about to ring Mike, but was curious to see what Spinner might have captured on video, so she took the cassette of Big Limp's exploits into her lounge area and shoved it in the VCR, flopping back gratefully, her injured leg propped up on the other arm of the deep lounge. Taxi appeared from under the sideboard and jumped up to make bread on her stomach. She hugged him and watched the grainy footage. It wouldn't win any Oscars, but it would definitely mean the end of Big Limp's free-loading on other people's premiums. Spinner's invisible digital video camera invaded the man's half-drawn blinds to show him striding round the house like Arnie Schwarzenegger, then hunching and shuffling like Christopher Skase the minute he opened the front door. And there he was limp-free in his fancy home gymnasium, pumping iron. Gemma lay back, watching his regimen. He was smart, too, she concluded, after a few minutes. He was doing twice or three times the work on one leg than he did on the other. This would make it nicely smaller than the so-called 'normal' leg, so that a doctor could see the obvious difference in size and give him the benefit of the doubt. Cheats, she thought. The world is full of cheats.

She rewound the Big Limp cassette, lifted Taxi off and struggled to her feet again, going back to her office to remind herself of the phone number of the local Thai and order take-away chicken curry.

She put the reports and the cassettes away, and switched on her computer system. Her heart lifted when she saw there were only four emails. Maybe I won't sack Mike after all, she thought.

The first two were from friends, the third a spam which she deleted. She opened the final one and the smile left her face instantly. It was very brief. '*Hullo Dirtygirl, I'm closer than you think,*' it read. '*I look forward to our meeting very much.*

It won't be long now.' Her blood ran cold. There was no signature and the sender was Jolly-Roger@hotmail.

Gemma immediately deleted it, wishing it and its writer to cyberhell. It was just a bluff, she knew. There was no way someone could discover a person's physical address purely from an email. He probably said that to all the girls. Even so, she shut down her system and felt like unplugging it at the power point, wishing she'd never switched it on. She didn't like the feeling that her home was an open conduit for this sort of pestilence. The dark sense of dread rose in her again, and she shivered, feeling compelled to go through all her rooms, checking them, switching on lights because it was already getting dark inside. She briefly understood Fayed's need to have closed circuit security cameras in every room. She wished for summer and the long days where the sun still shone at this hour. It was now only a little before seven but it might as well have been midnight. She went to the old carved cedar sideboard and poured herself a brandy then went to check her answering machine.

She heard a faint sound near the front door. She craned around to see what it was. Taxi was nowhere to be seen. The sound came again. It was a faint knocking.

Gemma put the phone down and went to the front door, squinting through the peephole. There was no one there. This is stupid, she told herself. Get a grip, girl. She went into her office and tried to catch a glimpse through the security grille of the entrance area, but could see no one. Slowly, she went back to the phone, dialling the number of Mike's flat. This time Mike answered.

'I've been waiting for you to ring,' she said, 'and tell me what happened to you. I think you owe me that at least.'

'I followed Belinda Swann like I said I was going to,' he said in a flat voice. 'She was with a girlfriend and I followed them to the Hellfire Club. They were both dressed up in bondage outfits—black leather, studs, cut-outs, boots up to the crotch. Just after you rang, someone spotted me with the camera. I did what I could, but they dragged me out of the car. Three thousand dollars' worth of camera.'

'What do you mean, someone spotted you?' Gemma asked. 'No one's spotted any of us ever before.'

'I know how it sounds,' said Mike. 'I feel bad enough as it is.'

'What about the footage?' she heard the heart-less professional in her ask. 'Did you get any good exposure?'

'I've got that,' Mike said, sounding better. 'And I managed to hang onto my camera.'

Gemma imagined the interest that video footage would create when contrasted against the pig-tailed schoolgirl who would doubtless appear in court. But she still felt very angry with Mike—and even more so now. None of her operatives had ever been burned like that before.

'I was attacked last night, too, Mike,' she said. 'It could have been a lot worse than it was. As it is, I can't walk properly.'

'Shit,' he said. 'That's no good. We must be the same star sign.' The joke went flat and after a silence he asked, 'What happened?'

She told him, feeling every ache and pain, every twinge, as she relived the assault.

'I'm sorry,' he said. 'I let you down.' There was a pause. 'Look,' he said, 'there's something I want to say. I don't want you to think I'm saying it to excuse myself. It's just something I felt last night when it was all going arse-up.'

Gemma waited.

'I reckon they were waiting for me, the pricks that attacked me. I got the feeling I was set up. How else would someone know I'd be there with a camera? You know yourself our equipment can't be seen through tinted windows. Especially when it's dark. They *knew* I'd be there.'

Gemma considered Mike's words. Maybe he was just trying to avoid responsibility. But what if it were the truth? Her blood ran cold. Someone knowing where Mike would be. Someone coming after her in a lane, someone breathing on her phone. Someone posting violent sexual email. Virtual reality stepping out from the shadows into the real world where she lived.

'But that's impossible,' she said. 'How could someone know?'

She rang off and remained sitting where she was. The wind had blown up outside and rattled the windows. She thought about what Mike had said. Maybe it was true or maybe he was just imagining it to assuage his discomfort at being sprung.

Gemma searched around for a plausible rationalisation. After all, Belinda Swann's father was a senior police officer himself: he'd expect this sort of move from the defence. Maybe he had his own people on his daughter. He could know what to look for in the traffic. Counter-surveillance could be quite simple; just a matter of getting a mate to tail you, to see if anyone else was doing the same. Maybe her attacker, the cyberstalker, Mike's attacker and even the breather were just a series of unfortunate, but random events.

She was limping to her bedroom to get a warmer jumper when she heard another sound outside. She grabbed a coat instead, pulled it on and hobbled to the window. Everything seemed more threatening now that she was handicapped. The sound seemed to be coming from the northern side of her place, outside her bedroom. She listened. She could hear rustlings and movements that were not just the windows shaking under the gusts from the south. There was definitely someone out there. She put the window up a little, grateful for the strong wrought-iron lace bars that protected her.

'Who is it?' she yelled outside. 'What do you want?'

The sounds stopped and Gemma started to feel foolish. No one answered. Maybe it was just the creator of Disneyland Pompeii next door pottering about, adding more sentimental goddesses to his pantheon. But the sounds she'd heard were not the sort a confident householder makes and it was already dark. This was a creeper. A stealth fiend. Something touched her leg and she jumped, biting back a scream. It was Taxi's whiskers as he checked her ankle. Right, she thought, angered by the sudden fright. I'm not putting up with this.

Gemma grabbed her long black torch which could double as a handy weapon and limped through the lounge area, pulling the sliding doors unlocked, stepping out onto the timber deck. The wind moaned in the recesses of the building and the heavy sea rolled beneath her, driven by salted gusts of wind. A tendril of the jasmine she'd planted near the rail of the deck whipped into her eye painfully, causing her to blink and swear. The bushes near the end of the garden showed dimly in the light from the room behind her. She saw movement to one side, as if someone or something was hiding in there. She remembered the curious disturbance she'd noted a few days before under the window of the office. Cautiously, keeping her weight as far as possible on her good leg, she stepped down onto the winter grass, following the torchlight ahead of her like the holy grail. She followed its beam to the edge of the garden where the stunted masses of coprosma and native heath formed a natural boundary. Below this rugged vegetation was the incline to the rocks.

She hobbled closer to the dense coprosma bush, frowning in concentration, shining the torchlight on something that looked like paper or fabric under the bushes. With hesitant steps, and keeping her eyes peeled for any peripheral movement, Gemma approached, flicking the torch sideways to take in the total scene, making sure she wasn't missing anything. She thought she could hear the tiniest sound. Something breathing. Maybe an animal. There were possums about, she knew, but possums didn't behave like this. She peered closer. Now she could see padded fabric, newspaper. Litter. Don't tell me, she thought with relief. It's a poor bloody dero's nest. It's not some dirty stalker, it's a fringe-dweller sleeping rough along the coastline, using people's hoses and taps and outside showers. She recalled the hollowed-out area she'd found earlier under her office window behind the bushes. Now she gingerly prodded at what she realised was the corner of a dirty sleeping bag with the toe of her injured foot. Still wary, she prodded harder.

'Come on, mate,' she said in her old police voice, getting a good grip on the heavy torch. 'Wakey wakey. You'll have to move along. You can't stay here.'

To her dismay, she heard the sound of crying. Her dismay turned quickly to irritation. 'Come on,' she said, more harshly than she'd intended. 'I don't need this. It's freezing and I've got things to do. Up and off my property. Go and have a good cry somewhere else. Now.' She leaned over and picked up a corner of the sleeping bag, pulling at it. Suddenly it gave way as whoever was huddled on it rolled off and ran away. Gemma fell clumsily backwards trying to protect her injured leg, putting an arm out to break her fall, ending up in a tangled heap. The torch went flying. In the silence she could hear the surf crashing below. She groped around for the torch, cursing under her breath. She could hear whoever it was running and falling and sliding down the incline. The slope was treacherous in the dark. Even Taxi had fallen and got himself pinned down there some years ago, vanishing for days. Gemma found the torch and grabbed it, hurrying as best she could to the edge.

'Come back! Don't try and climb down there in the dark. You'll fall!'

The torch beam lit up a scrabbling figure dressed in dirty jeans and anorak with tousled dark hair. 'Come on,' she repeated, remembering one of Aunt Merle's injunctions from a life time ago: no matter whether you can help or not, any situation is always improved by putting on the kettle. 'Come back,' she called into the wind, 'and I'll make you a cup of tea!'

Beneath her, the figure straightened up. Impossible to tell whether it was male or female, but at least the frantic and dangerous slide had stopped. Gemma shone her torch full on the upturned face, twenty metres below. She gasped. Under the grubby layers of clothing and heavy eyebrows a white face stared back at her. Both the face and the body were longer and thinner than she remembered. But there was no forgetting that face.

It was the Ratbag.

ELEVEN

'What on earth are you doing here?' she asked as he half crawled back up the slope, rocks and pebbles sliding under his worn sneakers. She stood at the top of the cliff, shining the torch so that he had a path of light to follow. In a few minutes he'd managed to scramble to the top, worm through the bushes and stand silently in front of her. She racked her brain for his real name. She knew it was the same as a famous nineteenth-century French novelist. She discarded Emile and Gustave. Hugo, that was it.

'Hugo! What do you think you're doing here?'

He stood there shivering and Gemma realised how cold she was.

'You'd better come in,' she said. He followed her meekly back over the timber deck and in through the sliding doors. 'You gave me a terrible fright,' she said.

'I was really scared you'd shoot me,' were his first words.

She took a good look at him. 'I don't shoot people much.'

Under an old maroon anorak were a jumper and jeans that looked as if they'd never been washed.

She ushered him into the kitchen while she put the kettle on and poured herself a brandy. Now they were inside, she could smell him, the mousey odour of unwashed boy.

He looked at the kettle. 'I don't like tea.'

'What about hot chocolate?' she asked, dimly remembering a packet she'd noticed on one of her rarely visited shelves. He nodded and she started looking for it.

'Look, Hugo,' she said, 'why don't you go and have a shower?' She remembered his favourite food. 'And while you do that, I'll make the hot chocolate and order a pizza for you. Then, when you're feeling fresher, you'd better tell me what's going on.'

She saw the relief and the gratitude in his face and he disappeared into the bathroom. She remembered the distressed little kid of a couple of years ago, almost in tears about the injured falcon he'd nursed in a cardboard box. She ordered the pizza and poured herself another brandy, the shower going as she searched her room, trying to find something the Ratbag might wear. She finally settled on an old brown jumper that wasn't too girlie, some black trackies and a pair of Steve's socks. That, she decided, would have to do.

The phone rang just as she was finding a towel for the Ratbag. She knocked on the bathroom door and shoved it and the clothes into the room, then hobbled to answer the phone, hoping it would be Steve, conjured up by his socks. That sort of thing often happened. But it was Angie.

'You're still working?' Gemma was impressed.

'I've got the autopsy report on Shelly, Gemster. I knew you'd want to know asap.'

Gemma listened while Angie skim-read it and her anger grew that anyone would treat another human being the way someone had treated Shelly. It was the same grim picture—knock-out blows with a heavy instrument, something that left an odd-shaped weal on the skin. Gemma's blood ran cold. *That's on my skin, too.* She shivered. *Those plaited marks—It's him.* She put her hand on her left ribs, and felt the tenderness.

'Angie . . .' she started.

'What?'

'Oh . . . it's nothing. Go on.'

Even though it was important evidence, she couldn't bring herself to admit it just now. The thought of going down to the morgue and having her flank compared with the blackening bruises on her friend's body was just too awful. Tomorrow, she told herself. Instead, she listened to the horrible catalogue of injuries: bashing, biting and finally rape and death. Gemma recalled Shelly in her golden aspect, slinking down the staircase, all platinum and smiles, available at an hourly rate. Just like me, she thought.

'Thanks, Angie. Fax it to me, will you? Something's come up.' She was about to hang up when the Ratbag's presence reminded her of something. 'What's happening with Naomi?' she asked, thinking of Shelly's fifteen-year-old daughter.

'Dunno. I'll find out.'

Gemma rang off. She stood near the phone, thinking of the odd-shaped weals. He would have killed me, she thought. It could have been me instead of Shelly. Except I was ready for him.

The Ratbag wolfed down two-thirds of the family-sized pizza she picked up for him when she took delivery of her chicken curry. When he'd slowed up a bit, she poured him a glass of orange juice, made herself some coffee and settled down on the lounge opposite him as comfortably as she could, her leg propped up on the low table to one side of the lounge. Taxi had run to hide under the cedar sideboard and she could just see the tip of a nose and the odd whisker in the shadow underneath.

'What happened to your leg?' he asked.

Gemma looked down at her bandaged foot. 'I was on a job,' she said, 'and the offender jumped me.' He wasn't going to change the subject like that, she thought. 'Right,' she said. 'It's payback time. I got your pizza. I answered your question. Now it's your turn. What are you doing here?'

The Ratbag looked much sweeter now, with his

long hair slicked back and her old jumper hanging off him. But there were dark circles around his eyes and his mouth seemed thinner than she remembered.

'I've left school,' he said. 'And come to Sydney to live.'

'But Hugo, you can't do that!'

'Heaps of kids do.' His insouciance was almost convincing.

Gemma frowned. 'You can't be any older than twelve—thirteen—max. Kids have to go to school. It's the law. Don't give me that bullshit.'

'But plenty of kids do it anyway,' he said. 'I've been hanging with them.'

'I can see that,' said Gemma. 'You've been living on the streets, haven't you?'

'I had a job.'

'Doing what?'

'Just helping around this sort of club. You know, running messages, that sort of thing. Helping this bloke. He gave me fifty dollars.'

'He didn't try anything on, did he?' she asked, alarmed.

There was a pause. 'One bloke did, but I ran away.'

'Tell me what happened.'

He shook his head. 'I told you. I ran away. He didn't touch me.'

'When did you leave Melbourne?' she asked after a moment.

'A while ago.' He was vague. Gemma persisted. 'A week ago,' he said.

'Oh my God! Have you rung your mother?'

He paused before shaking his head.

Gemma leaned forward. 'Hugo,' she said, 'you must ring her.'

He blinked at her, the steady, considered gaze of a much younger child. 'I saw you in that boatshed making those statues,' he said. 'What are they supposed to be?'

Gemma felt stung at his question. 'They're lions,' she said.

'They look more like dogs,' he said. 'Freaky-looking dogs.'

'You must ring your mother,' Gemma persisted. 'She'll be sick with worry.' The Ratbag suddenly looked very sad, pausing in his attack on the second last slice of pizza in his odd way.

'No she won't.'

'What makes you say that?'

'She sort of kicked me out, really.'

'What do you mean?'

The Ratbag pulled at a piece of stretchy cheese until it broke, then he lifted the remainder of the slice to his mouth. Gemma had to wait while he chewed and swallowed it.

'I wanted to go and visit Dad. And she wouldn't let me. Dad's got me every second weekend.' His voice became almost a whisper as if he didn't want to hear his own words. 'But he's only been able to come down twice since the divorce.' Then his voice picked up as the loyal child defended his father. 'He's very, very busy,' Hugo explained. 'He's the general manager for the whole of New South

Wales for his business. He hasn't got much time because he's in charge of everyone in the company.' Pain and pride showed in his eyes before he looked away.

'Sure,' said Gemma. 'Go on.'

'One night we had a fight and she was screaming at me. She told me that Dad doesn't want me. She even said . . . ' his voice faltered and he looked away, not wanting Gemma to see the tears that had welled ' . . . that she didn't want me either. That having me was the worst mistake of her whole life. That she could have been someone if she didn't have me to look after all the time.' He paused and collected himself. 'So I ran away. I knew the only reason Dad didn't visit me was because she'd made us move to Melbourne and he didn't have the time. But then—' He stopped.

'Go on.'

He shook his head. 'No,' he said. 'I don't want to talk about it.'

Gemma had a fair idea of what had happened. She spoke softly. 'You went round to your father's place and he didn't want you to stay with him, did he?' she asked.

For a second, it looked as if Hugo was about to cry, then she saw him set his jaw. 'He rang Mum. And he took me into town and put me on the Melbourne bus.' The Ratbag looked away again and for a second Gemma hated his father. 'But I sneaked off and got a refund.'

'Oh Hugo,' she said. 'What am I going to do with you?'

'Can I live here?' he pleaded. 'With you?' He saw her shocked face. *'Please?'*

Despite the seriousness of the situation, he was only a little boy and Gemma was moved. 'Look,' she said, 'you can stay here tonight. But tomorrow we're going to have to sort something out. Okay?'

He nodded. She remembered Will at that age, lost and neglected while Kit and her ex-husband made a battleground of Will's home in their marital fight to the death.

'Why can't I live here?' he said. 'I'm used to it here. I could go back to my old school. My friends will remember me. I'll get a job and give you some money. I've got a lot of clothes back in Melbourne. I could get them. You wouldn't have to spend anything.'

He picked up the last piece of pizza and then put it down again. 'I don't eat very much food.'

Gemma didn't know whether to laugh or cry; his plaintive words had touched her heart.

'Hugo, we've got to be sensible about this. It's not because of money or how much food you might eat. It's more complicated than that.'

He gave her the look that kids do when they know they've lost the fight before it's even started.

'I'm not set up to be a foster mother,' she said. 'It's not in my'—she groped for a word—'plans.'

Hugo bowed his head and she touched the damp hair.

'Look,' she said, 'you're a great kid and I like you. But you're someone else's kid. You can't just leave home and live with me.' She couldn't bear to look at him.

'I'll make up the lounge bed for you,' she said. 'You can have Taxi for company.'

Half an hour later, he was lying along the lounge. Gemma had banned the filthy sleeping bag from the house and piled up spare blankets and her fake fur coat over him.

'Do you sometimes see my falcon around?'

'Sure,' she lied, remembering the bird the Ratbag had found injured and kept safe until it was healed.

'You'd know him, because he was darker under his wings. The others were lighter.'

The phone rang and Gemma grabbed it, glad for the breathing space the interruption offered her.

'Steve!' she said, pleased to hear his voice.

'I can't speak long,' he said. 'The target's bought it. I'm in! The deal goes down in the next twenty-four hours. Everything's in place. Then I can come home and stay home for a while.'

'Steve,' she said, 'I know who you're dealing with. Please be very careful.'

'You know me,' he said. 'Old Cautious himself. I used to jump off my billycart when it went too fast.'

'If he finds out you're a cop,' she said, 'and set him up. You've heard what he does.'

'Don't know what you're talking about,' he said. 'We'll celebrate when I come home. Buy a nice bottle of the Widow.'

And he rang off. Gemma put the phone down. She didn't like Steve saying that. Usually he went for the Bolly on special occasions. 'Widow' was not a word that she wanted to hear just now.

•

Next morning, her leg felt less tender and she could put more weight on it. In the shower, she was pleased to see that the purple-black bruising around her ribs was changing into the green stage around the edges. Gemma made breakfast for herself, trying to keep the clatter to a minimum but it didn't seem to matter—the Ratbag was dead to the world on the lounge under a pile of blankets. Taxi blinked balefully at the stranger on his favourite bed and she fed him the last of his fish dinner. She scribbled a note: *'Had to go out. If you hear people coming and going at the front of the house, don't be worried. It's just my staff. I'll be back later today and we'll work out what we're going to do with you. Help yourself to whatever. Love, Gemma.'* She tiptoed in and propped the note on the table beside the lounge with a glass of orange juice.

She went into her bedroom and pulled out her red suit and cream blouse and, while shivering in her underwear, she turned to see the bruising on the left side of her back. Standing sideways in front of the mirror, she was shocked by what she saw. Although the marks on her ribs weren't too bad, it was a different story on her back: dark purple bruises in an ugly wave pattern, becoming deeper towards the centre of her back. God, she thought, he hit me hard. She recalled the moment of impact, and looked closely at her neck. There was a blurred bruise on one side. A wave of disgust and fear made her rush to dress. She hated the fact that he'd left his mark on her like a brand, a mark of possession. The mark of the beast, she thought, as she hurried to button her blouse. The sea and the sky were grey and overcast and the southerly still knocked around the eaves and the windows so she gritted her teeth and hurriedly pulled a cream cashmere vest over the blouse. She looked reasonably good, she thought, until the feet—sneakers were the only shoes she could wear comfortably over her strapped-up ankle. You might have marked me, she addressed her unknown assailant silently, but I've sure as hell marked you. With some satisfaction she recalled the crunch as her knee connected with his head and imagined the damage she'd inflicted on him. She applied a bright red lipstick and checked that her hair was in order.

Gemma closed the door to her living area behind her and checked that both offices were reasonably tidy before taking the Peter Greengate file from her desk and opening it, studying the photograph of Patricia Greengate, wondering what sort of woman she was, with her snaky jewellery. She gathered up her camera, her laptop and her notebook, shoving them all in a big carry bag. Tonight, I'm going to follow you, ma'am, she told the photograph. See what you're getting up to. But first, I've got a search to do.

An hour later, she pulled into Benjamin Glass's Recycling and Manufacturing Industries' parking area. The disappearance of the owner hadn't made any difference to his business, she could see. Behind the tall cyclone fences the yards were busy with trucks delivering goods to the long factory building. The reception and information area was marked with a red and white sign. Gemma checked her briefcase and found the letter Minkie had written, glanced at her hair and lipstick in the mirror and swung out of the car, careful to place her feet together before she stood up. She managed the three wide steps to the building and pushed open the glass door to the foyer where a receptionist sat. The long timber counter was bare apart from a phone and a tall glass of artificial magnolias.

In a few minutes, she was sitting in Rosalie Luscombe's office as Benjamin Glass's personal assistant read the letter from his wife.

'Here,' Rosalie said, handing over a key on a tag. She had short cropped hair and a clean-scrubbed face. Until she stood up she reminded Gemma of an American boy actor who'd played in a family sitcom. Then Gemma saw that she was over six feet tall, and built like a footballer. She looked up at Rosalie's unadorned face.

'Do you know, Ms Luscombe,' she asked, 'if your boss had a safe in the office?'

'I believe he has one,' she said, and Gemma noted her use of the present tense, 'but I've never known where it is.'

'Any ideas?'

'I'm not paid for guesswork,' said the hefty woman. 'And it was not my business.'

'Ms Luscombe, I appreciate your discretion. But your employer is missing, possibly dead, and his wife needs your assistance. Not to mention the police and the insurers.'

This reference caused a further tightening of almost non-existent lips. Rosalie Luscombe's features clamped down in distaste. 'The police and the insurers can make their own arrangements as far as I'm concerned,' she said. 'And I'm sure that woman doesn't need me.'

She led Gemma to the room at the end of the hallway, took the key back from Gemma and deftly unlocked the door, standing back to let her enter.

'Call me if you need anything,' she said. 'I can hear you from where I sit. I could always hear Mr Glass when he called.'

Gemma watched her walk back down the corridor. Then she turned to examine her surroundings. If the home office had been the elegant and richly furnished retiring room of a gentleman, this office was all briskness and efficiency, with a lot of black and white epoxy resin around the light fittings, the desk lamp and even the furniture, the whole space lit by frosted windows. It was a cool white place of business, a bit like the inside of a Tupperware box, Gemma thought. She looked around. She was starting to get a sense of the character of the missing man now. Someone with very clean-cut boundaries between the different components of his life, she thought. Someone who kept these areas widely separated. In this way, she imagined, he could be a man of moral contradictions without creating too much inner conflict: a philanthropist and cardsharp, patron and cheat, gentleman and ragpicker who made his fortune recycling garbage.

She went over to Benjamin Glass's black chair and sat in it, surprised to find it was covered in soft suede and not the leather she'd been expecting. Here was another little bit of information to add to the puzzle—someone with a love of comfort, a sensualist. Apart from framed certificates and awards, the walls of the office were bare of decoration. Gemma swung round and checked the desk, going all over it and even under it, looking for secrets. It was clean. She got down on the floor as she'd done in the Vaucluse study, taking great care of her injured leg, and patted her way across the serviceable grey carpet tiles, failing to find any irregularity. Then she went all over the walls, tapping and listening, but there was nothing. Just the solid sound of the timber framework, all in order, and all where it should be, behind gyprock cladding.

Years of experience had taught Gemma that men kept their secrets in the shed. It didn't have to be an actual shed, just somewhere completely personal and private. She'd found all sorts of things there over the years. She'd even cut down a couple of men who'd hanged themselves in their sheds. A man's shed was his bolt-hole, his earth. The study at the grand mansion Benjamin Glass shared with Minkie and the now destroyed work tower of the Nelson Bay holiday home were neither of them private enough, she thought, to be the shed, because they were both areas of shared access. But this place was different. In spite of its bareness, she felt that this arctic office was Benjamin Glass's 'shed'.

She stood in the centre of the room and looked around. Apart from a photograph of himself and his cat, there were no other personal items in the room. She picked up the picture and studied the missing animal, noticing its unusual patterning, like black and white checks. She put it down again, feeling dejected, no closer to discovering the lead, the break, the mysterious *something* that might help her in this case. Defeated, she turned towards the door and was walking out when she remembered something from an old police investigation. On a hunch, she went back down the corridor to where Rosalie Luscombe sat, frowning at her monitor screen. She looked up sternly at Gemma's approach.

'Ms Luscombe,' she said 'I can't find the safe. His wife says he had one, you say he has one. Why can't I find it?'

'I really can't help you,' said Rosalie Luscombe, a tad too happily, Gemma thought.

She cleared her throat. 'This might sound odd, but I want to ask you something.' Rosalie Luscombe cocked her cropped head, waiting.

'Have you ever . . . I'm not quite sure how to phrase this . . . did you ever walk into Mr Glass's office and find him in an odd position? An unexpected position?' She tried another way. 'Have you ever surprised him in his office when he wasn't expecting anyone?'

'I always knock.' The woman bridled.

'I'm sure you do. But sometimes people don't hear.'

Rosalie's eyes narrowed as she searched her memory. 'Once or twice over the years I've worked for Mr Glass,' she admitted, 'he hasn't heard my knock. Why do you ask?'

'Just tell me what happened on those occasions,' Gemma said.

'I had the feeling he'd just straightened up from doing something.' She sniffed. 'As if he was looking through the keyhole or something, near the door.' She picked up a blue folder and put it down again. 'I did wonder at the time what he might have been doing,' she said. 'Because we don't have keyholes anymore, do we?' She shrugged.

Gemma felt warmer towards her. 'You've been a great help,' she said, turning away from the puzzled secretary with a smile.

As fast as her injuries would let her, she hurried back to the cold white office. She closed the door and squatted down, wincing as she did, so that she was looking straight at the lock. Okay, she thought, looking around. There's nothing to see. Just the door. No one could see through a modern lock, she knew. So what was he doing down here? She looked down. On the floor on the inside of the door ran a metal strip trim, forming a division between the grey carpet tiles of Benjamin Glass's office and the even more serviceable rattan tiles of the corridor. Gemma focused all her attention on the metal strip, feeling along the length of it, studying the small brass screws that kept it firmly in position. And, sure enough, she saw what she was looking for: around each of the screws were innumerable tiny scratches, fine as cobwebs. These screws had been loosened and tightened many, many times. She pulled out her Swiss Army knife and started on the first one. It came away easily. In a few minutes, she had all six screws out and was lifting the metal trim up. Underneath the partly lifted carpet squares, Gemma could see dull metal, not the concrete slab that she'd expect to find here. Benjamin Glass had organised the safe so that the body of it lay in a cavity that started just inside his office and ran underneath part of the hall floor. She pulled the carpet tiles away. There it was, a plump solid safe with the door side exposed. Returning to her briefcase, she found the key and got down on the floor again. For a painful moment it wouldn't turn, but then the mechanism slid into place with ease and the door opened sideways.

Gemma peered into the metallic silver-grey

interior. There was no fortune in banknotes to tempt her integrity—just another two decks of playing cards, a surgical scalpel and a large envelope. Carefully, she drew the items out, closing the safe door, replacing the carpet squares, refitting the metal trim, screwing it back down and putting the objects safely into her briefcase. She went over to the desk and picked up the photograph of the millionaire philanthropist and his cat with its funny checked face. 'The cat's out of the bag now, maybe,' she whispered to them and left, locking the office behind her.

She walked back down the hall and said goodbye to Ms Luscombe but just as she was about to leave her office, she turned back.

'Ms Luscombe,' she asked, 'where's Mr Glass's cat?'

'The cat?' said the other, surprised. 'I have no idea. It's certainly not here. I imagine Mr Glass took it to the Bay with him. Poor thing must have perished in the fire.'

Gemma thanked her again and hobbled out of the building back to her car. So, the cat must have been in the house. It wasn't here and it wasn't at the Vaucluse mansion. But she was too eager to examine what she'd found in the safe under the floor in Benjamin Glass's office to worry about the missing cat right now. She couldn't wait to check out what she'd found so she drove a little way down the road, parked and pulled out the items to have a closer look at what Benjamin Glass had so carefully secreted away.

First she examined the cards, flicking through the deck. One pack was quite normal and the other had only a few of the flickering white marks when she whizzed the cards through her fingers. The marking process obviously hadn't been finished on this deck. She examined the fine point on the scalpel blade then turned her attention to the envelope and opened it. She looked through the contents. Wow, she thought. What have we got here? And, more to the point, *who* have we got here? She felt elated by this new line of inquiry, enlivened with new enthusiasm.

She shoved the items back in her carry bag, stowed it on the floor and drove home, finding that her injured foot was starting to ache. She was resigned to the fact that eventually she might have to hand the articles she'd found over to Sean Wright. Section 316 of the Crimes Act made that very clear. But there was nothing she'd discovered so far that suggested any serious crime and on this basis, she decided, she could give herself a little grace. This could be the breakthrough I need on the Benjamin Glass disappearance, she thought.

On the way home, she dropped into Gallery Europa. The same receptionist with the varnished helmet-like hair-do was behind the desk. As the woman raised her head to greet Gemma, she showed no sign of recognition.

'Anthony Love,' Gemma said. 'Any word of him?'

'As a matter of fact, he hasn't been near the gallery in the last week or so.' She peered at Gemma.

'You left your card, didn't you?' Gemma nodded. 'I said I'd give it to him when I see him. Haven't seen him, couldn't give it, could I?' Then she lowered the helmet again.

When Gemma let herself in, she could hear the sound of the television. 'Hullo?' she called. 'Hugo?'

He was sitting up on the lounge with Taxi, the two of them watching a video, and he jumped up, looking guilty, as she came in.

'I took the money from the kitchen,' he said, 'in the jar.'

For a second, Gemma didn't know what he meant, then she realised he was talking about the jar of change on top of the fridge that came in handy for the occasional bus fare and newspaper.

'You said I could help myself.' He looked away. 'The man at the video shop remembered me,' he continued sadly. 'He asked me if I was living back here again.'

She came and sat beside him. 'Hugo, just pause that film for a sec?' He did so, looking scared. 'It's okay, Hugo,' she said. 'But you must realise that a boy your age can't live here and just watch videos all day. It's not right. I'll have to ring your mum.'

His despairing face nearly broke her heart. Don't do this to me, she begged inwardly. It's not fair. You're not my responsibility. I don't even think of you for long periods of time. I don't owe you anything. Instead, she tried patting him awkwardly.

'Come on,' she said. 'Everything will be okay.' She knew from her own experience this was a stupid thing to say to a child. But she had so much to deal with—the pressure of work, the fears she had concerning her own safety, the worry about Steve. I've got so much to do right now, she thought, I can't have a bloody kid hanging round my neck.

'What's your phone number in Melbourne?'

The Ratbag looked at her. 'I don't know,' he said.

'Don't be so damn stupid, Hugo,' she snapped. 'Of course you know your own phone number.' Now she was really angry.

But his set face and determined mouth did not change.

Gemma jumped up. 'Look,' she said, 'we do it nicely or we do it hard. Which way do you want?' Now she felt mean, using the sort of pressure she'd applied to crims in the past on a little lost boy. 'If you don't tell me,' she continued, 'I'll have to go to the police. They'll track your mother down in ten minutes flat. So what's it to be?' She stood, hands on hips, waiting for an answer. Behind her, the paused movie clicked off and a television program took its place. Gemma swung round and snapped it off. Her phone rang and she snatched it up.

'Yes?'

'It's me,' said Angie. 'I've just heard that Sean

and the Crime Scene people found what looks like human remains at the fire site at Nelson Bay. I knew you'd like to know rather than have Mr Right teasing you about it. The bits and pieces are at the morgue right now. They were found in the lowest section of the place, probably protected when the building collapsed.'

'So they'll have him identified?'

'The lab out at Lidcombe is running the DNA tests soonest.'

'Has the wife been informed?'

'They had to go round and ask her for her husband's personal items to provide the DNA reference sample.'

'Angie, you're a major babe.'

'Put it on paper, honey. I might need it one day.'

Gemma rang off. She went into her bedroom and took the sneakers off, unwrapping the bandage from her ankle. She tried standing on it. It hurt, but it held out. She decided against a new bandage, replaced the sneakers and went back to the lounge room and stood in the doorway. The Ratbag was slumped on the lounge, staring at the blank TV screen.

'Hugo,' she said, 'I'm going out again now. But we're going to have to sort this out. By the time I get back, I want you to have remembered your phone number. I don't want to have a fight about it.'

He was hunched over, not looking at her, the picture of misery. She felt bad leaving him like this. She took a little time to scan and copy the contents of the envelope she'd found in Benjamin Glass's safe. Then she drove back to Vaucluse.

•

Minkie, wearing a long-sleeved red velvet body suit under her black trousers and large rubies on each ear, opened the front door and stepped back to let her in. Once in the grand drawing room, Gemma placed her briefcase on the marble-topped table. Minkie, rubies glinting, glanced first at her, then at the briefcase, as if it might have a bomb in it.

'The police were here,' she said nervously. 'They've found'—she made a funny little sound like a miaow—'*remains.*' She fiddled with one of the rubies. 'Can you believe it? Remains! After that inferno?' She waited for a reply, but Gemma said nothing. 'That young detective,' Minkie continued, 'the smart one, took some of Benjamin's personal things. His toothbrush, hairbrush, things like that.' She looked as if she were about to burst into tears. 'They said they needed them for a DNA match.' Gemma saw her straighten up and compose her face. 'Who the hell else do they think it would be in that house?'

'It's standard procedure,' said Gemma. 'The coroner must be satisfied as to the identity of the deceased. Nothing can be presumed.' God, she thought to herself, I'm sounding like a cop.

'What happens now?' Minkie asked. 'I mean, what will they do with the remains?'

'Didn't Sean Wright tell you?'

'He said something about tests and the morgue.

I wasn't really paying attention to the details. I was shocked. It's one thing to know that no one could have survived that fire, it's another thing to have it become really true.' She turned away, fishing a tissue from her red velvet sleeve.

'The pathologist will make an examination and determine the cause of death.'

'Good Christ! I could tell him that!' Minkie's voice balanced on the edge between anger and hysteria. 'A six-year-old child could tell him that!'

'Again,' Gemma said, 'it's a requirement of the coroner. I know it must sound a bit odd.'

Minkie looked as if she might have something to say about that, but then she noticed Gemma glance down at her briefcase and she was suddenly focused on it too. 'What have you got in there?' she asked.

She's really frightened, Gemma thought. She's not the cool customer I first met. This is what it must look like, Gemma realised, when a control freak starts to come unstuck. She opened the case and took out the decks of cards, the scalpel and the envelope containing the original photographs.

'These are the things I found in your husband's safe at his place of work,' said Gemma.

Minkie was startled. 'You found the safe?'

'Why? Couldn't you?' Gemma couldn't resist asking.

'I didn't even try,' said the other. 'That's why I obtained your services.'

So you tell me, Gemma thought.

'What have you got?' Minkie peered at the objects.

'Two more card decks similar to those I found here,' she said, indicating the drawers where the cards had been. 'It's my belief,' said Gemma, picking up the scalpel, 'that your husband used the sharp point of this instrument to prick out the tiny etched petals on the backs of the cards for his use.' Then she picked up the large envelope. 'But I'm much more concerned about these photographs.' She paused, proffering the envelope. 'What can you tell me about them?'

Slowly, Minkie put her hand out to take the envelope. She opened the flap and pulled out the three photos. Gemma heard the shocked inhalation of breath as she saw the first one. Then the pallor and the sudden redness of Minkie's face as she stared at each photo in turn.

'I don't believe it,' she said finally, throwing the photos down onto the marble table. 'I can't believe you found this . . . this . . . *trash*'—she paused, distressed—'in my husband's safe.'

'I can assure you I did,' said Gemma. 'And we need to talk about it.' The saintly philanthropist image was well and truly undone now.

'If you did, so what?' Minkie was rallying fast. She jabbed a contemptuous finger at the three photos. 'A lot of men use pornography. I just didn't think Benjamin was like that.' She sniffed.

'I don't perceive these photographs as pornography, Minkie,' Gemma said carefully. 'To my mind, these suggest the sorts of shots a man takes of his girlfriend. If you look at this one, I think you'll see for yourself that your husband took them.'

Minkie suddenly started sobbing, flinging herself around, away from the strewn photographs. Is this an act, Gemma asked herself, or is it real shock and anger? It was very convincing.

'I'm sorry to have to be the one who shows you this, but if we're going to work together, you've got to tell me anything you know about this woman.' Gemma picked one of the photos up. Kneeling in the middle of an unmade bed, in a room dominated by a huge nude portrait of herself, a good-looking blonde woman, wearing nothing except a smouldering half-smile and black lace gloves, stared straight into the camera. Her hair, like the bed, was tousled. She was gorgeous. About my age, Gemma thought ruefully, but with a hell of a lot more of everything.

Minkie blew her nose. 'Why do you say he knew her?' she cried. 'Maybe he just liked these sorts of photographs. Maybe she's a professional model.'

It was, Gemma thought, a variation on the usual denials she heard when she showed people a truth they found unpalatable. Gemma studied the first picture again. Beside the woman on the bed was a cupboard with its door angled open and inside the door was a long mirror. In the mirror, Gemma could see the grainy outline of the portly, naked photographer holding the camera. She pointed a finger at the figure.

'There's the photographer,' she said. 'Do you know that man?'

Minkie snatched the photo from her and stared at it a long moment. 'The bastard,' she said. 'The filthy stinking two-faced bastard!'

'Is it your husband?' Gemma persisted.

Minkie flung the photograph away from her, stamping away to the window. 'My husband!' she said. 'My *late* husband. My bastard of a husband. My fucking *dead* bastard of a husband!'

Gemma watched the drama. If this was how Minkie reacted to a mere photo, what would she have done if she'd stumbled upon the lovers? But would she behave like this if she'd had time to rehearse it? Surely she'd be composed and not let me see what looks like completely spontaneous naked fury and humiliation.

'The *bastard*,' Minkie repeated. 'Having me find out like *this*.'

Gemma had heard that or similar lines so many times from her clients that she wished she'd developed her own line in comforting them more successfully.

'There is no nice way,' she said finally. 'It's always going to be hurtful.' She turned her attention back to the case in hand. 'Do you know this woman?' she asked after a pause.

'Of course I don't!' Minkie snapped. 'I have no idea who she is. And I don't want to know.' She threw herself down on the lounge, her face bitten with rage. 'Oh!' she wailed, 'I'm just so angry! If he wasn't already dead, I could kill him!' She shot

252 • GABRIELLE LORD

a look at Gemma. Her features were hard and compressed. 'Does that shock you? What am I supposed to say?' she challenged her. 'Right this moment, I'm glad he's dead.'

True love, Gemma thought. Ain't it grand? The minute he plays hide the sausage with someone else, love flies out the window and we want his heart in a box. What would *she* feel like if she found out Steve had been sleeping with another woman? Steve sleeping over at another woman's house, even if she was fat and fifty, did make her feel some sort of jealousy.

'Minkie,' she said to the woman who was still sitting hunched with rage, 'you're going to have to accept that your husband had two big secrets. And either of them could provide a motive for murder. Taken together, it doesn't look good. So I have to ask you this: did you know your husband had a girlfriend?'

She saw something move across Minkie's face, but instead of answering the question, there was another, noisier outburst.

'God,' Minkie said, jumping up, 'it's only going to make things worse for me.' She swung around like a caged panther. '*Shit!*' she screamed, 'I don't know what I'm going to do!'

'What's going to make things worse for you?' Gemma asked.

Minkie swung round, eyes narrowed to a mean green blaze. 'This! *Her!* That slut! Now it's going to look like I killed him because I was jealous of some little tart!'

'And did you? Were you?' Gemma pressed.

'Of course I didn't! I didn't even know of her existence until you came barging in here with those damn photographs.'

'I didn't barge, Minkie,' Gemma said mildly. 'I'm investigating your husband's suspected murder. At *your* invitation.'

Minkie went over to a marble-topped credenza and upended a glass, pouring herself a brandy. She was putting the stopper back in place when she remembered Gemma.

'Do you want one?' she asked rather ungraciously.

Gemma thought it was past time she went, so she declined, gathered up the photographs and put them away. Then she took out the scanned copies and passed them to Minkie who was sipping brandy neat and screwing up her nose in distaste.

'I want you to start asking around,' she said. 'Find out if anyone knows who this woman is.'

Minkie looked at the copies. 'How many people are going to see these?' she said. 'How many copies are there?'

'Only the ones in your hand,' Gemma reassured her. 'I made them myself.'

'How humiliating!' she cried. 'Who am I supposed to ask?'

'Ask his friends, his staff at work,' Gemma suggested, impatient to be gone. 'Rosalie Luscombe may know something.'

Minkie threw her a look of disgust, then finished the brandy.

It was often the way, Gemma thought, with the wife and the secretary, the other woman in each other's lives. The androgynous Rosalie Luscombe had referred to her boss's wife as '*that woman*', Gemma remembered.

'No. I won't.' said Minkie. 'It's undignified.'

'So's being charged with murder,' said Gemma a little too smartly. She hadn't noticed anything very dignified in the woman's reactions of the last few minutes.

'Put yourself in my situation,' Minkie said, working up to her topic, 'me, the wife, going round with a photograph of that tart—asking people to tell me who she is. How would *you* feel? It's unthinkable.'

'It's in your interests to find this woman,' Gemma said. 'Once the police know about her, we lose the advantage of surprising her. I'm obliged by law to pass on this evidence. I could be liable if I don't within a reasonable amount of time.'

'Not the police too?' said Minkie. 'I can't stand the thought of them feeling sorry for me.'

Was Minkie protesting too much, Gemma wondered. 'Look,' she said, 'feeling sorry for people isn't part of police procedure.'

The conversation had come to an end and Minkie let her out of the house in silence. This time Gemma managed the path with only the slightest limp. The sense of foreboding that had surrounded her lately returned, haunting her with a sense of unformed dread. She shook it off once she was on the street, but still she couldn't keep herself from looking around, checking every car, making sure she wasn't the target of the insurance company's operative sitting off the Montreau-Glass mansion across the road, checking up on Minkie and her visitors, writing Gemma up in a report right this very moment. It was a cool, overcast day and something about the greyness of the light infected Gemma's mood. She crossed the road, walking right up to the T-intersection and back down the other side. All the parked vehicles were empty. No one was sitting alone pretending to read a newspaper, a street directory, or even napping. But that certainly didn't discount someone, some-where, with high-powered binos and a camera like her own, watching. Waiting. She thought of cyber-creep and his promise of seeing her sometime soon. She shivered and scrambled into her car. Angie's suggestion of the semi-automatic Glock 27 seemed more and more like a good idea.

•

She drove straight to the address Peter Greengate had given her, stopping to pick up a newspaper and two sausage rolls at her favourite cake shop, hoping that the fix of fatty pastry would lift her spirits. She drove slowly past the Greengate's mar-ital home, a pretty Federation-style cottage with a paved front yard and geraniums hanging in bask-ets from the verandah roof, turned at the end of the street and came back, parking on the side opposite the cottage. *'High! Voltage! Rock and Roll!'* screamed her radio and she automatically

sang along. According to her husband, Patricia
Greengate should be leaving the house soon.
Gemma ate the sausage rolls and read, her eyes
constantly moving above the top of the newspaper,
checking the front door behind the geraniums.

•

An hour later, she was recalling all the reasons why
she didn't go out on the road anymore. The bore-
dom and discomfort of sitting for long periods in
parked cars, was making her edgy. The sausage rolls
were now a regrettable lump of indigestion and she
wriggled in her seat, trying to make herself more
comfortable. She'd read the newspaper from front
to back. She checked her Telstra shares in the
finance pages and swore, then glanced at her watch.
A slight sound caught her attention. Patricia Greengate was leaving the house with a shopping bag, a
romantic vision in long skirt and misty shawls as
she turned around from locking the door, silver
jewellery shining in the light. No snakes today.
Gemma waited, fingers on the ignition keys, while
the woman got into her white Honda and drove
off. Gemma took off after her. In a few minutes,
the Honda reached Bondi Junction train station.
As Patricia Greengate signalled the right-hand turn
into the free parking area, Gemma considered her
options. If she couldn't find a parking place she
might lose her target. Luckily she noticed a one
hour spot on the road and quickly took it. Stuffing
the video camera into her large carry bag, she
jumped out to run across the road into the park-

ing area. It took her a few minutes to locate the
Honda in the middle section. Gemma looked
around and saw Patricia Greengate moving towards
the incline to the station. She hurried after her
quarry, and when she got to the bottom and looked
around, she saw the woman turn a corner and dis-
appear. Gemma walked as fast as she could with
her injured ankle and arrived at the same corner
only a few seconds later. She looked around. Mrs
Greengate had vanished. Impossible. She must be
on one of the platforms. Gemma limped rapidly to
check but it was soon apparent the woman wasn't
up there. There was only one platform for waiting
passengers to the city because the Eastern suburbs
line terminated here. Gemma retraced her steps,
cursing. Maybe Patricia Greengate was surveillance
savvy and had just walked right through the station
area and out the other side. Gemma ran through
and came out on the other side. But nowhere could
she see the figure in the misty trailing shawls. Then
she noticed the toilets. She must be in the loo,
Gemma thought, hanging back. She waited for
some minutes. Two women came out of the Ladies,
a mother and daughter from the look of them, but
apart from a non-descript man with an airline bag
who left the nearby Gents, absolutely no one else
had need of the facilities. Gemma waited and
waited. She eventually went into the women's toilet
to check it out. She looked in every cubicle. There
was no one there. Nor was there any other exit.
She'd lost her quarry. The simplest follow and she'd
stuffed up. She hurried back out and checked the

City platform again. The only people there were two backpackers, poring over a map. Gemma sighed. Her leg was aching and she'd lost her target. She still had the Ratbag to deal with when she got home. It had not been a good day.

TWELVE

Back in her car, Gemma stowed her camera back out of sight and left a message for Sean Wright to ring her. She felt angry with herself for letting Patricia Greengate get away. Losing visual connection like that was the problem. With her injured leg she just hadn't been quite fast enough to keep her target in her sights. '*Hollywood nights, those Hollywood nights*', sang the radio and she switched it off, irritated by a song that was usually among her favourites.

Her phone rang and she answered it, hoping it would be Sean. But it was a young woman's voice. Sean was at the morgue, she was told, waiting for the PM doctor's report on Benjamin Glass.

'Thanks,' said Gemma. 'Who am I talking to?'

'Melissa,' came the reply and Gemma remembered the smart young photographer at the fire scene, unloading cameras, quietly taking shots, going about her business without any fuss.

'Melissa,' she said, 'we've met. At the Benjamin Glass fire scene.'

'I know,' said the other. 'That's why I'm ringing you. You remember I did the photography for Physical Evidence, for the three high temperature accelerant fires.'

Gemma waited.

'Sean Wright won't tell you this, but I want you to know he found cat hairs at all three HTA sites.'

'But Sean said there was no trace of a cat,' said Gemma, starting to wonder why her erstwhile colleague might have lied to her.

'That's right,' said Melissa. 'But we always have a problem establishing an outer perimeter for fire scenes.'

Gemma remembered the difficulties of taping off a crime scene: where does it start? finish? how to decide how wide to tape?

'It was only at the widest perimeters we found the animal hairs.'

'But you said *cat* hair,' Gemma reminded her.

'The results only just came back, the animal experts are so overworked. I thought you'd want to know this.'

'Thanks, Melissa,' said Gemma, wondering why the photographer had bothered to inform her.

'Sean Wright is a total prick,' said Melissa, and Gemma wondered no more.

She put the phone down, frowning. Cat hairs at all three HTA fire scenes? An absurd image came to her—a wicked feline arsonist with a checked face.

•

She drove to Glebe through the heavy traffic, still trying to fit the cat hairs into a crime scenario that made sense. Finally she decided that they were irrelevant. Cat hairs would be found at almost every crime scene, given the nature of cats. She brought her attention back to the fact that she'd lost Patricia Greengate. I'll have to start again, she thought to herself, hoping her weird client wasn't in too much of a hurry. I might even offer him a reduced rate, she thought, feeling badly about losing the target.

She parked in one of the streets behind the buildings of the Institute of Forensic Medicine, walking to the back door and pressing an intercom buzzer for entry. She announced her name and was let in. Straightaway she could hear Sean's laugh. He was approaching along a narrow hallway holding a large manila envelope and flirting with a short girl beside him.

Gemma hurried towards him, hand outstretched, cheesy grin in place. 'Sean,' she said. 'I hoped I'd find you here. I've got something you'll be very interested to see.'

He smiled his superior smile and the girl ducked sideways into one of the rooms and disappeared. 'What might that be?' he asked.

'Come in here,' she said, indicating a small grey and pink sitting room nearby with kitchen facilities. She ducked her head around the corner to check that it was empty.

Sean followed her in. 'The lab rang through the DNA result,' he said. 'The crispy we found in the foundations was definitely part of the late Benjamin Glass.'

'That certainly makes things simpler,' she said.

'Not necessarily,' he said patronisingly. 'In this case it actually makes things much more complex.'

Gemma imagined Sean in years to come, boring the pants off people, with his pathetic little power games. But she'd dealt with him in the past and instead of letting her irritation show her eyelids were almost batting as she sweetly asked, 'How is that, Sean?'

'I only found a partial body at the crime scene,' he said. 'You saw what the fire had done. The only reason we found anything of him was because he'd fallen through into the cellar section of the building when the buildings collapsed. Otherwise it would have been incinerated too. Just a section of the sacrum, the doctor told me. But it was enough.'

Gemma waited, trying to keep a pleasant expression on her face.

'Beats me how they know which end is up,' Sean said, in a rare moment of humility. He paused deliberately again and only the knowledge that she had a red-hot clue in the form of a photograph of a lace-gloved naked blonde in her briefcase that Sean didn't know about kept Gemma calm. She adopted a look of rapt attention, and waited.

'But there was enough tissue apparently,' he went on, 'to reveal extremely high levels of carboxy-haemoglobin.'

'And what's that?' Gemma asked, sweet as pie.

'And as well, there was no vital reaction to the

effects of the fire,' he continued, ignoring her question.

Gemma at least understood this one. 'He was dead before the fire,' she translated. 'So it *was* murder?'

'He was dead all right,' said Sean smugly. 'He'd died of carbon monoxide poisoning *before* the fire.'

'And so it can't be suicide,' Gemma said recalling the brilliant flashes she'd seen on the video of the inferno. 'Unless he somehow sets up a timer with the HTAs and kills himself with carbon monoxide.'

'Except for the fact that there was no trace of carbon monoxide anywhere at the fire scene except concentrated in the tissues of the late Mr Glass,' said Sean. 'So how could he have done that?'

'Surely the fire would have destroyed any residues?' she said.

Sean lifted his shoulders and pulled a face. 'It's got to have come from somewhere, and in concentrations high enough to be lethal.'

Gemma went to the sink and poured herself some water using one of a stack of polyfoam disposable cups. This investigation was getting weirder by the minute. Benjamin Glass dead from carbon monoxide poisoning. Someone activating the house alarm, then swiftly switching it off and setting a fire with a rare accelerant that took the evidence with it but, at the same time, drew attention to itself and the dead man at its centre. Had

Minkie or Anthony Love, or both of them together, somehow gassed him in his car, dragged him into the house, panicked and forgotten to deactivate the alarm, then set up HTA fuel for ignition a short time later? It was too complicated. Why not just push him off the headland? Or knock him on the head? Or gas him and leave him in the car? It would be much simpler to make it look accidental or to simulate a suicide. Why then draw attention to the whole incident by making a fire with an accelerant so unique, so spectacular, that it would create immense speculation and interest? Nothing about this case made any sense at all. And yet the investigator in her knew that although the facts she could already see ran through a wall that made them invisible or went underground, they were there all right, as real and as solid as she was, just waiting for her to discover them and make the right connections. People never do things without reasons, she knew.

'I'll tell you something I've come to see about this job,' said Sean. Here we go again, thought Gemma, restraining her desire to say *please don't*.

'What we think we don't know about a case is too often staring us right in the face but we can't see it. And why's that?—because it's so big and obvious.'

Gemma looked up at him and this time didn't have to feign interest. Someone had gone to an enormous amount of trouble for the sake of this death. At this, a clear light suddenly shone into the murky conjectures that so far had only teased her. 'You're right,' she said. 'Sean, you're dead right.' A line of enquiry so clear, so obvious, that it was embarrassing not to have considered it before, had suddenly opened up with Sean's words. Gemma couldn't wait to get away and research it.

'Hey!' said Sean, thrilled at her response. 'How about a proper drink?'

His question barely registered with her as she tried to work out where to start chasing up her new idea. The university, she thought. Academic records. 'Uh?' She swung back to him, aware he'd just issued an invitation. She flashed him one of her best smiles. 'Another time, Sean. The cat. What about the cat?' She waited to see what he'd say.

'We didn't find any cat,' he said. 'But if all we've got left of an adult male is a small piece of rump we can't expect there'd be anything left of a cat, now could we?'

If he was disappointed about her not accepting his invitation for a drink, Gemma thought, he didn't let it show. Probably puts it on any female from fifteen to fifty. 'I'd give a lot to know if that cat was in the holiday house or not,' she said.

'I went to Benjamin Glass's factory,' he said, 'and found cat hair all through his office and a nice photo of the damn thing. Funny patchy chequerboard face.'

'I heard there were cat hairs found at all three fire scenes,' she said with relish.

'Oh that,' he said dismissively. 'It's got to be the *same* cat to mean anything,' he reminded her. 'Benjamin Glass's cat. What is it with you and that cat anyway?' he asked.

Gemma smiled. 'Don't you remember your lectures on Fraud Indicators?' she asked. 'Go and dig up your old notes and read the bit about arson and the family pet.'

'I never took notes,' he said. 'Didn't need to. Waste of time.'

'Maybe not,' said Gemma. 'So I'll tell *you* something for a change. One strong indication of arson is the discovery that the family pet just happened to be staying somewhere else at the time of the fire. The arsonist arranges a sleep over for Fido to make sure he's not killed or injured in the blaze.'

Sean shrugged his shoulders as if discounting what Gemma was telling him.

'I hear the widow's paying you to investigate the fire. You'd better be careful of that woman. I bet she didn't brief you that a yellow BMW was reported near the Nelson Bay house around the time of the fire. I did my homework. That's what Minkie Montreau drives.'

'Who reported it?' said Gemma, frowning.

'The policeman's best pal,' said Sean. 'Mr Anonymous Tipoff. Anyway, what are you doing here? Who have you come to see?'

His dominating manner was back in full force and in that instant, Gemma decided to give herself another twenty-four hours before handing over Ms Black Lace Gloves.

'You,' she said sweetly. 'I was told you were here. I just wanted to keep you informed.

On account of auld lang syne. I found a couple of things in a safe at Benjamin Glass's factory office. Obviously no one from your team had found it.' Sean looked extremely pissed off at that, but before he could say anything, Gemma continued quickly. 'I was acting on the instructions of Minkie Montreau. She wanted me to search the place thoroughly because she knew there was a safe but not where it was. I found a key hidden in his office at home.'

Sean's face was compressed with anger.

'Look,' she said, trying to placate him, 'I had all the advantages. I'm working for the wife. I was invited in first.' If you guys had taken these fires more seriously from the beginning, she felt like saying, I doubt if I'd even be here.

'That's no excuse,' he said. 'I don't have to remind you that your licence depends on you co-operating with the police whenever appropriate. You don't want a suspension.'

'That's why I'm here,' she said, handing over the decks of cards and the scalpel.

From down the hall, she could hear the sound of a vacuum cleaner moving closer. I'll hand over the rest tomorrow, she decided. After I've visited Sydney University. She brought her attention back to the present.

'Did the PM doctor say any more about the autopsy results on Shelly?' she asked, changing the subject.

Sean put the cards and scalpel back into the plastic bag, and slid them together into the large envelope he carried. 'The bruises on her body match the injuries we photographed on Robyn Warburton. The doc thinks it's probably a chain that he wraps round his fist. To give him more clout.'

Clout all right. Gemma shuddered. She remembered the terrible blow to her flank and how the bruises were getting darker under her silk blouse. Just thinking about it made her aware of how sore her ribs were.

'What's up?' Sean asked, noticing her wince.

'Nothing,' she said. 'My war injuries playing up.'

'You should let us do our job, Gemma,' he said in his patronising way. 'Just follow your insurance fraudsters and stay out of trouble. Little girls get hurt when they try playing with the big boys.'

'If the big boys were doing their job properly,' she said through gritted teeth, 'I wouldn't have even been there that night.' She flashed him a wide smile to undercut the criticism. The noise of the vacuum down the hall became louder and the cleaner came in, wrestling with a very noisy industrial-strength machine. 'I've gotta go,' Gemma said over the sound. She felt only marginally guilty about the photographs still in her briefcase.

At the door, Gemma turned to him. 'I'll ring you soon,' she said. 'We'll have that drink.' He opened the door for her and she hurried outside.

•

It was an unsettled evening and a light rain had fallen while she was inside. Parramatta Road was streaked with water, oil stains and the lurid reflections of red, white and green lights. To get to her car from the main entrance, she had to turn off the comforting busyness of Parramatta Road and into a darker Glebe street. She walked as briskly as possible, aware of her limp, yet as ready for action as she could be, her mind trying to make sense of a case that just seemed to get wilder and crazier by the moment. A card cheat, high temperature accelerants, a blonde with black lace gloves, a missing cat. And now carbon monoxide in lethal concentrations in the pathetic bit of tissue left after a conflagration like the fires of hell. Not to mention an anonymous tipoff that put a car similar to that driven by the dead man's widow at the fire scene. She stopped by her car, and stared up at the new moon, just visible through thin cloud. Her side was really painful now and she had to ease herself gently into the driver's seat.

When she arrived home, after rehearsing a few sentences to use on the Ratbag, she was puzzled to see her place in darkness. Maybe he'd gone to sleep on the lounge watching telly, she thought. But her puzzlement turned to alarm when she stepped up onto the small tiled area that led to her front door. Her security door stood wide open and her front door was also slightly ajar. She pushed it cautiously, spooked by this breach in her security.

'Hugo?' she called. 'Where are you?' He must

have gone out and left the door open. She didn't like this one bit. 'Hugo?' she called again.

But her apartment was darkly still. She stepped into the hall and could see the eerie glow of the screen saver in the operatives' office. She reached for the hall light and switched it on. Now she could hear the sound of the television in her living room. 'Hugo?' she called again, walking with more confidence in the light. She was about to lock the door when she recalled some advice: don't lock the exit until you're sure the place is empty. Remembering this, she walked to the door that opened onto her lounge room and switched the light on. The television was on but the rumpled nest of blankets and coats on her lounge was empty except for Taxi, curled up in a ball, half-opened eyes reflecting the colourful gleam of a television advertisement. She went through every room but there was no trace of the Ratbag or anyone else. She went out onto the timber deck. The old sleeping bag was gone. Back inside, she checked the small change jar in the kitchen. It was empty. Some part of her was relieved, but she hated to think of the poor little kid trying to keep alive on the hostile, predatory streets of Kings Cross. She had no idea of who or where his father might be, nor could she even remember his surname. And how dare he leave her house wide open like this?

'Damn you, Ratbag,' she said out loud. Somehow, the little fellow had weaselled his way into her heart, made her feel responsible for him, reminding her of Will at that age, and of herself, a lost and lonely child at boarding school. She tried to distract herself by looking in the fridge and found there was nothing left. The Ratbag had cleaned that out, too.

She felt too restless to stay home now. She could drive to the Cross, ask Kosta about the missing diary, do her shopping at the huge supermarket there, pick up her clothes from where she'd left them at the safe house and make enquiries about Shelly's stepfather. No doubt the police would have contacted him by now. Maybe she would be able to pick up any news on the street about Steve's dangerous target. And she could keep an eye out for a frightened little kid who had, by her reckoning, about eleven dollars in the world. She finally found Kosta's number in an old diary and although he was surprised to hear from her, he sounded keen to meet up with her again.

She drove to the Cross, turning Meatloaf up loud to drive her gloomy thoughts away and sang along with him that 'Two out of three ain't bad'.

In spite of everything, the lights and smell of the Cross lifted her mood. Maybe a drink in a bad dive would be fun later on. Just the one. Just to have a look around. Just a sniff of loud rock and bad company. I need cheering up, she told herself. Perhaps it would help dislodge the dark undercurrent that seemed to be undermining her spirits over the last month or so. She parked in a quiet cul-de-sac near the top of the Cross, did her shopping and loaded

272 • GABRIELLE LORD

it into her car, and returned to the café on the corner where she'd arranged to meet Kosta.

She took a table against the back wall and was wondering whether to order now or wait till Kosta arrived when she heard a couple arguing near the entrance. She looked up and then froze as Steve, gorgeous in black leather, halfway through the door, met her eyes. It was an electric moment and he broke the connection immediately as he swung around to the blonde woman behind him.

'No, Lorraine,' she heard him say in his authoritative voice. 'Not this place. Come on. Let's go.'

Gemma looked across to the black glass counter that ran half the length of the café. In its mirrored surface she could see that Steve was hustling the woman behind him, steering her, arm around her waist. Gemma's heart started beating hard. She could hear the woman protesting, complaining at this sudden change of plan.

'But why? Just tell me why,' she demanded, turning to look back into the café, as if trying to see what the problem was, knowing intuitively that there was a reason why Steve was making them go somewhere else. But Steve was adamant and Gemma knew that mood, too. Part of her understood exactly why he would do this. She would do the same thing in the same circumstances, pleading anything—bad vibes, a headache, anything— rather than enter a place where someone familiar was already ensconced.

But the woman with him was not easily persuaded. As the couple walked past the glass wall that separated the café from the street, Gemma took a chance and looked straight at them. The woman with Steve was not fat and fifty. She was probably less than half that age. Lorraine Litchfield was deadset-film-star-knock-your-eyes-out-drop-dead-gorgeous. Then, in a split second that Gemma would forever regret, her eyes and those of the blonde locked. Gemma looked away quickly, pretending her glance was casual, but it was too late. She'd broken one of the commandments: never make eye-contact with a target. Gemma cursed herself. From the corner of her eye, she could see Lorraine Litchfield trying to push past Steve and return to the café. But Steve was blocking her, steering her backwards, his gestures conciliatory. Finally, they started walking away. But Lorraine Litchfield kept turning her head back towards the café.

Gemma waited till they were out of sight, then jumped up and went to the front of the café, pushing aside the waiter bringing her a jug of water. She waited, peering cautiously round the door, watching as the couple crossed the road heading north towards Macleay Street. Gemma hated seeing Steve's arm around the blonde's narrow waist. How could I have made such a mistake? Gemma wondered, as she hastened across the street, ignoring an angry driver who'd had to brake suddenly in front of her. She remembered the newspaper and television images of the family at the funeral and Mrs Litchfield, her corseted body and face congested with anger, swearing at the photographer. Mrs Litchfield *senior,* mother of the murdered crime boss. The woman Gemma had presumed to be Litchfield's daughter or daughter-in-law was in fact, his wife, now widow.

Gemma ducked into a shop entrance as she saw Steve turn round to check behind him. She was sure he hadn't spotted her. But she hurried after them, always keeping a lot of people between herself and her quarry for cover. Suddenly Steve beckoned a cab and she watched as her lover helped the other woman into the back seat, sliding in beside her and the cab took off.

Gemma stood in the doorway, heart racing, trying to calm down. She started walking quickly, the pain in her ankle temporarily forgotten, not caring where she went, just wanting to keep moving, keep the anxiety at a bearable level. Why had Steve lied to her about this job? She went over their conversation in memory. She could feel her hackles rising and the beginning of raw anger. A few things fell into place. That odd pause in the conversation when her joke about Steve's interest in an older women had fallen flat. No wonder he hadn't laughed. There *was* no joke. He wasn't involved with an older woman at all. No wonder the atmosphere around her remark had been so charged that Gemma could still feel it now, mixed up horribly with all her present feelings of anger and jealousy. Steve had his chance to correct her right then and there and he hadn't done it. Now Gemma had to ask herself why. Her anger grew. She wasn't watching where she was going and almost tripped over. Was it just a lazy male thing?

Easier to stay silent and let the assumption remain rather than create a fuss and the potential jealousy that the truth might bring? *Bastard,* she thought to herself, if that was the case. And if it wasn't, and he genuinely had something to hide about this relationship, then things were far worse than she'd imagined.

Gemma's heart lurched and she almost cried out loud. Terry Litchfield's widow was young, beautiful and very, very rich. Unconcerned passers-by bumped into her as she stood in the street, dazed. That heavy brassy looking zodiac charm had been her gift to Steve and Gemma realised now its heaviness was because of the amount of gold in it. In the same way that she'd known the photographs taken by Benjamin Glass of the naked woman in the black lace gloves had not been taken by a client but a *lover*, Gemma suddenly realised that the zodiac charm was of a similar order. Gemma knew this was a classic situation reversed—the crim, Lorraine Litchfield, had fallen for the middle-class man, Steve. She stumbled on, unseeing, uncaring about the other pedestrians who had to get out of her way. '*Steve*?' her rival had called out when Gemma rang him, '*it's some woman*'. And Gemma had found it faintly amusing then. But not now. Steve *said* that business was hotting up and he was under Fayed's surveillance and forced to be scrupulously careful. But the fact was he'd dropped right out of her life over the last week. Could there be another reason, something else, something that chewed at her consciousness and worried at her heart?

She had walked almost to the El Alamein fountain before she became conscious of her surroundings again. A group of Koori kids sat in a silent row nearby. She sat too, staring sightlessly past the kids as they pretended not to look at her. Their silence was broken by whispered comments and laughter. Maybe about her. She didn't care. She didn't care about anything except one thing. She prayed that Steve was simply acting his role. Of course he'd put his arm around a woman's waist in public if he was supposed to be her boyfriend. It went with the undercover script. But did the arm drop away once they were alone together? She prayed that Steve had not stepped over the line that kept him both professional to the job and true to her. Behind her the fountain hissed and tiny droplets chilled her face. Tears started at the very thought that she and Steve might be through. I need to get right out of here, she told herself. I need a drink. For a second, the petulance cleared and she had a detached insight into herself. Steve's not the only one who might be acting unprofessionally, girl, she heard an inner voice say. Look at you, carrying on like a lovesick adolescent, not only interfering with an important police operation, but also endangering your man with your own unprofessional behaviour, making dreadful tactical mistakes just because you can't handle the pressure. Gemma made a decision to maintain her standards, no matter what personal pressures bore down on her. As she moved to get up, her injured flank twinged savagely and she stopped, forced to stoop for a few long moments till the spasm passed. God, what a pathetic creature I'm becoming, she thought to herself. This time, she stood up slowly and squared her shoulders.

She walked over to the group of kids, reminded of the Ratbag's predicament. They all looked away, hoping that she wasn't trouble. Thinking of that little kid, and all the others alone in the world on the savage streets of Kings Cross took her mind off her anguish over Steve.

She pulled a twenty-dollar note out of her wallet. 'Have any of you guys seen a young kid around, not Koori. About twelve, thirteen? Dark hair. Thick eyebrows. Worried look on his face. Wearing a green parka, pretty grubby.'

Two of the kids didn't even turn at the sound of her voice; the others shook their heads. Gemma pulled out one of her business cards from the same pocket.

'This is me,' she said. 'I'm not a cop or a social worker. I don't want to make any trouble for you kids. But if any of you see this kid, or find out where he hangs, give me a call on this number and I'll make sure it's worth your time. Okay?' She handed the note and her card over to the oldest girl. 'Get yourselves something to eat, eh?' she said.

The girl looked at the business card and then shoved it in a pocket. One of them jiggled his feet and they were silent. It was almost as if she didn't exist, that she hadn't just spoken to them, given them money.

'Where are you kids from?' she asked, suddenly touched by their youth, their lostness.

The smallest girl tossed her wild hair. 'All over the place,' she said. 'Come from everywhere, us mob.'

'You let me know?' Gemma asked again. 'If you see this kid?'

'Your kid?' the girl asked.

Gemma shook her head. 'No,' she said. 'I'm just a friend. He's run away from his mother in Melbourne. He doesn't know anything about living on the streets.'

'He'll learn pretty quick,' said one of the boys. The silence fell again.

Gemma walked back to the café, trying not to think of where Steve might be with that beautiful girl. She noticed two black Mercedes drive by and for a moment, thought some eccentric funeral was taking place. It was almost impossible to see into the interiors through the tinted windows. The two cars turned the corner and into Macleay Street, vanishing from her sight.

At the café she saw Kosta sitting morosely at the same table she'd vacated twenty minutes before. He'd almost finished a half bottle of red as Gemma approached.

'I thought you weren't going to show,' he said, raising his droopy eyes to her. 'Grab a glass.'

'I was here earlier,' she said, 'but I had to leave. Something came up.' She turned her glass over and he poured her some wine. Gemma tossed it down and felt the glow of it spreading downwards. It hit her behind the knees and she realised she hadn't eaten for too long.

'Trouble?' he asked.

Gemma shrugged. There were more people at the tables than had been there earlier and as she looked around, she caught the waiter staring at her. Kosta looked heavier and more compressed than she remembered from the last time she'd seen him. She wasn't sure how he supported himself these days but she knew he'd made a living of sorts in the past as a small-time dealer, buying several grams and cutting them to sell on. He had moved in and out of various rehab places, and generally made himself available to anyone who could use either him or his services. He'd tried to be a standover man, but as Shelly had told Gemma years ago, he just didn't have enough mongrel in him for that. Even now, despite the bloating from too much beer and baklava, and the wear and tear of substance abuse, shreds of good nature still showed in his face.

He looked miserable. Was it because, Gemma wondered, he really had cared for Shelly, or was it because a reliable meal ticket was gone for good? She pulled out her note book. Kosta waved it away.

'No, no,' he said, a little blue and black evil eye earring wobbling on his right earlobe. 'Before you get going, let me tell you, *I* got something for *you*.' He wagged a forefinger at her. 'You know that diary the cops were looking for everywhere? Naomi had it all the time. She said her mum didn't want the police to get hold of it. She said it's okay for me to give it to you.' He pulled out a good sized black leather diary and placed it on the table.

'Where's Naomi now?' Gemma asked.

'She's at school,' he said. 'She comes home on the weekends.'

'Home?' Gemma said.

'She goes to Shell's mum at Rockdale,' he said. 'Her grandmother's place.'

'A few years ago Shell told me about her step-father,' said Gemma. 'From what she said he's not fit to be anywhere near a young girl.'

'He had me bashed once,' said Kosta. 'But it's okay, Naomi's safe. Shell's mum kicked him out a while back.'

Gemma turned her attention back to the diary in her hands. 'Tell Naomi thanks for this,' said Gemma, thinking of the motherless fifteen-year-old. 'Tell her I'm very sorry about Shell. And I'm not going to rest until the person who killed her is locked up.'

She turned the diary over and flicked through it. There seemed to be a lot of entries, names, addresses, phone and email contacts. She wondered how long she could decently hold on to this piece of information too, knowing that the police were looking for it. Strictly speaking, she'd have to hand it over to Mr Right pretty smartly. But after the shock of seeing Lorraine Litchfield, nitpicking issues like withholding information didn't seem to matter much anymore. They're as important as my licence, she reminded herself, recalling the promise she'd made to herself at the El Alamein fountain, to remain faithful to her professional standards. It's all a girl's got when the shooting starts, she remembered Angie saying a long time ago. Gemma leaned down and stowed the diary safely in her briefcase.

'I really miss the Shell, you know,' Kosta was saying. 'We were together on and off for nearly fifteen years. Since I was twenty-five. It's a long time.'

'It is,' said Gemma whose history with Shelly covered roughly the same period.

'I'd do anything to get the bastard who done that to her,' he said.

'That lawyer who was hassling her to sell up,' said Gemma. 'What do you know about him?'

Kosta leaned forward. 'That pig. For sure he's acting for George Fayed,' he said. 'He was putting the pressure on Shell. He wants to take over everything, the houses, the girls, the Litchfield dealers and distributors. My mate reckons he wants to own Sydney and everyone in it. I just saw him in his Mercedes with his baboons behind him.'

Gemma recalled the two black cars while Kosta upended his glass of wine and drained it, then leaned forward, looked around to make sure no one could hear him.

'I reckon Fayed had Shell killed,' he said, 'because she wouldn't sell Baroque.'

'The police don't think that,' she said. 'It looks like the work of whoever's been targeting the sex workers.'

'That's right,' said Kosta. 'Him! It's the same person!' His manner revealed that he thought it was obvious. 'He's got thugs out there bashing them, getting them off the streets. He doesn't want them taking the custom. He wants to frighten them off the streets so that all the mugs have to use his places.' He put his glass down. 'Whatcha drinking?'

'Scotch and ice,' she said. She pulled out a twenty and Kosta took it to the bar, returning with the drinks. Either there was no change, or he'd pocketed it. He sat down, delighted that he had Gemma's attention.

'You heard of the French Connection?' he asked.

Gemma nodded. Here we go again, she thought.

'His thugs pick you up, keep you somewhere for a few days, keep injecting you, then chuck you out again. Just like in that movie.'

'Kosta, listen to me. Men like Fayed don't waste time and valuable substances like that. They just break people's legs.'

Kosta raised a scolding finger, suddenly looking very Greek and patriarchal as he waggled it from side to side, the little evil eye earring bobbing.

'No, no,' he said. 'You don't get it. It's like his *mark*. He *likes* to do that. You know how animals mark their territory? Like that. Plus, he's showing he doesn't care about wasting gear, he's got so much of it. He's showing off. He wants to be king of the city.'

Gemma remained unconvinced. Men like Fayed, just like anyone in the public eye, attracted the products of the rumour mill. But Kosta had warmed to his subject.

'He's been buying up all the houses. Then he puts his own addicted girls in and doesn't pay them nothing except their medication. When they're really sick, he just chucks them out. My mate I mentioned to you? He worked bodyguard for Fayed. Says you never saw anything like the security. Won't drive anywhere without his two cars. And other cars a little way behind him to make sure no one's on his arse. External and internal security all through his place, closed circuit cameras everywhere. In every room.'

Gemma looked up with renewed interest. She remembered Angie telling her about the closed circuit television inside the Fayed fortress. She could corroborate this part of the information herself. Maybe Kosta's mate was a reliable source after all.

'He doesn't trust no bastard,' Kosta was saying. 'He has terrible nightmares.' He finished his drink. 'No way the Shell was going to let someone like that get his hands on her house.' He swayed a little in his seat. 'George Fayed likes to kill women. He's gutless.'

'He's killed at least one man,' said Gemma. 'He got rid of Terry Litchfield.'

Kosta again raised his admonishing finger. 'Let me put you straight on that point, Gemma. I know for a fact he did not,' he said.

'What are you saying, Kosta?'

'I know that everyone *thinks* Fayed killed Tezza,' Kosta was saying, 'but I know for a fact it was his missus. That blonde bitch, Lorraine. She did for him.'

'Are you sure about that?' Gemma said, picking up her drink again.

'True,' he said. 'She'd been playing up. Some rich buyer from interstate. You know the type,' he said. 'Tall, dark, handsome. Armani shirts.'

Steve! Gemma thought.

'Lorraine gets really keen on this bloke and has poor old Tezza knocked off for twenty-five grand.'

Gemma tried to think rationally. Terry Litchfield's been dead for months, she thought. But the way Kosta was telling it made it sound like Steve had been around for quite a while. She felt a chill all through her body.

Kosta raised his empty glass to a waiter who walked straight past him.

'Darryl Tunks did the drive-by. Right outside the bloody mansion poor old Tezza had just bought for the bitch. Straight through the gates. Poor bastard managed to get out onto the street and that's as far as he got.' He paused to attract another waiter. 'Some women,' he added, as the waiter took his glass.

'Who told you this?' she said, trying to keep her voice normal.

'Friend of Darryl's.' He sounded vague.

'Can you tell me his name and address? I want to talk to him.'

'He hangs around here.' Kosta waved vaguely in the direction of the street. 'Dunno where he lives.'

Gemma cross-referenced the two versions: Terry Litchfield killed by George Fayed or killed by his wife. Either way, Steve's presence was very much part of the drama. Either he *was* Lorraine Litchfield's lover in reality and had been for some time, well before the period of the undercover operation, giving Lorraine a good reason to get rid of her husband, or Steve was invited in as part of the wronged widow's revenge on Fayed. Both stories were completely possible; both worked. But which version was the truth? One version just lodged quietly in her mind like any other information. The other broke her heart and made her mouth dry up just contemplating it. She remembered the conjecture she'd been assuming, that the police had enough evidence to convince Lorraine that it was Fayed. If Lorraine *had* killed her husband, she'd know that the police 'evidence' against Fayed was bullshit right from the start. So why team up with them in the first place? There was only one answer to that and she resisted it vigorously. But the more she fought it, the more plausible it seemed. Lorraine Litchfield wanted Steve so badly she was prepared to set up a phoney deal with Fayed to draw him into a relationship with her. To give him the keys to her kingdom: the wealth, the glamour, the good life in paradise, Sydney. But what if Steve had been intimately involved with the woman all along? He wouldn't be the first DUC to find himself with a leg in both camps. And he wouldn't be the last, she thought. What if the two of them, Steve and Lorraine Litchfield together, had planned the destruction of Fayed with the aim of becoming the new king and queen of the Sydney crime empire?

Gemma felt shaken. Don't go down that line of thought, she told herself. Get back onto one of your cases. You're here to investigate the death of your friend. She recalled her conversation with Shelly in the hospital lift.

'Shelly said she was working for a pair of psychologists,' she said to Kosta, whose eyes were clouding over fast, as the latest drink started taking effect. 'Sex therapists. Did she mention this to you? Some sort of sex surrogacy?'

'Don't know about that sort of stuff,' Kosta said, shaking his head. 'You've lost me.' But then he thought of something and visibly brightened. 'You mean the can't-get-it-up clinic?'

'That would be one name for it,' Gemma said.

'I can even tell you where it is,' he said, pleased to be helpful.

Gemma duly noted his directions. Her heart was heavy, her head spinning from the late night and the smoke-filled bar. She stood up. 'I've got to go, Kosta,' she said, pulling out a twenty-dollar note. 'Thanks for giving me the diary.'

For a moment he looked as if he were going to say something more, but his eyes filled with tears and he cleared his throat instead. Gemma touched his shoulder before she left.

•

Gemma wasn't sure how it was that she found herself in Indigo Ice some time later, nursing a ten-dollar glass of fake champagne, watching the flashing couples on the crowded dance floor, her head filled with the *thump thump thump* of the bass speakers. In front of her snaked a jet-black man, fabulous in cool white chinos, with a golden woman, their dancing so beautiful, so provocative and synchronised that Gemma envied their harmony. She was staring at them, lost in admiration and the incessant beat of the music when the couple danced away from each other in order to come together again in a sinewy *pas de deux*. Through the gap suddenly opened between them, another couple was revealed, the woman with her arms around the man's neck, the man holding her closely around the buttocks, as they swayed together.

Gemma froze. The woman was Lorraine Litchfield and the man holding her was Steve. Gemma jumped to her feet, unnoticed in the flashing light. Suddenly, the woman turned, and her eyes bored straight through Gemma in a syncopated, strobic stare. Gemma turned and fled, leaving her drink, pushing her way through the crowd, not bothering to apologise, blind with tears and jealousy.

She hobbled up the sticky carpet of the staircase and back onto the street, clutching her briefcase. She almost ran all the way back to her car. In the safety of the locked vehicle she pulled out her mobile, aware of how her hands were shaking. Dialling Steve's number, she was aware in some part of her mind of how stupid this was, but was unable to stop herself, her heart rushing with fear, anger and pain. She realised she was rocking herself with anxiety and jealousy, something she hadn't done since she was ten.

'Yes?' His voice was cool and wary and behind him she could hear the noise of the dance club.

'I've just left Indigo Ice, Steve. I saw you dancing with her! What the fuck do you think you're doing?'

'My job,' he said. His voice didn't warm or change in any way. 'I can't give you a result right now, I'll call you later, okay?'

'No, it's *not* okay!' she said, almost in tears.

'This is not a good time to talk.' Steve's business-like voice inflamed her further.

'I'll bet,' she yelled, 'with Lorraine bloody Litchfield's tongue halfway down your goddamn throat!'

'I'll call you later,' he said, in the same flat voice. And then he was gone

Wilfully, she rang straight back but he'd switched on voice mail. Furious, she tried again. But it was no use. Eventually, her breathing slowed down and she shoved the mobile back in her briefcase. What am I going to do? she thought, gripping the steering wheel so hard that a stab of pain seared through the injuries on the back of her fingers. She started the car, and screeched away, taking the back streets home, risking the Breathalyser.

•

She couldn't get to sleep and ended up taking half a Mogadon. Next morning, when she woke, her first image was of Steve's hands cupping Lorraine Litchfield's neat little bottom. She swung herself out of bed, trying to banish the picture. The movement as she stood up sent another painful spasm through her bruised ribs. She checked herself in the mirror, twisting to get a better view. Although the bruising on her flank was fading, for some reason the pain was still quite sharp. Maybe he cracked a rib or two, she thought. A hairline fracture.

She put on some coffee, wrapped herself in the coat that had covered the Ratbag, and huddled on a corner of the lounge, close to the heater, while the coffee brewed. I really should see a doctor, she thought. She phoned a local GP she'd visited once or twice over the years and made an appointment to see her. She rang off from the call, even more dispirited. The haunted feeling that undermined her as soon as she was alone or took her mind off her work, deepened into desolation. She didn't want to eat anything. She poured the coffee, strong and sweet. She rang Kit.

'I think Steve's involved with another woman,' she said as soon as Kit answered.

'You'd better tell me.' And Gemma did.

'You have to trust him, Gems. What he said its true. It is his job. Come round for dinner tonight.'

'It might be his job but I don't like it.'

'You know how I feel about your job,' said Kit. 'It's the same sort of thing.'

'I guess I just have to wear it,' said Gemma. 'I'll call about dinner.'

'Okay.' Kit rang off.

Later that morning Gemma visited Sydney University and had a brief interview with Dr Jacob Susskind, head of the Chemical Engineering School. Afterwards, she limped back to her car, climbed in, glanced over the notes she'd taken then pushed her note book back into her briefcase, where it fitted next to Shelly's diary.

She sat staring sightlessly at the twisted aerial ropes of a large fig tree whose subterranean roots were already lifting the footpath on either side, considering the information she now had about Minkie Montreau. The woman *had* been a doctoral student there twenty-five years ago and although Dr Susskind had not been her supervisor, and Ms Montreau had never completed the doctoral thesis she was working on, the university records showed she had been awarded a Masters degree. Dr Susskind suggested that Gemma approach Archives and have a look at the bound copy of her thesis. Minkie Montreau, Gemma thought, was turning out to be a very complex character. She could almost hear Kit's words in her head again: *'we express who we are in everything we do.'* Complex character, complex murder, a voice in her mind suggested.

A research fellow, thin and tall with a slight tic in his left eye, kindly helped Gemma through the mysteries of archival filing and finally located the gold-embossed fake-leather binder.

'Here it is,' he said, winking. 'Someone else looked at it a while ago. It's funny with these research theses. Years will go by and no one takes any notice of them, and then suddenly you'll get people wanting to see them. There's one there about the action of a rare protein in the CNS and four people wanted to look at it last week.'

'CNS?' Gemma was puzzled.

'Sorry. Central nervous system. Hadn't been touched in four years before that.'

He wanted to chat, Gemma knew, but she wasn't in the mood. She thanked him and took the volume from him.

'Sure there's nothing else I can get you?' he asked.

Gemma shook her head. She opened Minkie's thesis at the title page. The research fellow who'd been filing nearby turned back, hearing her intake of breath.

'Found what you wanted?' he inquired.

Gemma didn't answer, just kept looking through the stiff pages of the thesis. It didn't make a great deal of sense to her, but she could understand enough to know that once this information was given to the police, Minkie Montreau was in lethal trouble. Circumstantial evidence is never conclusive in the way physical evidence is, but when a series of circumstances starts piling up inexorably into an overwhelming mass of damning facts, a jury is forced to draw certain conclusions. She pulled out her mobile and rang Angie.

'You'll never guess,' she said, 'the title and subject matter of Minkie Montreau's Masters thesis.'

'How to marry a rich old codger and then knock him off?'

'Just about.' She quoted the title of the thesis to Angie.

Her friend's low whistle rang down the line. 'That looks very bad for the widow,' said Angie. 'You'd better pass that on to Mr Right.'

'Not till I talk to her,' said Gemma. 'After all, she's employed me to investigate her husband's death. I'm just doing my job, officer.'

'That's very important information,' Angie warned.

'That's why I'm telling you, Angelface.'

'Hey, don't put it on me, girl. It's not my case.'

'Relax, Ange. I'm going to check with the insurers, Australian Magister.' But she couldn't keep up the lightheartedness; memories of Steve and Lorraine Litchfield from the night before assailed her. She lowered her voice. 'I saw Steve last night. Accidentally. He was dancing with Lorraine Litchfield in Indigo Ice. Cheek to cheek. Ange, he had his hands around her bum!'

'Listen, hon,' said her friend. 'He's a professional. He's got to make it look like they're a serious item. If that's the script they've got to look right—he's got to have his hands round her bum in public.'

'It looked too damn right to me,' said Gemma, her voice wobbling. 'What if they stay there in private?'

'Gemster,' said Angie sternly, 'stop carrying on like a girl. I'm doing some shooting practice today. And I think you should take better care of yourself, considering the woman you're working for. Come to the range. Shoot the crotches out of some B12s. Write Steve's name on one of them. You'll feel heaps better.'

'No, I won't,' said Gemma, feeling like a five-year-old. 'I don't think I've ever felt worse.'

'Go to the gym, then,' said her friend. 'Do a few laps. Listen to your girlfriend. Men aren't worth the heartache. They're good for one thing only, and if you want my honest opinion, they're not all that good at that.'

•

Gemma rang off and instead of driving direct to Minkie Montreau's, as she'd planned, she took a detour via the boatshed. Angie's suggestion of doing a few laps was a good idea. Visiting her boatshed was another. She parked on the narrow road and looked down at the tiny thumbnail-shaped inlet. A few fishing boats were piled on one side, and the rocks of the southern end rose steeply to the clifftop house where Gemma sometimes lived in her fantasies. She could see the corrugated iron roof of the boatshed from here, tucked away under the shoulder of the southern headland. Gemma got out of the car and walked to the white railing that separated the path from the sloping beach-front. A gusting south-westerly chopped white-tipped waves over a glass green sea. She exhaled, realising how tightly she'd been holding herself. Here, she wasn't Gemma Lincoln PI, or anyone's girlfriend, or soon-to-be-ex-girlfriend, or sister. She was just a woman standing looking at the sea, someone who wanted to make something beautiful and extraordinary out of nothing but cold, damp clay. She saw the scalloped edges left on the sand by the retreating tide, embroidered with tiny shells and pebbles. There is something about waves, thought Gemma, curving over the sand then diminishing, that is like the breathing of the world. Despite everything, she felt a rare, brief peace standing there watching as a crew of gulls squabbled along the waterline and a small dog contemplated them, wondering whether or not to give chase.

Gemma walked down the path and was about to unlock the boatshed when she saw the colourful iridescence of oil on water. The rainbow marbling ran down the small freshwater runoff channel from the higher ground behind the beach. Now the water's edge, as well as being decorated with the usual pretty foam and seaweeds, sported a wide band of pollution that appeared to be spreading. Gemma went over for a closer look, tracing the flow back to its source. It was the big beached launch. You brute, she thought, noting its registration, intending to contact the Council. She returned to the boatshed.

The second she walked in, she sensed something different. Even the air seemed agitated and not the still coolness she was used to. Warned by instinct, she looked around. Everything seemed untouched and just as she had left it. On the counter, the shrouded shapes of the two lions loomed, one almost finished, the other barely started. She went over to the first one to pull the sheeting off it, but hesitated. For a crazy second she feared what she might find underneath the shroud. Stop being so silly, she told herself, whipping the sheet off it. The familiar, block-like head and open jaw, sightless eye and crouching hindquarters were all exactly as she'd left them. She touched the lion's fine, proud snout, noticing that now it felt completely dry. All was exactly as she'd left it. You're being paranoid, she told herself, replacing the sheet. She shivered. It was very cold in here, so she walked outside, relocked the padlock and stood for a few moments in the weak sun. Because of the narrowness of the inlet, and the long arm of headland that stretched out to sea on the south, Phoenix Bay was calm.

Her desolate mood now had an overlay of anger and jealousy that even the soft winter sun and the wash of the sea couldn't dislodge. Steve's comments to her after her rash phone call to him seemed increasingly unconvincing. She knew her boyfriend had to pass with George Fayed. He had to talk, walk, think, speak, act, dress, *smell* like a big time interstate drug dealer in the company of a man who had honed his survival skills in refugee camps and the savage crucible of a war zone, where the slightest false note could mean death. Steve's fictional history had to hold up to scrutiny and checking; he had to ensure he didn't make some tiny slip that could bring him undone to his increasingly paranoid enemy. She tried to find some empathy with Steve, living the lie of undercover work, his life in the hands of a woman who had at best only teamed up with him out of a desire for vengeance. Even if Lorraine Litchfield imagined herself in love with him, Gemma knew how fast that sort of 'love' could fly out the window if Steve did not do her bidding. In fact, Gemma realised, the only thing standing between Steve and a very bad outcome, was the fragile goodwill of Lorraine Litchfield. Like it or not, she concluded, Lorraine Litchfield was Steve's partner in this operation.

She turned and retraced her steps back to the roadside. As she got into her car, she realised fully the danger she'd placed Steve in last night. I can't keep behaving like this, she told herself. Angie's right. I've got to get right off Steve's case or I'll go crazy. She pulled out her mobile, looked up a number and rang Australian Magister. She spoke with one of the brokers and what he told her added another brick to the cell that Gemma felt sure would soon wall up Minkie Montreau.

'How recently?' Gemma asked.

'Last week, according to our records,' said the broker. 'Posted Monday before last.'

So a few days before the fire, Minkie Montreau had requested a copy of the policy be sent to her. Taken together with the title and content of Minkie's Masters thesis, Gemma could see a long gaol sentence in the offing.

Gemma rang off and drove to the widow's mansion but found no one at home. She left a message for Minkie to ring Gemma urgently and then she drove home.

•

Gemma felt hungry and cooked some chicken and herb sausages, eating them without tasting, her mind, despite her earlier intention, preoccupied with Steve. She tried to confine her thoughts to the certainty that she now had Minkie Montreau in the bag. But it was almost impossible to suppress the anxieties that forced themselves into her consciousness. In order to distract herself, she pulled Shelly's diary out of her briefcase and made herself comfortable on the lounge. Taxi immediately pounced on her, settling on her stomach.

Gemma worked her way through the diary. Many of the entries were self-explanatory: engagements with Kosta, reminders to buy items for Naomi, business meetings with accountants, men's first names and references to jobs for the discreetly named Chester Clinic—Kosta's 'can't-get-it-up' clinic. On two of the Chester jobs, Shelly had written '*Me or S. Confirm*'. Gemma looked away, remembering. '*Two of us work for them*', Shelly had said in the hospital lift. Gemma looked out to sea. Was 'S' the other worker? She turned to the last day of Shelly's life. There was her friend's neat writing. 'Peter,' she'd written. Peter Fenster and his ugly remarks about the attacks on the scx workers leaped into Gemma's mind. He certainly had the right attitude, and his car was involved in one of the attacks. He needs further investigation, she thought. The phone rang.

'I've just got the result on your clothes,' Tim Conway from Kings Cross police told her. 'Nothing doing as far as DNA goes.'

'I'd already formed that conclusion myself,' said Gemma.

'But they found something. Fibres of some sort.'

'What about the Ford? Any results back yet?'

'I haven't heard anything,' said Tim.

'Why is it taking so long?' Gemma grizzled. Then she sighed. 'Here's something for you, at least. The name of Shelly's last client was "Peter" And a Peter Fenster owns the Ford.'

'There're a lot of Peters in the world,' said Tim.

'I'll go to the lab and see Ric Loader myself,' she said. She knew it was time to come clean about the fact that she had the same bruises on her flank that Shelly had. 'I was attacked by the same man,' she said. 'Unless there are two chain-wielding maniacs attacking women on the streets of Sydney.'

'I'll send that statement you made on the night to Sean Wright,' said Tim.

'It won't help him much,' said Gemma remembering how she'd been unable to give any description.

'The girls are still out there,' he said. 'Getting into cars. Not using the safe house. You can't talk reason to them.'

'You can't talk reason to a habit, Tim,' she reminded him. 'Have you heard the theory that

Fayed's behind these bashings? That he's moving into brothels?'

'It's been around for a while,' he said. 'Fayed's got his digits in a lot of pies.'

She rang off and dialled Kosta.

'God, man, what time is it?' he said, sounding hurt.

'Time you were out of bed and talking talk to me, Kosta,' she said. 'Does the name "Peter" mean anything to you?'

There was a long pause at the end of the line.

'Hell,' he said, 'she saw a lot of Peters over the years. Peters, Johns, Toms. You name it. Why you asking?'

'Shelly wrote "Peter" down in her diary as her last client on the day she was killed.'

'Peter,' he said, and Gemma could almost hear his effort to think over the line. 'Oh,' Kosta suddenly said. *'Peter.'*

'That's exactly what I'm asking you,' said Gemma, rolling her eyes heavenwards.

'No way,' said Kosta. 'Not *Peter.'*

'Peter who?' she asked.

'But he's a *teacher.'*

Artists and now teachers, Gemma thought, are apparently thought to be incapable of committing homicide. 'So tell me about Peter the teacher.'

'He was one of the guys referred to Shelly from the can't-get-it-up clinic.' There was a pause. When Kosta spoke again, his voice was stronger. 'She told me about him. Said he was a hopeless root.'

Kosta and Shelly must have had a refreshingly

honest relationship, Gemma thought. Then she remembered something Shelly had told her. *'Sticks it in, wiggles it around a bit, comes in thirty seconds and dribbles on my neck.'*

'Kosta,' she said, 'I think she might have told me about him too. Or at least described him to me.'

'The fucking cops were at me again last night,' he said and now his voice was angry. 'After you left. You're talking bullshit, I told them. Get out and find the killer, the mongrel who did that to Shell instead of wasting time harassing me.'

'We'll get him, Kosta,' Gemma promised him. There was a silence filled with the presence of Shelly. 'Tell me more about this Peter.'

'I only know what the Shell told me,' he said. 'She worked with him a couple of times. That's it.'

Gemma tried another angle. 'Shelly told me that she was doing this surrogacy work with another girl. It's possible that her name might also start with an "S" too. Does that suggest anyone to you?'

'Nah,' he said. 'I dunno any names, but I know she worked with some other girl.'

'If you hear anything about her, will you let me know?' Gemma said. 'It's important, Kosta.

'All I know for a fact is that this other girl always wears black lace gloves when she does the business,' Kosta said.

The nameless blonde kneeling on the bed, gloriously naked except for her gloves filled Gemma's imagination.

'It's like her trademark,' Kosta was saying. 'Kinky, eh?'

Black lace gloves. The portly photographer captured in the mirror as he snapped the photo.

'Hell, Kosta,' she said. 'That's great information.'

'What I say?' asked Kosta, bewildered.

But Gemma rang off and sat, stunned, for a few seconds. Black lace gloves. With these three words, it was as if two transparencies, each etched with pictures from two completely separate worlds, had suddenly been laid one over the other, and a whole new world, deeper and more complex, was now emerging. Investigation is all about building up links and connections, creating a mosaic of information until one day the picture emerges. And boy, was it starting to emerge.

She jumped up, heart racing. Shelly and the lace-gloved blonde were now linked together— they both worked as sex therapists. And the woman with the gloves was inextricably entwined with Benjamin Glass. Shelly was dead. Benjamin Glass was dead. But now they were dead together in the same picture. What the hell was going on?

Cherchez la blonde, thought Gemma.

THIRTEEN

R ic Loader took her into his room at the end of the corridor. The Analytical Laboratory was a warren of offices, examination rooms, laboratories and sterile rooms housing specialist equipment for reading the traces sent to them by the Crime Scene examiners.

'This attacker you're after,' Ric said. 'We're starting to think he must be in the rag trade, we collected so many wool and rayon fibres from the driver's seat of the Ford. That blouse you sent us?' Gemma nodded and he continued. 'Microscopic fragments of the same wool and rayon all over it.'

'Maybe he's a traveller,' she said 'a salesman, who stacks up samples in his vehicle.'

'On the driver's seat?' Rick looked incredulous. 'It doesn't make sense.'

'So it was the same guy?'

'You know we don't say things like that.' Ric smiled. 'All we can confirm officially is that we found traces of the same material in the Ford and on the blouse you sent us after you were attacked.'

Gemma's injured flank twinged painfully. Even though the DNA testing result was not reportable, things seemed a little lighter now.

'That's good enough for me,' she said.

•

The new information Gemma had unearthed about Minkie Montreau's Masters thesis and the connection between the glove-wearing blonde and Benjamin Glass had changed the energy of the whole day. Now she could take her focus off Steve and Lorraine Litchfield.

Impressed by Gemma's ID and the seriousness of the matter, Pauline Chester, the therapist from the Chester Clinic, a tall woman with a neat page-boy haircut and a woollen jersey-knit dress, ushered her into a discreetly furnished office.

'We have to be very cautious,' Pauline said, gesturing Gemma to a chair opposite her desk, 'about the wrong sort of publicity. You can appreciate how sensitive this issue is for our male clients. We have to be able to guarantee complete confidentiality. That's why I have to be so careful about giving out any information. And with Mr Glass's disappearance such a shock to us all . . .'

'Of course,' said Gemma.

'And that's why,' said Pauline, 'we only use women and girls with particular skills. We like to take graduates or women who've studied Applied Psychology, but'—she shrugged—'just plain common sense and trainability can be sufficient, given the right person. We deal with all sorts of clients, from self-made men like Mr Glass to academics, poets, scientists, wharf labourers. All sorts.'

'I need to talk to the other woman who worked with Shelly. It's important.'

'Oh dear,' said Pauline. 'I hope we're not going to lose her, too. It's so hard to get surrogates with the right experience and the right attitude.'

'Purely routine,' said Gemma.

'I can give you her business card,' said Pauline. 'There's nothing confidential about that—she left a pile of them here. It only has her phone number. So then it's up to her if she wants to take things further.'

'Of course,' said Gemma, flashing her brightest smile, taking the business card. Beneath the phone number, the name '*Skanda*' was embossed in flowing magenta on a black lace background.

Gemma's CD-ROM back-to-front phone book program did the rest and she soon had the street address of Skanda Bergen, Private Consultant.

Less than half an hour later Gemma pressed the security buzzer for apartment number 12 in a handsome 1930s block at Elizabeth Bay. Slender, with just a hint of neo-gothic in the shapes of architraves and door lintels, the building rose out of a small garden of dense green shrubs.

A breathy woman's voice answered the intercom.

'It's Gemma Lincoln,' Gemma said in reply. 'I'm a friend of Shelly's. I need to talk to you.'

There was a silence finally broken by the hum and click of the front door unlocking. Gemma pushed it open and stepped inside the entrance hall. It was panelled and carpeted and smelt of good wood polish, faded perfumes and somewhere, just a touch of tomcat piss. She walked up to the first floor and the door was opened before she'd had time to knock.

'What do you want?'

The woman standing in front of her was as attractive in the flesh as she was in her photograph despite the gloves she was wearing—no trademark black lace today, thought Gemma, but pink rubber household gloves. Seizing the opportunity, she stepped through the open door, aware that her presence could become extremely unwelcome very quickly.

'I want to talk to you about Shelly,' she said.

Skanda Bergen closed the door and now that she was safely inside, Gemma focused on her hostess. Close up, she was still beautiful, although in the clear northern light of the open windows, Gemma noticed a rough, matte-like finish to her skin, as if she'd been scrubbed or sandpapered and there was a wildness in her eyes. Maybe too many men does that to a woman's skin, Gemma thought. Or maybe she's had one skin peel too many. But apart from the sharkskin, and the hypervigilant, darting eyes,

306 • GABRIELLE LORD

Gemma had to admit that Skanda's features were flawless, as was her figure. Only the tiny lines around her eyes and mouth indicated her maturity. Gemma guessed late thirties, but because of a certain tweaked look of constant surprise around the eyes, surgical intervention couldn't entirely be ruled out. She could even be older than me, Gemma speculated.

'You a cop?' Skanda asked. Gemma shook her head.

'I'm a private investigator,' she said.

The woman picked up a cloth and started to clean table tops, window sills and chairs. The apartment was neatly furnished, in soft understated pastels. Nothing too demanding to frighten the mugs, Gemma thought. Opposite the front door, through the open window, Gemma could see two doves sitting on the terracotta ridge tiles along the top of the angled roof outside. Beyond the doves, a few intrepid sailing boats leaning hard into the wind dotted the harbour. Skanda sprayed something out of a container over everything and went over the surfaces again. The place was already spotless and in the corner of the room, a space age vacuum cleaner stood ready for action. Several photographs on top of a cabinet caught her attention and Gemma drew closer to see: Skanda and another blonde woman laughing together, a group of children at a picnic, and separate framed photographs of a man and a woman. Family shots, Gemma surmised.

'I only have a few minutes,' Skanda said, wiping

over the backs of steel piping furniture that already gleamed, 'and housework is never ending.' She flashed Gemma a glance of complicity. 'So you'll forgive the lack of hospitality. I have to get this finished before the next client.'

Never-ending housework had never been a problem to her, Gemma thought. Never-starting would be more accurate.

'I can't tell you much,' said Skanda between further swipes at the coffee table and chairs, 'except I've been really scared that whoever attacked Shell might come after me. You know?'

'What makes you think that?' Gemma asked.

'I'm convinced that it was someone from the clinic. The Chester Clinic. Shelly and I worked with the psychologists there, Pauline and Jerry Chester.' Skanda pulled the rubber gloves off and threw them expertly across the small living area into the kitchen sink. 'I've got clients who love it when I wear those,' she said, looking at them as they lay on the shining stainless steel. 'Can you imagine getting off on rubber gloves?'

Despite Skanda's precautions, Gemma noticed that the skin on her fingers was peeling. That's what too much house-cleaning does, Gemma thought fleetingly and with satisfaction.

'No,' said Gemma. 'I can't. Why do you think it's someone from the clinic?'

Now Skanda was washing her hands, sleeves rolled right up, rubbing soap over her hands and forearms. It's how a surgeon washes, Gemma thought. Or a theatre nurse. No wonder her skin was so dry if this was a regular routine.

'Ask yourself this,' said Skanda. 'How come Shell's worked the street and the houses for years and never come to any harm—well, not real harm. She's been working over twenty years. And then she does just a couple of jobs for Pauline Chester and *whack*. That's it. She's murdered.' Skanda rinsed her hands and arms, drying herself thoroughly, then applying some sort of moisturiser over the just-washed area, rubbing it right up to her elbows.

'Shelly worked with someone called Peter,' Gemma said. 'Did you?'

Skanda shook her head. 'He was one of Shelly's clients,' she said. 'The mugs get used to one woman. They're regulars.'

'Do you know what he looks like?' Gemma asked, pulling out the envelope with the picture she'd printed from her visit to Peter Fenster's house.

'He looked like a mug,' snarled Skanda. 'Like they all do.'

Gemma handed her the picture and she studied it then shook her head. 'That's not him. He was a skinny-looking thing.'

'Do you know anything about this Peter?' Gemma asked, putting the picture away.

Again, Skanda shook her head. 'The men we see are psychologically disturbed,' she said, screwing the lid back on the tube of moisturiser. 'I've had just about enough of this sort of work. It's bad enough dealing with mugs off the street without having to deal with murderers as well.'

'But these are men who *want* to be helped,' said Gemma. 'They're hardly your free-ranging psychos.'

'All I can say is, you think about it,' Skanda said, pulling her sleeves down. 'You don't have to have a major in psychology to work out that men who can't get it up feel threatened by women. And people hate and fear what threatens them.'

She disappeared behind the fridge door. 'That's not psychology,' she continued, 'that's just how it is.'

Gemma had a fleeting glimpse of what looked like a small pharmacy in the white interior—jars, bottles, tubes and assorted containers with their prescriptions attached. Then the fridge door closed. *She* should talk about nutcases, Gemma thought, with her compulsive cleaning and her fridge full of pharmaceutical products.

'And do you have a major in Psychology?' Gemma asked, picking up on the cue.

'Yes, as a matter of fact I do,' said Skanda as she turned from the fridge with one of the phials, poured some of its contents into a glass, added water, stirred it and drank it down. 'It was one of the strands in my degree.' She picked up the empty glass, added a little water and swirled it round to collect any remaining sediment. 'You look surprised,' she challenged, 'at the notion of a well-educated whore?' She toasted the ceiling, before draining the glass. 'Sydney's full of them.

And that's not counting all the women married to wealthy men.' She laughed, but the effort wasn't convincing. 'I wasn't so lucky,' she said, and Gemma caught a glimpse of some personal disappointment, some failed relationship behind this remark. 'I couldn't find work apart from very low paid postgraduate positions. The universities are in their death throes. There's no money for research anymore. So I ended up going back to work in my area of expertise.'

'Which is?' Gemma asked, wanting to be clear on this point.

'I am very good at being the sort of woman a certain sort of man likes to buy. How else could I have paid my uni fees and survived?' she said. 'They think they can buy a woman, but that's not so,' she added. 'What they buy is a service, but some of them forget that.'

Gemma considered this and decided on a sudden pounce. She kept her voice very low and expressionless. 'And did Benjamin Glass fall into that category?'

Great shot, girl, Gemma congratulated herself. It was a direct hit. The question had shocked Skanda Bergen so much that Gemma thought she was going to drop the glass, but slowly it was lowered onto the spotless surface of the kitchen counter. All colour left her face, leaving her lips as pale as her suede-finish skin, and her tweaked blue eyes widened even further.

'Why are you asking me this?' she whispered.

'Did he?' Gemma repeated.

'I don't know what you're talking about,' said Skanda, turning away and picking up the cleaning agent.

'I find that hard to believe,' said Gemma, 'because I have photographs in my possession of you and Benjamin Glass.'

Skanda's face hardened, then changed to a careless mask. She put the container down again and Gemma watched closely. She thinks she's worked it out, she thought. And now she's come up with the defence.

As if on cue, Skanda turned around, the colour returning to her collagen-plumped lips. 'So what if you have?' she said. 'He was just another client at the clinic.'

If that were true, Gemma thought, you wouldn't have looked as if you were about to drop dead when I mentioned his name. Now Gemma could see something else in the woman's face, a nuance she wasn't sure about, something masked and dangerous.

She chose her next words carefully. 'I have reason to believe,' Gemma said, 'that he was more than just a client.' She thought of the hidden cache in the safe—the marked cards and the photos of this woman—the two loves of Benjamin Glass. 'The police will certainly want to talk to you once they know about the connection.' For a moment, Gemma felt guilt about the information she was withholding from the police and in her mind Section 316 of the Crimes Act wagged a scolding finger at her. She overrode it.

'What do you want? Money?' Skanda's contemptuous voice brought her back to the situation.

Gemma shook her head.

'Then why did you come here with your bullshit about being a friend of Shelly's and then do this business with the photographs?'

'It's no story,' said Gemma. 'Shelly was a friend of mine. I met her when I was a cop years ago and I kept in touch. I cared about what happened to her.'

She looked through an open door to the small bedroom and caught a glimpse of a large portrait of Skanda over the bed, wearing just her sandpaper skin and her black lace gloves. Her signature image. Gemma looked back at the living original and saw that Skanda was shaking.

'It's such a shock,' she said. 'Benjamin and now Shelly. It's like a curse on me, my friends dying like this.'

And not real cheery for your friends, either, Gemma thought, intrigued by the woman's self-centredness.

'I'm really, really scared,' Skanda was saying, as if Gemma didn't believe her.

You're scared all right, Gemma thought. But of what?

Skanda returned to the kitchen, pulled on the rubber gloves again, picked up another spray cleanser and started rewiping the already spotless surfaces. Gemma wondered what Kit would make of this cleaning compulsion and she thought of Lady Macbeth.

'You'd better go,' Skanda said without turning around. 'I have a client due any minute.'

Gemma started to walk towards the door and only then did Skanda swing round, still ashen-faced.

'Those photographs,' she said. 'Who has them?'

'Only me at the moment,' Gemma lied. 'So far, no one else knows who you are.'

'You don't have to tell them about me,' Skanda said. She put the spray container and cloth down. 'Please. I was just a sex surrogate. I've got nothing to do with Benjamin Glass or his life. I was just someone who worked for him, like his cleaner or his driver. No,' she added. 'Not even as important as that.'

'If that's the case,' Gemma said 'why do you need to keep it secret? What's the big deal?'

'Oh for God's sake! Don't be so stupid!' the woman snapped. 'Why would anyone—especially someone like me—want to get dragged into a fucking murder investigation?'

Gemma decided to be cheeky. 'Your duty as a citizen who respects the rule of law and supports democratic principles?'

Skanda stared at her with blank hostility.

'When did you meet Benjamin Glass?' Gemma said.

'I've told you. Through the Chester Clinic. A while ago.'

'How long?'

Skanda screwed up her pretty face as if it was hard to remember. 'Bit over a year.'

'And he was still undergoing sex therapy with you?'

'Yes he was.'

Gemma thought there'd be no harm in a straight question. 'Ms Bergen,' she said, 'did you kill Benjamin Glass?'

Skanda's wide eyes became wider. 'Why the hell are you asking me a question like that?' she said. 'Do you think I'm the sort of person who goes round killing people?' Her jaw had dropped in shock. 'You must be crazy.'

'I'm not crazy,' said Gemma, 'I'm investigating the case. I've been retained by a client and I want to know the answer.'

Skanda viciously sprayed cleaner on a spotless wall and scrubbed hard. 'I've told you everything I know,' she said. 'Benjamin Glass came here with a referral from Pauline or Jerry—'

'From the clinic?'

'Yes.'

'And?'

'We'd do what we had to do.'

'And what was that?'

'Book a time, darling, and I'll show you,' Skanda snarled, grabbing the vacuum cleaner and pushing it aggressively in Gemma's direction. 'I don't have to answer your damned questions. I can tell you to go to hell, you know.' She switched on the machine.

'You can,' Gemma shouted above the noise. 'And I can tell the police about you. Right now.'

Skanda lunged around the room with the vacuum cleaner.

'Turn that damn thing off and tell me what I want to know,' said Gemma, 'and I might be able to lose your name for a while. Tell me what you and Mr Glass did.'

Gemma waited. Finally Skanda switched the cleaner off. Then she stamped around like a crazed parlourmaid, straightening a pile of magazines, putting on a CD, plumping up cushions, generally tidying an already perfectly tidy room.

'Sometimes it was just body work, you know, massage. Pressure points. Breathing techniques.' Her mouth curled down in distaste. 'Most men are so fucked up about sex they find it impossible to enjoy full body orgasm. They're fixated on their pricks. They just do those little spurts and grunts and think they've climaxed.'

She opened the front door and stood waiting beside it. Gemma took the cue and stood in the doorway, ready to leave.

'And was that the case with Benjamin?'

'He was improving a lot.'

Skanda's face showed a hard, bitter expression that was gone almost the moment Gemma noticed it. Gemma stepped outside, said goodbye and Skanda closed the door. She took her time going back down to her car, thinking over the interview. Skanda Bergen was a case, that was clear enough, with her crazy cleaning routines. And she was furious. Was she so self-centred that she took Benjamin Glass's death personally, angry at the loss of such a rich client? Gemma jotted down a few notes about the angry, defensive nature of the woman and her obsessive compulsion to clean. She couldn't quite find the words she needed to describe whatever it was that lay in those darting eyes. Something volatile, dangerous. She looked forward to discussing it with Kit.

Across the road, under the spreading protection of a huge Moreton Bay fig, a couple were embracing. All the pain and jealousy about Steve came rushing back again. She stared at the pair, wondering where her man was, and what he was doing. Just in this moment, Gemma didn't care that she had a teasing new lead into the Benjamin Glass investigation. Right now, all she could think about was the fact that Steve was living with another woman, sleeping under her roof, putting his arm around her waist. Gemma straightened her shoulders and got into her car. Earlier, she'd made an appointment to visit Mike. It was time to clear the air in that direction, at least. On the way to Mike's place, she couldn't shake the feeling she was being followed. Uneasy, she checked her mirror. The traffic behind her seemed innocent but she checked her rear-view mirror more often than usual.

•

The house Mike Moody shared with another deserted husband was a small Victorian terrace not far from the University of New South Wales at Kensington. Mike opened the door at her knock and she was shocked at his appearance. One eye was black, there was a stitched split over his eyebrow, another on the cheekbone, and the right side of his mouth was grazed and swollen.

'God,' she said. 'You do look terrible.'

'This is good,' he responded, 'compared to how I was the other night.' His voice sounded flat, bruised lips hardly moving. He watched as she hobbled in. 'And anyway,' he said, 'you're not too smart yourself.'

'All right,' she said. 'I forgive you. I didn't think I'd ever want to see you again,' she said, 'let alone employ you.'

'Thanks,' he grunted. 'Can I get you something? Tea? Coffee?'

He busied himself in the kitchen and Gemma looked around. It was definitely a rented bachelor domain. An old sunken lounge in front of the television, a dying indoor plant, a few chairs and clothes drying on a clothes horse near a small heater comprised the furniture of the living room. Mike came back with two coffees and set them down on an uncomfortably low coffee table, a refugee from the '70s, all orange and lime-green ceramic tiles.

'Excuse the mess,' he said. 'I'm not much of a housekeeper.' He went into the kitchen again and returned with a large round cake tin, opening it to reveal an elaborate chocolate cake and offered her a wicked looking slice.

'Whipped it up yourself, did you?' she joked.

Mike nodded. 'Actually, yes, I did. I'm working through an international cake cookbook. This is a

Bavarian recipe. Bit like Black Forest cake. Every week I make the next cake in the book.'

Gemma stared at him. 'I'm astonished,' she said.

'Why?' he asked. 'Most of the great chefs are men.'

'It's not a skill I associate with police officers,' she said. 'It's delicious,' she added, when she'd tasted it.

Mike replaced the lid on the cake tin and took it back to the kitchen, returning with a small piece for himself. He ate with difficulty, chewing only on one side of his jaw, and barely moving his wounded mouth. What a pair we are, she thought. But at least Mike caught his target on video. Mine got away.

'Want to see what I got?' he asked.

Gemma blinked, wondering for a moment what he was talking about. Then he slid a cassette into his VCR. The image was blurred for a second until the automatic focus hardened the edges around a young girl, tall, full-breasted, her upper body encased in a low-cut bustier in black leather, held together with studs, her back completely naked. Thigh-high boots with dangerously high heels covered tight leather hipster pants, revealing a trim tanned belly with a jewelled navel. Belinda Swann, Gemma thought, looking like a vision from Miss Kitty's House of Bondage. No one seeing this would imagine the girl could possibly be fourteen. It was the sort of image that would be very helpful to Belinda Swann's ex-boyfriend's counsel.

'How old would you think she was if you didn't know?' Mike asked.

Gemma considered. Taking into account her make-up, her height and mature-looking figure, Gemma tried to forget she knew the girl's age. 'I think if you said twenty-six no one would argue,' she replied.

'Watch this bit,' said Mike. 'You can see the two guys there'—he pointed to two murky figures standing behind the queue near the door of the nightclub—'the ones who bashed me.'

Gemma studied them as they loomed closer.

'I kept filming,' said Mike. 'You never know when it might be needed in court.'

The men's features became clear as the automatic zoom righted itself. Young, fit, dark, dangerous, she thought. They started walking towards the camera and then it all happened. The camera angle suddenly swerved, swung upside-down and the images became incomprehensible. Then came the grainy black and white tweed pattern as the picture was lost. Mike stood up and switched it off.

'That's it,' he said. 'But we've got those two cold if we ever meet up with them again. I've already printed off copies for the cops.'

Gemma turned to him. 'Mike,' she said, 'I owe you an apology. I was furious with you. I thought you'd just stood me up.' She didn't tell him she'd really wanted to see him to make sure his injuries justified his no-show the other night.

As if reading her thoughts, Mike attempted a

lop-sided smile. 'You came round to check me out, didn't you?' he said. 'Make sure I was fair dinkum?'

He'd got it in one, she thought.

'I'd do the same,' he said, 'if I'd been in your shoes. After all, you don't really know me very well yet. It takes ages to build up a working trust in a game like this one. I just hope you believe I'm trustworthy. I like working with you.'

It was hard to know if he was trying on a low grade flirt, or merely speaking his mind.

'That's nice,' she said vaguely before continuing. 'I didn't realise you'd been so badly assaulted, Mike. And then your dopey flatmate lost my mobile number and couldn't ring. So I didn't know what the hell was going on.'

Mike rehoused the cassette in a black cover and put it away.

'My flatmate is now my ex-flatmate. He moved out a few days ago,' he said. 'He's always got to keep one step ahead of his ex. She finds out where he lives and does terrible things to him.'

'Like what?'

'Mean things. Prawn heads in the hub caps. Graffiti on the walls. Shit in brown paper bags type of things. That sort of stuff. She broke into one of the places he was renting and destroyed everything in his wardrobe. But she'll get her comeuppance.'

'What do you mean?' Gemma asked, uneasy at the turn the conversation seemed to be taking.

'I ran a check on her new boyfriend,' he said. 'And he's got a criminal record. Real nasty.'

Gemma stood up, brushing crumbs off her knee. 'I'd better get going.'

'I won't be far behind you,' he said, picking up the cups and plates, taking them back into the kitchen. Then he went into the bedroom, leaving Gemma perched on the arm of the lounge. From that position, she could just see into the bedroom, painted an ugly green, with stacks of CDs and books, and on the wall, a poster of a naked woman, a bullseye target on one breast.

The door moved slightly and Mike came back out carrying a coat.

'I want to do a full forensic on that computer of yours,' he said. 'Make sure everything's ridgey-didge. You'll definitely need to upgrade your security.' He checked his wristwatch. 'I'll need it for a couple of hours. You can have it back as soon as I've finished. Is that okay?'

It was more of a statement than a question, and Gemma nodded.

'Just excuse me for a moment,' Mike said, vanishing into the bathroom, closing the door. While he was occupied, Gemma crept into the green bedroom. An old suede jacket hung from the doorknob. Gemma felt around in its pockets and found a man's handkerchief. Gingerly, she pulled it out. It was heavily bloodstained. Pinching it between two fingernails, she folded tissues from the nearby box around it and slid it into her pocket. Close up, she could see that the poster of the naked woman had been further defaced, not only by the bullseye over her heart, but also by what appeared to be small stab wounds around her other breast, belly and groin. Both eyes had been scratched out with a sharp instrument. It was so ugly that she jumped in fright when she heard a sudden sound. It was only the toilet flushing next door so she limped back to the living area and was innocently loitering near the front door when Mike came out, drying his hands. She felt the purloined handkerchief, safe in her pocket. I'll get this matched against any DNA traces from the previous attacks, she thought. I *have* to eliminate Mike from this or I'll forever be unsure about him. The two assaults were hours apart; it's possible for him to have been involved with both. And I need to see Kit soon, too, and talk to her; do whatever it takes to get our relationship back on track again.

Her mobile rang. It was Minkie Montreau returning her call. Gemma arranged to see her but first she dropped the handkerchief off to Angie at the Police Centre who parcelled it up neatly for the Analytical Laboratory and promised personal delivery later that day.

'Tell Ric to match it against the attacks on Robyn Warburton and Shelly.'

'What are you up to?' Angie asked. 'Whose is this?' And she indicated the package.

'Just do it,' said Gemma. 'I'll explain later.'

'You're not withholding anything from the relevant authorities, are you, girl?' asked Angie.

'It's just a real wild card,' said Gemma. 'Elimination purposes only.' But Angie's words reminded her of another package. She fished it out of her briefcase. 'And give these photographs to Sean?' She handed over the pictures of Skanda Bergen in her birthday suit and gloves. 'Tell him I found them among Benjamin Glass's possessions.' She wondered how long it would take Mr Right to track down the late philanthropist's bedmate.

Half an hour later, Gemma was knocking on Minkie Montreau's huge front door. Minkie's face was apprehensive as she opened it. Not all your locks and bolts and castle gates can keep this away from you, Gemma thought, as she walked into the spacious foyer.

'What is it now?' asked Minkie nervously.

Gemma swung round to face her. 'Three things,' she said. 'First, someone has reported a yellow BMW in the vicinity of the beach house prior to the fire. Secondly, I checked with the company which insured your Nelson Bay property. You asked for a copy of the policy to be sent out to you only last week.'

'I did *not*!' said Minkie indignantly.

'Your broker's records prove it,' Gemma continued relentlessly. 'And thirdly, I went to Sydney University and tracked down a copy of your Masters thesis.'

She watched Minkie's face as she pulled out her notebook. A look of pure terror contorted the usually regular features and too much of the whites showed in the strange green eyes.

'Why did you do that?' she said in a barely audible voice.

'And this is what I discovered,' Gemma said, finding the notes she'd scribbled down in the university archives. 'A Masters thesis submitted by Miriam Montreau titled "Applications of synthetic and natural polymers in the production of high temperature accelerants".' Gemma read from the title page.

She turned on the woman who was now huddled on a chair like a frightened child, twisting a handkerchief between her fingers.

'I can't believe this is happening,' whispered Minkie. *Who is doing this to me?* Her voice was like a smothered scream.

'Minkie,' said Gemma, 'you've lied to me every time we've met. And every time I've discovered something else you haven't told me. I've had to drag the truth out of you. I don't know what your game is but I think it's only fair to warn you that when I hand this information over to Sean Wright, the police could well believe they now have enough on you to charge you with the murder of your husband.'

'No!' cried Minkie. 'That's ridiculous.'

'Personally,' said Gemma, to drive it home, 'I think they've got more than enough for a committal hearing.'

'But they can't do that!' she said. *'I didn't do it.*

You've got to believe me. Please don't pass this on. You're working for me, not the police!'

'Why should I believe you?' Gemma asked. 'You've lied and continued to lie.'

'Only about things that have nothing to do with Benjamin's death,' she said. 'I've told you the truth about everything else.' Tears ran down her face. 'I've had a very difficult life,' she said. 'People only see this'—she waved her hand vaguely at the lavish surroundings—'they don't know what it was like to grow up with parents who were Communists in the '50s. Ideologues are the pits when it comes to parenting. I was a political *ideal,* not a little child.'

Here we go, thought Gemma. The sob story to soften me up again.

'I'm not going to give you the story of my unhappy childhood,' Minkie said, as if reading Gemma's mind, 'but I was forced to do that wretched Engineering degree and that bloody Masters thesis by a woman who'd didn't even finish her own degree. I was halfway through my doctorate before I cried enough! Even then, I didn't start living my own life. I started designing and manufacturing sexy underwear. You know why? To get right up my mother's nose! I knew she'd hate it and I was right. But after a while, I found that I couldn't sustain my interest in it. It wasn't what I really wanted to do either. But by then I'd met and married Benjamin.' She paused. 'It took me years to discover what I really wanted in life. And years to find what was important to me in matters of love.' She walked to the long window and looked out at the garden for a moment before turning back to Gemma. 'I know I've appeared dishonest. But I've only tried to keep some things . . . someone . . . out of the picture.'

'Why?' asked Gemma. 'Who cares if you've got a boyfriend? Your husband's dead. What's the big deal?' She remembered the time she'd rung Anthony Love and a woman had answered. 'Is he married?' she asked. 'Is that it?'

'It's much more complicated than that,' she said. 'Anthony could be in real trouble if the truth came out.'

Gemma swung round, ready to leave. 'I'm going. I've had enough of this,' she said. 'I'll total up what you owe me and fax it to you.'

She went to the door. Minkie made no move to open it for her.

'You don't seem to appreciate the very real danger you're in,' Gemma said. 'Stop pretending to be noble. If all these lies have been to protect Anthony, you're wasting your time and energy. It only makes everything look worse. As a person connected to a murder investigation, he'll have to be interviewed by the police.'

'No!' Minkie's voice was a shriek. 'That mustn't happen. The success of his latest work depends on it. You don't understand!'

'It's you who doesn't understand,' snapped Gemma. 'Now please open this door for me.'

For the first time, she felt a shiver of fear. If this woman had murdered her husband, Gemma might be next on the hit list. She wondered how well she'd be able to defend herself, with her strength compromised by her injuries.

Minkie, however, proceeded to open the heavy door and Gemma went down the path as fast as her leg would let her. By the time she got back to her car, it was aching again from the effort. Once or twice, she fancied she saw a black car in her rear-vision mirror that made all the same turns as she did, but she dismissed the idea as paranoia.

•

Next morning found Dr Heather Pike poking and probing around Gemma's ribs. Gemma had told her about the events of the night in the lane and the injury to her leg and flank. First, Heather had checked her knee and ankle, and pronounced herself satisfied at the way it was healing.

'You've taken a terrible whack across the ribs,' she observed.

Gemma shuddered, remembering. But there was another danger to address, and this was the main reason she'd made the appointment.

'Heather,' she said. 'There's something else I want to talk about,' she said. 'It might sound crazy, but here goes—I want a Naltrexone implant.'

Heather's dark eyebrows rose in surprise. 'What on earth are you asking me, Gemma?' Her shock registered on her clear, intelligent face. 'I don't know what to say. Surely you're not a user, are you? If you are, we need to have a talk.'

Gemma shook her head. 'Certainly not. But I might be put in a situation where heroin could be forced on me,' she said. 'That's why I want you to give me an implant.'

'You don't understand,' said Heather. 'I can't just go putting implants of potentially dangerous drugs into people to avoid something that *might* happen. You're asking me to do something I can't.'

'Please, Heather,' said Gemma. 'I don't need you to understand. Just tell me whether or not you're willing to do it.'

'Naltrexone implants are still at a very experimental stage,' said Heather. 'It could be dangerous.'

'It could be much more dangerous for me without it,' Gemma said, wishing she'd talked to Steve about it before he went undercover anywhere near George Fayed. 'I wouldn't be asking you to do it otherwise.'

Heather's frowning face irritated Gemma. 'Look,' she said impatiently, 'I'll get someone else to do it if you won't.'

Heather picked up her pen and wrote something down on a pad. 'Give me a couple of days to research this, will you?' she said. 'I'll ring you.'

'Promise?'

'Promise.'

Gemma walked out of Heather's surgery and down the hallway. She was aware of a child crying in the busy waiting room, the sound wailing like a siren as she stepped outside into the cold air. She had skipped breakfast and, instead of crossing the road towards her car, walked without thinking around the corner, hoping to find a milk bar. She found herself in an ugly back lane. Piles of cardboard and newspapers lined the narrow footpath, reminding her of the scene of her attack where she had been hurt so badly that even now, days later, the ache in her flank had not stopped. Ahead of her, she was aware of two men coming towards her. Every instinct signalled danger. Her melancholic mood vanished immediately, replaced with the hot ice of adrenaline. She swung round on her heel and barely had time to register shock when she collided with two more men who'd suddenly materialised behind her. One of them grabbed her in a painful wristlock and before she could scream, fight or kick, Gemma felt herself lifted off her feet, something was thrown over her head, the briefcase snatched from her shocked hands, and her body was crushed in a powerful grip. The sound of a car screeching to brake behind her had her screaming '*Let me go!*' uselessly into a suffocating gag of denim. Not into the car, she told herself. Once they've got me in the car I'm gone. Gemma struggled with all her strength. She tried to kick but both legs were already pinned. She heard a car door open. Then she was flung painfully onto the back seat, pushed down to the floor. Someone leaned on her back, wedging her between the front and back seats. Her face was grazed on harsh nylon carpet; she felt the bite of disposable cuffs around her wrists. Helpless, she tried to breathe, moving her head to one side, trying to dislodge whatever it was that was over her face, stinking of male sweat and engine oil. Doors slammed, and the weight of someone's boot slammed onto her. The pain in her flank was agonising. George Fayed had her, her frightened brain told her. She was helpless. He was going to force-inject her. Her scream was drowned in the gunning of a V8 engine.

FOURTEEN

Gemma lay terrified, unable to move from shock, not to mention the heavy boot that still lay on her. Now she was half-lying, half-crouched around the differential hump, her body shivering with adrenalin, fright and fight. She'd have to try and escape when they dragged her out of the car. The conversation around her, desultory though it was, was not in Lebanese. It was, in fact, very ocker. She thought of the cyberstalker. Could he have organised this? Was she going to be raped? Murdered? She tried to concentrate on keeping track of the turns the car made, imagining the roads they were taking, trying to remember how the lights went along William Street, sensing they were driving towards the city. But then came a turn south and she imagined College Street and the

Avery building full of armed police, just metres away but useless to her. A few minutes later she heard the noise of trains and thought they must be near Central. The sound faded and in a matter of minutes, Gemma gave up. It was no use: they could be anywhere. She lay there, planning the next move, knowing that her only chance of escape would present itself when the car stopped and these men transferred her to wherever it was they were taking her. She wondered if her briefcase was with them in the car, or whether its contents lay scattered on the lane.

'Listen, girlie,' a voice said, close to her ear. 'I don't get no thrill from hurting women. But you come quietly when we get out of the car, or I'll break your fucking arm. What's it to be?'

Gemma was aware the car was slowing, and in a few minutes, had stopped. The voice continued, not so close now.

'Lorraine just wants a chat with you. Nothing to worry about. I'm going to let you get up now.'

Lorraine? she thought, relieved that she wasn't going to be forcibly injected or raped and murdered by a computer nerd. But the feeling was short lived. Her fears had materialised. Lorraine Litchfield, whose eyes had blazed through her the night before, *had* recognised her. Please God she didn't know about her relationship with Steve. God, Gemma, she asked herself, what have you done?

'Just move real quiet and easy,' her captor was saying. 'If you start chirping and carrying on, I'll cover you over again just like my budgie. Get it?'

'Okay,' she said, although her answer was largely muffled by the carpet. The coat was removed from Gemma's eyes and she struggled awkwardly with her legs and left arm, backing out in a crawl to get out of the car. She stood up and looked around as her captor cut the cuffs off. She was standing in a courtyard. Before she could think any further he applied a wristlock, hard on her right arm and hand. She straightened up to see who held her, a solid block of a man, short back and sides, dressed in an aqua Hawaiian shirt printed with pineapples. He could have been a barman at a beachside pub. He loosed his hold on her arm as soon as he realised she wasn't going to fight him.

'This is depriving a person of liberty,' she said to him. 'It's kidnapping.' It was a stupid thing to say, but it was what had come to her lips, unbidden, in her shocked state.

His face softened. 'Don't be like that, darlin',' he said. 'You're just making a social call.'

'People usually ring first,' she said, her voice shaking, 'and issue an invitation.'

'That's right,' he said. 'That's exactly what we're doing.'

She tried to walk, but the shock of her abduction suddenly hit in waves again and her legs felt wobbly beneath her. The car, a big black Commodore, was parked in the courtyard of a project builder's idea of a Tuscan villa, but there was nothing artificial about the three-metre lime-washed wall that surrounded the two-storeyed house, or the security cameras trained onto the barren,

prison-like yard. As she approached a paved terrace where a row of classical urns grew weeds and
grasses in their chalices, the double doors of the
large house beyond opened, and the blonde who'd
been hanging round Steve's neck the night before
walked out. Behind her and still inside, Gemma
saw Steve. She quickly looked away, fearing her
face would betray her.

'Bring her in here, Murray,' said Lorraine to the
budgie man as she went back inside.

Gemma offered no resistance as she was hus-
tled up the couple of steps from the bare garden
area onto the tiled patio. She blinked as she went
inside, her eyes adjusting to the light as she took
in her surroundings. Lorraine Litchfield's taste in
furnishings ran to the extreme end of neo-rococo.
Mother-of-pearl chairs and tables were reflected in
huge gilt mirrors, which also reflected elaborate
chandeliers as well as the group of three people,
her captors and Gemma, that now stood in front
of Lorraine.

Gemma kept her face averted from Steve and
focused on two carved mother-of-pearl cherubs,
twined together and surmounting the back of a
chair, aware of the slender figure of Lorraine Litchfield lighting up a cigarette. The cloud of smoke
that surrounded her kidnapper as she exhaled and
shook the match away was a similar hue to the
baby-blue angora-trimmed suit that hugged Lorraine's perfect figure, its short tight skirt revealing
long legs ending in silver high-heeled sandals. The
wristlock had suddenly dropped away and Gemma

focused all her attention on the powder-blue vision in front of her.

'You're in a lot of trouble, lady,' said Gemma in her best cop's voice. 'You'll go a row for this. Assault, deprivation of liberty, they'll throw the book at you.'

'Listen to her,' said Lorraine, not even addressing Gemma. 'What a joke.' Then she came right up to Gemma, jabbing her cigarette frighteningly close to Gemma's face. 'You're the one in trouble, you little slut.'

Hatred and jealousy blazed in her eyes and Gemma grasped the situation fast. She really has fallen for Steve. She's fallen for the man who is playing the role of her boyfriend. Gemma took a deep breath. Please God it's not reciprocal. I've got to have all my wits about me, she told herself. I've got to stay calm and reason this out. I've got to stay detached.

'I don't care for your language, lady,' Gemma said. 'It sounds vulgar.'

Lorraine swung away, turning on the silver Italian heels.

'Listen Miss-up-Yourself, I'll tell you what's vulgar. Kev and Murray,' she ordered. 'Out!'

Gemma watched in alarm as the two men who'd brought her inside left. Compared to this acid-spitting blonde, these men now seemed positively decent and caring and Gemma didn't like being left inside with Lorraine Litchfield and Steve. The other two seemed to have vanished. Maybe, thought Gemma, they were only there to bring me

336 • GABRIELLE LORD

in. It was a cheering thought in an otherwise bleak situation.

'Okay,' Lorraine said to Steve. 'Now let's hear her version.'

'Lorraine, stop this,' said Steve in an unnaturally mild voice. 'This is silly.'

It was a mistake.

'Don't you dare call me silly!' she hissed at him, her whole body writhing in a whiplash of anger. Again, she coiled herself round to face her rival and Gemma was reminded of a snake, doubling itself up to rear and strike.

'Her version,' the woman had said, implying Steve had already given his version of whatever it was Lorraine Litchfield wanted to know.

'How do you know this man?' Lorraine said, pointing a long manicured finger at Steve.

Gemma's mind raced. So that was it: she wanted to know where she stood, and where Gemma stood in relation to Steve. Somehow, Gemma had to come up with an answer that matched Steve's explanation. She knew, and she knew that Steve knew, that telling the truth is always the best policy when it comes to interrogation and cross-examination. But a qualified truth, with certain areas of omission. Steve would have told Lorraine as much of the truth as was safe, Gemma thought. That gave her a clue.

'*Answer me!*' Lorraine had come too close again, pushing into Gemma's space, provoking her. If the woman had sent four men to bring me in, thought Gemma, she must already know something of my history.

'Him?' she answered, sounding as uninterested and careless as she could. 'You want to know how I know him?' she said, shrugging and throwing a glance at Steve, who had turned away and was leaning against the mantelpiece underneath the most ornate of the gilt mirrors. 'I know him from the job.'

'What job?'

Again, Gemma prayed that her answer matched Steve's. 'I used to be a police officer,' she said, then continued with a tone of distaste that was partly genuine. 'So was he, but I guess that's no longer the case, given the company he's keeping.'

Lorraine tossed back her white-blonde hair. 'That's rich, coming from you,' she said, with an ambiguity that was worrying. Did she already know of their relationship? she wondered. Lorraine went to the sliding door and turned back, her figure silhouetted against the light.

'How well did you know him?'

'You see people in the corridors. In the lift. Different divisions. I knew his face. Why?'

Lorraine shoved her face bare inches from Gemma's. 'You knew a damn sight more than his fucking face, you moll!' she screamed. 'I saw you looking at him last night.'

Gemma resisted backing away, standing her ground, narrowing her own eyes as she confronted her enraged rival.

'When a face is familiar,' Gemma started to say, 'it's perfectly natural to—'

But her words were interrupted. 'I'll give you natural!' shrieked Lorraine, snatching something up from the depths of the cushions on the mother-of-pearl three-seater lounge. Gemma froze when she saw what it was. The crazy woman was pointing the nasty end of a Colt M1911 at her, the barrel trembling and jerking about at Lorraine's every word and movement. Gemma felt her courage drain away and she was suddenly cold.

'Hey, Lorraine! Baby.' Steve's voice was calm and unhurried, as if it were a gin and tonic Lorraine Litchfield was waving around, not a pistol. 'Put that down, baby.'

Gemma saw his eyes meet hers briefly in the mirror and they were hard as stone. He turned back to Lorraine and in that second she swung the M1911 round on Steve, her hands shaking as she pointed it at his face.

'Baby,' he said, holding a conciliatory hand out to her, and Gemma felt her heart go cold. 'Baby, put that down. You don't have to worry. This woman means nothing to me.'

Lorraine swung the pistol back towards Gemma. 'Then you won't care if I kill the bitch right here and now, will you?'

Gemma held her breath. Her eyes flickered to Steve and back. He was coolly ignoring her.

'You're overreacting, baby.' Steve's voice was soft and steady. 'Don't make a big fuss about nothing. Just take it easy and put that damn thing down.'

'Don't you start telling me what to do!' Lorraine yelled. 'I had enough of that from that bastard Terry.'

She swung the gun back towards Steve then around again to Gemma who realised she was clenching her toes up into little fists inside her shoes. She tried to relax them but Lorraine's next words had her toes curling again.

'You've gotta choose, Steve,' she said. 'Right now. Who's it to be? Me or her?'

Gemma felt trapped in someone else's nightmare. The unreality of the scene she was witnessing, its craziness, its hysteria, made it even more terrifying. Part of her was finding it hard to believe her eyes. But the Colt was more real than anything else in that pearl-infested room. Her rational mind told her that of course Steve was playing it as safely as he could, telling Lorraine what she wanted to hear. Keeping Gemma safe. But there was another voice saying *he's been involved with her all the time. She killed her husband for him. They're in this together. This has been going on for a lot longer than the police operation.* Gemma clenched her jaw. No emotion moved on her face. She stood still as death.

'Baby,' came Steve's soft voice as he moved closer to Lorraine, coming up behind her. Now Gemma turned away to watch the scene in the mirror. It was easier somehow to watch this insanity in mirrorland than to face the pistol that still wavered in her direction, the deadly snout revealing the dark hollow through which sudden death could blaze. Now Steve was almost touching Lorraine. His eyes met Gemma's briefly, expressionless. Then he looked deliberately away, turning towards Lorraine.

'Baby doll, look. Just use those beautiful eyes of yours and look. Look at her. Then look at you. Just do that for me?'

Gemma found it impossible not to do what Steve was suggesting to Lorraine. She had a clear view both of herself and Lorraine. The woman pointing the gun at Gemma in the mirror, despite the snarl pinching her features, was extremely beautiful: willowy, tall, perfectly proportioned and gorgeous as only twenty-something can be, the soft sheer suit a haze around her slim figure. Gemma, on the other hand, with the pallor of shock on her face, dishevelled, lips bloodless and hair tangled from the denim coat that had half-suffocated her, knew she looked every moment of her thirty-eight years and had never been a beauty in the first place. The ugly sister, she thought to herself, and the perfect princess. She steeled her jaw. This could be life or death, she knew, for both Steve and herself. Or betrayal so big and deep that she didn't even realise she was falling into it.

'Baby,' Steve was saying, 'calm down and take a look.'

Lorraine lowered the pistol and Steve drew her to him. He took the weapon from her hand, checked the safety catch with a deft flick and shoved it well out of the way onto the cushions behind him. Then he turned Lorraine round to face him, looking into her eyes.

'She means nothing to me,' he said. Then he looked Gemma straight in the face. 'There's no contest.'

And Gemma had to stand and watch them embrace, watch Steve's dark head close to Lorraine's, their mouths pressed together, see Steve's arms sliding around this woman who had ordered Gemma's abduction and humiliation. Then Lorraine surfaced from the kiss and snaked her head around to look at Gemma triumphantly. Gemma stared back, using her old expressionless face, the blank she'd perfected as a defenceless child surviving in a world of hostile, contemptuous adults. Behind her stony mask, Gemma wondered if she could stand all this much longer. Her flank was aching, her head spinning with grief, jealousy and fear. Her mouth was dry and something weird was happening to the back of her head. She hadn't eaten anything since yesterday and the hateful victory in Lorraine Litchfield's wide blue eyes blazed like a death ray.

'Murray! Get in here!' screamed Lorraine.

Murray appeared.

'Take this piece of shit back where you found it!' she commanded. 'And give her a good seeing-to!' Gemma felt a sudden rush of nausea, the golden mirrors and mother-of-pearl finishes melting and pouring together as her vision wobbled. As she staggered, an insight suddenly came to her—she'd seen this woman somewhere recently, completely separate from Steve. Then she felt her legs go under her. Oh no, she thought on the way down, as something happened to space and time. Then she knew nothing.

FIFTEEN

When she came to, she was in the car again, but this time lolling against the back seat. The budgie man was driving. She saw his eyes in the rear vision mirror checking her out. 'I'll drop you off somewhere,' he said. 'I don't mind doing that.'

'Let me out!'

'You were really smart, passing out back there. Fainting like that was the neatest thing you've ever done. Otherwise you would have got a good seeing-to.'

'Seeing-to?' Gemma yelled. 'Where's my brief-case?'

'Here.' He looked at her in the mirror.

'Let me out,' she demanded. 'Right now. Here.'

'Girlie . . .' he started saying.

'Right here!' Gemma was shocked at her own scream. He screeched the car to a halt so that she jerked forward and would have banged against the front seat had she not saved herself with out-stretched arms.

'All right!' he said.

She scrambled out of the car, not caring, not even knowing where she was.

'Here. Take this!'

He flung the briefcase out onto the footpath. Gemma grabbed it. The car, a black Commodore with the LITCH registration, roared away. Gemma looked around. I will never forget that car, she thought. And I will never forgive Steve for this, no matter what he was doing.

She recognised Norton Street forming a right angle to the street she was in. It was the suburb of Leichhardt. She stood dazed for a moment. Then she pulled out her mobile and rang Kit but all she got was the voice mail. I was nearly killed, she reflected. She saw a café on the corner and made her way to it, grateful just to sit and breathe. She ordered coffee and, although she was starving, realised she'd throw up if she tried to eat anything just now. She stared out the door, watching cars crisscross on the street outside. She drank the coffee and when she went to pay, found that her wallet was missing. The face of the woman behind the counter changed from disapproval to shock as her customer burst into tears.

She scrambled for her phone, remembering Mike would be at the office by now, working on her computer. She'd have to get back to her car. She felt immense relief when his voice answered.

'Mike,' she said. 'Something's happened. Can you come and pick me up?'

'What is it?'

'Come and pick me up,' she said, 'corner of Norton and Marion streets, Leichhardt.'

He waited.

'I'll tell you what happened when I see you.'

When Mike's car drove into view, Gemma limped out to him, borrowed ten dollars, paid for her coffee and scrambled into the front seat, the line of vehicles behind them honking.

'What the hell happened to you?' he asked, looking at the long streak of grease smearing her slacks, the dirt and scuffing on her shoes.

She looked sideways at his swollen mouth and the black edges of stitches that showed under the plaster on his forehead. He seemed worse now than yesterday. She pulled down the sun visor on the passenger side and checked herself in the mirror. Her heart sank. God, I'm getting old, she thought to herself. Another dark smudge on one side of her face, streaked mascara and no lipstick made her look like the woman in a poster about domestic violence. She slammed the mirror up again, grabbed a tissue from her briefcase and started rubbing at her face.

'I was abducted off the street,' she said. 'A woman with a grudge against me.'

Mike swung round towards her. 'Who?' he asked.

'Lorraine Litchfield.'

'Are you going to lay charges?'

'It's not as clear cut as that,' she said, and gave him a simplified version of events. She couldn't bring herself to tell Mike about her own role in the affair—following Steve through Kings Cross, making eye contact with his companion, reacting in jealous fury, putting her man and herself at risk with her ill-conceived actions.

Mike frowned.

'This woman wants Steve,' she said. 'She has a . . .' she groped for words that wouldn't hurt her too much ' . . . a personal interest in him. And she suspects my involvement with him. There was a scene. It was horrible.' For another moment, she thought she was about to cry again. 'Then I went and fainted.' She put her head in her hands. 'I don't know what's happening to me.'

Mike drove on in silence. 'I don't know what to say,' he said finally. He swung a glance her way. 'I've never known what to say to women.'

She studied his profile and noticed the way the low winter sun shone on the golden hair of his powerful forearms, relaxed behind the steering wheel. Despite her suspicions, Gemma warmed to him. She felt very glad he was sitting beside her. 'I'm a mess,' she complained. 'I've never fainted in my life. I've never burst into tears in a public place.' She bit her lip. 'I'm a *professional*,' she said.

'You're a human, too, Gemma. All of us have a breaking point.'

'I thought I was tougher,' she said, almost ashamed of her admission.

'Better get you home and cleaned up,' he said. 'You look like you could do with a decent feed. And a good sleep.' He concentrated on the driving for a few moments. 'Gemma, you've got to report this to the police,' he said. 'It's a very serious offence. What if she decides to get at you again—in a more permanent way?'

Gemma shook her head, thinking of Steve's cold words, his dismissal of her, his comparison between Gemma, smeared with oil and smudged with dirt and the lovely blonde princess in the fluffy powder-blue suit.

'I don't believe I'm in any further danger from her. And anyway, this is a personal matter,' she said. I'll talk it over with Angie, she decided to herself. Angie will give it to me straight.

'But what did she want? Why did she do it? How did it all come about?'

'She wanted to find out about something.' Gemma's heart was still aching from the memory of the kiss she'd unwillingly witnessed and the struggle she was having, believing it was only theatre, part of Steve's role, and necessary for Gemma's own safety. 'And she did,' she added sadly.

Sitting in the car with Mike driving her, heading for home, with the winter sunlight filtering through molten clouds, she calmed down a lot. The rate of her dejected heart was almost back to normal and she realised only now how much she'd sweated during the incident, despite the cold day. Her blouse was soaked back and front under the jumper.

'How are things back at the ranch?' she asked.

'There are one or two reasons for concern,' he said.

Gemma sensed his unwillingness to continue, fearful of the understated remark.

'What's wrong?' she asked, frightened.

'Look,' he said. 'I don't want to talk about it just now. Let it wait till you're feeling a bit stronger.'

'Mike, tell me. You're really frightening me. What's happened?' Has something happened to Kit, she wondered, to Will? Taxi? 'Has someone been hurt?' she asked, dreading his answer.

Her companion was concentrating on making the turn at the roundabout into Bondi Road and his tanned face frowned at the rear vision mirror, then at her, but he shook his head and she felt some relief.

'I feel bad telling you this now,' he said, 'knowing what you've just been through.'

'Tell me!' Gemma was shocked at the terror in her voice.

'Things aren't good back at work,' he finally said.

Gemma felt immediate relief. It must be problems with Louise, or a client. 'What's happened?' she asked.

'You know I did a full forensic on your hard disk,' he said after a pause.

'Yes,' she said. 'Like I asked you to. Go on.'

Mike negotiated a lane change before speaking. 'You've got a Trojan attack zombie in your system.' He looked at her to see if she knew what he was talking about.

Gemma stared back at him, angry and shocked.

'But what about my firewall and the virus shield?' she asked.

'I'm afraid this got through your defences,' he said. 'And it brought you a complimentary copy of Hydra7Slave as well.' The tone of Mike's voice again told her clearly that this complimentary copy was not something to treasure.

'*Shit*,' she said. 'What's that?' Now on top of everything, her computer was infected, possibly files lost, deleted or distorted.

'Hydra7Slave Trojan was downloaded by your machine from a free web page server as a single file,' he said.

'But that's impossible. I've never done that,' she said. 'I've never downloaded a web page server. And why would I download a Trojan?'

'You wouldn't have known you were doing it,' he said. 'You would have just opened an email attachment and this damn thing comes in like the midget Japanese submarine under the Manly ferry. You wouldn't even know it was there. Then if you went looking for it, you'd never find it because the minute it gets in, it breaks into two randomly named files and deletes its original file name.'

'God, Mike,' she said. 'How bad is it?'

He was turning past Wonderland Avenue approaching Phoenix Crescent and now Gemma dreaded arriving home. She wondered how long it would take to put everything back together again. She had backed up all her files but wished, too late, she'd been more assiduous with some of the other material in her hard drive. She pulled out another tissue and blew her nose, concentrating on what Mike was telling her. I just want to run away somewhere nice and safe, she thought to herself. She thought of the boatshed, of camping there and locking the door. I need a break. I don't want to deal with all this right now.

'I used a packet sniffer running on my machine adjacent to yours so I could keep yours under observation,' he said. 'The minute I turned it on, your machine immediately went into action. I didn't touch it.'

'What? *By itself?*' Gemma was incredulous.

'It knew to connect with an ICR client.'

'Who?' she asked.

Mike shook his head. 'Some International Chat Relay,' he said. 'I couldn't keep up with the speed of the damn thing.'

'But how does that affect my computer?' she said.

'It joined a special Hydra7 ICR chat server where it posted everything,' Mike said.

Gemma's voice was barely a whisper as she tried to comprehend the full impact of this information. 'Does this mean I've lost everything?' she whispered.

They had pulled up outside her place. Along the horizon, a low white ship piled high with containers slid out of sight. In spite of everything, Gemma was aware of one of her favourite songs on the radio. '*Total eclipse of the heart,*' wailed the singer reflecting Gemma's mood. A cold wind blew through the window. Mike's silence alarmed her more than anything he'd said so far. She'd copied a lot of her records onto more permanent files but not all of them. What if the floppies had deteriorated? She imagined the horror of losing sensitive and irreplaceable records. It was unthinkable. All her work of the last seven years, contacts, associations. All possibly beyond retrieval.

Mike pulled the handbrake on and turned to face her. 'I'm afraid it's much worse than that,' he said. 'The minute you switch it on, the damn thing phones home to the zombie master. It tells him all your necessary connection details. Then it reports on you. Every keystroke you make. It's just the same as if a hacker was standing behind you, copying everything you do.'

Gemma turned to him in horror. 'Someone, somewhere,' Mike continued, 'has complete control over your computer, your entire file system and access. Someone now knows as much as you do about your business.'

She shook her head in disbelief, incomprehension.

'*Everything* is posted out there,' Mike said. 'Everything anyone would need to know about your files. All publicly available.'

Gemma stared at the horizon. Someone had got into her most confidential files, sensitive reports, methods of subterfuge. Someone now knew everything about her business—the names of all her clients, the results of all the surveillance work she'd ever done. Her whole system was burned wide open. She put a hand over her mouth as if to block a silent scream, hardly aware of Mike's arm around her shoulder.

'But my password! No one could know that but me!'

Mike glanced away, then he turned to her again.

'It's out there for anyone now.'

Gemma sat like a block of stone.

'Your password is "Ratbag",' Mike said.

'My God,' she said. 'This is a nightmare.' She still couldn't move. Shock on shock. She felt numb, immobilised.

'I've closed it all down, Gemma,' he said. 'Chances are it's just a smart-arsed script kiddie of fifteen who'll lose interest now and it'll all just blow over.'

Slowly, she turned to look at his concerned features. She recalled the effort someone had gone to so that her system would be flooded with ugly email, the phone call that might have been a breather, the odd feeling she'd had in the boat-shed—that someone had been there. She shook her head, shivering as every instinct chilled her.

'This is no script kiddie,' she whispered.

She watched while Mike ran through her system again, making sure everything was as clean as possible before he closed it down completely. 'Don't use this machine,' he said, 'until I've gone right through it and checked what changes it might have made to the registry.' He looked more closely at her. 'Gemma, I think you should take the rest of the day off and look after yourself,' he said. 'You look terrible.'

She waved him away. 'We'll have to change everything,' she said. 'We'll have to start again.' She limped down to the door of her lounge area. '*I'll* have to start again.'

Mike had never been into her private domain before and he paused as she went through. Taxi fussed around her ankles and she kicked him aside, turning to Mike.

'Come in, Mike. Do you want a drink before you go?' She didn't feel she wanted to be alone just then.

'Yes,' he said. 'It's been quite a day.' He followed her down the hallway and walked around, looking at the view. 'I should only have something soft with my injuries. But what the hell.'

She had poured them both a Scotch and handed Mike's drink to him when the phone rang. She picked it up. She hardly had a chance to say a word.

'It's Jenny Porter here, Gemma. Risk analyst with Social Security.'

Gemma wondered why her erstwhile colleague was sounding so distant, so formal. 'Jenny,' she started to say, 'of course I know who you are.' Jenny would be able to advise her in this situation, but the tone of the voice at the other end of the line stopped her in her tracks.

'I just turned my printer on,' Jenny said, 'to do a few queued jobs. Imagine my horror when instead it started printing out the confidential records of a security business.'

Gemma felt herself sinking onto the arm of the lounge.

'*Your* business, Gemma.'

In the chilly silence between them, Gemma felt more of her world collapsing, sliding in great chunks into a bottomless ravine.

'Can you explain to me,' Jenny was saying, 'how such sensitive—*inappropriate,* I should say—material of yours happened to get itself into my system?'

'Jenny, I can't . . . I only just found out about it myself.'

'It is a shocking breach of security from your end, Gemma, and an appalling inconvenience to us. Our system is in complete meltdown. We can't get into our own files. I can't believe you could let this happen.'

'As soon as I've found out what's going on, I'll be straight on to it, Jenny. I can't tell you how sorry I am . . .'

'My 2IC,' Jenny continued, 'is telling me now that this is happening as we speak to other security operators. Your stuff is jamming everyone else in the business. We're going to have to close down our system while we make sure the hacker hasn't sent us anything worse that we don't know about.'

Gemma closed her eyes. Just when she thought Jenny had finished with her, her erstwhile colleague spoke again.

'You better find out who hates you enough to do this.' Then she put the phone down.

It was a long minute before Gemma spoke. 'That was Jenny Porter, the risk analyst at Social Security,' she said in a faint voice. 'Jenny was so impressed with the results my business was delivering, she was going to give me the contract for the department's out-sourced fraud investigations. All the work I'd ever need. Solid government contracts.'

Mike put his drink down, watching Gemma as she fell back onto her blue leather lounge chair.

'It would've meant a huge increase in business. I was looking to put you and Spinner in as manager and assistant manager, put on more road operatives. I would have been a rich woman by the time I was forty.' She looked at him.

'I take it you won't be getting the work now?'

Gemma slowly shook her head. 'That's the least of what Jenny just told me.' She put her drink to her lips but put it down again, sickened. She couldn't swallow anything at the moment, let alone alcohol. Her voice was almost a whisper. 'Mike, all the confidential details of every job we've—Mercator's—done, the surveillance operations, the identities of all the frauds we've caught, the names of their employers, our methods of surveillance, the unfaithful spouses—their names and addresses, who they did it with and how often—all my reports and everyone else's, problems and personal comments—every single detail started printing out on Jenny's printer when she switched it on a little while ago.' She took a gulp of Scotch. 'Jenny naturally was horrified. And as if that's not bad enough, she just told me that all my files have been sent to every serious operator in the security business.'

'You'll have to ring her again,' Mike said. 'And tell her that her system is being corrupted. You must warn her about the zombie.'

Gemma picked up the phone again and braced herself.

'Jenny,' she began as soon as the other answered, 'somewhere in your system you'll find a Trojan called Hydra7Slave,' she said. 'Get your technician to talk to mine.'

She put the phone down and realised not only her hand, but her whole body was shaking.

'Stay there,' said Mike, taking the glass from her as she tried to get up and putting it safely down. 'You look like you're going to fall over.'

'She said I should find out who hates me enough to do this.'

'That's a very personal interpretation,' he said. 'This sort of thing happens to lots of people in the world we live in.'

'Not like this,' she said. 'Not tailored like this to do me maximum harm. This isn't just a random cyberblitz. This is personal.'

Mike went to the sliding glass doors and his big figure blocked out the glare of gathering cumulonimbus towers.

'You know what this means,' she said. 'It means I'm finished as an investigator. And Mercator is finished as a business. It's the end of the line for me. And you and Spinner and Louise.' She tried to recall how much money she had left in the bank. Not much, she knew, after the refit and the upgrade of her business. Her investments weren't doing well. She had several thousand in available cash at the most, she calculated, maybe just enough to cover severance pay for her operatives. 'I'm busted. I'm finished.'

She sat at the dining table and Mike came over to join her. They sat in silence, listening to the roar of the sea.

'You know,' said Mike after a while, 'how I told you that I had the feeling I'd been set up? The night I was bashed?'

'And I found it hard to believe,' she said.

They stared at each other.

'I was bashed the same night,' she added. Did invisible filaments connect these two separate incidents?

'It makes sense now when I think that someone has known every move we make. All the time. Since God knows when,' he said. 'They *were* waiting for me.'

'So much for your script kiddie,' she said.

Another long silence and then Mike picked up her drink and handed it back to her. 'Come on. This is the last one you're having. I'll go up the street and get some take-away. You need to eat something, not drink. No wonder you passed out.'

Gemma hardly heard him. She stood up, the numbness gone, and felt the old anxious need to pace and move around. She opened and closed the sliding door to the timber deck, agitated, restless and filled with fear and anger.

'*Who is doing this to me?*' she said finally, echoing Minkie Montreau's desperate question. 'Who is trying to destroy me?'

Gemma went to her bedroom and pulled on her coat.

'I couldn't eat anything just now. I need a walk.' She grabbed a banana from the fruit bowl and peeled it, tossing the skin onto the counter.

Mike followed her up the hall then turned into the operatives' office while Gemma continued outside and up the steps to the road. On the other side of the street, an electrocuted flying fox, hanging by the spurs of its feet from two telegraph wires, swung stiffly. She put her head down into the southerly and walked past the beaches around the coast to Kit's place. Normally she'd enjoy the view, but today she barely noticed the build-up of clouds in the south-east and the ominous silver-black anvils sheared off by the fury of unseen wind forces thousands of feet above.

She could hear strains of music from the kitchen as she put her hand through the cut-out hole in the sturdy wooden door that sealed Kit's back garden. It wasn't padlocked so she was able to open the gate and go up to the kitchen door. Kit looked up from paperwork covering the kitchen table, and immediately stood up and came out, putting an arm around Gemma, drawing her close in a gentle embrace.

'Oh Kit,' said Gemma, 'I don't know what I'm going to do.'

Kit didn't say anything, just pulled another chair closer to the table, pushed her accounts out of the way and put the kettle on. In a few minutes over a fresh brew, Gemma told her sister what had happened. Kit listened without interrupting or asking questions. When Gemma had finished, her older sister poured herself another cup of tea.

'Everything's crashed,' Gemma said. 'My business. Everything that is important to me. And I'm worried about Steve and my own indiscretion there.'

They sat together in silence. Thank God Kit wasn't the sort of person who was worried by silence, Gemma thought, or felt she had to say cheery things. Although she could barely keep still, it was comforting sitting here, in the kitchen with its friendly herbs and cooking smells, listening to the wind and the sea. 'I don't know if I'd ever forgive myself if anything happened to Steve,' she said finally.

'Steve is a professional,' Kit reminded her. 'He's been trained for this sort of thing. It's not as if he's an amateur who's stumbled in over his head. He knows what to do even if things go wrong. He knows how to stay out of danger.'

'I don't think he ever factored in that I would be the one to endanger him,' Gemma said.

Kit gave a little shrug. 'Maybe not,' she said, 'but the result is the same. He'd have a back-up system. He'd have someone partnering him.'

'Ian Lovelock,' said Gemma.

'What's he like?'

Gemma shook her head. 'I don't know, Kit,' she said. 'I should have thought about what you said to me the other day. None of this might have happened. Instead, I just pushed it away. I didn't want to hear it. I didn't want to know about it.'

'What did I say?' asked Kit in surprise.

Gemma reminded her. 'You said I was compelled to act out and put myself into dangerous situations.'

'Like about ninety per cent of the human race,' said Kit, 'except they don't usually have the job you've chosen. They do it more quietly with stress or whisky and pills.' She noticed Gemma hadn't touched her tea. 'Speaking of which,' she said. 'Would you like something a little stronger?'

Gemma shook her head. 'I've already had a drink. I think I'd be sick if I had another.'

The two sisters sat at opposite sides of the table, not looking at each other.

'I'm sorry, Kit,' Gemma said.

'What for?' said her sister. 'Don't punish yourself. You haven't done anything bad.'

'But look what's happened. My business has been blown right open. And I've jeopardised a police operation that's been carefully put in place for God knows how long.'

Kit came around and stood behind her, giving her neck and shoulders a massage.

'Police operations crash for lots of reasons,' Kit said. 'Things go wrong. People make mistakes. It's

how things are. Don't waste energy blaming yourself or anyone else. You're going to need everything
you've got to deal with this crisis.' She gave
Gemma's shoulders a final squeeze and went to the
sink, rinsing her cup.

Gemma pushed herself out of her chair. 'I've
got to go,' she said. 'I've got to *do* something.'

'What?' her sister asked.

'I don't know.'

'Let's go for a walk,' said Kit. ' I'll walk part of
the way home with you.' She went to the fridge
and pulled out half of a lemon chiffon pie,
wrapped it up and put it in a bag. 'This is for you,'
said Kit. 'You need a bit of sweetness in your day.'

They went out together, back along the cliff path
that Gemma had just taken, while lightning flickered on the horizon. The storm was blowing up
from the south, and grey veils of rain fell from the
sky to the distant edge of the sea. The sisters
walked through the cemetery, past the stone angels
and Celtic crosses, the kneeling cherubs with their
heads knocked off.

'Gems,' said Kit as they climbed the hill towards
the main gates, 'if you can think of the sort of crisis
that you're going through now as a very important
part of your life, and not as some unrelated, alien
attack out of the blue, it mightn't feel so tough.'

'I don't understand what you're saying.'

'What's happening is part of your business, your
work. It's not a random event. And you have the
resources to deal with it.'

'But someone's attacking me, Kit. Deliberately

hacking into my system, then publishing all my confidential records to my competitors. That's not part of *my* life, that's part of someone else's malice.'

Kit took Gemma's arm and tucked hers around it. 'Your work has been a factor in other people's malice,' she said. 'This sort of stuff is sticky. For years now you've been working closely with those who perceive themselves as aggrieved, helping them track down the people they believe have betrayed them.'

'Are you saying that somehow I've asked for this?' Gemma looked at her sister in disbelief.

Kit shook her head. 'Not at all. No one asks for this sort of thing. But it's an inevitable part of life. My life, your life, anyone's life. Because now in turn, you've become the "enemy" for someone else. Can you hear what I'm saying?'

Once, Gemma thought to herself, I would have just stormed away in exasperation from this sort of conversation with Kit. Instead, she stopped walking and turned round, reflecting on Kit's words. She surveyed the graves as they sloped down to the sea, the elaborate miniature temples, wreaths of stone roses, hearts of marble and pious female figures, their graceful hands draped over an anchor, a star on their forehead, representing the Victorian iconography of death.

'You're part of a malice circuit,' Kit went on. 'It's not a matter of blame or fault. You're part of a set-up that makes the world go round.'

'I thought love made the world go round,' Gemma said bitterly.

'Whatever gave you that impression?' Kit said.

Gemma leaned against the railings considering, watching a falcon stall above the cliffs ahead of them, its body motionless between its wings, hooked profile glancing from side to side, occasionally altering the trim of its rudder feathers.

'I want to get out of the world then,' she said. 'I don't want this sort of thing happening again, or anything like it.' She covered her face with her hands then ran her fingers through her hair, pulling it back from her face, twisting it into a coil and pushing it down the back of her collar to keep the wind from whipping it round her cheeks. 'I didn't know things could go so horribly wrong,' she said. What else didn't she know about, she wondered, that might bring more public humiliation and private ruin?

'You've got to make a choice, Gems. Choose life, not despair. There's no situation so bad it can't be redeemed in some way. Get out on the street. Find out what's going on with Steve. Take action. You can come through this muddle.'

'Muddle?' said Gemma, angry at this minimisation. 'It's not a muddle, it's a fucking nightmare.'

'You have the resources to deal with it and come through it. You're a professional woman with a lot of experience and a lot of skill. You've been trained to deal with crises. You know how to stay cool in a dangerous situation. You've got what it takes to sort this business out. I know you have. And when you've thought about it, you'll remember that you have it, too.' Kit kissed her on the cheek. 'But more importantly, I know you and I know your inner strength.'

'I feel helpless and powerless,' said Gemma despairingly, 'not strong at all.'

'I remember you when you were a tiny thing,' said Kit, 'standing there, shaking in your tiny boots, but standing up to *him*. That's something I can never forget.'

Without realising it, they had come to the place of their mother's grave. Both of them paused, looking at the simple headstone giving their mother's name and her birth and death dates. The rose bush Kit had planted last spring had one shrivelled bud and grass had grown up around it. They stood a moment in silence, and Gemma thought about this woman whom she could barely remember who had died too young.

'Go back and talk to your staff,' said Kit, as they started walking again. 'Talk to Mike and Spinner, work out what you're going to do. Talk to Angie. You have powerful allies. Use them. You can either fall in a heap and pull the doona up over your head or you can find your way through this. It's your choice.'

Over the cliff, the falcon, in pursuit of invisible prey on the rocks, folded its wings and dropped from the sky.

Gemma strode back with the strong wind behind her bunting her along. Kit's right, she thought. I've got to find a way through this. *My* way. She was suddenly aware that her injured leg was behaving reasonably well and that apart from the slightest tenderness when she took up the weight of her stride, it was functioning almost as well as her right leg. The last few days, she thought, I've had no time to do anything. Except damage control. The fire investigation seemed light years away. And the job she was doing for the sex workers. Even Shelly's death seemed a distant tragedy, hidden by Gemma's fears for Steve. And for herself.

Mike was still at work when she got back, fielding phone calls.

'The phone hasn't stopped,' he said. 'I told them to ring back later. A couple of the insurance companies want to break their contracts. Reckon they've got legal grounds to do it.'

'Tell them we'll complete any outstanding action free of charge,' said Gemma. 'First things first. I'm going to contact Spinner and Louise and tell them everything that's happened. If they keep their records on tape or paper, I can transfer it later when everything's settled down again.' *When everything's settled down again,* Gemma echoed in her mind. When my business has been forgiven for an unforgivable security lapse, when the identity of whoever is doing all this is revealed, when Steve is safe in my arms again.

She called up Spinner and Louise, asking them to come in straightaway for an urgent briefing. She only gave them the barest details over the radio. Spinner's shocked voice brought her back to earth and Louise's softly spoken words of comfort came as a pleasant surprise. I don't know this woman at all, Gemma thought to herself. Then she made herself some toasted salmon sandwiches and ate a good slice of Kit's lemon pie, then drank a huge vanilla milkshake, sitting at her dining table, looking out at the sea, watching clouds building up along the horizon.

An hour later, the four of them sat in the operatives' office.

'In case you're not sure what's just happened,' Gemma said, 'someone did a mass email of this business's private records to every competitor in Sydney.' She amazed herself by saying the words without choking and paused while that sank in. 'Someone hacked into our system and our whole organisation is compromised. The only phone calls I've had today are from journalists or insurance companies who've contracted with us over the years. You won't be surprised to hear that all bets are off.'

'It's already in the news,' said Spinner. 'I checked after you called.'

He logged on to the office computer and soon had the newspaper on screen and printed off. He handed it to Gemma.

'*Security Unsecured,*' ran the sub-editor's line.

'The confidential records of one of Sydney's private security firms were faxed to competitors today in what has been described as one of the worst cases of electronic industrial espionage to date. A hacker penetrated the confidential records of Mercator Security and Business Advisers, a well-known and, until today, well-respected Sydney-based security firm run by ex-cop Gemma Lincoln, specialising mainly in insurance fraud. Other areas of Mercator's business include spousal infidelity. The names and addresses of people targeted by the firm for fraud and other investigations of a sensitive nature were made public by the wide exposure.'

There was more, but Gemma couldn't bear to read on.

'There's a bit here in a box,' said Spinner, 'describing a job you did on some woman who was playing up. And how your own records reveal that you falsely gave her husband a negative report.'

Gemma closed her eyes. That wretched case would forever haunt her, surfacing like a rotting corpse to expose foul play.

'They've suppressed the names,' Spinner was saying, 'but I reckon there's enough detail for the parties involved to identify themselves.'

Gemma's heart sank even further. What if the aggrieved husband, now himself the victim of a

368 • GABRIELLE LORD

fraud, decided on some sort of civil action? He could take her to the cleaners, ruining her reputation for good. She thought of years in litigation, the destruction of relationships, friendships, her privacy. And what would the licensing board have had to say about someone taking a fee from a client and then lying about the services rendered?

Spinner was trying to be stern, but she could see his deep concern for her. 'It's a terrible mess,' he said.

Louise sat there, biting the nail on her little finger and Gemma noted for the first time what tiny hands she had, with stumpy, short fingers, almost like a baby's. Mike looked over her shoulder, reading more of the report from the screen.

'I'm going to have to lay you all off,' she said. 'There'll be no work after this. I don't know what I'm going to do. I'm so sorry. You're all good workers. You'll have no trouble finding employment and you can count on me giving you very good references. Not,' she added bitterly, 'that a reference from me will carry much weight anymore.'

'But do you think anyone will want us after this?' Louise's babyish voice was tinged with misery. 'We're stuck in this shit, too.'

She stood up and went to the door, watched in silence by Spinner and Mike. She seemed stunned, Gemma thought, noticing how remarkably thin Louise was. Had she always been like that and Gemma just hadn't noticed?

'It's all gone wrong,' said Louise. 'Terribly, terribly wrong.'

Gemma could only agree in silence. Louise left and Spinner walked to the window.

'I'm not going anywhere,' he said, a frown turning his wrinkled little jockey's face into a leprechaun's. 'What else can I do? I'm unemployable in any other area. Give me something to do. You're still my boss as far as I'm concerned.'

'Look through the outstandings and take your pick,' she said, feeling a little comforted.

'What about this one?' he said, picking up the Minkie Montreau folder.

Gemma shook her head. 'No,' she said, taking the folder from him. 'I have to tell her I'm handing the evidence I've collected against her over to the cops. Then she can pay me. As far as I'm concerned, that case is closed.'

'Get her cheque first,' warned Spinner, '*then* tell her what you have to do.'

Gemma turned to Mike. 'What do you want to do?' she asked.

He didn't answer immediately, but sat fiddling with the corner of the elastoplast over his eye. Finally, he got to his feet, picked up his jacket and pushed his chair in under the desk.

'I'm thinking about it,' he said. 'I'll call you later.'

•

This is my last visit to Minkie Montreau, Gemma thought as she drove towards the Vaucluse mansion. If I ever see her again, it will be when I'm in the witness box, being cross-examined during her trial. She thought back to when the case first came to her attention. It seemed ages ago now that Steve had come round with the wretched Scorpio charm around his neck, smelling like a stranger. Now, with her world lying in shards around her, she found some comfort in just doing the job she knew so well, tying up the ends, presenting her account. God knows how long it might be before she got another cheque. I have no idea how I'm going to survive this business, she thought. Maybe it will be just Spinner and me again, like the old days, until the scandal dies down and people forget. I'll create a new business, let the work slowly build up again. It didn't seem fair to have to start all over again at her age, but she knew the alternative was to collapse into aggrieved victimhood.

The sight of the familiar canary-yellow BMW parked in Queen Street diverted her thoughts immediately. On full alert now, Gemma looked around for a place to pull over. I should just go straight past, she thought, go on to Vaucluse and stick my account and report in her mailbox. It doesn't matter any more, the case is finished. But a rare parking spot alongside Zigolini's tempted her more than her curiosity could bear. She swung into it, copping the admonishing angry horn of the driver immediately behind her, who'd had to use his brakes. She switched off the ignition and waited.

It wasn't long before she saw Anthony Love in a brown velvet jacket, his hair tied back in a romantic ponytail, help Minkie Montreau, spick and span in a crisp charcoal pantsuit, both laden with shopping, climb into the BMW. Gemma followed them home, parking on the high side of the street some way off. From here she had a good view of the house. Through the lacy iron gates, Gemma noticed a lot of giggling as the two lovers unloaded the car unpacking what looked like gourmet delicatessen treats and wine, Gemma thought, from the clinking of bottles. A baguette stuck out of a paper bag and Anthony Love angled the shopping bags he was carrying so that from Minkie's point of view, it looked as if he were sporting a huge, crusty erection. Minkie's features were creased with laughter. It was hard to imagine her as a ruthless murderer.

Gemma waited while they went inside. And she waited a little longer. Then she climbed out, taking her briefcase and camera. Silently, she opened the gate and walked up the path through the formal wintering gardens, but this time, instead of pressing the doorbell, she crept around the building, tip-toeing along the sandstone flagging of the low verandah that surrounded the house. She had a pretty accurate idea where Minkie's private sitting room lay, and she thought that would be the first place Minkie would take her lover, once they'd prepared their feast. As she circumnavigated the house, careful to make no sound, she saw the harbour ahead of her, the sea a deep winter navy, and the small craft going about their business. She continued creeping towards the back of the house, hoping her actions were obscured from people passing on the road by the lush growth of the flowering japonicas, pink, white and mauve, that edged the verandah. As she neared the windows of Minkie's private sitting room, she could hear the sound of voices and the occasional burst of laughter.

Gemma drew her camera out of the briefcase, silently switching it on, making sure it was ready. Why am I doing this? she asked herself. Insurance? She wasn't entirely sure, but she had an idea that a video of these lovers together could one day provide her with some sort of bargaining power. She waited until things became quiet and then went right up to the barred window. The rich fabric of the two curtains didn't quite meet in the centre of the window, and the lace under-curtain was very fine, allowing a narrow view into the cosy room. Gemma poked the camera towards the glass and checked in the viewfinder. Oh boy, she thought. What a picture! On a beautiful pale blue rug in front of the open fire, two bodies writhed. The tables around them were loaded with smoked salmon, cheeses, the broken baguette, a silver bowl of impossibly perfect fruit and two glasses of wine. But the couple on the floor were satisfying other appetites.

She stepped back, looking round, again checking that her own activities were not being seen by neighbours. This is the Benjamin Glass arson case swan-song footage, she announced to herself. I'll make Madam Minkie a copy of this and she can perhaps find some comfort in it in her prison cell. Again, she pressed the video camera silently against

the glass, checking the viewfinder, selecting the best
focus before starting to shoot. It was always expe-
dient to keep the exposure the same, so that later
it would be impossible to tell from the film how
close she had been, in case issues of trespass were
ever raised later in court. She studied the picture
in the digital viewfinder: the lace curtain gave the
image a misty, arty look complemented by the walls
of the sitting room which were covered with paintings and beautifully coloured hangings. Ignoring
the art display, Gemma started recording, focusing
on what was happening on the floor in front of the
fire. Despite the hazy quality, it was very clear that
one of the parties mutually engaged in heavy pet-
ting was a partly undressed Minkie Montreau. Her
jacket and silk blouse lay discarded on the rug, her
slacks were round her ankles, revealing shapely
white legs and as she lifted her head to kiss her
lover, Gemma's camera caught her flushed,
smeared features in full. Then it was eclipsed by
her partner's bowed head. His hair seemed much
longer than Gemma had previously thought,
spreading across his narrow shoulders, like a
woman's. His wide rump was clearly visible and
although Gemma puzzled over its unusually effem-
inate contours, it wasn't until the pair disengaged
somewhat from their mutual caresses, that she
became aware of two extraordinary things: first,
that both the bodies involved in this coupling
were female, and secondly, that the other party,

whose face, ecstatic from the attentions of Minkie Montreau, was now turned partly towards Gemma, was none other than Mrs Patricia Greengate.

SIXTEEN

Gemma stared, first at the viewfinder, then through the curtains to the real thing. What had happened to Anthony Love? Slowly she lowered the camera while she peered at the clothes spread out around the couple on the floor. There was the brown velvet jacket, the man's trousers, shirt and black shoes. The couple were now laughingly feeding each other, playfully making a smorgasbord of each others bodies: brie was spread on breasts and licked off, wine was drunk, slices of smoked salmon were draped erotically across thighs and neck. She turned away. She didn't know whether to storm the front door in a fury or burst out laughing. All Minkie's caginess and blushing around the topic of 'Anthony Love' suddenly fell into place. 'But he's an artist!' she'd said. Indeed, thought Gemma. Patricia Greengate's greatest piece of art had been herself, or rather, himself. As in all other worlds, Gemma thought, it's more profitable to be a man.

Gemma leaned against the wall, incredulous to

think how she had been duped. Yet it all fitted neatly together when she thought back on it. 'I found her washing some clothes,' the gaunt Peter Greengate had said of his suspicions. '*Men's clothes.*' And of course the exotic, shawl-trailing figure she'd been following at Bondi had transformed itself into a stocky man carrying an airline bag. None of this, however, exonerated the unwitting woman sporting with her girlfriend a wall-width away from murder. Had Benjamin Glass found out about his wife's affair? Was Minkie, who'd showed her disdain for the conventional in some areas, squeamish about a lesbian romance becoming public knowledge? Gemma stowed the camera, and, after hesitating near the front door, walked back to the car. Minkie Montreau was no longer her business. Now, she had to face the tangled mess of her own life instead.

She sat in the car, looking at the beautiful house. Nothing was as it seemed. Minkie Montreau had done it again. Why on earth did she employ me in the first place? Gemma asked herself. The woman was an enigma. I'm surrounded by complex and possibly dangerous women, she thought, recalling her visit to the compulsive and crazy Skanda Bergen, her kidnapping by jealous Lorraine Litchfield. She recalled the photos on top of the cabinet in Skanda's spotless apartment. And as she did, her mind made a connection.

Her mobile rang. It was Dr Heather Pike.

'I must be mad,' she said, 'to even consider

doing this. I've got that Naltrexone implant you wanted.'

They made an appointment time and Gemma drove back to Phoenix Crescent. There was no way, she decided, she would ever show this video to Peter Greengate.

Spinner was the only person in the office when Gemma got back and while she prepared the video, she told him the story of what she'd witnessed at Minkie's place.

'Just goes to show,' said Spinner 'how we can't ever assume anything in our game.'

'Spinner,' she said, 'tell me something. Why would a person kill someone with carbon monoxide and then use an HTA to burn the place down, especially if by using the HTA they knew they'd be drawing attention to themselves in a very dangerous way?'

'Aren't there more important questions you should be answering right now?' Spinner asked.

'So answer me this instead,' she said. 'Why would Lorraine Litchfield be in a family shot with Skanda Bergen?'

'In a box of photos?' Spinner asked.'Or on display?'

'Right on top of the shelf,' she said. 'With all the other icons.'

Spinner stared at her. 'You know the answer to that one yourself.'

She did. 'It indicates that Skanda and Lorraine

have a relationship that is very important to Skanda,' she said. 'A relationship that she wants to display.'

'That would certainly be similar to the conclusion I'd come to,' said Spinner in his cautious way. 'If there's a photo of the two of them on show.'

'I want to pay her a visit and ask her a few more questions,' said Gemma.

'I'll go with you,' Spinner said. 'Can't have you going by yourself to that place.' Then he went a little too far. 'Why don't you come with me to church tonight? We can pray over you.'

'You can pray for me when I'm dead, Bede,' she said, warning him off by the rare use of his real name. 'And I'm not dead yet.'

Her phone rang and it was Angie.

'I've just heard the bad news,' she said. 'You and your business going very public. Mr Right was squawking about it to the whole floor. Gemster girl, what happened?'

Gemma gave her friend as brief an account as she could bear. Angie listened in sympathetic silence.

'I just want you to know,' she said when Gemma had finished speaking, 'that *I* know what it feels like to have your whole world shattered.'

Gemma recalled the time when Angie was suspended. 'But Angie, Mercator is finished. *I'm* finished,' she said, tears stinging the backs of her eyes.

'You can go down with the ship and accept that the end has come,' her friend said. 'Or you can remember that you're a professional. And have a look at the fact that someone has set out deliberately to sabotage you. Are you just going to collapse and let an arsehole like that win? There'll be a bit of gossip and scandal about this for a while. Then it'll blow over. Things like this always do. And meanwhile you can track down whoever it is that's set out to bring you down. If this had happened to another operator and they came to you about it, what would *you* do?'

'I'd tell them we'd investigate for them,' she said. 'I'd ask them for a list of people they thought might do something like this to them. Then I'd start asking around.'

'Okay,' said Angie. 'Then that's what you're going to do. I've never liked the name '"Mercator Security and Business Advisers'" anyway. You could come up with a brand new business name, something flash and keen. Something like '"Angelface Solutions".'

Despite everything, Gemma smiled. 'And my other worry is Steve,' she said. 'I'm scared he's gone in too far, one way or another.'

'What would you tell someone else who came to you saying they thought their boyfriend was in trouble with a major crim?'

Angie was right. So was Kit. She had two good women saying almost the same thing to her in their different ways. 'Angie,' she said. 'About that Glock.'

'Hush your mouth, Gorgeous. I'll call you back

on an outside line.' Angie rang off and Gemma put the phone down.

'I was hoping that would be Steve,' said Spinner, indicating the phone.

She shook her head. 'I wish he would ring.' She considered. 'Spinner, I *have* to do something. Have things in place so that if Steve's in big strife he's got more than just departmental rules to fall back on. I want us to be there.'

They both looked up as Mike came into the room. 'Have you decided already what you want to do?' she asked.

'I want to stay and work here. I reckon we can ride this out. I want to be involved in anything going down.'

'I'm not even sure what to do,' said Gemma. 'I've never been in this situation before. My business is destroyed and my boyfriend is involved in a dangerous undercover operation'—she paused, reluctant to continue—'which I may well have compromised.'

'I'll need to know a few things,' Mike said, 'if you want me to help.'

'Why would you want to?' Gemma asked. 'There's nothing in it for you. What are you going to live on? If you had any sense you'd be out looking for a job.'

'I like seeing the good guys win,' Mike said.

Gemma thought about it. She did need Mike, it was true. 'I don't like the feeling of owing anyone,' she said reluctantly.

'You don't have to,' he said. 'Pay me the usual rates.'

'I may not have the money.'

'Borrow it,' he said.

She remained indecisive.

'You'll have to trust me,' he said.

'I suppose I will,' she agreed. It wasn't very gracious, but it was the truth. There wasn't time for the niceties.

'You'd better tell me what you know about Steve's operation, then,' said Mike.

'What if you're working for George Fayed?' she said, only half-joking.

'I'm not. Now tell me what you know.'

'Terry Litchfield's widow believes George Fayed had her husband murdered. She's working with the police to expose him. I believe Steve's been introduced to Fayed as an interstate buyer with a lot of money and someone who has a lot of influence over Lorraine.' She managed to say the name without stumbling. 'The set-up is that she wants a business merger with Fayed. That way, they combine two big crime businesses. So Steve is on the scene as an attractive potential investor, perhaps even partner, in Fayed's business. However,' she added, 'I have heard a rumour that Lorraine Litchfield paid someone to get rid of her husband.'

'Either way,' said Mike, 'Steve's in a tricky situation. How much do you know about Fayed?'

'He has an elaborate security system, both external and internal,' Gemma said, 'and he's paranoid about everyone and everything.'

'With good reason,' said Mike. 'Let's say the worst has happened,' he continued, 'and Fayed has exposed Steve.'

Gemma swallowed hard. Even imagining this was unbearable.

'That would play right into his paranoia. Fayed would be very, very rattled. He might do a couple of things.'

Gemma closed her eyes, knowing one of them.

'He might want to make Steve an offer he can't refuse and get him to work as a double agent,' said Mike.

'Steve might agree to that to save his life,' she said. 'But they'd never trust him. They'd always be on him and then they'd dump him when he was no longer useful to them. He'd be disgraced. Or worse,' she added, 'they could easily set something up. Make him an addict. Kill him.'

She recalled their last meeting and Steve's coldness. Maybe he had already agreed to work for them. Maybe Steve's partner, Ian Lovelock, already knew this. Maybe not. She remembered all too well how convincing Steve had been in his distaste as he compared her with Lorraine Litchfield. She nearly jumped out of her skin when the phone rang.

'Ring this number,' said Angie. 'Re the package we were discussing earlier.'

Gemma scribbled the phone number down. 'He's a registered dealer,' Angie added, 'but he does special orders for friends. It'll cost you, but.'

'Thanks, Ange.' Gemma rang off.

'Okay, Mike,' she said. 'I've got some business to do tomorrow morning. Then I'll call you.' She paused. 'And, Mike?'

He looked up.

'Thanks,' she said.

She worked till late, driving around, pulling in favours, cruising the streets of the Cross, asking about Fayed, and in some cases, Steve. Everything was quiet. No one knew of anything unusual. There was no street talk around, just the usual rehash of what she already knew, that Fayed wanted all the parlours, that he punished people with his 'French Connection'. None of her usual sources had anything to say. It felt ominous. Back at home she lay awake most of the night with Taxi heavy on her feet.

•

First thing in the morning, she rang the gun dealer and drove to a meeting with him, ringing Angie from his office. For five hundred dollars—a special deal because she was a friend of Angie's—Gemma bought a Glock 27. She paid for it in cash and, when she stowed it in the car, found she couldn't stop looking at the large black plastic box on the back seat.

Later in the morning, Angie helped her through the paperwork at the Firearms Registry. 'You'll need to do the Glock course at the range. Do it this morning,' Angie urged, 'so you can get out there and feel good.'

'I haven't got time to feel good,' said Gemma.

'I'm not letting you run loose with one of these without any training,' said Angie, 'and that's that. Do as you're told for once in your life.'

Angie drove them to a private range south of Sydney run by an ex-SAS friend.

'It's a beautiful weapon,' Angie said, as they drove. 'It's a slightly smaller edition than the police issue Glock 19. I know you're going to fall in love with it,' she added. 'It's chambered for the venerable 9 mm Parabellum cartridge, it's got heaps of stopping power. It's got good sights, it's safe, it has a very nice military matte finish. Just the thing for those sweaty situations a lass occasionally finds herself in. It has exactly the same fine qualities as its big brother. It's chopped and channelled nicely and it's a true pocket pistol. See? The safety engages automatically so you don't have to worry about a misfire. Just the accessory for the well-dressed investigator.'

She looked across at her friend. None of her technical talk had raised a bite. She tried another tack.

'Okay,' she said. 'I think you'd better tell Aunty Angie what's going on.'

'I did something really silly,' she said. 'I think I've compromised Steve's operation.'

'Shit,' said Angie. 'You'd better tell me.'

Gemma told her everything except the Lorraine

Litchfield beauty pageant and Steve's choice of queen.

Angie took a corner too fast and corrected the skid. 'Sorry about that,' she said. 'Hey Gems, you're really doing it tough just now.'

At the range Angie demonstrated operating and field-stripping and made Gemma do the same until she was reasonably proficient in her handling of the gun. Then they both put on safety goggles and ear muffs and it didn't take long for Gemma to start bonding with her Glock 27. As Angie had said, it was controllable, user-friendly and reliable, recoiling straight back. And it balanced and fitted nicely into the web of her firing hand. She liked the feeling of lightness, compared to the weightier .38.

'I'll need a shoulder holster,' said Gemma. 'Have you got one?'

'FBI carry, girl,' Angie said, 'that's what you need.' She pulled out her own Bianchi holster and rig and fitted Gemma with it so that the holster was snug against the small of her back, with the Glock's butt facing outwards.

'Okay,' Angie ordered. 'I'll show you how you do it from there. Let's do the Glock foxtrot. Drop your right hip a little. That's it. That opens your jacket coat if you're wearing one. Now hand to butt in one nice smooth movement. That's the way. Then a neat rotation on the axis of your wrist. Don't labour it. Just nice and easy. If you need to, you can shoot while you're still drawing it forward through the wrist rotation. With this weapon, you don't even have to hit a vital spot. Hit someone anywhere with one of those and the hydrostatic shock kills them stone motherless.'

Gemma practised the movement a few times without firing until the manoeuvre felt more comfortable. Then she shoved the gun back behind her in its holster. She suddenly covered her face with her hands.

'What is it?' Angie said.

'Angie,' she said, 'I haven't told you everything.' She felt shame reddening her neck and face but kept going. 'Lorraine Litchfield sent some brutes to pull me off the street, just like you'd pick up some little lowlife. Then she pulled out this bloody great Colt and she made Steve choose between her and me. At gunpoint. I felt sick!'

'Lorraine Litchfield is dead!' said Angie, grabbing her portable.

But Gemma put her hand out to block her. 'No, no,' she said, 'don't do that. I need to tread very carefully from now on. I've got to think of Steve. Pulling her in will only make Fayed nervous.'

She dropped her hip and practised the draw one more time, freezing with the weapon in the firing position. Here I am, she thought, ready to fire, but at what? At whom? In the dark interior of the shooting range, her sense of seeing and hearing distorted by the goggles and the ear muffs, the difficult situations of her life seemed more distant.

'Someone hates me,' she said as she turned around to Angie, removing the protective gear. 'I know that attack on Mercator was personal. That means malice. That means I must know the person who sabotaged my records.'

'Love the way you get there, honey,' said Angie. 'Could it be someone who feels wronged?' she suggested. 'Someone feels wronged by your business?'

She started to repack the weapon, then stopped. 'You should be doing this,' she said, passing the Glock and case over to her friend.

On the drive back to the city Angie turned to her.

'Is there anything I can do?'

Gemma shook her head. 'Not right now, Ange,' she said. 'But switch your stand-by light on, will you?'

Angie patted Gemma's knee.

'Gemster girl. You know it's always on for you.'

Heather made a tiny incision under local anaesthetic.

'You're not pregnant, are you?' she asked.

Gemma shook her head. Heather pushed the Naltrexone implant into place on Gemma's good flank, closing the incision with a couple of stitches. She straightened up.

'There,' she said. 'That should cover you for several days. It's a slow-release design and will counteract the effects of any heroin introduced into your system. You might find you'll get a reaction to it, though.'

'Like what?' Gemma asked, pulling her clothes back on.

Heather shook her head. 'You tell me,' she said, 'if you start noticing anything. I've found people start manufacturing side effects to order if I describe them.'

Gemma started to rebutton her blouse but Heather pushed her hand aside gently, checking the bruising on her other ribs.

'That bruising is a long while going,' she observed.

'And the bastard who did it is still out there,' said Gemma. 'But I've got other things on my mind just at the moment.'

'You might get a bit of local irritation around the implant site over the next couple of days,' said Heather. 'Then it should settle down.'

Her gloved fingers tracked Gemma's damaged lower rib.

'You're a doll, Heather,' she said.

'More like a dill,' said her friend.

'I owe you one.'

'I'll remember that.'

•

Now, she and Spinner sat outside Skanda Bergen's apartment block. The Naltrexone implant was behaving itself, and apart from some topical soreness, unless she leaned against it, she forgot it was there. She wondered if the strange spacey feeling she had and the slight headache around her eyes were something to do with the drug's side effects, or whether these symptoms were simply the result of stress. '*Someone feels wronged by your business,*' Angie had said.

'Spinner,' she asked, 'can you think of anyone we've really offended? I'm talking about someone who might have a personal grudge.'

Spinner's shrewd little monkey eyes widened. '*Some*one who might have a grudge?' he repeated. 'You're joking! Just about every lying cheating bastard that we spring would have a grudge against us. You know what they're like. It's not *their* behaviour that lands them trouble, oh no. They never see it like that. *We're* the bad guys because we record their dishonesty. You're asking me about *some*one, shouldn't you be looking at *everyone*?'

A silence filled the front of the Holden and she knew that Spinner was struggling to say something. They'd been on too many jobs together over the years for her not to know this particular silence.

'Spit it out, Spinner,' she said.

He darted a nervous sideways glance at her. 'This is hard for me to say,' he started.

'Go on,' she encouraged, rearranging the contents of her briefcase so that everything fitted neatly and her camera and mobile were within easy reach.

'Haven't you ever asked yourself,' Spinner enquired 'how come Mike Moody gets those injuries to his face the same night you kick some guy's head in?'

Gemma looked away and out the window to where a pair of Indian mynah birds sat on a bare tree.

390 • GABRIELLE LORD

'Tell me you've never wondered whether that bloke you kneed in the face that night was Mike.'

The silence grew, broken only by a hoon roaring past on a motorcycle.

'That's a question I've been trying not to ask too seriously for a while now,' she finally said.

One of the mynahs squirted a nasty mess onto the footpath.

'Why the hell not?' said Spinner. 'That's not like you.' He paused. 'Remember that the truth shall set you free,' he added.

'Not in my position it won't,' Gemma snapped. 'Not if I start suspecting my own staff.'

'Boss,' he said, 'it's way past the time you should start suspecting your own staff.'

She turned to him, gaunt little Bede McNamara, with his wrinkled face, grown too heavy for the gallopers, and now a rider of the highways with his laptop and his binos and his precision in reporting and connecting things.

'Spinner, I wish you hadn't said that,' Gemma said after a silence. 'I took a bloodstained handkerchief from his place,' she admitted, 'when I visited him. It was simply to eliminate him.'

'Or not,' said Spinner. 'When will you get a result?'

Gemma shrugged. 'We'll know soon enough,' she said.

Spinner picked up her mobile from where it lay, on top of her briefcase.

'I had to bring it up,' said Spinner. 'It's been worrying me stupid for days. What with all the other things that have been going down in our little camp ever since he started with us.'

'He said he was mixed up in a brawl that night. Dragged out of his vehicle and beaten up outside the Hellfire Club on the Belinda Swann follow.'

'So he says,' said Spinner.

Have I made such a mess of things, Gemma was thinking, that I bring a traitor into my own camp?

'Right now,' said Spinner mercifully interrupting her thoughts, 'I need to concentrate on first things first.'

He was busy with a scanner and her mobile and some arcane program on his laptop. 'What I'm doing is tuning into your mobile's frequency,' he explained. 'Mike's not the only one who can do this sort of stuff.'

Gemma stared. Was Spinner resentful of Mike?

'Then,' Spinner was saying, 'if you can get her to talk to Lorraine Litchfield, offer her your phone.' He handed it back to her. 'Mobile phones broadcast over airwaves just like radios,' he said. 'I'll pick up any conversation on your phone and record it. She might say something useful. Something we can use at a later date.'

Gemma took the phone from him, put it in her briefcase and got down from the truck. She walked up to the front door of the building thinking about the intimate photo of Skanda and Lorraine laughing together. Gemma leaned on the button. But there was nobody home. Or at least no one was answering. Maybe Skanda is working, Gemma thought, in her spotless, oversprayed, overpol-

392 • GABRIELLE LORD

ished, overdusted bedroom wearing nothing but her black lace gloves and a man.

Gemma wandered back down the path, irritated at this hold-up. She wanted to grab Skanda Bergen and shake her, force her to use her connection with Lorraine Litchfield to get closer to Steve.

'What's up?' Spinner called from the Holden.

'She's not answering,' Gemma called back. She walked round and climbed back into the front seat. Nothing was going her way, she thought. She felt frustrated and angry. And Spinner's words about Mike Moody wouldn't leave her alone. She was just about to tell Spinner to start the truck and leave, when the front door of the apartment block opened, and a well-dressed middle-aged man walked out. Something about his hunched, gaunt figure made Gemma look twice. Within seconds, she had jumped down from the Rodeo and was running after him.

'Mr Greengate!' she called after him. 'It's me, Gemma Lincoln.'

Peter Greengate turned and baulked when he saw who was calling him. She thought of the potentially explosive video footage she had back at the office with his wife as one of the stars, an R-rated piece of tape that would blow apart his perceptions of the woman he had married—if she gave it to him. Gemma remembered the weird way he'd stood on her doorstep, staring at the closed door, how she thought she'd seen hatred in his eyes. 'Could I have a word with you, Mr Greengate?' she said.

He stood in the street, embarrassed and angry, poised for flight. Gemma too, waited awkwardly, marshalling her thoughts, picking her words carefully before speaking to him. She needed to tell him that her business had been completely compromised, and that she would not be able to furnish him with the information she'd contracted to provide. But before she could begin, Peter Greengate stepped backwards, moving further away from her. That's odd, Gemma thought. He's frightened.

'It's not what it looks like,' he was saying. 'I didn't do anything with that woman.'

Gemma was astonished. Did Peter Greengate think that because she was a PI she had some sort of X-ray vision? Or that she knew everything that went on in the area?

'Mr Greengate,' she said, 'I couldn't give two hoots what you've been up to. I simply want to let you know—'

'She's got some sort of disease,' he interrupted. 'It might be contagious.'

He obviously wasn't listening to her but Gemma pressed on. This was one less phone call she'd have to make over the next few days.

'I can't do that job for you,' she said. 'We'll sort out the money.'

'It was a proper referral,' he said. 'Through the Chester Clinic.'

'Do you understand?' Gemma said. 'I can't do the work you wanted.'

'What?' he said.

394 • GABRIELLE LORD

She realised he hadn't heard a word she'd been saying.

Then he suddenly turned and hunched down even further, hurrying away. She felt like laughing out loud. Foolish man, she thought. He thinks I've sprung him buying sex and losing the moral high ground regarding his wife. She watched him get into a car and drive away, then she waved at Spinner and hurried back to the intercom which she pressed again. This time, Skanda's voice answered.

'Yes?'

'Gemma Lincoln, Ms Bergen.'

'Fuck *off!*' There was a click as the woman hung up the intercom connection.

Gemma pressed the intercom again. 'Ms Bergen,' she said, 'I still haven't mentioned your name to the authorities. If you don't let me in now, I'm driving straight to the Sydney Police Centre and handing over your name and details to the officer in charge of the Benjamin Glass murder investigation.'

There was a long pause. Finally, the front door lock clicked and Gemma pushed through. She hurried up the stairs to Skanda's apartment and knocked on the door. It was opened and Gemma walked straight in.

'Lorraine Litchfield,' Gemma said, as she entered and turned, noticing how frightened Skanda looked. 'I want you to tell me how you know Lorraine.'

The place was smelling of bleach and disinfectants, and already Skanda had the vacuum cleaner out. She's a total loony, Gemma thought, looking around at the insane neatness of the place, its clinical sterility. Obsessive compulsive disorder, she remembered from a conversation with Kit. Skanda pulled disposable gloves off and went back into the bedroom. Gemma saw she'd already stripped the bed and then became aware of the churning sound of a washing machine somewhere out of sight. I'd hate to have her laundry bill, Gemma thought, if she changes the bed after every mug.

'Tell me about you and Lorraine,' repeated Gemma. 'Or I go straight to the detectives in Homicide.'

She watched the woman's pretty face. Gemma thought she could see a whole range of contingency plans move through her mind. It must be hard being a liar, she thought, trying to work out which falsehood will serve best, not ever being sure when you'll bring yourself undone by using the wrong one.

'Then you'll become a suspect,' she went on, 'and you'll be questioned closely. Your life will be exposed to the press. You'll be hauled over the coals. I don't have to tell you what that might be like for someone in your position. All that "discretion assured" nonsense you've promised your mugs will be shot to bits. No one will come anywhere near you again. You'll be out on the streets with the other girls who have no alternative. So tell me about Lorraine.'

Once Gemma would never had made such a threat, too concerned for her licence. But life, she

396 • GABRIELLE LORD

realised, creates situations that have no precedents and we have to do what we can. I won't have a licence by the end of the week anyway, she thought. This idea toughened her up even further.

'I'm running out of time, Skanda,' she said. 'Tell me everything you know about Lorraine or I'll tell everything I know about you.' She paused to let that sink in. 'What's it to be?'

Skanda Bergen's struggle still showed in her face and Gemma imagined she could almost pick up the electrical charge coming from the woman's anxiety.

'How do you come to know her?'

'How do you think?' snarled Skanda, her expression pinched with unwillingness. 'She was a worker too.'

She moved a couple of pornographic magazines and wiped the surface of the low table. Gemma could feel her anger at being forced to talk.

'And then she went and married Terry Litchfield,' Gemma prompted. 'And now she's a rich widow.'

Skanda stared at her. 'If you know so much, what do you want from me?' she asked.

She turned to the kitchen annexe where she went to a cupboard and pulled on another pair of disposable gloves. Gemma wondered if there was a proper name for a glovaphiliac.

'A friend of mine is a friend of hers,' said Gemma. 'I want to find out if he's all right. And where he might be.'

'How would I know?' said Skanda, and there was a cocky insolence in her voice that Gemma hadn't heard anyone use since about third class at school.

She moved nearer to Skanda, noticing the tiny flecks of skin around her nose and cheeks flaking from the sharkskin surface.

'Listen to me, bitch,' she whispered, using one of Angie's techniques. 'You find out everything you can about a man called Steve Brannigan, friend of your girlfriend Lorraine. Otherwise, as well as giving you up to the cops who will be looking all over Sydney for you, I'll make sure my old colleagues in the job fit you up with anything that comes into my head. And then some. You'll be fat and forty before you get outside again. Got it?'

Skanda looked wildly round, almost throwing off sparks. 'But I hardly ever see Lorraine anymore!'

'You're about to change all that right now,' said Gemma, keeping up the pressure, pulling her mobile out of her pocket. 'And don't even think of disappearing. I'll be watching you like a hawk. I've got operatives all over Sydney. Stalking people is my job. I'm a professional. Okay?' She thrust her mobile at her. 'Use this. Now, ring her.'

'What, *now*?'

'Now.'

Gemma waited while Skanda reluctantly took the mobile from her and dialled a number, looking up at Gemma from time to time. She waited for the other party to answer and turned away to speak.

'Hi, Lorraine,' she said, sweet as pie. 'It's

Skanda. Listen, honey, I'm in a bit of a fix. No, it's not money. I need to talk to you about somebody. Someone called Steve Brannigan.'

Skanda's startled face matched the way her body jumped at the response. Gemma could hear the high pitched yelling on the other end of the line, even though Skanda had moved away to the window for the call. Then it was only a few moments before Skanda thrust the mobile back to Gemma, a sly smirk on her face.

'Lorraine's not talking to anyone,' she said. 'About anything. She's flying out of Sydney.'

'What did she say?' asked Gemma.

Skanda turned away, triumphant. 'Lorraine is running for her life,' she crowed. 'And you can kiss whoever Steve is a big goodbye.'

Gemma wanted to hit her. But she restrained herself, trying to bring her shaking body under control. A sudden plop behind her made her spin around. A cat had jumped onto the windowsill from the roof outside. Skanda rushed at the animal and it vanished, to reappear in a higher position, near the roof ridge, but not before Gemma had noticed the distinctive harlequin pattern of its face.

'That cat,' Gemma said. 'I know that cat!'

'It's just a stray,' said Skanda. 'It's a pest, always trying to come in here.'

'It's not a stray at all,' said Gemma. 'I know whose cat that is!'

'Get out of my place!' Skanda yelled.

'Why have you got Benjamin Glass's cat?'

'I don't know what you're talking about! It's just some damn stupid stray.'

Skanda lifted a pile of lacy underwear, grabbing something that Gemma recognised only too well.

'Get out of my place now!' Skanda screamed.

'Okay, okay,' she said. 'I'm going.'

Skanda advanced, capsicum spray in front of her.

'Get out!' she screamed again. 'Get out of my apartment. Leave now!'

Gemma backed away. 'You're in deep shit, lady,' she yelled just before she turned and raced back downstairs. She saw Spinner look up at her sudden reappearance and he leaned across to open the door for her as she scrambled back inside.

'Spinner,' she said. 'Skanda has Benjamin Glass's cat!'

Spinner, who was still holding her mobile, looked at her wide-eyed. 'Whose cat?'

'The HTA case,' she explained. 'I've just spotted the missing cat.'

Skanda Bergen and Benjamin Glass's cat, she thought. All the connections were there, just as Sean had said. They'd just run underground where I couldn't see them, where I couldn't make sense of them.

'She just chased me out of her place with capsicum spray. I'm going to have to tell Sean Wright about her and the cat.'

That's two women I'm giving him, she thought, Skanda and Minkie.

'I got the conversation,' said Spinner. 'Wanna

hear it?' He played the recording he'd taken of the call Skanda had made to the widow. It was difficult to make out the words Lorraine Litchfield was screaming.

'I can't talk to anyone! I'm not here. Okay? All hell's broken loose. I can't talk now. Call me later.'

Spinner played it back a few times. 'She's shit scared,' he said.

'Of what? Of who? Fayed?'

Spinner shrugged. 'Anyone who brasses up Fayed has got to be in deep shit.'

Gemma thought for a moment. 'Fayed must have found out about the undercover job against him. Lorraine must have dobbed Steve in. But then Lorraine must have realised that her own position would also be compromised. It wouldn't take Fayed long to work out that the police operation couldn't have happened without Lorraine's assistance in setting it up.'

'She could play the injured innocent,' said Spinner. 'Pretend she's only just discovered—oh shock and horror—that her new boyfriend is an undercover cop. That's the only safe way to go.'

'Why didn't she see this coming?'

'We're making a huge assumption here,' she said. 'We don't know what's happening, really. Damn Skanda. I didn't get what I wanted.'

She felt her body tighten in frustration as Spinner gunned the motor.

'Come on,' he said. 'I'm taking you home.' He paused, his hand on the gear stick.

'Why does Skanda have that cat?' he asked.

'And why is she compulsive about cleaning?' she asked back. 'She's always wiping and spraying like something out of a '60s television ad.'

'Maybe it's cat hairs,' said Spinner. 'She's allergic to cat hairs.'

'She's allergic to something. I saw inside her fridge,' said Gemma. 'It's like a pharmacy in there.'

On the drive back to the office, Gemma went over and over the facts of the Benjamin Glass case in her mind. Now it seemed far more complicated than it had when she'd been prepared to hand over the evidence to Sean Wright and wash her hands of Minkie Montreau. Now Skanda Bergen was suddenly in the frame as well. But her mind kept returning to Steve's position. Had something happened to him? Is that why Lorraine Litchfield was panicked?

'I've got to make Steve my first priority,' she said. 'I can't think about anything else right now.'

'Think about Mike Moody,' Spinner said. 'Think about what I said.'

SEVENTEEN

Spinner dropped her home and she went straight to the bathroom for a shower, trying to wash off the day but she couldn't shake its problems. The complete destruction of her business almost eclipsed other concerns. Then there was Mike Moody, recently separated, angry with his wife, batching and making cakes. Could he have the necessary psychological profile for someone who attacks women? So many men, she knew, believed their estranged wives 'owed' them, believed they were guilty of something. Anything. That they needed punishing. Would this justify attacks on women? She recalled the cases she knew of violent men, their rage kept in check during the years they had the services of a wife or steady girlfriend, but who, when those services were lost, lashed out at other women, strangers to them. Was Mike one of those? Quite a few police officers turn out to be very nasty indeed, she knew.

She put on a new silky tracksuit and sneakers, and went into the operatives' office to the desk where Mike usually sat. It was unlikely that he'd leave anything incriminating here, she knew, but sometimes even master criminals slip up. I don't even know what I'm looking for, she thought, going through his drawers. They were neat and innocuous: files of the jobs he was working on, notes on Belinda Swann. The trouble is, Gemma realised, he's so far ahead of me in technical know-how that I could be looking straight at the proof of his guilt and not even recognise it. She pulled his large blue desk diary over and opened it, flicking through the days and months. Details of jobs she remembered, times, meetings. She was about to close the book and push it back into position, when a familiar phone number jumped out at her. She looked closer. It was Angie's. Why would Mike have Angie's number? she wondered. She frowned, then stared. Underneath that was George Fayed's name, spelled out large and clear, together with a mobile phone number. Gemma jumped to her feet. What's going on here? she thought. Why did one of her colleagues have the mobile phone number of a drug lord? She recalled that the external security gate was standing open and was on her way to get the key. She nearly jumped out of her skin when the desk phone rang. She came back to answer it.

'Ric Loader here, Gemma. I've got something for you. You're not going to like it.'

'What are you talking about?'

'That sample you gave me.'

Gemma remembered the bloodstained handkerchief taken from Mike's coat pocket.

'I ran it through Genotyper and we got a match. Two matches, actually.'

She remembered the bedroom, the ugly defaced poster, the woman's breast targeted and stabbed.

'What matches?'

'Whoever attacked Robyn Warburton and killed Shelly Glover is the same person.'

Her mind tried to put it all together as Rod continued.

'And we found the same profile on that handkerchief.'

Gemma's could hear nothing for a few seconds except the sound of her pounding heart. To Ric, the traces left on objects were simply the matrix from which to extract a profile. He had no knowledge of how or where the objects might be connected, let alone connected to Gemma herself. She recalled the fringed cowboy jacket in which she'd found Ric's sample; now she understood why she'd had the impressions of ribbons flying from her attacker.

'My God, Ric,' she said. *'He works for me.'* She thought of something. 'And probably George Fayed as well,' she added. My enemy has been here all the time, she thought.

She heard a sound outside and jumped back from Mike's desk.

'What!' Ric's shocked voice shrilled in her ear.

'His name's Mike Moody and he works for me!

His address is 646 Todman Avenue, Kensington.
For God's sake get to him fast!'

Another sound out the front and she wished
she'd locked the security door earlier.

'Someone's here!' she said. Her heart contracted
as she realised it could be Mike himself.

'Ric!' she said, her voice hoarse with urgency,
'call triple 0! Tell them a Signal One! Unit two,
number 8 Phoenix Crescent, Phoenix Bay!'

Ric started to say something. 'Just *do it*!' she
screamed, repeating her address, dropping the
phone.

She ran into her bedroom, unlocked her gun safe
and pulled the Glock out of its case. Fingers trembling, she loaded it and slipped it into her tracksuit
pocket. Its comforting weight pressed against her
thigh and she kept a hand in her pocket, ready to
pull it out in an instant. She peered into the hall.
Mike was coming in, opening the unlocked grille
door.

She ducked back behind the door that separated
her apartment from the two front rooms off the
hall. She could hear Mike moving around in the
operatives' room. Then she pressed back against
the door as he walked across the hall and into her
office. She crept through the door, sliding her feet
along the floor, slow and soft, until she came to
her office. She paused outside, then ducked her
head around the doorway. Mike suddenly turned
from where he sat in front of her computer and
caught her, peeping around the door.

'Gemma!' he said. 'You gave me a fright!'

406 • GABRIELLE LORD

He sat back in the chair, which he'd swivelled round in the first second of seeing her, relaxed and perfectly at ease.

She raised the Glock into the firing position, bracing herself near the doorway.

'On the floor!' she yelled. 'Now! *Get on the floor!*'

She saw his shocked face. He half-tried to stand up and she moved closer.

'You heard what I said! Get on the fucking floor! Ric Loader just rang. Your DNA was all over Robyn Warburton and Shelly! Do it now!'

Mike slid out of the chair and awkwardly knelt on the floor. 'Who? What are you talking about?'

'Right down! Down!'

Mike opened his hands, pleading.

'Gemma, I don't know what you're talking about. I don't know why you're doing this!'

She moved into the room. 'Get down. On your stomach,' she yelled as he dropped to all fours.

'It was you all the time! Get down!'

Keeping the gun trained on him, she moved in closer, willing her ears to hear the wail of sirens, praying that car after car was speeding towards Phoenix Bay.

'I don't believe this,' he said. 'You can't be serious! This is crazy.'

He made as if to stand up.

'Don't move!' she screamed. 'The cops will be here any moment. Just stay where you are.'

She saw him look up at the Glock, only a metre

away from his face, and duck his head again. 'Tell me what's going on, for Chrissakes,' he said.

'I should have realised it was you. You're in touch with George Fayed. I found his number in your diary. You're working for him. You're being taken to the cleaners by your ex-wife. You hate women,' she said. 'You want to punish them, so you attack street girls, not only for pleasure, but because your filthy boss pays you for it! You killed Shelly. I saw that ugly poster in your bedroom.'

'This is totally insane,' he said, his voice muffled, from the floor. 'I don't know where to start. I've got nothing to do with any attack on anyone. What ugly poster? What filthy boss?'

Even in her fizzing high adrenalin mode, Gemma recognised that Mike's responses seemed genuine, the reactions of an innocent person shocked by someone else's extraordinary and unreasonable behaviour. But there's no arguing with a DNA match, she reminded herself.

'You can't deny a DNA profile,' she said. 'You raped and bashed Robyn, murdered Shelly and came after me! I got you in the face with my knee.'

'Gemma,' he pleaded. 'These injuries,' he said. 'Take a good look. They're not from a knee. Fists caused this'—cautiously he raised a finger to point to the split on his brow and near his mouth—'and this. Not a knee. I can get a pathologist to certify that, if you like. And I can get eyewitnesses to that brawl outside the Hellfire Club. I've already lined those guys up for an assault case. Against them and the bloody copper who paid them.'

'You could still have had time to attack me in the lane. I saw the fringes of your jacket. And Ric Loader got a perfect match from your bloodstained handkerchief.'

'What jacket? What handkerchief are you talking about?'

'Stop lying!'

'I'm *not* lying. I haven't got a fringed jacket, for Chrissakes. What the hell are you talking about? This is ridiculous.'

She could hear the bewilderment in his voice wearing off and the anger starting up.

He struggled to stand.

'Stay down,' she warned.

'This is ridiculous,' he repeated. You can't do this to me. For God's sake, Gemma, I had a party recently with about forty people at my place. There were coats and bags all over the place. I'm still finding things people left there.' He lifted his upper body up and made a gesture of appeal. 'That jacket you're talking about has been hanging on the doorknob of the bedroom since the party. It could've come from anyone who was there that night.'

It was true. She'd forgotten the party Mike had thrown.

'That poster was just a joke,' he said. 'I'd completely forgotten about it. We played darts, that's all.'

'I didn't find it particularly funny,' she said.

'Come on,' he said. 'What about you shooting the crotch out of those B12s?'

Gemma hated to admit he had a point.

'Look,' he said, 'be reasonable. Do you really think I'd be working here with you, knowing that you're investigating those bashings and the murder? Think about it. I'd want to be on the other side of the state, not across the hallway from the very investigator who's taken on the job.'

'If you were working for George Fayed,' she whispered, 'it makes perfect sense.'

'I'm not. I can explain why I have his number.'

'And Angie's,' Gemma added. 'How do you know Angie?'

'It's a long story,' he said.

Gemma lowered the Glock. Now she could hear the sirens.

'I can understand your fear,' he said. 'And I can see how you got there—my house, my bedroom, my jacket, my handkerchief. It all makes perfect sense except that the jacket and the handkerchief aren't mine.'

She was starting to worry that squad cars might be about to pull up on the road above and a dozen armed police come crashing into her place. Now the sirens were wailing down the main road. Any minute now, she'd hear the screeching of brakes.

'Last year I worked on a JTF with the New South Wales police. Angie was part of it.'

'Angie never mentioned any Joint Task Force to me,' Gemma said. 'She's my girlfriend.'

'There's this thing called the Official Secrets Act,' Mike said.

'I don't know what to do,' she said. 'I don't know what to say.'

She could hear the cars skidding to a halt up on the crescent, the thud of running feet, the sound of disembodied radio voices. She went to the door and opened it.

Three police officers faced her, Glocks drawn.

'Drop it!' one of them screamed.

For a second, shock froze her. Then she let the gun fall and even as she heard it hit the floor, so did she, pinned in a painful wristlock.

'What's going on here?' said a pockmarked heavy, twisting his face down to hers, battle madness already showing in his eyes. 'We heard you got a Signal One here.'

'Please, Officer—' she started. 'Officers. There's been a misunderstanding. I can explain. Please can I get up?'

EIGHTEEN

When Gemma had explained it all and the police had left, Mike followed her across the hallway as she collapsed on a chair in her office. He stood at the door, not stepping in. Her embarrassment was fading. Better to have a red face than a dead face, she remembered someone telling her a long time ago. She looked around. I have to let the police concentrate now on finding the street girl basher. I've got plenty to do in my own house. I've got Steve to worry about. I have to find out who is sabotaging my business and clear my name. Am I just doing it all over again? she wondered, recalling how she'd once wanted to clear her father's name. Am I compelled to live my life constantly trying to prove that I'm all right and that my family is all right? Am I just another less obvious version of Skanda Bergen's compulsion to clean and wipe everything up?

'You've been under a lot of stress lately,' Mike said. 'It'd make anyone jump at shadows.'

'George Fayed's number in your diary is hardly

a shadow,' she said. 'If I rang that number, what would happen?'

'Nothing,' said Mike. 'It was a connection we set up with him for a while. It's long been disconnected.' He paused. 'I can tell you this much,' he said. 'It was a joint operation with the Federal Police, the National Crime Authority and the State police. A surveillance operation on George Fayed. ASIO was involved.'

Gemma felt restless. She stood up and went to the window where the coprosma bush made a green darkness outside.

'I don't know who to trust, Mike,' she said. 'I'm clutching at straws. My business and my life are just going down the gurgler so fast. Now I'm hearing things that I knew nothing about. It's not a good feeling.'

'Look,' he said, 'you couldn't have known. Your response was understandable under the circumstances. I'd have done the same.'

'What else don't I know?' she asked. 'Any more surprises?'

Mike shook his head.

'I'd never know anyway,' she said, 'with that cloak and dagger stuff.' She sat down, feeling suddenly drained. 'Sean Wright will want to pull in everyone who was at your party once Ric Loader gives him that information,' she said, thinking of the voluntary DNA samples that would have to be given. 'It'll be the end of your social life. Your friends won't like it.'

'I don't care about that,' he said. 'And neither

will anyone who's innocent. It's a worry to know that one of my acquaintances is a real bastard.'

'It mightn't have been one of your friends,' she said. 'Maybe someone has a new boyfriend?'

Mike laughed. 'Could be my ex's new boyfriend,' he said.

'You astonish me,' said Gemma. 'You invited your ex?'

'Only joking,' he said.

Spinner went to that party, Gemma remembered. He wouldn't mind providing a cheek scrape in the slightest.

'I've been working on Fayed,' Mike said.

Gemma forced herself to focus on Steve's situation again.

'I got some really interesting stuff out of the air near his place,' said Mike. 'I borrowed a van from a mate. Now I need to go to Mum's for a while, run a few things.' Mike checked his watch.

A lot of coppers, Gemma knew, used relatives' homes for a safe house, as a storage facility. She also knew that wireless networks, despite their built-in security codes, transmit publicly over the airwaves, providing the medium for television receivers, for cell phones and radios. Any decent technician could surreptitiously grab and analyse data, pulling it out of the air, find the master password and gain access to pretty well anything transmitted.

'I'll come and pick you up,' Mike said, 'when I know more about what I've got.'

She turned from the window to face him. She

nodded, keeping her fingers crossed behind her back for luck.

'Okay,' she said.

I have to trust him, she told herself. I really don't have an alternative right now. She went to her desk, pulling a drawer open. There lay the Scorpio zodiac charm. She picked it up and turned it over in her hands, hardly seeing it, feeling its weight. Be safe, Steve, she prayed. Be safe wherever you are.

•

Gemma limped into Kings Cross police station. Deb shook her head from the other side of the counter.

'If you're looking for Tim,' she said, 'he's not here. Someone found a body in a bag in a lane behind Springfield Avenue and he's gone down to check it out.'

'I wanted to ask him about a friend of mine,' Gemma said. The only people around the Cross she hadn't checked with about Steve were the police.

She thanked Deb and left, deciding it would be quicker to walk than try to find another parking spot. In a few minutes, she noticed a small group of police clustered in front of the police vehicles blocking each end of the lane. She caught Tim's eye and he nodded at her, allowing her through. On the footpath near an overflowing wheelie bin squatted the Crime Scene examiner and, as Gemma hurried over, he stood up. The laughter took her by surprise. Someone must have made one of their usual bad taste Crime Scene jokes, she thought, until she came closer. She saw the corpse in the same moment, where it lay stretched out in the now opened green garbage bag. She put her handkerchief to her nose in a useless gesture and thought of one more use for a dead cat. On top of the putrefying remains of what might have been old cuts of meat, the stiff body lay, legs stretched fore and aft, tail up. Already, interest in the scene was evaporating as people walked back to their cars.

'Got called out to a bag under a bridge once,' the Crime Scene officer was saying as he repacked his case. 'Took me an hour to get through all the wrappings without disturbing things too much.' He paused, snapping the case closed. 'It was half a goat.'

He nodded at Gemma as she came to stand beside the stinking rubbish and the dead cat. Suddenly she looked closer. She'd seen that cat less than twenty-four hours ago. The distinctive houndstooth check marking left her in no doubt. There were no obvious marks of violence on the animal. Underneath it, she could see what looked like a can of hairspray. She pushed the carcass aside with the toe of her boot and stooped down to read the label on it. What she saw made her run after the Crime Scene Examiner, who was just stepping into his station wagon.

'Please,' she said, 'come back for a minute?'

'Who are you?' he wanted to know, frowning in partial recognition.

'Gemma Lincoln,' she said. 'I used to work with you, remember?' She steeled herself for a lie. 'I'm a mate of Sean Wright,' she added.

Ahead of them, she saw Tim's van moving out of the lane, allowing passage again. 'Talk to Sean if you want, but there's something in that rubbish that he'll want to know about in connection with a murder investigation.'

'A dead cat?'

The young man's face was a picture.

'You'll want to bag that cat and what's underneath it,' she said. 'In fact, I don't want to tell you your job, but you'll want to bag everything in and around that garbage. I believe that cat belonged to Benjamin Glass.'

His face registered a faint interest at the name of the dead man.

Gemma hurried on while she had his attention. 'And underneath the cat's body is a canister of carbon monoxide gas. Benjamin Glass died of carbon monoxide poisoning.'

'I thought he died in a fire,' said the crime scene examiner. 'A high temperature accelerant fire.'

'That's what everyone thought. But lethal amounts of carbon monoxide were found in tissue samples from the deceased. I believe that dead cat is his. And under the cat is something you should look at.'

'Look, ma'am,' he said, with heavy-handed correctness, 'I'll tell Sean Wright. On account of you're a friend of his. But that's all I'm doing. No way I'm bagging a dead cat.' He threw her a look of amused contempt.

That look, thought Gemma. All my life I've copped that look from men. She struggled to keep the anger out of her voice.

'It's not just a dead cat,' she said, 'The cat and the canister underneath it could be vital evidence in a murder investigation. Can you get that?'

'My job,' he said, speaking in a loud, slow voice as if she were stupid, 'is to attend crime scenes, to notice, record, collect and collate physical evidence.' He paused for effect, turning away to open the door of the wagon. 'It is not my job to pick up dead cats off the street.'

Gemma watched as he drove off. Then she went back to the garbage and carefully teased the canister out, using her toe. It rolled towards the gutter and she blocked it with her foot, looking around for something to put it in. An empty plastic bag fluttered at the top of the wheelie bin, and Gemma pounced on it, swept the canister into it without touching it and dropped it into her briefcase. Only then did she head back to the main drag.

She was about to flag a taxi when she spotted two of the Koori kids she'd spoken to near the El Alamein fountain.

'Hey,' Gemma called. The girl turned. Gemma saw recognition in her eyes. 'Have you seen that kid I asked you about?'

The girl's eyes followed Gemma's hand as it

pulled a twenty-dollar note out of her briefcase. The boy clutched a heavy suitcase closer.

'Look,' she said to them, 'he's not in trouble. I'm just worried about him.' She felt a sudden rush of intense sadness as she spoke. 'I know what it's like to be little and for no one to want you.'

The girl looked at Gemma in silence for a long minute. 'Yes,' she said at last. 'We see him around a bit.'

'Where?'

The girl shrugged.

'Where's he living?'

'Just around.'

That's the Ratbag, Gemma thought. Just crashing wherever he can.

The girl's mouth compressed and she turned her dark eyes away, pocketing the note. Her younger companion tugged at her sleeve. 'Give it to me,' he said but the girl pushed his hand away.

'When you say "just around",' Gemma tried again, 'what do you actually mean?'

'He beds down all over the place. Like us. Sometimes people let us stay at their place. Sometimes we get into a refuge. Mostly we sleep around here'—she made a vague sweep of her arm—'lotsa different places. Maybe he does, too.'

'Do you wanna buy some stuff?' the boy asked, tapping the suitcase.

'Like what?' said Gemma.

The boy shrugged. 'Got it off a friend,' he said.

'I'll have a look,' said Gemma.

He opened the suitcase and Gemma peered in.

It was a typical minor thieves' haul: CDs, bits of jewellery, a decent watch or two, several pieces of china, clothes, some pharmaceuticals.

'No,' she said, 'there's nothing here I'm interested in.'

'Give you the lot for fifty bucks?' he said.

Gemma looked at the pair. What would become of them? Where would they end up? Why did nobody care? Instead, she found herself groping for words of encouragement, suggestions of what they could do to improve their lot. But she knew they would sound stupid and ineffectual. She opened her wallet and pulled out another twenty. It was all she could do. The girl grabbed it and the kids took off with their haul, vanishing round a corner.

Gemma stood a moment under the bare plane trees where dejected Indian mynahs pecked at plastic litter. Poor little wretches, she thought, turning her steps towards Kosta's place.

•

Kosta took her in his big Ford with the gold *komboloi* dangling from the rear-vision mirror. 'There's someone who wants to meet you,' he said as they drove towards the end of Victoria Street. He parked outside a large terrace house and Gemma got out of the car and followed Kosta through the open door. 'I'm working as doorman here now,' he said. 'But I don't knock on till later in the day.' Together, they walked through the narrow hallway of the house, with its bedrooms down one side, until they reached the kitchen at the back. Shelly had renovated this area into a pleasant north-facing living room with a heavy door that locked these rooms off from the rest of the house. Like my place, thought Gemma. We stalkers of the night have a lot in common. The public and the private worlds.

'Girls,' Kosta called out as they stepped down into the living room past the heavy door, 'I've got a visitor for you.'

Two young women turned round from where they'd been sitting together at the wooden kitchen table, their cigarettes smoking in the ashtray, coffees steaming. As soon as she saw the girl nearest her, Gemma knew who it was. She reached out her hand to the younger woman, who had her mother's golden fingernails as well as her determined jawline.

'Naomi,' she said, 'it's lovely to meet you again. Last time I saw you, you were going off to child care.' She paused. 'I'm so sorry about your mum.'

Naomi's blue eyes filled with tears and she nodded, unable to speak for the moment.

'She was a good person,' Gemma said, 'and a friend of mine. I want to go to the funeral.'

'I'll let you know,' said Kosta. 'And this is—' He was about to continue when Gemma interrupted.

'I know who this is,' she said, nodding to the girl. 'Robyn. I'm pleased to see you out of hospital. You look much better than when I last saw you.'

A lot of the swelling had subsided, but Robyn's face was still darkly bruised, and her left eye was covered with a patch. It wasn't till then that Gemma saw the pair of crutches leaning against the table. 'I met you with your mother at the hospital a little while ago,' she explained. 'I wouldn't expect you to remember.'

The bruised girl shook her head. 'Sorry,' she said. 'I don't remember much about the first few days.'

'You needn't be sorry,' said Gemma. 'Whoever did this to you is the one who should be sorry.'

'Mum's determined to track the animal down,' said Robyn.

Gemma remembered the athletic woman with her powerful shoulders. 'I really hope she does,' she said. 'Save us all a lot of bother.'

'We were just talking then,' said Naomi, 'when you came in. Wondering what sort of man does this sort of thing.'

'A real mean one,' said Kosta, settling himself down in a gingham-dressed kitchen chair. 'Gemma wants to know if anyone's heard anything about George Fayed. Or anything unusual. A friend of hers might be in a bit of trouble with him.'

'I haven't heard anything about Fayed *personally*,' Naomi said, looking across at Robyn who also shook her head. 'But no way he's getting his hands on this place. We're all going to run it now.'

'Like a proper family business,' Kosta added. 'Rob here is off the gear.'

'You bet,' said Robyn. 'Nearly got me dead, that stuff.'

'Naomi's going to do the books,' Kosta continued, 'and this young bloke here'—Gemma turned around to see who Kosta meant and there was the Ratbag, large as life, stepping down into the lower level of the living area, still wearing the dirty maroon anorak, hair slicked back like a gangster from a '30s movie—'this young bloke is going to be gopher. He'll keep cocky for us.'

The Ratbag didn't see Gemma until she spoke.

'Hullo, Hugo,' she said. He seemed to stop in mid stride like a character in an animated cartoon, and his eyes were huge in a face that was slowly blushing.

'Fancy meeting you here,' said Gemma.

NINETEEN

She took him out for a milkshake and a pizza and they sat in the relative warmth of the pizza joint, away from the scudding winds of the street. As usual, he was hungry and ate a family-sized pizza without showing any signs of struggle.

'Hugo,' she said as yet another slice vanished into his mouth, 'you can't live in a brothel.'

'It's not like that,' he protested. 'It's a live-in job. Kosta said I can have the little back room off the kitchen. I like Naomi. She said she'd look after me.'

'There's no way you can do this,' Gemma said. 'The minute DOCS finds out, you'll be sent home to your mother. You should be at school.'

'But I hate school,' he said. 'It's boring. And anyway,' he added, 'how will they find out? Unless you tell on me.'

'Will you give me your mother's name and address at least?' said Gemma. 'I promise I won't dob on you. But she'll be out of her mind with worry.'

'She's not,' he said.

'Hugo,' Gemma said, 'she would be.'

'Uh-uh.' He shook his head. 'I rang her the day before yesterday.'

'What did she say?'

He shrugged. 'Nothing much.'

'Nothing much?' Gemma repeated, incredulous. 'Don't give me that crap.'

'It's not crap,' he said in his mild way, shoving down another triangle of pizza.

'You told her you were staying at your dad's place,' Gemma said on a sudden inspiration and the Ratbag looked away, sheepish.

'You did, didn't you?' she said. 'You little dog.'

'But I really might be soon,' said the Ratbag. 'So it's not like a big lie. Dad's only got a one-bedroom place for him and his girlfriend at the moment. But he said he might be getting another place with enough room for me. If he moves, then I can most likely live with them.'

'If?' Gemma repeated. 'Most likely? There are too many ifs and mights, Hugo,' she said. Good on you, Dad, she thought with a flash of fury. Top marks for fathering. That's great. Your son *is* far better off living in a brothel, you arsehole. Memories of her own father with his total disregard for his daughters started to surface, but she pushed them back down again, focusing on the present matter.

'Oh Hugo,' she said finally, 'what am I going to do with you?'

'Is your cat okay?' he asked.

'He's fine,' she said. 'Stop trying to change the subject.'

'I wanted to see you after I ran away from your place,' he said 'but I was scared you'd dob on me.'

Despite herself, she was touched. 'That's nice,' she said. 'But Hugo, I don't know how long you can stay living at Baroque.'

'I could live in your boatshed,' he suggested. 'Then would it be all right?'

'You can't go round living in other people's back rooms and sheds. And it's not even just a question of where you're going to live. At your age, the law requires you to live with a parent. Or a guardian. And attend school. Word's going to get round about you. Business people will notice you around the Cross. They'll mention it to youth workers and the cops. The Koori kids already know about you. It's only a matter of time before the authorities get to you.'

He looked away in deep dejection. 'All these people,' he said, 'telling me what to do. I just want my dad back and all of us to be together like we used to be. If the authorities are so smart, how come they can't do that?'

'You can't make people do what they don't want to do,' she said.

'Unless you're a kid,' he said. 'Then everyone can make you do what you don't want to do.'

Gemma remembered from the events of her own childhood that he was quite correct.

'For goodness sake, stay out of sight,' she said. 'At least for the next day or so. There're some

426 • GABRIELLE LORD

things I've got to do, then I'll come back and we'll talk about what we're going to do about you.'

'You could adopt me,' he said.

Gemma started to laugh then stopped herself when she saw the boy's face. He wasn't joking.

'I saw Steve,' he said after a pause. 'Your friend Steve.'

'Hugo, so you remember him. Where?'

'He was coming out of that nightclub, the one with them big purple icicles round the doorway?'

Gemma remembered the crystalline entrance foyer to Indigo Ice and the fabulous couple parting to reveal Steve dancing close with Lorraine Litchfield. 'And then what?' she asked.

'He was with a man. Then he got in a car.'

'A man?'

The Ratbag nodded.

'What sort of car?'

'Big black Mercedes,' said the Ratbag, slurping the last of his milkshake through the straw.

'Don't make that noise. When was that?' she asked.

'This morning.'

Gemma glanced at her watch. 'What time?'

The Ratbag shook his head. 'Early.'

'Do you know who the man was?' she asked.

The Ratbag nodded. 'Naomi calls him the Lebanese drug lord,' he said. 'All the girls know him. George Fayed.'

Gemma felt her heart contract. If the meeting

doesn't work out, she thought, Steve will be in dead trouble.

Mike rang to say the analysis program was going to take longer than he'd anticipated because Sean Wright wanted him to give the names and addresses of every male who'd been at his party before he did anything else. Gemma diverted to Phoenix Bay, and made her way to the boatshed, finding in its cool silence a place of retreat from the chaotic events of her recent life. I might have to sell my apartment, she thought. Never mind Hugo, I might end up living down here. She took out the carbon monoxide canister she'd fished out from under the dead cat and carefully placed it on the shelf above the cold water tap. If that cat were autopsied, would its tissue, too, reveal lethal quantities of the deadly gas? Gemma's brain was working on overdrive, pushing pieces of this puzzle together, then pulling them apart. Nothing seemed to make sense.

She gave up and turned to the shrouded figures. For a second, her overworked brain betrayed her, suggesting that two assassins crouched under the damp drapes. She shivered at the thought and lifted the damp cloths off both shapes, needing the reassurance of seeing her handiwork. Again, she admired the more complete figure, running her fingers over his staring eyes and open jaw. She picked up a clay knife and found herself scraping away at the second figure, finding the clay hard and very

428 • GABRIELLE LORD

cold, difficult to shape. She only meant to stay for a little while but it wasn't long before she became fully involved, all her anxieties vanishing for the moment in the focused attention she was giving the work under her fingers. She decided to work up the basic shape, as she'd done with the first figure, straining with effort as she pulled and stretched the surface of clay. She wanted the line of it to suggest the straining tension of the beast's powerful hindquarters.

As she worked, bits of clay dropped to the floor and soon her shoes were covered in small lumps and blobs. I'd better not commit any major crimes, she thought, until I clean myself up thoroughly. These traces would come straight home to me, and the Physical Evidence people would just snap me up. While she was concentrating on the sculpture, her mind free from anything to do with the investigations, something happened. She was smoothing the now more pliant clay up and over to make the leaning neck of the second lion when one of underground connections of the case suddenly surfaced, and the question she'd previously put to Spinner— why would someone use an HTA?—found an answer. To obliterate *all* traces, came the reply in her mind. All traces of *what*? she asked herself. Gemma looked down at her shoes, now covered in fine clay dust. Traces of something that is left with every step, she answered. Gemma stood there, her hands immobilised on the cold clay of the second lion's embryonic shoulders as Locard's famous words came into her mind. '*Wherever he steps, whatever he touches, whatever he leaves, even unconsciously, will serve as a silent witness against him.'* Wherever I went, she thought, I'd be shedding tiny flakes of clay, leaving a trail that could be followed. The murderer at Nelson Bay was so fearful of leaving a trail that could be followed, that only an HTA inferno would do—the equivalent of a hellfire which would obliterate every trace. But every trace of *what*? Again, the question came back at her.

Gemma flung the cloths back over the clay lions and scrubbed her hands at the paint-stained little sink. Minkie Montreau's thesis had lain in the archives unexamined for years, according to Dr Susskind's assistant, and then 'suddenly you'll get people needing to see them'. What people? Who? Who was the person who had recently viewed the thesis, apart from herself?

She hurried to lock up, then climbed over the rocks at the back of the small inlet and was practically running by the time she reached her car. She swung out from the beachside road and turned back towards the city, heading for the university. I've got to find out who else asked to see that thesis, she thought. Already, a conclusion was starting to form, like clay starting to take shape. I think I know who it is, she thought. I think I know now who killed Benjamin Glass and why it all had to be so complicated. As she thought it through, the facts surrounding the murder—an event that had previously seemed maddeningly mysterious or crazy—started falling logically into place. As she knew from all her experience in the game, whatever people do, no matter how weird it might seem to an outsider, *always* makes sense to the individual concerned. And it's an investigator's job to crack that. I only need to check up on a few things to be one hundred per cent sure, she thought, and then Sean Wright can kiss my arse.

•

She hardly noticed the drive, moving through the gears on automatic, thinking of the disappointment that had led to murder. Envy is a terrible thing, as Gemma knew. If the person she suspected *was* in fact the murderer, Gemma imagined her stewing in envy while two women of her acquaintance had acquired wealthy husbands, one some time ago, one quite recently, while she herself remained single and probably broke. Then, perhaps it had looked like she might snare her own sugar daddy. For a while, as long as his infatuation lasted, she'd entertained hope that he might leave his marriage. Then, Gemma imagined the anger building as her suspect realised that her lover was never going to leave his wife. Finally, the envy and the anger had hardened into hatred. Enough to kill. It had all been there, beneath her level of consciousness. and now it seemed so obvious.

She drove through the gates of the university and parked near the library, hurrying across the wide lawns, adding more and more detail to the events that lead to a homicidal tragedy. Marked cards, a lover's photographs of his mistress, a cleaning compulsion, a man's missing cat. Someone who knew the security code at the Nelson Bay beach house. Someone who'd taken a great deal of interest in her rival, made it her business to find out about Minkie Montreau's Masters thesis. Even though an ordinary house fire would have been quite adequate, she *believed* that the traces she would leave behind her needed a fire of more than ordinary intensity to remove. A lifetime of preoccupation and self-consciousness about her condition had created the belief in her that nothing less than the extreme temperatures of an HTA inferno would suffice. Then there was the added bonus of such a fire pointing directly at her hated rival, the wife her lover would not leave. Had she decided on the HTA scenario before or after finding out about the thesis?

By the time Gemma reached Archives, she had the whole ugly story, laid out in her mind's eye. It didn't take her long to hunt out the gawky research assistant, delighted at her return.

'You're getting hooked, aren't you?' His eyelid twitched—or was it a wink? 'It happens.'

'Tell me,' she said. 'The other person who asked about Miriam Montreau's thesis. I believe she's a friend of mine.'

'How blessed I am that two such handsome females have visited my hallowed shrine in recent times,' he said with a whinnying laugh. His tic was going demented and Gemma wondered what it was about hanging around large collections of books

432 • GABRIELLE LORD

that had such a negative effect on a man's behaviour.

'You are indeed,' said Gemma. 'Although she's much better looking than I am.'

The research assistant was gallant. 'Well,' he said, 'it depends on what you fancy.'

'Come on,' said Gemma. 'My friend is a real beauty. You'd have to admit it. She's pretty close to perfect.'

The research assistant nodded. 'Almost perfect,' he agreed, 'except for her ichthyosis.'

Gemma thought of the photographs, the beautiful face, breasts cupped by black lace gloves that she believed would not only hide the scaly surface of her fingers, but also limit the shedding of microscopic flakes of skin.

'Ichthyosis?' Gemma tripped over the unfamiliar word.

'Yes,' he said. 'Scaly skin.'

•

She took a diversion to the Kremlin. Sean Wright was out, but Angie came down to the foyer.

'Tell Sean to pull Skanda Bergen in for questioning. Tell him she's the woman in the black lace gloves.'

Quickly, she filled Angie in. 'The reason was there all the time. This woman has some sort of chronic dermatitis. She'd be shedding skin cells all the time, everywhere she goes. So she's not content with an ordinary fire. And she knows enough about DNA capabilities to know that we could match her against any cells found at a crime scene. She believes that only an HTA will be powerful enough to destroy any skin flakes she might shed.'

Gemma knew she had her friend's complete attention. 'Skanda Bergen has ichthyosis,' she said. 'It's like a bad case of dandruff of the skin,' she added, responding to Angie's questioning look. 'It's not terribly obvious, although I noticed something rough about the skin on her face as soon as I met her. I visited her twice, and both times she was frantically dusting and vacuuming. I just thought she was obsessive-compulsive. But then I made the connection. She's obsessed with the skin flakes she's always shedding.' She paused before explaining. 'She was having an affair with Benjamin Glass, not just a sex worker–client relationship. I believe he fell for her, for a while at least. The photographs I found of her hidden at his office weren't pornography. They were more like love letters. Her colleague Lorraine Litchfield marries a wealthy crim only a few years ago. Why shouldn't *she* marry Benjamin? She asks him. He's infatuated, but he's not going to leave his wife for Skanda. Skanda is enraged. Maybe she asks him one more time, maybe he refuses one time too many. Now Skanda hates him and hates Minkie for being in her way. My guess is that Benjamin Glass would have been very proud of his wife's academic achievements and most likely told Skanda about his wife's thesis. So that puts her on the trail of HTAs. It'll be very interesting to discover where she got the accelerant from. Maybe one of her clients is a scientist?'

Angie made a note in her book, and Gemma continued.

'So she sets a couple of practice fires to make sure this is going to work and at the same time creates the possibility that an arsonist is on the loose. And she gets hold of a bright yellow BMW and off she goes up to Nelson Bay with her little cylinder of CO. Let's assume she's spent time with Benjamin previously at Nelson Bay. She could have easily found out the security code to the house. Benjamin is there on his own. Maybe she gives him one last chance to redeem himself. We'll never really know. Then'—Gemma paused—'it might have gone something like this: she opens her bag, grabs her spray and lets him have it with a good blast of CO. He's shocked and coughing. He wouldn't know that he's inhaling pure carbon monoxide. This girl wants to make sure he doesn't escape. He's dead very quickly. She sets the fire and off she goes. She's practised the detonation time on the other two fires. But she's got no fight with his cat so she takes that back with her. Maybe she'd always liked it. But then I drop in on her and by sheer bad luck, the cat appears on the windowsill. She denies all knowledge of it, of course, but now the cat has to go. So she kills it with her little canister and dumps it in a garbage bag somewhere in the Cross, knowing that there's no way she can now be connected with the dead man.' She paused, aware of Angie's amazement. 'How am I doing?'

Angie nodded. 'Pretty impressive, I'd say.'

'And I haven't finished yet,' said Gemma. 'She's a smart girl. She's set up a murder that she hopes will destroy his wife as well as the man she's come to hate. So she creates a path of powerful circumstantial evidence that seems to lead straight to the door of the person with the most to gain from Benjamin Glass's death. It only takes a phone call to the insurance brokers and a copy of the policy is sent to Minkie Montreau's address. Skanda knows that's going to look bad for Minkie.'

Angie nodded. 'As far as she's concerned,' she said, 'it's perfect payback. The man who rejected her dead, and the woman he wouldn't leave, her rival, serving life for his murder.'

'And one more thing,' said Gemma. 'Tell Sean to make sure he collects cat hair from Skanda's flat. Match it with cat hair from Benjamin Glass's factory. You could even suggest he goes and collects the dead cat. If it's still there in the lane. Then get Lance at Paradigm Laboratories on the job. He specialises in mitochondrial DNA. I can guarantee he'll get a match.'

'If you say so,' said Angie.

'Ms Bergen's already admitted knowing the dead man,' said Gemma. 'But the presence of a lot of cat hair will help a jury establish she had his cat at her place, not just him. And they'd have to ask why that might be so. Tell Sean to find the yellow BMW she hired and he'll get cat hair from that,

I'll bet. He should put it to her that she'd do well to come clean about it. There's a canister of carbon monoxide with her on it. She'd probably wipe prints, but with her skin condition, the analysts might get lucky and find plenty of material for a profile.'

'Where's the canister?' Angie asked.

'I'll get it,' said Gemma. She paused, thinking back. 'There was much more to it than the sex worker and client relationship.'

'There's always more to it,' said Angie. She shrugged. 'Humans are funny critters.'

'So I'm discovering,' said Gemma. 'I didn't know you worked with Mike Moody last year.'

'Who?' Angie looked genuinely puzzled.

Gemma filled her in and Angie nodded.

'Hardly remember him,' she said. 'It was one of those joint operations. People coming and going. I think I only spoke to him once.'

Two grubby-looking creatures with dreadlocks, wild facial hair and torn jeans walked past Gemma and Angie through the security gates, surrounded by a stench of engine oil, flashing ID as they went.

'Will you look at them?' Angie said.

'Drug Squad?' Gemma asked. Angie nodded.

Gemma said goodbye and walked out of the building, remembering the old days when she'd worked there when anyone could walk in and out almost unchallenged.

On her way back to the car, she decided to double the account she would finally present to the widow Glass. After all, Minkie had had her running around in circles. Gemma drove home, worked out the amount, then thought of the insurance pay-out coming to Minkie and tripled it. It came to a tidy sum. She put it in an envelope with her business card and posted it.

•

Now, she sat perched uneasily on a stool in the operatives' office, watching Mike as he sat hunched in front of his laptop.

'Ouch!' she exclaimed, as the pain in her lower rib reminded her not to lean against the desk. Still, it felt good taking action like this, even if she didn't fully understand what Mike was doing. Her knowledge of electronics was limited and she knew how much she relied on the expertise of the operatives she employed and felt grateful that Mike knew what he was doing. Now, as she looked at him, she wondered how she could ever have thought he was a spy.

'Mike,' she started to say, 'I'm sorry about what happened earlier. I've been very concerned about Steve—'

'Don't worry about it,' he said, as he started up a program. 'You've been under diabolical stress lately.' He turned to her and flashed his white-toothed grin. 'I'm feeling lucky that I got out alive. You looked very serious with that Glock.'

'I was serious,' she said. 'It looked like you were the man in the frame.'

Mike turned back to his keyboard and screen. 'The more intelligence we can get on Fayed, the better for Steve,' Mike continued. 'If something's gone wrong, this way we've got a good chance of finding out what it is.'

'Tell me.'

'I did a complete RF sweep of all the frequencies in Fayed's area,' he said, indicating the laptop. 'And what I'm doing now is running a merge program so I can analyse what I've grabbed from the air around Fayed's joint.' He tapped the side of the screen, busy at its work. 'I've got a searchable data base on a CD-Rom with the details of every *licensed* transmission in the area. That way, we can eliminate all the transmissions we expect to see. Then I'll see what's left. The exception report will show me the ones we don't know about. Anything that shouldn't be there could prove to be very interesting.' He saw Gemma's face and paused.

'Look,' he said, 'what I'm going to do is what any analyst does—take a sample, put it on a slide and see what we've got. Or, in this case, see what's floating around in the airwaves.'

'Okay, Mike,' she said.

'And I found an Optus micro cell up a telegraph pole about twenty metres from his castle. I picked up beacon signals from that and, would you believe, I found an extra little something—a low output transmission? That's very interesting.'

'I didn't notice any micro cell on a telegraph pole,' she said 'and I've cruised past his place.'

'You don't see what you're not looking for,' said Mike.

That, at least, she understood.

'Optus and Telstra both utilise telegraph poles for their networks. At the higher frequencies,' he continued, 'height is might. For very short range, you need to be in the line of sight for transmission.'

'Mike, I'm the one losing transmission,' Gemma said.

'Look,' he said, 'you don't need to know all that. Basically what I'm saying is that I picked up a signal that could belong to a Federal agency.'

'You should know,' she said drily. Mike laughed.

'But what's the point of gathering in police intelligence?' she asked. 'So far, the police have been spectacularly unsuccessful in touching George Fayed.'

'Gemma, I'm interested in the police operation because it gives us a way in.'

'A way in where?' she asked.

'You know from other situations that the best way to go is to use assets already in place.'

She nodded. It was classic strategy.

Mike turned his attention back to the screen. 'See there?' he said, indicating wave-like patterns. 'That shows us what's going on in the lower frequencies. Nothing very exciting. Remote controls for things like televisions, signals from babies' sleep monitors, garage doors, that sort of thing. But if you have a look *here*, at 5.6 gigahertz—'

'5.6?' she repeated. 'That sounds familiar.'

'It is,' he said. 'It's the surveillance operation we were talking about. You remember how police operations are always stymied by the Listening

Devices Act? And how they grizzle about that. All they can do is pick up pieces of mosaic intelligence—watch whatever address it is that interests them, make a note of who comes and goes, check out the visitors, track them back to where they come from, check out rego plates. Slowly gather the bits that make up a picture of what goes on in and around the place.'

Gemma nodded. She remembered diagrams on white boards, flow charts that demonstrated criminal connections. 'I've been through all that,' she said.

'I want to do something a bit cleverer than police surveillance,' said Mike. He closed down his program. 'I did a few things last night,' he said. 'I've got a van and I've found a garage we can rent not far away from Fayed's place. We don't want to be on the street.'

He jumped up and grabbed his coat. 'Come on,' he said. 'Let's do our job.'

A short while later, Gemma huddled with Mike in the back of the borrowed van, watching him as he went to work.

'What we can do first,' he said to her, 'is pick up the police surveillance frequency modulations.'

'But you said you were going to do something smarter than that.'

She wondered if he'd even heard her.

'When I was doing my analysis of this set-up here,' said Mike, 'I picked up another signal in the

1–10 megahertz, very weak and close to the noise floor.'

'And?' she asked.

'I detected the "noise" of closed circuit television screens.'

'George Fayed has CCT inside and outside his place,' said Gemma. Things were getting interesting now, she thought.

Mike nodded. 'And with the right equipment and know-how, receivers can also act as transmitters. Receivers are transmitters are receivers are transmitters . . .'

'You mean, his closed circuit system could work the other way and transmit out to us?'

'That's exactly what I mean,' said Mike.

Gemma felt a wave of hope lift her spirits. 'We can see inside Fayed's place right here?' She indicated Mike's screen.

'All I have to do is find the cables,' said Mike. 'Once I find the cables, we're in. We can piggyback in on the police surveillance frequency. I've just got to make sure there's zero interference with the Optus system.'

If we can see inside Fayed's house, Gemma thought, and if Steve's there, I might be able to help him. And redeem myself for my earlier behaviour.

Gemma waited in the cramped van, the only sound the soft chattering of Mike's keyboard as he worked.

'Okay,' he said finally. 'It's time to get off the street. Let's go and take cover.'

They climbed into the front of the van and drove away from Fayed's corner and around into a tree-lined street running at a right-angle to it. Before they parked in the rented garage Gemma glanced up at the sky. It was dark with a threatening storm and the oppressive coldness chilled her to the bone.

An hour later, she was in the back of the van again, more cramped up than before, watching Mike's fingers manipulate the arcane figures and symbols that appeared on his screen.

'The Feds are using a broadband, frequency agile transmitter,' Mike said, 'capable of four video channels.'

Gemma grunted. Her body was seething; the inaction was frustrating.

'Mike,' she said, 'I'm going crazy just sitting here. I need to be out there doing something.'

Mike, busy with frequency modulations and demodulations, translating these from one electronic 'language' to another, barely looked up, just nodded and kept working. She started to uncurl, feeling pins and needles shoot down one leg. Outside, the storm was building, coming closer and she could see the effects of its interference from time to time, shivering Mike's screen. There was a silent brilliant flash and Gemma nearly jumped out of her skin as the thunderclap broke right over the roof. The figures on Mike's screen convulsed and disappeared, returning seconds later.

'Hey! Look.' Mike said, utterly absorbed. A picture appeared on Mike's laptop and Gemma noticed his forehead gleaming with sweat in the bluish light of the screen. 'Picture and sound.'

'What is it?' She leaned forward to peer at the images on the screen in front of her. She saw the opulent, heavy furnishings of a bedroom as they flicked into view for a few seconds. Then the picture changed. Now she was looking down past a giant chandelier into some sort of reception room with grandiose gilt furniture. 'What am I looking at?' she asked. The screen flickered and the picture switched to a living room with heavy Italianate furnishings.

'We're in!' Mike said, clapping his hands together. 'Welcome to Casa Fayed's closed circuit television home movies.' Despite the chill of their surroundings, Mike wiped his forehead with a handkerchief, wincing as he touched the stitches over his brow.

Gemma held her breath as she stared into an ornate dining room, complete with long baronial table, carved chairs and heavy curtains. Twisted pillars featured beside the entrance. The decor was reminiscent, Gemma thought, of Hollywood biblical epics, circa 1960. The picture switched to a view of the kitchen where two handsome strong-featured women, possibly Fayed's wife and mother, Gemma thought, busied themselves.

'He's got internal cameras everywhere,' said Mike. 'We can see what he can see now.'

Gemma leaned forward in excitement, her

worries momentarily forgotten, as the screen changed yet again. They had access to a series of dress circle views into the house of the drug lord. Marble and gilt bathrooms, storerooms, a generator room, external and internal corridors, all were covered in the system of rotating closed circuit television angles. Anywhere an assassin might conceivably hide himself, Gemma thought, Fayed has cameras to make sure it can't happen. Even the laundry, and what looked like a drying room, where sheets and towels hung. A generous lap pool, sauna and gym area took up half of one level. It was like a small city in there, Gemma thought, with all the services anyone could reasonably want. She sat transfixed, staring into the secret world of the drug lord.

'Smile, George Fayed,' she said. 'You're on reality TV.'

'He'd have a control room in there somewhere,' said Mike and as he spoke, as if by magic the heart of the security system itself was revealed on the screen: a small room with banks of monitors and a heavily geared security man who lounged beneath them, glancing up from time to time to survey the screens, each one showing a section of the huge fortress. After watching the repetitive rotation several times, Gemma started to get an idea of the layout of the house.

'Looks like the whole ground level is mostly a service area,' said Mike, 'car park and air conditioning and a mechanic's work area. He's even got his own machine shop.'

Gemma noticed the machining tools, vices, lathes, and benches crowded with tools and spare parts. Room after room, in orderly rotation appeared on the screen. Then it changed to a murky darkness.

'What's that?' Gemma asked.

Mike peered closer at slow-moving coloured shapes, blobs of green, yellow and blue, with occasional red centres.

'I don't know,' said Mike, frowning. 'Looks like the images you get with ultraviolet light.'

'Maybe his solarium?' she ventured.

Mike shook his head, doing what he could to improve the picture on his screen, using his zoom and focus to try and make more sense of the moving shapes, but the images became even more incomprehensible at such close quarters. Another frame change and a huge coloured shape loomed through the murk on the screen, reminding Gemma of a predator swerving through dark water. Then it was gone.

'What the hell *is* that?' she asked.

Mike peered more closely at the screen, then shook his head. 'Buggered if I know,' he said. 'They're heat images, but I don't know what that is. It's possible it's some sort of machinery.'

Now another room came into view, equally dark and mysterious. 'Might have better luck with this one.' He focused his attention and skill on the screen.

'This room is totally dark,' said Gemma. Almost as she spoke, someone must have switched the light on because the room on Mike's screen jumped into perfect illumination and focus. A man lay unconscious on a bed. Gemma gasped, then covered her mouth with her hands to stop herself from screaming out loud. It was Steve. For what seemed like minutes, Gemma froze. She hunched, mouth covered, staring at the inert figure on the screen. Then, as suddenly, the image vanished.

'What's happened?' she said, her voice a harsh whispered scream.

'It's okay, it's okay,' came Mike's calm voice beside her. 'It's just the light being switched off again. Listen. This is a good result. We know for sure now where Steve is.'

'He's injured, I know it,' she said. 'Why is he unconscious?'

'He might be sleeping,' he suggested.

Gemma tried to stand up, knocking her head, the tears already in her eyes springing onto her cheeks. 'I've got to get him out of there,' she said. 'I've got to get Steve.'

Mike's hand on her arm steadied her. 'Take it easy,' he said. 'Take a few deep breaths.'

'You don't understand,' she said. 'It's my fault he's in there. I did something really stupid and now Steve is—' She stopped. 'God, Mike. What if he's dead?'

'People don't switch lights on to check a dead man,' said Mike. 'And they wouldn't be keeping a body there. Anywhere else, but not in Fayed's private home. If Steve were dead, he'd be at the bottom of the Gap, not here.'

It was true, and Gemma knew it.

'We've got to get him out of there,' she said. 'We've got to get an SPG team together. Raid the place and get him out.' She was hardly watching the procession of images on Mike's screen, all she could think of was Steve lying there, unconscious, vulnerable.

'I've got it,' she said. 'I'll call Ian Lovelock. And Angie. Between the two of them, they can organise a big party. We can give them the layout of Fayed's place now.' She indicated the rotating pictures on Mike's screen. 'We get in there and we get Steve out.' Her mind was racing. She was aware of her heart beating hard against her ribs.

Mike shook his head. 'Better we contact Fayed and we deal. He gives us Steve, or—'

'Or what?' she asked. 'We threaten a joint raid. Tear his fortress down and find—'

'What?' Mike asked.

'That dark room we saw. It might be a store room.'

'No way he'd keep anything at his house, Gemma. That's for the lieutenants.'

He was right. God knows how they could compel George Fayed to do anything.

'What are you doing now?' she asked.

'I'm copying the video feed,' he said. 'This way, we can build up a map of the place.'

Gemma's mobile rang. It was Angie.

'Angie,' she said, 'we've got into George Fayed's place. Steve's in there. Mike's piggybacked in on

448 • GABRIELLE LORD

Fayed's own closed circuit security system. Tell Ian Lovelock if he doesn't already know.'

'Great,' said her friend. 'Police intelligence will love that. Make some copies for us. Send them over anonymously. The Drug Squad boys will wet their pants over it.'

'Tell her I'm sending it electronically asap,' said Mike. 'Then she can deliver it to Lovelock.'

'What about Steve?' said Gemma, after passing on Mike's message.

'That depends on the Drug Squad,' said Angie. 'What they decide.'

'Where's Ian Lovelock?'

'Could be anywhere,' said Angie. 'I'll pass on the information right now. Give us a couple of hours to look at the pictures.'

'We might not have a couple of hours,' Gemma said, thinking of Steve lying in the dark in the drug lord's fortress.

'They'll have to do a quick target appraisal. I'll get back to you. Oh,' she added, 'I nearly forgot why I rang you. Ric Loader got a perfect match from the assault on Robyn Warburton with the DNA from those attacks from the late '80s and early '90s.'

Gemma remembered immediately. 'I *knew* it,' she said. 'The door handle MO. So it was him. Something happened and he got active again.'

'His missus probably left him,' Angie suggested.

'And now he's on the loose again.'

'Or he was doing ten years for something simi-lar,' said Angie. 'Did Ric get anything off the clothes you were wearing the night you were attacked?'

'It was a negative,' Gemma said.

Angie rang off.

'Okay,' said Mike. 'Feel like ringing George Fayed?'

'You said that number wouldn't work,' said Gemma.

'I've picked up the frequency of his new one.'

'What can I deal with?' Gemma asked. 'We haven't got anything.'

Mike picked up his phone and handed it to her. 'Use mine. Tell him if he doesn't let Steve walk out of there his status as a registered informant will be circulated to his friends. There are a couple of men serving life sentences who will be very interested to discover who betrayed them.'

Gemma was stunned. 'George Fayed?'

Mike nodded. 'He's been passing on information about the Chinese to ASIO for a couple of years. Don't ask me how I know this and you didn't hear it from me.'

One of the country's most unsavoury and powerful crims, Gemma thought, has been in bed with the Australian Security and Intelligence Organisation all this time. Slowly, she took Mike's mobile and keyed the numbers. She didn't have to wait long. Almost immediately, the phone was answered; a man's guarded voice.

'Yes?'

'George Fayed?' Gemma asked.

The voice changed. 'Who is this?'

You'd better hear me real good, she thought, because I'm going to bring you down, George Fayed.

'My name is Gemma Lincoln,' she said. 'You're holding an acquaintance of mine.' She paused, listening to the silence humming between them. 'And I've got a deal you might consider,' she continued. The silence continued until she spoke again. 'I'm a licensed private investigator and we know you are holding a man inside your house.' Again, he said nothing. It was unnerving, she realised, to have her voice just sink into nothing like this. 'Are you there?' she asked.

'I'm here,' he said. 'What's this deal you're talking about?'

'You give me back Steve Brannigan,' she said, 'immediately. He comes out of your place in good health.' She paused. 'If that doesn't happen, not only will your house be raided by the State Protection Group and you will be charged with kidnap and attempted murder'—she paused herself, for effect—'but also files demonstrating your status as a registered police informant will be copied and sent out to interested parties.'

She heard the shocked intake of breath. 'I don't know what you're talking about,' said the voice. But he was rattled.

'I know Steve Brannigan is in your house.'

Let your paranoia feed, George Fayed, she prayed. Are you looking around, wondering which of your lieutenants has betrayed you? Let's destabilise your empire, she thought. 'You've got a spy in your camp,' said Gemma.

The long silence continued. Gemma could just hear what sounded like whispered consultations going on, away from the phone line. Cop that, you bastard, Gemma thought. Is it you? Is it you? she imagined Fayed thinking, as he looked around. Her spirits had lifted enormously in the last five minutes. Now she had the power. She had the negotiating upper hand. She could almost feel the drug lord's mind ticking over, working out his position.

'Listen, you little bitch. You've got nothing to deal with. If I see as much as a probationary constable anywhere near my house, your friend dies of an overdose. I found him lying on the street and had the goodness to pick him up and put him to bed while I found out who he is. I've got witnesses who can testify to his growing drug habit.'

Gemma could hear her heartbeat pounding in her head. Shock dried her mouth. She found she couldn't swallow. This was not how it was supposed to work out.

'If you do anything to move on me, he'll be dead—by his own hand.' Fayed stressed the last few words. 'So call it off now,' he said. 'Or your friend dies like the dog he is.'

The line suddenly cut out.

Gemma stared ahead sightlessly. 'Oh Jesus,' she whispered, 'what have I done?'

'What happened?' Mike asked.

The seeming safety of the dim garage suddenly

452 • GABRIELLE LORD

felt like the dark chill of the tomb, the dull glow
of the van's interior light funereal and threatening.

'What happened?' Mike repeated. Outside the
storm raged while Gemma told him.

'Look,' he said, 'this is a gambit. He can't win
this round. It's foolproof. If he's exposed as an
informant, he's finished. He wouldn't dare kill
Steve.'

'He's killed other people and never even been
charged,' Gemma said. 'He could do it. He could
get away with it. And he knows it.'

'But not a cop,' Mike added. 'He wouldn't do
this.'

Gemma swung round to him. 'How can you be
so sure? You're just saying that to make me feel
better.'

'I believe he'll do what we want,' Mike said.
'This is just a gambit while he plans a way out.
Steve's going to be okay. He's going to have to give
him up or be exposed.'

'How can you say that?' Gemma said, her hand
shaking as she picked up her mobile. 'He's got
nothing to lose! If he's to be exposed as an informant, what's another dead man to him? I have to
call the raid off.'

She nearly jumped out of her skin when her
phone started to ring.

'Hullo?' she said.

'It's the cavalry,' said Angie. 'As soon as the
briefing is over we're on our way!'

Gemma panicked. 'No, no!' she screamed down
the phone. 'You can't! You mustn't. Fayed's threat-

ened to kill Steve the second there's any hint of a police raid. Please, tell them to back off!'

'I'll tell them,' said Angie, 'but you can't expect them to do it. Eventually they'll have to go in after Steve. Ian Lovelock received a coded signal from him saying he was in strife and would ring again. When he didn't, Ian reported it and we're treating it as a Signal One.'

'But Fayed will kill him!'

'Gemster, we've got to move! This is kidnapping. This is very serious.'

'You bet it's serious!' Gemma screamed. 'Tell them what Fayed told me,' she begged. 'Steve will die if he sees anything like police activity.' Gemma felt desperate. 'At least get them to wait till Mike transmits the layout of Fayed's place. Tell them they can't act without that sort of refined intelligence.'

Angie lowered her voice. 'I'll do my best, but you should know there are people higher up in the job who think that something like this is just what they need. They'll get increased funding, more press coverage. More get tough on drug barons bullshit.'

'Angie I'm talking about Steve's *life*! Not some goddamn PR operation for the brass to wank over.'

'Girl, I know it. I'm just passing on what I hear. You know how stupid some of those clowns are!'

'Call them off. Right now!'

'I'll do my best,' repeated Angie.

'*No!*' shouted Gemma. But it was too late. Angie was gone. 'God, Mike. What am I going to do?'

'Ring Fayed again,' urged Mike. 'Tell him we'll do everything he wants. Calm the whole situation down a few notches. He can't win. It's only a matter of time before he sees that.'

'Steve could be dead before he does!' Gemma made a decision. All the fear and frustration in her mind and body suddenly coalesced and her resolution not only seemed possible, but also the only direction to take. 'I know what has to be done,' she said. 'I'm going in myself.'

'That's crazy,' said Mike. 'What the hell do you think you can do by yourself in there?' Almost without a pause he added, 'I'll come with you.'

'No,' she said. 'I need you on the outside. You told me how you can translate—demodulate the radio frequencies,' she said. 'Okay. Start demodulating right now. Get me the code for that metal roller door.'

'You'll just end up in the same mess as Steve,' said Mike. 'At least wait until the SPG people get here.'

'I've got to get him out before any SPG operation,' said Gemma. 'Or Steve dies.'

'Let the experts do their job, Gemma,' Mike said. 'They'll get him out.'

'Experts? There's no time!' Her voice was almost inaudible. 'Do you know how long it takes to depress a plunger full of heroin into someone's arm?' she asked. 'Death is almost instantaneous.'

She couldn't bear hearing her own words. She jumped out of the van and walked around it, stretching cramped legs and back, needing to move, to pace, to plan. How could it all have gone so terribly wrong? Why hadn't she thought of a Naltrexone implant for Steve earlier? Why didn't he think of it himself? How could Fayed have turned what seemed to be their unassailable position of strength into a threat, and one that was only too easily carried out? The questions whirled in her mind as the storm seemed to gather strength. He'd get away with this murder as he'd got away with others. He didn't have to deal with other criminals like the Litchfield family. He didn't have to make alliances at all. Was it possible he was big enough and powerful enough to crush any other rival, even if he were exposed as a police dog?

She returned to the van.

'I have to go in,' she told Mike. 'At least that way, I can get to Steve. There's a chance I can get him out safely.' She turned to him. 'If I can't . . . ' Her voice faltered. Naltrexone might defend her against the effects of a hit, but it was no magic shield. If the dose of heroin was large enough, it would depress her system and kill her. It would be the end of her life and Steve's too. She didn't want to think about their two bodies lying in Fayed's fortress. But maybe that's what it would take to bring Fayed down.

'What I mean is that with two of us found over-dosed,' she said, 'Fayed's far less likely to get off a murder charge. One death might be "accidental". But two deaths is evidence in a successful murder trial.'

'Noble but crazy,' said Mike. He looked up from

the screen of his laptop. 'Listen, Gemma, if you're determined to go in, I must go in with you. The second you operate that door code, they're going to come after you.'

'That's why you must stay here. I need you to create a diversion to cover me. Something that won't endanger Steve.'

'Anything I do could be dangerous,' Mike said. 'You know Fayed's paranoia.'

'The storm,' she said. 'Make it look like the storm is interfering with his security system. Can you blank out his screens for a while from out here?'

Mike looked as if he was about to argue with her, but he agreed. 'Okay. It's crazy but it's worth a try. Let's have a closer look at the layout.'

So now she was crouched down on the floor of the passenger seat with Mike in the driver's seat, the Glock sitting in the small of her back. She hardly dared breathe. She and Mike had roughed out a map of the internal layout, matching up the doorways and the corridors, using the furnishings as navaids and landmarks. They had studied the changing views until Gemma felt she had some understanding of where Steve was in relation to the rest of the space.

'That room where Steve is,' said Mike, 'doesn't appear to be up with the living areas. My bet is that it's underneath the second and third storey, at street level, with the parking area and the machine shop. The flooring looks to be the same substance—heavy-duty cement with some sort of finish.'

Gemma listened to the rain on the roof of the garage.

'We have to move now,' she said. 'The storm will start losing intensity.'

Mike started the engine and Gemma swallowed hard. He had given her the numerical code to the roller door in case she needed it again and the numbers were branded in her memory. She swayed a little as the van turned out of the garage, slowly making its way back towards Fayed's huge bunker. Mike turned the corner, and parked the van out of the sight line of the fortress building.

'The next big lightning strike,' he said, 'I'm going to use a broadband video jammer. I can splatter the bastards with a noise attack every time there's lightning. Their security screens will go scrambled eggs. Pray that they think it's connected to the storm. But I can only make it last a few seconds, otherwise they'll get suspicious. So you'll have to get in fast and move around fast with every crash of thunder. Then presume that all the cameras are live again. We don't want them thinking there's more than electrical interference involved. Okay? You've got a few seconds after the lightning flashes. It's not much, but if you can move fast, you've got a chance.'

He pulled out and drove slowly down the street as if he were going to drive right past, but at the last moment, slowed briefly.

'The minute you see I've got Steve safe,' Gemma

458 • GABRIELLE LORD

said, 'start sending a live feed of what's going on in this place to the police Intranet, attention Ian Lovelock.'

She slid the door of the van open. Rain chilled her face and Mike touched her arm.

'I'd say break a leg,' he said 'but you've already done that.'

Gemma jumped at the next rolling peal of thunder and flattened against a wall, cold, wet and scared stiff, watching the tail lights of the van disappearing. The only thing that kept her going was the thought of Steve lying in there, already doped to the eyeballs. She heard the rumbling of the metal roller door and silently blessed Mike. As soon as it was opened sufficiently, she rolled under it. Already, it was descending again and she prayed that Mike had crashed their screens for that moment. She crawled through the dim garage, ducking behind one of several black Mercedes. The roller door was home again. She crouched, keeping in the shadows, between the three parked cars. Cautiously, she made her way to the small partly enclosed machine shop at the right-hand back wall of the underground parking area. She hunched near the door, knowing that there was a camera angle that picked up this area, waiting for the thunderclap that would give her a little free time to move.

She could hear footsteps. Gemma closed her eyes in dismay. It didn't work, she thought. They know I'm here. She flattened herself in the dim corner, willing herself invisible. The footsteps were louder now as the two men ran into the parking area. Too scared to move, Gemma listened. Were they searching for her, moving from one area to the next, finally coming in here, to find her shaking with fear near the workshop?

She waited. Then she heard the sound of car doors slamming, the rumble of the roller door as it went up. She breathed a sigh of relief. A black Mercedes drove out, leaving the stink of engine and hot metal behind. She heard it take off in the same direction as the van and prayed that Mike had taken the necessary evasive action and hidden both himself and the van with its precious documentation of the Fayed family's domestic epicentre.

Now she tried to orient herself. Mike had thought the room in which Steve lay was further underneath the house, to the left of the roller door, in the bowels of the building on this level. Pressing herself against the walls, and desperately trying to remember the camera angles and how to avoid them, Gemma eased her way out along the back wall. She crawled along in the semi-darkness until she came to a security gate. She pressed the same numbers Mike had demodulated for the garage. Nothing happened for a second, then she was rewarded by an electronic hum and the sound of the gate unlocking. She pressed it open, trying to keep as close to the wall as possible, remembering the bank of monitors somewhere upstairs, and the man who sat under them, keeping an eye on the inner and outer worlds of George Fayed.

She was in a narrow corridor, lit only with a

weak naked globe hanging from the ceiling a little way ahead of her. On her right was what seemed to be a wall of black glass. She was reminded uncomfortably of the black faceted meteorite of her nightmare. She tried to look through its shiny surface, but all she could see was her own outline, and the edges of her face reflected. She moved past the black window towards a lit area further down the corridor. Her mouth had become very dry and she didn't know if it was because of the action of the Naltrexone in her system or the fear that seemed to bang her heartbeat through her head. She strained to listen for any clue, or sound that might let her know where Steve was. Upstairs, she heard the scraping of a chair. Then she heard the clatter of boots on polished floors. She pressed up against the wall, and the hard edges of the Glock were a comfort. The sound of running was getting louder. It was too late to concern herself with being cautious, Gemma realised. Already, they must have seen her on the interior cameras. She broke into a run, crashing down the hall, aiming for the relatively open space of the underground garage and the machine shop where there was some cover.

But the security door she'd previously opened was closed, and no longer responded to her keyed-in digits. She swore, not knowing what to do. Lie low somewhere, she thought. Keeping low, and praying that the cameras would miss her, she pressed onwards until she came to a closed door. This door had a conventional door and handle. Maybe a storage area, she thought. Slowly, she

turned the handle. It wasn't locked. She peered in.
The heat and the smell hit her in the face the
second the door opened and she bit back a scream.
Shit! She'd almost walked into George Fayed's
snake room. For a split second, Gemma was para-
lysed. Dozens of glittering eyes targeted her. Heads
raised, they twined, some escaping, some darting
forward until she'd slammed the door shut. She
recalled the puzzling heat map that had glowed on
Mike's screen in the van. Had it been a heat picture of the snakes?

She hesitated outside the room, shaking, her
mouth so dry she could hardly swallow. Steve
where are you? she whispered silently. Almost in
the same instant she heard something. Again, she
tensed, not knowing what direction it had come
from, disoriented by her recent fright and the
musty closeness of the narrow corridor. Again
came the sound. Someone was whistling. And she
could smell cigarette smoke, fresh, as if someone
was smoking quite nearby. She crept down towards
the end of the corridor. Now she could see that
the corridor she was in ended at a T-intersection
and the sound she'd heard seemed to be coming
from around the corner to the right. Gemma crept
to the end of the wall and peered around. Another
corridor, but this time, she could see a small table
and chair halfway down the hall beside another
doorway. A cigarette was smoking itself to death
on an ashtray on the table. She moved quickly and
silently towards the table and the door just beyond
it. She heard the sound of a man cursing and in

462 • GABRIELLE LORD

that second she knew it was Steve's voice. Keeping a lookout for the owner of the cigarette, Gemma ducked into the room.

Steve was standing in front of a mirror, shaving.

'Steve! What are you doing?' she said. 'What the hell's going on?'

Steve put the razor down and wiped his face with the towel around his neck. He turned to her, his eyes raised casually to a point above her head.

'You shouldn't be here,' he said in a low, toneless voice.

'I saw you,' she said. 'I thought you were nearly dead.'

She looked around. The room they stood in looked very different from what she remembered. It had a bed and desk and through a sliding door, Gemma could see a small shower recess. It reminded Gemma of the self-contained units of hospitals or hotels where staff sometimes stay overnight. Gemma stood in shocked silence. Steve seemed perfectly at home here in the monster's lair, whistling and shaving as if everything was quite normal.

'That's a camera up there,' Steve said, pointing the razor at the top of the doorway. 'They'll be on their way down now. You shouldn't have come in here. It was crazy.'

Behind his words, Gemma could hear the boots thudding upstairs.

'Steve,' she whispered. 'Tell me it isn't true. Tell me what I'm thinking isn't true. Please.'

She was almost in tears. Now she could hear the

shouting and the thudding getting closer and closer.

'Gems, I'd like to be able to help you,' Steve said, 'but really there's nothing I can do.'

'You bastard!' she cried. 'You've done a deal with Fayed, haven't you!'

He frowned. 'I hope you're not armed.' He darted forward and as she dropped her hip and reached behind her for the weapon, he had her wrist in a crushing hold.

'Drop it,' he whispered. 'Now.'

He wrenched the Glock from her fingers. Gemma stared in disbelief, her crushed hand helpless as he shoved the gun out of sight and turned back to the mirror. The footsteps thudded closer. Although it was useless, she looked around but there was nowhere to hide.

'I can't believe this is happening,' she said. 'I can't believe that you could do this. I put my life on the line to come in and get you out of here. And you just—' She was beyond words, beyond heartbreak.

Steve shrugged and affected a rueful look. 'You shouldn't have,' he said. 'I told you to stay away. I thought I made it very clear the other day at Lorraine's.'

Gemma felt one last desperate surge of hope, that Steve was still true to her, and just playing for time.

'Steve,' she whispered. 'Tell me what's going on.'

But before he could answer, two huge men burst into the room and Gemma was grabbed, fingers bruising into her upper arms. She felt all the fight go out of her. It wasn't just the overwhelming odds; it was the final blow—the defection of the man she'd loved and been faithful to, in her fashion, for years. All the while, Steve continued to shave, whistling as he did, barely looking around when a voice shouted down the corridor and George Fayed materialised at the doorway, smaller than he'd appeared on television.

'Let's have a look at what we've got here,' he said, his voice aggressively Australian in its accents.

He wore a silver-grey bespoke suit and his heavy eyebrows hid eyes that Gemma couldn't read in the dim light of the underground corridor. She stared defiantly at him, determined not to reveal how scared she was feeling, how her heart was breaking over her faithless man.

'Let's see what a licensed private investigator looks like. Of the female variety.' He said the last words with withering contempt.

'We look a damn sight better than you,' she said.

'I patted her,' said Steve, turning casually from his shaving. 'She wasn't carrying.'

The lie caused pieces of Gemma's heart to stir.

'I don't like people breaking into my place,' Fayed said, moving too close, sharp jabbing fingers feeling around her body. He stepped back, satisfied she was unarmed. 'You have absolutely no right to be here. Even the police try to find some reason for their pathetic warrants.'

Gemma felt the grip on her arms relax a little. She looked across at Steve. He ignored her.

'Apparently you thought this man was being held here against his will,' said Fayed indicating Steve. 'Does it look like that to you?'

Gemma said nothing.

'Tell me. Does it?'

He let the silence answer as Steve completed his shaving, splashed his face with water, wiped it with the towel and then applied some cologne. The scent of it reached Gemma: it was the exotic fragrance she'd smelled on him in her bed.

'So now I get it,' said Fayed. His smile made his eyes look even colder. 'You're the ex-girlfriend.' He stepped back, glancing across at Steve. 'I've gotta say Lorraine's a great improvement, mate.'

Gemma tightened her jaw and throat, determined not to let her heartbreak show. 'I'm not here as this man's ex-girlfriend,' she said in as tough a voice as she could muster. 'I'm here as part of an operation to bust you, Fayed. You've got no show at all.'

Gemma stared at Steve. As if reading her thoughts he turned to her. 'I don't live in your world anymore, Gemma,' Steve said in a flat voice. 'That world never did a damn thing for me.'

The grip on her arms became sharp as Fayed jerked his head and the bodyguard practically lifted Gemma out of the room and down the corridor, pushing her towards another doorway. Gemma struggled but it was useless. She could hear Steve's footsteps behind them.

'You know,' said Fayed with the same cool display of contempt as before, 'you've really made things very difficult for yourself. And for me. Those threats to call the police in here are quite distressing for me and my family. If they do come here, they'll find nothing. I have interests in Indonesia who own houses where a woman like you can be put to work. For a while, at least. White women tend to age quickly in the tropics. Especially if they have a drug habit.'

'No!' said Gemma. 'We had a deal. I called the police operation off.'

'Shut up, bitch.'

'You *bastards*!' Gemma screamed at them all, seething with helplessness.

Fayed gestured. 'Medication for the lady, please. She's getting overexcited.'

Gemma saw the largest bodyguard pull out a plastic packet. She stared harder. It was a loaded fit.

'Give her a good whack,' said Fayed. 'Knock her out till I decide what's the best thing to do with the interfering little moll.'

Her eyes pleaded with Steve's impassive stare as she struggled against her captors.

'You're going to pay for this!' she screamed. 'People like you think you can get away with murder.'

She was lifted bodily, crushed in the hostile embrace of the bodyguard, thrown into a windowless room just like one of the sacks that covered the floor. Still held in the same vice-like grip, Gemma could only watch while a tourniquet was applied to her arm and a brimming syringe held up before her. Please let the Naltrexone work, she prayed, as the man approached her, his face as impassive as fate. She shuddered as the needle stung its way into her arm. Something surged through her, a dark, alien energy. She felt her knees wobble and had only a glimpse of the stacked shelves as she fell and the light went out. The door was slammed shut, she heard it being locked and then she was left in the darkness.

Gemma lay there, stunned by everything that had happened in the last few minutes. She rolled over onto her stomach and cried. Steve was lost. Instead of just visiting the realms of hell, as the job required, bringing back the information he'd been entrusted with, he'd made the decision to take out citizenship.

She couldn't tell if the terrifying imbalance she was experiencing was because of emotional or drug overload. She stumbled around in the dark, feeling her way with her hands. She fell heavily over something and lay there a moment, overwhelmed by grief, anger and fear. She pulled herself up until she was half-lying, half-sitting across some of the sacks she'd noticed before the light went out. She waited, trying to determine how she felt, whether she was about to be whirled away on heroin's outrageous ecstasy, or knocked out by sheer emotional pain. She became aware that the sacks she was sitting on seemed to contain some lumpy material but she couldn't work out what it was, although it smelled strangely familiar. She felt her way to a clear piece of floor and sat down, shivering, wishing she'd worn warmer clothes. She wondered if there was a camera in here and if so whether it was one of the mysterious murky rooms she and Mike had already seen in the van. Would he recognise her human shape in the coloured blobs on his screen? She scrambled to her feet at sounds from the corridor. Running footsteps and shouts outside. The door suddenly rattled and Gemma dived to the floor and sprawled there, eyes closed, as the door opened. Voices yelled orders.

'Get rid of her!' Fayed's yell pierced the melee. 'Lock her up with the aura.'

Gemma shuddered at the words. What did he mean? Was 'aura' the code name of some death-ray? Being sealed up reminded her of ancient pharoahs, or desiccated vestal virgins mummified in tombs. She tried to control her breathing so that she might pass as unconscious. Breathing in deep also served to calm her. I'm supposed to be stupi-fied, she thought. And it's not far wrong. She was aware of someone coming in, nudging her body with a toe, then half-carrying, half-dragging her out of the room.

Gemma fluttered her eyelids to see. One of Fayed's bodyguards was hauling her along towards the door, behind which Gemma knew snakes writhed. It took every ounce of willpower for her not to scream and struggle. She could at least hope that the door of that room would remain unlocked so she could escape. She stayed floppy, a posture made more realistic by the relief that surged through her as they passed the door to the snake room. Now the bodyguard hauled her out of the corridor and into the underground car park. The man let her slide to the ground and she heard the sound of a door being unlocked. He opened a doorway concealed in a recess in the bedrock and unnoticed by Gemma until now, near the workshop area. But before she'd finished working out how to dive sideways and roll towards the workshop area, the man had shoved her through the half-opened door and slammed it shut again.

All was silent. Despite the fact that they were underground in winter, the air here seemed sticky and humid. She groped around the walls to find she was in some sort of cellar carved out of rock. A repulsive stench filled her nostrils: the odour of rotting meat, made even more disgusting by the sickly warmth of her prison.

For a few moments she sat huddled against the wall, trying to make sense of her surroundings. Something moved in the murkiness, reminding Gemma again of the huge looming shape she'd seen on Mike's screen. Her mouth went dry and this time she knew it wasn't Naltrexone or heroin. It was terror. *There is something in here with me,* she realised. Despite the shock and pain of Steve's cruel rejection and betrayal, her survival instincts sounded a desperate alarm. She froze, straining to see in the dark, to listen in the surrounding stillness. Nothing moved or made any sound and the stink was overwhelming. *I've got to get out of here,* a panicky inner voice screamed. Gemma recalled the areas covered by Fayed's surveillance. This room had been shrouded in darkness, though a murky shape moved in it, like the backdrop to a nightmare. Despite her fear she seized on this thought. If *we* couldn't see what was in here when Mike had it up on his screen, then *I* can't be seen either, she thought. Fayed's system can't pick me up on the security monitors. Hope allayed her tension. I've got a chance of getting out of here, she realised. Carefully, she tried the door. It was locked. She felt around in her pockets for something, some weapon, some tool. But she knew Fayed's locks would be sophisticated and her skills were far from advanced.

Her attention was diverted by a series of loud noises from above. Angie, is that you? Are you in? Gemma prayed. Then she went cold when she remembered that Steve was now an enemy. She quietened the confusing emotions this knowledge caused by listening intently to the growing uproar. The crashing sounds in the building around her were growing to a crescendo of thudding footsteps and shouting. Beyond the door that locked her in, she could hear cars revving up. Then the noises stopped. In the silence that followed Gemma jumped as she heard a terrible sound, a guttural coughing, coming from somewhere in the cellar. She froze. For a second, she imagined a huge carnivore, a powerful tiger, five times her weight and size. '*Lock her up with the aura*', she'd heard Fayed yell. But he hadn't been referring to a death-ray. Gemma recalled Fayed's logo, the stylised golden lizard, and the name of his company, 'Oradoro'. And it didn't mean anything like El Dorado, the city of gold, she now realised. It meant 'golden ora' and the *ora*, she knew, was the huge carnivorous monitor lizard of Indonesia, the komodo dragon.

Gemma stared blindly into the darkness, rigid with terror, imagining the sudden pounce of the enormous reptile, being knocked to the floor, torn open. Oh God, she thought. I've got to get out of here.

She jumped to hear a sound behind her. The door was being unlocked. She spun around. A man stood outside the partly opened door and in the dim light behind him, Gemma could see it was Steve. She pressed back against the wall. My God, she thought, he's come to kill me. I'm the only witness to his treason. Desperately, she tried to press herself further away from the entrance. Steve peered into the cellar, his eyes still unaccustomed to the dark, and Gemma stayed motionless. He hadn't seen her.

'Gemma,' he called. 'It's me. Come on.'

She shrank back further into the gloom, wishing there were more recesses to hide her.

'Hurry,' he said. 'You've got to get out of here.' His eyes suddenly focused and she realised he'd seen her, flattened though she was against the projecting rock face.

'Why?' Gemma's voice was a whispered scream. 'What are you planning next?'

'Gemma, *come on*! You've got to get out.'

'So you can betray me again? Shoot me this

472 • GABRIELLE LORD

time? With me out of the way, you can just go back to Ian Lovelock and your job. Tell them some bullshit, maybe even get decorated. You treacherous, two-faced bastard!'

'Just come on!' he yelled, lurching forward to grab her, 'or we're both dead. There's a glass screen in here that operates just like in the banks,' he said. 'If it goes down and you're still in here, you'll die. Come *out*!'

'Bullshit!' she said, ducking backwards and avoiding his grasp.

Steve cursed and half-came into the cellar, his hand out, attempting to drag her out by force.

She fought with him. 'I'll take my chances with the reptiles,' she said furiously. 'They'd be more trustworthy than you.'

Gemma stopped struggling and measured up the distance. If she could get to the exit, she could still get out of this situation. There was another growl behind her and she twisted round, still held fast in Steve's grip. It was too dark to make out anything in detail but her peripheral vision alerted her to movement somewhere in the murky darkness. She twisted back to face Steve, unable to see his features in the gloom.

'Fayed's sent you to deal with me, hasn't he?' she said. 'You're here to kill me. Otherwise why hasn't anyone noticed that this door's open?'

'Christ, Gemma. There's a full-scale joint raid happening up there. Fayed's got other things on his mind just now,' said Steve.

Gemma strained to listen. It now sounded as if

all hell had broken loose. The entire building, right down to its footings and bedrock was throbbing with ground reverberation as the staccato chop of helicopters sounded. The bastard's telling the truth about that, at least, she thought. This sounds big. Must be Federal, State and everything else.

'Come on, woman. It's like the fall of Saigon upstairs. Hurry while we can still get out of here alive.'

Gemma barely heard him. 'I called off that raid because Fayed said he'd kill you.' Her voice faltered. 'I came in here to get you out. I risked my life for you,' she said in a whisper.

'Don't waste it then,' he said, 'on being completely fucking stupid.'

She was irresolute.

'If you don't believe me, turn around,' said Steve. 'I've been trying not to stir it up, but take a look behind you.'

Gemma stood facing him. 'No way am I going to make it easier for you,' she said, barely able to speak for the tears. 'If you're going to shoot me, do it while I'm facing you.'

She saw his flank drop and his hand move towards his jacket. Gemma dived to the ground, rolling away, uselessly closing her eyes against the bullet. It didn't come immediately. She opened her eyes to see that Steve was standing holding a powerful torch ahead of him so that light shone into the recesses of the sandstone area in which she'd been imprisoned. She was surprised to see no weapon. She followed the beam of light as Steve moved it around. For a few seconds, she couldn't see anything except the reflections from the glass wall ahead that sealed off half the area in which she now stood. Adjusting to her focus, her vision penetrated the reflecting wall. Something moved in the darkness behind the glass.

'Oh my God!' she screamed. 'What is that?'

Lumbering towards her, tongue flickering, was a monster, jaws dripping, saurian eyes refocusing in the sudden light.

TWENTY

Gemma slowly backed away, no longer caring about the danger that Steve posed. The dragon raised its lowered head and stood right up against the partition, towering horridly above her. If that glass screen suddenly dropped, thought Gemma . . .

'Now will you get out?' said Steve, jumping forward and grabbing her arm. 'Or do you want to be eaten alive by the time the cops break through?'

He jerked her backwards and the two of them stumbled out into the corridor, Steve slamming the door shut. Gemma huddled against the wall, feeling sick to her stomach.

'I had to play along with them,' said Steve. 'Fayed never trusted me. If I'd shown the slightest sort of interest in you, we'd both be dead, sweetheart. I had to let him think I was happy to go onto his payroll, that I only wanted to save my own skin.'

'And so you were!' Gemma screamed. 'Don't you dare sweetheart *me*, you arsehole!' She leaned back against the wall. Screaming at Steve had taken the last of her diminishing energy.

'You were brilliant,' he said. 'Because of you, I'm armed and dangerous.' He patted the Glock. 'But how are *you* feeling, after that jab?'

She felt groggy, weak from fright and the pharmaceuticals were fighting it out in her system. Then she remembered the closed circuit cameras. She looked up and, sure enough, there it was, a little hooded camera watching the corridor, sending back all the details of her escape and Steve's actions to Fayed's central control room. In a minute the place would be crawling with his stooges and she'd be dead. This time, there would be no reprieve.

'They'll be watching this,' she said, indicating the camera. 'You're stuffed, you treacherous, double-dealing prick.'

As Steve looked up, Gemma gathered her remaining strength, knocked him off balance and barged past him, back into the underground parking area and the workshop. Around her, the building was exploding like a war zone. Voices shrieked incomprehensible orders upstairs. Shouts from the street were drowned by a crushing noise. Gemma could hear the labouring tracks of an earthmover outside. The metal roller door bulged from the pressure. She realised now why the cars she'd heard starting up earlier had stopped. There was nowhere for them to go, except straight into the arms of the waiting Special Operation officers. At least Steve was telling the truth about this; Fayed and his people sure had other things on their minds.

Ducking between the parked cars, she searched for a safe hideout. She could hear Steve calling her, her name echoing around the car park, punctuated by the crash of metal and the screaming and shouting from upstairs. Now a deafening noise shook the car park area and the whole building trembled. Gemma spun round, trying to work out what was happening. The earthmover had given up on its attempts to move the roller door and now seemed to be battering the very walls of the building. She saw Steve weaving his way through the cars, calling to her. Another mighty crash and great cracks appeared in the wall near the staircase, zig-zagging as she watched. Another surge of gears from the earthmover and the first of the bricks near the frame of the roller door started crumbling. She saw Steve crawling towards her.

'Gemma!' he yelled through the din.

'Piss off!' she shouted. 'Get out of here and start running now. There'll be a hole in that wall any minute.'

'Will you listen to me?' he yelled.

'The whole place is going to be overrun with the people you've sold out,' she yelled back at him. 'I'm giving you one chance to get away.' She tightened her throat against the tears she could feel. Go away, tears, she ordered.

'Gems,' he pleaded. 'Will you see reason? I set this raid up, for Chrissakes.' He pushed his dark hair back from his eyes in a gesture that once used to make her heart stop. 'How do you think the guys out there knew to come here now? They're acting on information received. Received from *me*!'

'You lying bastard!' she shouted. 'This is *my* raid. With Ian Lovelock and Angie. I told Mike to send live video feed!'

'We haven't got time to argue,' he said, making a move towards her.

'Steve,' she warned, 'don't touch me. I never want you to touch me again. If you run now, you can get lost in the confusion. Get your cheating arse out of the country. Do it now. Because I swear I'll do everything in my power to haul you in once I'm out of here.'

Steve continued to stand in front of her, hands helplessly beside him, palms out-turned, beseeching. A frightful sound made her look around. Huge cracks appeared in several of the wide pillars supporting the centre of the car park area. Smaller cracks radiated from the larger rifts. The damage was spreading fast, no longer confined to the side of the building being charged by the bulldozer.

'Where am I supposed to run to?' Steve bellowed. 'The whole joint is collapsing!'

Ahead of Gemma, one of the large central pillars seemed to tremble. She pivoted round. This is crazy, she thought. A hole punched in a downstairs wall can't do this sort of damage. What the hell's going on? For a wild moment she even wondered if an earthquake could be happening simultaneously with the raid. And Steve was right: there was nowhere to go.

The roller door buckled and sagged, bending under the weight of walls that could no longer support themselves. She stopped thinking about Steve, her only thoughts now on survival. Raised voices and racing footsteps alerted her to the arrival of people down the cement staircase. Steve dropped out of sight and Gemma did the same. But she wasn't quite fast enough. One of the two leading bodyguards saw Gemma and raised his weapon, taking aim on the run. She jumped with fright when the Glock fired nearby. The first bodyguard fell. Good shot, Steve, she thought, in spite of everything. The second man disappeared from sight as the sound of the shot reverberated around the disintegrating car park. Maybe he got both of them, she thought. More likely he's dived for cover.

She glimpsed the heavy figure of George Fayed turning the corner of the stairs as she ducked back into her hiding spot. Further shots rang out. The roof started to fall, small chunks crashing around her from the rippling ceiling. I don't want to be buried in here, she prayed, scrambling along the ground. She started crawling away, using the cars as cover, aiming for the collapsing wall near the roller door. Behind the tumbling brickwork, she could see bright light.

This was no earthquake, Gemma realised. The building had been structurally damaged. She remembered Angie telling her how the first floor had been opened out in a continuous space for a wedding reception. And you do that, Gemma thought, by removing the weight-bearing pillars. A thousand people jumping around at the party would have further weakened the structure, and now a D12 battering at the walls and garage door is the last straw.

Fayed's fortress is coming down like the walls of Jericho.

She scrambled past another parked car, making her way to the roller door. Maybe I'll be able to hack my way out, she thought, looking around for an implement. But she knew she wouldn't have the strength. I'm going to die down here, she thought, crushed to death in a drug lord's fortress.

She was aware of more brilliant light and lifted her head cautiously. Someone with oxy gear was cutting through the metal door. Had the raiding party realised the imminent collapse of the building and now changed their mode of entry? Please don't fall down on me now, she pleaded. It was then she noticed George Fayed edging his way towards the workshop, a 9 mm Browning double-action automatic in his hand. She saw Steve crouched underneath a car near the workshop and as she watched, he positioned himself at the end of the vehicle, closer to the workshop's entrance as Fayed circled the area, wild-eyed, sweeping his gun before him. More of the screeching, blinding oxy light now showed as the torch cut through the steel garage door. In a few moments, Gemma realised, there'd be a hole big enough for entry. That's if the whole building doesn't fall down first and crush us all to death. Almost as she thought this, several more chunks of concrete fell from the ceiling, crashing through the windscreen of the car she was beside. I want to be out of here, she prayed, back home with my Taxi cat, licking my wounds, safe in my nest.

The shocking sound of further gunfire in a closed space startled her into red alert. She peered out. What she saw both took her breath away and made her heart start to question her judgment of the man who now had George Fayed pinned down, kicking and cursing, on the oily ground near the workshop. Steve had straddled Fayed and was trying to secure his firing arm, still free and dangerously equipped with the Browning automatic. The Glock was nowhere to be seen.

'Steve!' she screamed, scuttling like a crab towards the struggling pair. The frightening whine and skid of ricochet a nanosecond after a bullet shot, made her swing round to see the second bodyguard coming for them, firing as he weaved between the cars. He disappeared, then jumped out to take aim. Gemma dived between two cars. Steve had all the trouble he needed trying to control the powerful and desperate drug lord. She would deal with his offsider. A piece of concrete the size of a small fridge crashed almost on the exact spot she'd just vacated. She peered around it, trying to pinpoint Fayed's bodyguard. The blaze and glare of the oxy-cutting and the sound of the building above her folding in on itself, distracted her for a second and in that moment, the bodyguard was suddenly in front of Steve, blocking Gemma's view. She saw the Glock lying on the ground out of Steve's reach. *He's going to kill Steve,* she thought. Without thinking, she grabbed the gun and fired it directly at the bodyguard. Down he went, and an arc of blood painted the cracking pillar nearby as he knocked Steve down, then rolled to a standstill. Gemma executed the best combat roll of her life, flipping right side up with the Glock in her hand again. Steve bellowed something which Gemma couldn't understand. Fayed scrambled to his feet while Steve, stunned, tried to regain control of his adversary. She swung the weapon at Fayed.

'Don't even think about it,' he said. Gemma slowly lowered the Glock. Fayed's Browning was now just inches away from Steve's face. 'You're going to get me out of here!' he said to Steve. He kicked him. 'Dirty'—kick—'lying'—kick—'copper *bastard*'—double kick.

Gemma could hardly bear to watch.

'Stop it!' she yelled uselessly. Fayed didn't bother turning towards her when he spoke. 'We're getting out of here—you and me. Get in the car. Your bitch girlfriend can negotiate with the police. *Now!*'

Fayed had slowly stooped until he'd picked up the other automatic dropped by his dead bodyguard. The sight of the Browning's square profile so close to Steve's half-closed eyes was horrible. One of the Browning twins was trained on Gemma as she froze midstep. 'Okay, okay,' she said. 'I'll get you out of here.'

Another shout from Fayed and she started moving towards the roller door.

A terrible ripping sound made Gemma turn her head to see the staircase down which Fayed and his now dead bodyguards had run start to buckle, folding in on itself as the corner around which it turned started to collapse. The treble crash of glass smashing accompanied clouds of choking cement dust. Tiny stones stung Gemma's face.

'Get me out of here now or your boyfriend's dead!' Fayed shrieked through the dust.

Gemma stumbled round fallen debris, past the cracking pillars towards the roller door. Three sides of the square had now been cut in the door and the torch was just starting to eat its firey way through the fourth side of the armoured steel. She flinched as another chunk of ceiling fell down, revealing the underlying criss-crossed steel rein-forcements.

Through the dust, Gemma saw something move. At first she thought it was one of the body-guards, recovering from his wounds. But then she realised that the large, low-moving shape darting among the debris was not human. It was the huge, dinosaur-like reptile, its drooling head swinging fast from side to side, long tongue flicking, rear-ing up against a pillar. She turned and ran and was about to yell a warning, but the sound of the oxy-grinder rendered her voice useless. And yet a terrible scream penetrated even that. Gemma swung around. A huge torpedo-like weapon struck Fayed, smashing him to the ground. She couldn't comprehend what was happening. She was aware of Steve rolling to one side, away from the flailing arm that held one of the Brownings. Then he vanished in the gloom. Another frightful shriek, cut off by a choking gurgle, was the last sound George Fayed ever made. Transfixed with horror, she screamed as something loomed up out of the dust and grabbed her. It was Steve. Gemma couldn't believe her eyes. Despite the imminent collapse of the building around it, the beast continued to disembowel George Fayed, shaking the body from side to side, entrails and shredded flesh flying in ribbons.

'C'mon,' Steve shouted. 'We're getting out of here!'

In the midst of all the carnage and filth, the din of the oxy gear, the crash of falling masonry, Gemma was aware of the heavy scent of his cologne. Then it all came together in a sickening crescendo—the heavy fragrance, ribbons, shredding, her attacker. Out of the confusion, she tried to grasp something, some insight. Then the roof fell in.

•

Heather Pike's was the first face that swam into view as Gemma woke up. She looked around, taking in her surroundings: pastel shades, hospital bed, drip posts nearby, and a huge arrangement of late roses in a vase near the black screen of a television. Gemma struggled to get up.

'It's okay,' said Heather. 'You're okay, and so is

Steve. Mostly. The surgeon just cleaned you up and I think you should stay in for observation. We don't know how hard you hit your head.'

A young nurse hurried into the room. 'Your sister's on her way,' she said.

Gemma took a deep breath. 'What happened?'

'The building you were in collapsed. You and Steve were pulled out. Others weren't so lucky.' There was a pause. 'Do you remember it?' Heather asked.

Gemma nodded. 'I just hope the dragon made it,' she said and started to laugh when she saw the glances exchanged by Heather and the young nurse. She stopped as suddenly, as a spasm of pain hit her flank. 'I need to make a phone call.' She reached over and picked up the phone.

As she did, Angie walked in.

'Speak of the devil,' said Gemma as Angie leaned over and kissed her. She'd brought an early bunch of jonquils.

'Ange,' she said, 'I was just going to ring you and tell you. His jacket was slashed to ribbons. The night I was attacked. His jacket was cut into strips.'

Angie whipped out her notebook and noted this. She looked up, a puzzled frown on her face. 'Why does a man wear a slashed jacket?' she asked.

TWENTY-ONE

The doorbell sounded and Gemma peered sideways out the window. Minkie Montreau was on the doorstep, no longer dressed in her usual black elegance but glowing in a dark red velvet suit over a figure-hugging leopardskin print sweater, a little black hat, iridescent feathers curving round one subtly rouged cheek. Gemma opened the door and was wondering whether or not she should ask her visitor in when Minkie resolved it herself.

'I'm not staying,' she said. 'I won't come in. Anthony and I are about to leave on a nice cruise together. Courtesy of the Stanford Macquarie Prize.' She winked. 'You didn't know he won? Isn't that wonderful?'

'Art prizes have not been uppermost in my mind lately,' Gemma said.

Minkie continued. 'Patricia Greengate has been entering the Stanford for years and years. *And* many other art competitions. Patricia Greengate has never won a sausage.' Minkie waved the envelope she was holding to make her point. 'But

Anthony Love wins the first major prize he ever enters! Just you wait till the time is right and I ring my contacts in the industry Can you imagine what sort of furore this will create in the so-called art world? Art snake pit, more like it.'

She almost handed Gemma the envelope she was holding, but pulled it back to flutter it around a little more.

'Your account,' she said. 'I'm settling it in person to say thank you. I'm so grateful to you for not saying anything about that little matter on the video you sent me.' Gemma took the envelope next time it came near, fearing Minkie might never relinquish it.

'It doesn't matter now what Patricia's tiresome husband says or does anymore. She's divorcing him. I presume it was he who procured your services?'

'I took myself off the case,' said Gemma, 'as soon as I realised there was a conflict of interest.' Not to mention the fact that my business has collapsed, she didn't say.

'It's a small world, isn't it?' laughed Minkie as she trotted off with a wave.

It sure is, thought Gemma, when you're engaged to work for two parties who happen to share a spouse. Especially when that spouse creates a whole new identity.

She was about to close the door when she saw Mike's van pulling up. Minkie and Mike passed each other on the top step, Mike turning to take a second glance at the extraordinary feathered figure. Gemma was reminded of some strange mythological beast, half-bird, half-woman. But not, after all, a harpy, she thought. She stood in the doorway, waiting for Mike to come down. He was looking much better than when she'd last seen him, tense and exhausted. She stepped back to let him in, closing the door after him. She looked up at him and he paused on his way down the corridor.

'Thanks for everything you did, Mike,' she said.

'You weren't too bad yourself.' He grinned and walked into the operatives' office. Gemma followed.

'I'm just picking up a few things,' he said. 'And I also wanted to warn you,' he said. 'The pictures of George Fayed being eaten by the Komodo dragon are all over the Internet,' he said. 'Just in case someone thinks it's funny to send them to you. The CCT frames just kept rolling on right up until the roof caved in.'

She shivered. 'I never thought I'd get out of there alive,' she said. 'And I thought Steve was a goner, too.'

'How is he?'

She shook her head and looked away from him. I can't even think about Steve at the moment, she thought. 'He's still in hospital,' she said.

'What's up with him?'

'I'm not sure,' she said. 'I heard there were a couple of fractures and lacerations. He was protected from the worst of the cave-in by the same pillar that saved me. It half-fell and then got wedged across at an angle. We were lucky enough to be in the corner pocket.'

'You heard?' said Mike. 'You mean you haven't visited him yet?'

She put a hand around to feel the injury on her side. 'I don't trust him, Mike,' she said. 'I can't believe in him anymore.'

'You've got to talk to him,' said Mike.

I've got to talk to him, thought Gemma, as she drove to St Vincents an hour later. She'd been putting this moment off but Mike was right. She remembered the horrible moment of Steve's unblinking choice, the humiliating difference between herself, dishevelled and dirty, and the beautiful swansdown powder blue vision of Lorraine Litchfield.

By the time she'd found him, sitting up on a small enclosed verandah, working on his laptop with one hand, the other awkward in plaster, one plastered leg stuck out onto a chair opposite, she'd composed herself.

He turned at her presence, moments before he could have heard her approach and his face softened into the smile she'd always loved to see. His hair was shorter than she'd ever seen it, and shaved patches on his scalp were criss-crossed with stitches.

He put the laptop aside and crookedly began to stand up, groping for the crutches angled against the chair.

'Don't get up,' she said.

But he was already standing, gripping the crutches. 'Look at me,' he said. 'What a pathetic figure.' He looked into her face. 'I didn't think you'd ever come,' he said, in a voice so low she had to strain to hear.

She started to move forward on automatic, then stopped and stepped back, not knowing what to say, how to start. 'I can't trust you anymore,' she blurted out. 'I don't think I can ever trust you again.'

Steve hung between his crutches, the iron stirrup under his plastered leg scraping as he adjusted his position, his face suddenly serious. 'I guess we've both got issues of trust to hammer out,' he finally said.

'What do you mean?'

'You know what I mean. Your cyberstalker. Your chat room flirting.' He saw her shocked face. 'Remember how you wouldn't tell me how it all started? Did you really think I wouldn't work it out?'

Sometimes I forget, she thought, that my boyfriend is a highly intuitive detective.

Steve's face was dark now, no hint of the earlier pleasure in seeing her. 'It's such a crap thing to do. All the lying that goes on there. A person doesn't even have to show their face.'

'I know it was silly,' she said. 'And I regretted it straightaway. Hell, Steve, I'm only human.' She paused. 'And *you* should talk. You *work* in lying. Your living is lying.'

With unflinching eyes locked onto his, Gemma spoke. 'Did you do a deal with George Fayed?'

'Yes,' Steve said. 'But I had my fingers crossed behind my back.'

Then he patted another chair on the verandah. 'Sit down, Gems,' he said. 'It's time we talked.'

She felt her stomach turn at the words. He's going to call it off, she thought. He's going to tell me he's in love with Lorraine Litchfield and he and I are finished.

'I've got something to tell you,' he said and her heart contracted. 'I'm going to be off work for a while with this—' He indicated his bandaged limbs. 'When I get out of here, why don't we jump in my car and take a drive up the coast somewhere? Find some sunshine, take a break?'

She leaned across and gently kissed him. Her eyes were filled with tears. 'I thought you were just about to sack me,' she said. 'I'd love to, but I won't be able to afford it. I've got to lay everyone off and by the time I give them severance pay, I'll be flat broke. I could take a week off, maybe,' she added. 'But that's all. I'll have to hire myself out. Become a Pinkerton's girl, or something.'

He smoothed her hair. 'Just so long as you don't get into mischief again on the Net.'

'I didn't actually *do* anything except pretend to be someone else in a chat room,' she continued and it sounded pathetic. 'That gold Scorpio charm,' she began, 'it's still somewhere at my place.'

She could tell from his frown that he didn't know what she meant for a moment.

'That thing?' he said. 'I don't want it.'

She geared herself up emotionally for the question she had to ask. 'I've got to ask you this,' she said. 'Have you been having an affair with Lorraine Litchfield?'

The expression on Steve's face suddenly changed and he looked past her.

'Oh shit,' he said.

Gemma turned to see a vision in a fluffy white angora long-sleeved, short-skirted figure-hugging dress, knee-length white boots and a cascade of finely tuned and tousled hair approaching them. Behind her was the budgie man, still wearing the pineapple Hawaiian shirt. Lorraine Litchfield propped like a startled horse when she saw Gemma. Gemma noticed her new, thick, collagen-enhanced lips glistened wet with scarlet lipstick.

'What's *she* doing here?' she yelled, jabbing a long purple nail in Gemma's direction.

Gemma saw Steve get a firm grip on his crutches.

'Lorraine,' he said, 'I could ask the same of you.'

Lorraine's blue eyes narrowed into navy slits. 'I'm here,' she announced to the whole corridor, pouting her impossible lips, 'visiting my fiancé. And *that* woman'—the purple nail jabbed towards Gemma again—'has got no business here at all.' Lorraine clutched a fluffy little bag and Gemma wondered if the M1911 was stashed inside and wondered also when hospitals would become more security conscious.

'Your *fiancé* must be on another floor of the hospital,' said Steve. 'I'm having a private conversation with my girlfriend. I'd like you to leave us in peace now.'

Lorraine looked from one to the other, for a few seconds speechless with fury. 'Your *girlfriend*?' she shrieked. 'That bitch? You chose me! You said there was no contest!'

'That's right,' said Steve. He swung closer to Gemma on his crutches and they stood together, blocking Lorraine's entry into the enclosed area. 'And I meant it. There isn't.'

'Come on, Lorrie,' said the budgie man. 'This isn't the time or the place. Let's get out of here.'

'You promised me!' she screamed. 'What can you see in her? She's *old!*'

'Leave now, Lorraine,' said Steve, 'or I'll get security up here and have you forcibly removed.'

The budgie man attempted to steer Lorraine away. 'You can see how things are here. This isn't doing any good. Come on.'

Lorraine swung round on him, shoving him. 'Piss off, limpdick!' she yelled.

Then she turned on Gemma and her face was distorted with hatred. 'Why don't you tell your so-called girlfriend about what we did in Tezza's bed! I'll bet you haven't told her that!' Her eyes had turned black with fury and her chin was lifted in triumph and somehow, the plumped-up lips had become tight and mean.

Despite feeling her heart give a great lurch, Gemma didn't miss a beat. 'Of course he's told me about it, Lorraine,' she said. 'My boyfriend tells me everything.' And in that moment she could feel a wave of loving gratitude emanating from Steve as he grasped her hand and squeezed it. Inspired, Gemma continued. 'He even showed me the proof that you murdered your husband. Come near either of us again, and he hands it over to the investigating detectives. By the time you get out of Silverwater, you'll be even older than me!'

Lorraine Litchfield's face paled with shock. She was struck speechless. The plump lips gaped. Kosta's source was right on the money, Gemma realised. You did kill your husband. Steve pressed the red button in the wall with the end of a crutch and Lorraine, still stunned, backed away.

'Goodbye, Lorraine,' Steve said.

Lorraine looked from Steve to Gemma, her gaze filled with poisonous hatred.

'Lorrie, come on.' The budgie man hauled her away, but she swung round, screaming. 'You're *dead,* bitch! Do you hear me?'

The lift doors opened and a nurse and a security officer hurried down the hallway as the budgie man squashed Lorraine into the lift before the doors closed on them.

'What's going on here?' asked the nurse as she hurried over. The lift hummed downwards, Lorraine Litchfield's last hysterical curse floating in the air like a bad smell.

'Who was that?' asked the nurse, turning round at the sound.

'No one important,' said Steve. He tightened his arm around Gemma.

On the drive back home, Gemma was preoccupied with two things: she wished she'd asked Lorraine why she always dressed like a matching bathroom set and she wondered how long it would take before she could completely forgive Steve.

When she arrived home, Mike was sitting at the desk in the operatives' room watching the news on the small portable TV.

'Look at this,' he said as she walked in. On the screen, despite the blanket she was clutching over her face, Gemma saw the sharp profile of Skanda Bergen between two suited detectives, being pressed down into the back seat of a police vehicle.

'She was refused bail,' said Mike, leaning over to turn the set off.

'I should hope so,' said Gemma.

'How did it go?' he asked, referring to her visit to Steve.

'I'm not sure,' she replied, turning on her way into her office. 'Lorraine Litchfield turned up and created a scene.' She paused. 'And I heard something I didn't want to hear.'

'Look,' said Mike standing up. 'Give yourself a break. And Steve. You've been through a hell of a lot lately. You've cracked a major murder investigation, you've been through a fire fight, you've been badly beaten up, you've only just escaped from a collapsing building, and your business has almost been destroyed by some malicious bastard. You need to take it easy for a while.'

'I can't afford to take it easy,' she said, going over to her desk. 'I have no idea how I'm going to climb back out of this hole.' She indicated the pile of bills on the spike on her desk to Mike who stood at the doorway.

'I had a dream,' she said, 'of a meteorite rushing towards me. I didn't realise it would hit so hard.'

She ripped open the envelope Minkie Montreau had given her. 'Here's a bit of good news for a change,' she said, barely glancing at the cheque in her hand. 'I tripled the bill and rounded it up before I sent to Benjamin Glass's widow, and she's paid up without a squeak. Ten grand will keep me solvent for just a little while longer.' Gemma remembered the bills that waited to be paid: credit accounts, rates, an astronomical telephone bill, the bank card.

'I wish you'd use a decent bookkeeping program,' Mike said. 'I can set up a straightforward one for you.'

'I can just afford to pay your severance payout as it is,' she said. 'I can't afford any extra services.'

'Bill me later,' he said, 'when things improve.'

'God knows when that'll be,' she said. 'But I've got to get back into work. How's my computer system?'

Mike smiled. 'As clean as I could get it,' he said. 'While you were in hospital I installed the latest virus scanner for you. You're all cleaned up and ready to go.'

'Can you guarantee it will never happen again?'

Mike shook his head. 'There's no guarantee,' he said. 'All we can do is keep up with the hackers. Just keep banging out incremental improvements, day by day.'

'So any time something like this could happen again?'

'If you never open email attachments, you can stay a lot safer,' he said.

Gemma nodded.

'Get your correspondents to include their information in the body of the email. Most of the problems are caused by script kiddies mucking around because they can.'

'You said 'as clean as you could get it,' she quoted.

'I want to do one more thing,' he said. 'It's something I should have done right at the start.'

He sat at her desk and Gemma stood behind him, watching.

'I'll have to come up with a nice new business name,' she said. 'I've never been crazy about the Mercator etcetera.'

Mike leaned forward, concentrating on the screen.

'It's time for a name change and a new image.'

'What about komodo dragon?' Mike suggested, fingers still moving over the keys, running through arcane programming.

'I don't think so,' she said.

Mike stopped work and stared at the screen. 'Well, bugger me,' he said.

'What?'

'Just let me check if this is right.'

'If what is right?' Gemma said. 'What are you talking about?'

Mike saved his work and leaned back in her chair. 'Are you ready for this?' he asked.

'Ready for what?'

'All the mess generated by the exposure of your password and records, the zombie, everything,' he said, 'distracted me from one very basic fact.'

'*What?*'

'The original security breach didn't happen via some cyberstalker out there,' he said. 'The initial security breach happened right *here,* in this office, on this very machine.'

'But,' she said, 'the only people who have access to this machine are myself and the people who work for me.'

'Exactly,' said Mike. 'And I know it's not me who broke in to your system.'

'And I know it's not me,' she said.

'That leaves only two possibilities,' she said.

Mike made a face. 'It's either that self-righteous little religious fanatic or Miss Mouse,' he said.

It took him a while but it was when he retrieved Louise's deleted email that he found what they were looking for. 'She was talking to the enemy all the time,' Mike said. 'Telling Solidere Security everything we were doing.'

'You were right about being set up,' Gemma

said. 'Why would she do such a thing? I should feel really angry about it.'

'I bloody do,' said Mike. 'Because of her I got a thumping.'

'Looking back now it all seems so clear,' she said thoughtfully. 'She always had an air of grievance. She never went anywhere. She had that wretched mother to take care of.'

'She would have looked at you,' said Mike, 'and it must have seemed that you had everything going for you. Looks, brains, your own business, a boyfriend . . .'

'That's all gone now, just as she planned' said Gemma. 'She must have resented me for not giving her the jobs I gave to Spinner and you. But she just wasn't up to your standard. And then she said something that I wondered about later. "*It's all gone wrong,*" she said. "*Terribly wrong*".'

'She hadn't planned on the escalation,' Mike said. 'She probably just did some spiteful thing like giving your password out and that opened the floodgates to all the other creeps.'

'She's destroyed herself as well as my business,' said Gemma. 'I don't know why I ever employed her in the first place.' She paused. 'I think I felt sorry for her.'

'Not good enough,' said Mike. 'Who's sorry now?'

After Mike had gone, she went out into the kitchen and made a coffee, carried it back to her desk and sat down at the computer. She opened her email program and found she had a message. Only one. From Steve. That's odd, she thought. Steve's never sent me email before. All her investigator's instincts were alerted. Something unusual was happening. Something out of the ordinary. Something *wrong*. She hesitated. If I don't open it, she thought, it can't hurt me. Outside, the coprosma bush moved in a gust of wind and she went to close the window right down, pleased to have the strong grilles between her and the outside world. She came back to the screen and clicked the message open. It didn't take her more than a few seconds to realise that it wasn't from Steve.

'Hullo Dirtygirl,' she read. *'How are things in your apartment at Phoenix Crescent? I've posted your address to all the men who want to help you out with your home invasions and rape fantasies.'* It was signed JollyRoger@hotmail.

Gemma stared at the screen, feeling sick. This wasn't Louise. This was someone else. The cyber-stalker. She hit the delete button as fast as she could. But it was too late. Now every perv and psychopath on the net knew exactly where she lived. All the crazy and famished creatures who believed that sex would satisfy their starving souls could drop in, park in her street, hang round her place. The little apartment that she loved so much now felt dark and menacing. *Who is this Jolly Roger creep?* she asked herself. Her mind was in too much turmoil to think clearly. Just pretend, she told herself, that you're a client who's had this happen to them. Would you think it was just some random loony out there?

She paced around, unable to be still, anxiety driving her. If this were someone else's case, she reasoned, I'd have to say 'no way!'. This is someone who knows you, lady. This is someone very close to you who knows your address and your boyfriend's name. This is someone acting out of personal spite and malice, someone who wants to punish you. For what? For some offence. But I'm not an ex-wife, she thought. I haven't taken some bloke to the cleaners. I haven't put prawns in anyone's hubcaps.

Her mind kept coming back to Mike Moody. Why? she asked herself. Because he fits the profile, he knows me and he's got an angry ex-wife. DNA material matching the assault on Robyn Warburton and the murder of Shelly had been found at Mike's house. On a handkerchief he said wasn't his. From a coat he denied owning. Over a dozen men had been contacted by the police, she knew, to give a sample so as to eliminate them from the investigation. The coat itself had been taken away. If it isn't Mike, it's got to be somebody he knows or somebody who came to his party. Someone's partner perhaps. Gemma racked her brains, trying to remember Mike's flatmate's name. Robert. Roger. Roger something. Jolly Roger. Roger Hollis. Roger Hollis with the familiar voice on the phone. Why was the name, too, familiar? Was it simply because it sounded so ordinary? She went into her program explorer, and typed in 'Roger Hollis'. She waited the few seconds it took to scan through her files.

There was a file in that name from nearly seven years ago. She opened it. As she scrolled through the case, memories returned, clarified. She'd been reminded of someone when Peter Greengate came seeking surveillance on his wife because she'd seen the same hatred in Peter Greengate that she'd seen in another man: the client from whom Gemma had withheld salient facts about his wife's behaviour because of fears for the woman's safety. She read the last comments she'd noted down about the case and gasped. The client from whom she'd withheld information all those years had been *Roger Hollis*!

'*We share similar interests*,' Mike had said of his ex-flatmate, and Gemma had assumed he meant grievances about 'the missus'. But Roger Hollis could also be another cop who knew about her and Steve, a techno-freak, like Mike. A hacker. In Gemma's imagination, the cyberstalker took on the physical dimensions of the man who'd attacked her in the lane. She remembered the ribbon-like streamers that flared from his jacket as she kneed him. Roger Hollis's ex had destroyed his wardrobe. Did that mean she'd slashed them into ribbons? *So now when he plans his attacks on women, he wears the jacket. To remind him of what *she* did, to consecrate his violence.* In Gemma's mind, the stalking figures merged and became one. The cyberstalker, the attacker in the lane, the man who left the DNA traces at Mike's place, were all the same person!

She jumped to her feet. Oh my God, she thought. I've got to get out of here. She raced into the bedroom, packed the Glock in a bag with a box of ammunition, grabbed up her coat, mobile, a rug from the bottom of her cupboard, a packet of chocolate biscuits and left. Roger Hollis now also knows that I lied to him about his wife years ago. He could easily identify himself as the husband in the damning newspaper report about the exposure of her confidential records, cheated on not only by his wife, but also by the very investigator to whom he'd paid good money to catch her at it. Now I'm another woman who's betrayed him. Another woman he has to punish. For a split second, she thought about going to Kit's but rejected the idea, remembering another time she'd led a killer to her sister's house. She ran up the steps, ringing Angie on the way, leaving a message for her.

'Angie, check out a man called Roger Hollis, until recently living at 646 Todman Avenue, Kensington. Bring him in. Match him against the attack on me, Robyn Warburton and Shelly. I'm lying low for a while, because he knows my address.'

She headed for her car, then stopped. He might easily know my car, too, she thought. She hurried through the dusk down to Phoenix Bay. It was deserted except for a dog chasing seagulls but even he trotted off home as night fell and the beach darkened under the pallid light of a rising moon.

With trembling hands, Gemma unlocked the pad-lock on the boatshed, pulling back the half-jammed door, squeezing in and slamming it shut again, pad-locking it on the inside. She switched on the light, bumping it as she did so. The swinging shadows, moving back and forth with the light, startled her and made unsettling patterns on the shrouded shapes of the two lions on the workbench. She reached up and stilled its motion, feeling sick at heart, and looked around. One of the shrouded lions looked wrong somehow, its sheeting hanging right down from the bench to the floor, curtaining the dark area underneath. She knew she hadn't left it like that. She stayed rigid with fear. Someone was under the bench, crouched low. She started to reach for her gun but remembered Angie's warn-ing: *'Gun in bag with zipper get you dead, lady.'* Without taking her eyes off the shrouded area under the workbench, she reached around behind her and her fingers closed on a clay tool, an awl with a sharp point.

'Who's there?' she yelled. She jumped back in alarm, fingers scrabbling for the zip on her gun bag, as the shrouding moved a little. 'Who is it?' she screamed. 'Don't move, just tell me. I've got a gun.'

She'd managed to half unzip the bag and was fishing round blindly for the Glock, too terrified to take her eyes off the veiled hide-out under the counter.

'Don't shoot! Don't shoot! It's me!'

Gemma's body sagged with relief. 'You little bastard, Hugo. Get out of there!' She stood back, as the dishevelled figure crawled out. 'What do you think you're doing here?' she said. 'I could've shot you!'

He crawled out, standing up, face white in the caged globe's light.

'How the hell did you get in here?' she demanded.

'The window,' he said. 'I could just squeeze through.' The two small windows on the northern side of the shed had always been jammed shut. 'I found an old rusty fishing knife,' he said. 'And I got it open. I didn't have anywhere else to go.'

She went to the window and saw where the rotting wood of the window frame splintered.

'Someone dobbed on me and DOCS came round to Naomi's place to get me. I had to make a run for it.' He looked shyly proud. 'Have you got anything to eat?' he added.

She unzipped her bag, pulled out the packet of biscuits and passed them to him.

'Wow,' he said, spotting the Glock. 'Do you carry that everywhere with you?'

'No,' she said.

'Can I hold it?' he asked.

Gemma shook her head. 'It's not a toy, Hugo,' she said sternly, but pathetically glad of his company. She shivered and put on the small one-bar heater, heating up some water for pan coffee from the packet of ground beans under the sink while the Ratbag, seated on the little low foldaway bed, wolfed his way through the biscuits. She switched

506 • GABRIELLE LORD

on the tinny radio, sat in the nineteenth-century wooden office chair and began to breathe again. No one knew about this place except Kit and Steve and he was in hospital. She was safe. She could relax. She had a small flask of brandy on the shelf over the sink and she thought she'd earned one. She was rinsing the glass prior to pouring a shot when she heard something. She turned the tap off but then had to wait until the water had gurgled its way down the drain. She strained, listening. Just the wash of the waves against the rocks, the distant sound of traffic up on the road.

'Did you hear anything?' she asked the Ratbag. He shook his head. He wouldn't have heard a thing, she thought, over the crunching of the biscuits.

Her mobile rang and she nearly jumped out of her skin. Steve, she thought, moving to pick it up.

'Hullo?' she said. For a moment, she didn't get it, thought that someone was playing a joke. A rhythm and blues song was coming down the line and a man's raspy, whispery voice was singing along with it; the voice she'd heard in the lane. '*He sings along,*' Shelly had said, '*while he's doing that to them.*'

He was here. He'd come here, down the phone line, singing into her most private sanctuary. '*Baby did a bad, bad thing,*' she heard, the syncopation jumping ahead of the beat. For a moment, disbelief prevented every other emotion. It isn't possible, she was thinking. How could he trace her like this? The answer was immediate. He knew her mobile number. Now she remembered the breather and the music in the background. That was the song she hadn't quite remembered. Mike's flatmate had rung her at home, claiming to have lost her mobile number.

'What's that music?' asked the Ratbag. For a frozen moment, she stood there as the spidery sound floated out of her mobile. She felt sick. She remembered Mike's words: '*Receivers are transmitters are receivers are transmitters . . .*' With the right scanning equipment, Roger Hollis could pinpoint her via her mobile phone signal. Maybe, even at this very moment, her number active and lit up on a monitor screen, his scanning program was homing in on this little wooden box on deserted Phoenix Bay. And he was speeding closer to her every second. She punched the call off button and threw the handset down as if it were a poisonous snake. It slid off the bench and fell to the floor. Frantic, she checked the bolt locks, wishing like hell she'd secured the place properly. At least he wouldn't be able to fit through the windows. But the boatshed was not safe. The whole place could collapse in a strong wind. And why would I want to huddle here like a sitting duck? We're getting out of here right now, she thought.

'Who was that?' the Ratbag wanted to know, pausing his munching.

'Hugo,' she said. 'We need to get out of here smartly because someone's on his way here. Someone very unpleasant.'

'Who?' he said. 'The singing man?'

'Yes,' she said. 'So it's best we're not here, wouldn't you say?'

'But what if he's already out there now?'

'That's why I'm going to ring Waverley police right now to send a car down here just in case. Okay?'

No, I can't ring out, she realised. This mobile's number will light up on his screen, give him more time to refine his search. She remained immobilised. A triple 0 call could be her death warrant. She prayed that the message she'd left for Angie was being acted on.

'I'm hopeful they might be just about to pick him up anyway,' she said. 'I left a message with his name and details.'

'But what if they don't?' he asked.

'We've still got to get out of here,' she said.

The Ratbag cocked his head to one side, listening.

'What was that?' he said.

She felt fear rising from the pit of her stomach and leaned against the counter for support.

'Did you hear that?' the Ratbag asked. 'There's someone out there.'

Gemma felt the hairs on the back of her neck prickle. She sensed, rather than heard, the presence outside. She grabbed the caged globe and switched it off, pulling the Ratbag down onto the floor with her. 'Don't make a sound,' she said. 'We're ready for him.'

Down on the floor in the dark, her senses were sharpened. Now she thought she could hear the tiny facets of shellgrit scraping together at every stealthy footfall. Was he only yards away beyond the weathered timber of the boatshed?

They crouched in the silence of the night. The waves washed up along the boat racks, tinkling shells on the ebb flow. All was silent and still under the waning moon.

'What do you think you heard?' she whispered.

'Dunno. Something.'

They waited. But nothing happened.

'Maybe I was imagining it,' he said. 'It might've been one of those birds.'

They waited a few more minutes in the silence. Gemma slowly stood up and, keeping well back, peered through the frosted panes. In the bluish murk outside, nothing moved. Under the ghostly light of the moon she could see, just past where the sand met the darkness of the rocks, the molten curve of the riptide, cutting an arc through the modest swell. Maybe we could hide under a boat and wait it out till help arrives, she thought, noticing the dim hulls of the overturned fishing boats. The bulk of the old surf club building on the northern curve of the beach offered some sort of shelter.

'Hugo,' she said, 'we're going to make a run for that building over there, and then, when we're sure the coast is clear, go around the rocks to the inlet of Tamarama beach.'

Dangerous, she thought, in the dark and over uneven ground, but by the time he got here, we'd be safely away. She tiptoed around to the other

510 • GABRIELLE LORD

window and checked the southern side. Again, nothing. Just the blurred shapes of neglected, waterfilled boats near the higher ground, the pale railing along the path and the dark bush reaching up to the road. If the killer had pinpointed her by way of her mobile, he could be cruising the road above, trying to fine-tune her location, waiting for her to use the mobile again to call for help.

'Come on, Hugo,' she said. 'We're moving camp.'

She tucked the Glock into her belt. So much for your fancy Bianchi holster, Angie, she thought. She snatched up the box of matches she used to light the gas rings, wishing she'd brought the torch, and unbolted the double doors. She could feel the Ratbag close behind her.

'The faster we're out of here,' she said to him, 'the better. Okay?'

'Okay.'

She could feel his body keeping close, and couldn't tell who was trembling more.

'Ready?'

He nodded.

Gemma flung open one of the doors, stepped out and started running.

'Come on, Hugo,' she hissed, grabbing his hand as they sprinted along the sand.

They were halfway to the surf lifesaving building when they heard a splintering sound and she swung around, trying to pinpoint the source of the noise in the darkness. Had someone trodden on a rotten board on one of the old boats? She pushed the Ratbag down next to an overturned aluminium dinghy, dropping down beside him.

'Stay there!' she whispered. 'Whatever you do, don't move until I tell you. I have to know where you are at all times. Otherwise you might end up getting shot.' She paused, listening. 'Do you understand?'

'Yes.' His voice barely audible.

She drew the Glock out of her belt. I'm ready for you, you bastard, she thought. You don't know about this nice little piece of plastic in my hand. The stink of petrol was strong here away from the wind and the silence seemed deeper, apart from the hum of the surf on the rocks. Maybe the splintering sound had simply been a piece of rotting timber falling away. Gemma raised her head. All was dark and quiet on Phoenix Bay. She tugged Hugo up and hurried across the sand, lit by the fading moon, the Glock in one hand and Hugo's hand in the other. I've overreacted, she thought. There's no way he could've pinpointed me in that time. Even so, she decided, I'll give my place a wide berth until he's safely locked up.

They had almost reached the old surf club building. Gemma could see the moon shining on its broken windows. 'Nearly there, Hugo,' she said, jollying him along.

And then the shadow struck. Out of nowhere, jumping down from the ramp of the surf club from some dark lair, something pounced and Hugo screamed as he was snatched from Gemma's grasp. Gemma's uncomprehending eyes saw that a powerful man now had Hugo viciously around the neck, a knife blade to the boy's throat. As his arm moved, the slashed jacket he was wearing danced like the strands of a hula skirt.

'Throw the gun down,' he snarled.

Hugo struggled briefly then went limp. God, Gemma thought. He's died of fright.

'*Do it!*' Roger Hollis ordered. It was the weird voice, harsh and whispery. In the dim moonlight, Gemma could see the point of the blade pressing hard into Hugo's soft skin and a thin black stream start to make its way down his neck.

'Okay, okay,' she said, not daring to take her eyes off him, throwing the Glock as far as she could away from him. She heard the splash as it hit the shallows. Hollis's face was in darkness, but there was no mistaking the hatred in his voice. With a shivering thrill, Gemma suddenly recognised the landscape of her nightmare, the waning moon lighting the water. But this was no sacred lake on Delos. Hollis scrambled sideways towards the water's edge and the weapon, dragging Hugo with him. The boy was crying, softly and hopelessly. You bastard, Gemma thought, her eyes filling with tears of rage. She felt the red surge of anger move up from the base of her spine, firing ideas in her brain. I could tackle him while he's trying to get the gun, drag Hugo away, maybe disarm him. Hollis continued to back towards the shallows, dragging Hugo with him. But a slight turn of his head as he sought for the dark shadow of the Glock provided Gemma's chance. She dived, flying at the man, knocking him off-balance, wrenching Hugo away. Now she was running as fast as she could towards the surf club, but Hugo was a handicap. She gave him a mighty shove.

'Get up to the path!' she screamed, pushing him towards the dark shape of the building. 'We have to split up! Get help! Hurry!'

Behind them, Hollis roared. 'Stop right there, or I shoot the boy.'

Gemma stopped. She saw Hugo scramble to climb up the old surf club's cement rampart, slip and fall.

'Both of you,' he yelled. 'Neither of you move.'

Gemma turned to face him. Her enemy was now close to them, the Glock secure in his hand.

'Okay, Miss Private Investigator,' Hollis whispered. 'Climb up there.' He indicated the cement edge of the rampart that had foiled Hugo's flight a few seconds ago. 'We're all going to walk nice and quietly up to my car. To a more private location.' He dragged Hugo to his feet, pulling him roughly to him. 'Do it now, or I snap the kid's neck.'

Gemma considered her chances but a cry from Hugo caused her to wince and move to obey.

Roger Hollis, still clutching Hugo, backed over to the rampart. He laughed and it was a horrible sound. 'Up there now,' he ordered. He indicated behind him and Gemma placed her hands on the edge, about to pull herself up, her mind whirling as she searched for a way out of this nightmare.

So that when another figure materialised out of

the darkness of the club's shadows, flew through the air and landed on Hollis's back, bringing him face-down in a head-high tackle, Gemma threw herself on the downed man with a yell of triumph, kicking the Glock from his hand.

'Get the kid away!' a woman's voice screamed close beside her. Whoever it was had shoved Hollis's face into the sand and twisted his arm behind him in a wristlock.

Gemma dragged the Ratbag out from under the killer. She recognised the woman sitting on top of Hollis. It was Brenda, Robyn Warburton's mother, intent on using all her strength to restrain Hollis who was squirming like a snake, getting purchase on the sand, trying to lift his body and throw her off.

Gemma crawled around, searching for the Glock, lost somewhere in the sand.

'Help me, Hugo!' she called and he started ducking down between the old dinghies, feeling around in the sand for the gun while Gemma ran back to help Brenda.

Roger Hollis was very strong. Even with the two of them, he was putting up a terrific fight. Gemma, still handicapped by the injuries he'd inflicted on her in the lane, and Brenda, although extremely strong for a woman, was no match for him. The three of them rolled towards the beached launch, kicking and struggling. Hollis was getting the better of them. He broke free from the armlock Brenda had applied with a vicious twisting punch.

Brenda's head jerked back and he jumped to his feet.

Then the world exploded. Gemma turned to see what had happened. To the sound of the echoing shot, blue-gold flames shot up near her, and she scrambled further away. What was happening? A wall of fire sprang up, obscuring the beached launch.

'Hugo!' she screamed. 'Where are you?'

She stared in disbelief. Hugo, limping towards her, was silhouetted against the flames, the Glock held out in both hands. Hollis had regained his feet but Brenda, hurling herself onto him again, blocked him. Again, he punched her aside and jumped into the sea on a running dive.

'He's getting away!' Brenda screamed.

But Gemma's attention was no longer on him. She realised what had happened. The 9 mm bullet the Ratbag had intended for Hollis had instead struck the fuel-tank of the large launch, its sparks igniting a river of flame that ran from the fresh-water channel and into the surf, while along the shoreline, the fuel that had been leaking for days blazed into fire.

'God, Hugo,' Gemma said, 'give me that!'

By the light of flames, Gemma saw his strained, unhappy face. She turned to see Brenda who was leaning against the cement wall near the surf club, head down.

'Brenda, are you all right?' she called.

Brenda lifted her head. 'My nose is bleeding,' she said. 'And the bastard got away.'

'I meant to get him,' said the Ratbag.

'Come here,' Gemma said, taking the Glock from him, tucking it away and putting her arms around the boy. 'You were fantastic,' she said. 'You saved the day, Hugo. You and Brenda.' The pain in her side seared.

'How come the water is on fire?' he asked, sheepish about the hugging.

Gemma let him go and the two of them strained to see Hollis. It wasn't possible past the glare of the flames, now burning down.

'Hell,' Gemma said. 'The whole launch is going to go up. Quick.'

She grabbed the Ratbag's hand and dragged him over to where Brenda was now sitting on the rocks near the cement wall. As Gemma approached, she saw a sports jacket lying in the sand. She picked it up and saw that it had been slashed to ribbons. That's all they'll need at the Analytical Laboratory, Gemma thought. That and the DNA on it.

'He's out there now,' Brenda said, pointing towards the gap in the wall of fire. Gemma looked out in amazement. The Phoenix Bay rip had drawn the fire into itself, and as the wall of flame died down along the shoreline, a brilliant curve of fire, twice as long as the beach itself, followed the semi-circular current as it ran out to sea.

'Look!' she said to the others. 'The rip is on fire!'

She thought she could just make out Hollis's dark head, speeding out to sea, carried further and further away as they watched. To avoid the spurting fire, Hollis had swum into the clutches of the rip. The three of them stood mesmerised.

Gemma limped over to Brenda, her arm still around Hugo. 'Thanks, Brenda,' she said. 'You and Hugo saved my life.'

Brenda took a handkerchief away from her bloody nose, and shook her hair off her tanned face.

'I told you,' she said. 'I'd do anything to get him. I knew he'd come after you again because he couldn't bear the idea you'd got away. I just stayed close to you. I used to live around here,' she added, looking around at the few houses above the road. 'I've still got friends here.'

The big launch exploded in a shower of flaming debris. They could feel the heat of it even here, at the other end of the beach, Gemma's little boatshed silhouetted against the roaring blaze.

Now, they could hear the sound of sirens. The two women and the boy walked up to meet them.

TWENTY-TWO

Next morning, Gemma woke the Ratbag with a cup of hot chocolate. Now they sat at the big dining room table looking out at the sea, rugged up against the early cold, the smell of dead fire heavy in the air. A light sou'westerly chopped the sea in low running diagonal ridges. She wondered if Roger Hollis's body would ever be found, washed up somewhere on the coast.

She examined her injured side in the mirror in her bedroom. The bruising was fading, losing its edges. She searched for another warmer top and as she was about to close the drawer, the gleam of gold caught her eye. It was the Scorpio charm. She picked it up and looked more closely at it. It seemed even uglier now, a gaudy lump of gold. The phone rang and Gemma answered it, still holding the charm. After a brief conversation she turned to the Ratbag who was sitting up on the lounge, slurping his drink.

'Hugo,' she said. 'My friend Angie has contacted

your father and he's going to pick you up this morning.'

The boy looked frantic.

'It's okay,' she said, putting a hand on his arm. 'I've explained everything to Angie and she's already told your father what happened. I'm going to recommend you for a bravery award.'

'Me?' he said, blinking.

'You,' she said. 'You made all the difference last night. How about pizza for breakfast?' She rang and ordered one.

He was resigned to going back to Melbourne, Gemma knew. Although he wasn't doing handstands about it. She made herself coffee and by the time it was ready, the pizza arrived. Gemma took a wedge out for herself and handed the Ratbag the rest of it. They went back to the dining table and Taxi perched like a vulture on the sideboard, hopeful of a taste.

'I want you to know, Hugo, that you can come up and spend holidays here with me. I'd like to have a friend like you. We could go to the pictures, maybe do some rock climbing. You could ask those friends of yours over, the ones you liked at school here.'

He nodded over a mouthful, looking cheerier.

'Look, Hugo,' she said, 'it won't be long before you'll be leaving school. Who knows, you might even get a job with me.' If I'm ever back in business again, she thought.

His eyes widened. 'That would be heaps cool.'

Her phone rang again and she picked it up. 'Yes?'

'I'm allowed out tomorrow afternoon. I said you'd pick me up. Will you?'

'Steve,' she said with all her heart, 'I will always pick you up.'

She cleared away and tidied the kitchen. I nearly died last night, she thought. An immense gratitude filled her heart. Okay, she admitted to herself. I've got a few business problems. But I'm alive and Steve's coming home.

While Hugo sat swivelling on a chair in her office, she pulled the bills off the spike and smoothed them out. It was time to face the music. She started calculating her expenses and her financial position didn't look promising.

'What about the singing man,' the Ratbag said, interrupting her thoughts. 'What if he comes back?' He touched his throat where she'd put a strip of plaster over the cut from Hollis's knife.

'I doubt if the singing man will come back again,' she said. 'There'll be a search for a while. Maybe he'll wash up somewhere.'

'Why would people look for a man like him?' asked the boy.

Gemma put a few cheques in an envelope to be banked. It was a good question.

'Because,' she said, 'he's a human being no matter what he's done. And some of us believe that human beings are valuable, even if he doesn't think so.'

She was folding the cheque Minkie Montreau

had given her to tuck into the banking envelope, when she noticed something. She looked closer.

'Holy shit!' she said.

'What?' said the Ratbag, delighted at her language.

She stared at the cheque. I was so preoccupied with everything, she realised, that I didn't notice the placement of the comma! A grateful Minkie Montreau had written a cheque for $100,000. Her heart lifted with more gratitude and relief. It was only a trifle for someone who'd be as rich as she was now, Gemma thought, but very few people would act with such generosity. Now she had plenty: enough to go away with Steve for a while. Enough to establish a new company name and, with a bit of luck, enough to put Mike and Spinner back on the payroll again. I'll call the business Phoenix, she thought, after the street I live in and the bird who rises out of the ashes. Maybe there would even be enough for a trip to Delos with Kit to look at those lions and the sacred lake.

'What's that gold thing?' The Ratbag pointed to the chained scorpion, now lying on the table near the window.

'It's a zodiac charm,' she said.

'Do you believe in that?'

Gemma shook her head. 'I'm going to take it down to the beach and chuck it into the ocean,' she said.

'Maybe a fish will swallow it and someone on the other side of the world will catch the fish and find it,' he said.

'Maybe someone will.'

'Why don't you want it?'

'A lot of reasons,' she said, smiling at the boy, spinning round on her swivel chair.

'Hugo,' she added, 'what would you say about me shouting you and your Dad lunch today before you leave?'

She went to the sliding doors and opened them. The stench of wet charred timber was stronger outside. Later in the day, she would go down to the beach, throw the gold charm into the sea as an offering, for her life, for Shelly, for Steve, for her family, for everything good and growing. Then she could work on her lions again, free from all other pressures. It was a clear winter day, dark blue water, light blue sky. She noticed the long jasmine buds swelling in maroon clusters on the deck railing. Spring would be here in a few weeks. In this expanding moment, all things seemed possible to her. She stood there, taking it all in, the quiet joys of her life, and the small white horses rising and vanishing in turn on the sea as the sun shone on a redeemed world.

Following is an extract from Gabrielle Lord's
new book *Lethal Factor*

CHAPTER ONE

I could hear my own breathing, sounding like the surf against the rocks at Malabar, as the cartridge respirator kept me safe from any external contamination. Behind the clear mask that protected my eyes and face, and a little awkward in the space suit, I manoeuvred as delicately as I could. It's something like dry-land diving, and in my world, there are just as many reefs and sharks to outmanoeuvre.

Outside the house I was searching, the HAZCHEM boys from the Fire Brigade were champing at the bit, wanting to get in here with their solvents and their powerful sterilising equipment. But the Fire Brigade would just have to wait a little longer while I searched and recorded everything in the dead man's house. As a senior analyst with Criminalistics at Forensic Services of the Australian Federal Police, and one-time New South Wales police crime scene examiner, I take precedence. Especially with this sort of death.

I'd been called out early this morning, away from a couple of days of hard-earned leave and I knew my daughter Jacinta would take a dim view of this if she woke up while I was away. We'd been planning a walk around the coast and brunch at Maroubra. Instead, I was searching a dead man's house.

Dr Tony Bonning's analytical laboratory had been similarly searched and found to be completely clean. Accident had been ruled out and suicide was most unlikely, given that Dr Bonning had just been promoted and was looking forward to a working holiday in Scotland. And who, except the floridly insane, would use such a means to end his life? I even knew the man slightly.

Tony Bonning wasn't a friend, but he was a colleague, because in our game eventually you get to know the names and faces of just about everyone in similar and related fields. Over the years, I'd bumped into everyone connected with forensic science at various functions and conferences. Tony Bonning was a nice fellow with whom I'd chatted on those sorts of occasions, but nothing more. Until now. It felt odd, to be searching his house now. His special area had been in the chemistry of toxins and he had sometimes given evidence as an expert witness.

Behind me, I was aware of our young trainee, Vic Agnew, lent to me by the Federal Police for a training course. Similarly kitted out, Vic followed, filming my every move with his video camera. Occasionally I said something for the recording if I felt it was important, even though I knew the sound quality would be very poor because of the breathing apparatus. Vic also passed a rare comment, but mostly we worked quietly, focused and attentive to the surroundings.

Part of a crime scene examiner's job is to cover the scene of the crime so thoroughly that it can be presented to the judge and jury as if they had seen it for themselves. Usually, the police do this, but because of the nature of Tony Bonning's death, and the possible danger lurking in his home, I was carrying out these procedures.

The other aspect of crime scene examination involves finding, collecting and recording evidence. Already we had searched every room, a visual search first without touching or disturbing anything, recording in a methodical way, so that nothing was left unnoted, marking the door to each room as we left it, to show any following police officers what we'd covered. 'Every contact leaves a trace' taught the great nineteenth-century French criminologist and scientist Edmund Locard. In the normal run of homicides, I would expect the killer's presence to be betrayed by some sort of trace. But this killer had not needed to visit this house in person. Instead, he had sent a gift-wrapped emissary on his behalf, a silent, deadly and agonising assassin.

Because the autopsy results were public, and I already knew what had killed scientist Dr Bonning, and how, I was concentrating my efforts on food and drink items, taking wipe samples from everywhere, sealing them in sterile containers, detailing their origin. So far, the kitchen had been most disappointing, with the refrigerator almost empty apart from a block of cheese, some shrivelled bacon and bottles of wine and beer, still sealed.

The freezer was empty of food, almost filled by a glacier that could have been formed during the Ice Age. Nothing there excited my interest. Or suspicion. But I'd taken particular interest in the small kitchen bin, and would check the samples I'd taken very thoroughly, firstly in one of the brilliantly lit examination rooms at my workplace, then under the high-powered light microscope.

Now there was only the dead man's bedroom to search and I paused at the doorway a moment, letting the scene talk to me, just like I used to do in the old days, to tell me something of the individual who until a few days ago had slept there. You can tell a lot about a person from how he lives and what he has around him. This was a well-furnished bedroom, a masculine space, untidy but not dirty. Messy, but not chaotic.

Now, at the doorway to Dr Bonning's bedroom, I imagined him waking on the last morning of his life. Outside, the sudden laughing of kookaburras startled me, incongruous in this place. Did the kookaburras laugh for him that last morning? The unmade bed still showed where Bonning had flung the doona aside on rising. Against the wall on the left-hand side of the doorway was a tall chest of drawers with a mirror on top. Was he already feeling the first effects of the disease when he looked in the mirror? Did he feel something that he thought was just indigestion and decide to tough it out and go to work anyway? From all reports he loved his job.

It was on the floor near the closed window that I gained a poignant insight into the dead man's character. Over the small wastepaper bin, like a halo against the wall, was a novelty basketball goal ring, complete with net. The kookaburras' laughter reached hysterical heights then all at once stopped and I imagined them flying away with a flash of blue.

I went into the room and Vic came up behind me. Again we started the systematic search and recording left to right, floor to waist. Finally, I approached the wastepaper bin, noticing a couple of screwed up balls of foil in it among the other bits and pieces. My suspicious mind immediately thought of illegal substances in foil wrappings, but closer inspection revealed them to be sweet or chocolate wrappers. I imagined Bonning lying on his bed, perhaps reading a journal, eating sweets, exercising his basketball skills, throwing the screwed-up wrappings into his bin from the bed. One, a half crushed ball of red silver foil, excited my interest. It was much larger than the others and I felt a sweat of excitement, thinking of what my old partner Bob Edwards had told me.

'Tony wondered when he got it, if he had a secret admirer,' Bob had said.

Someone was thinking of him, all right. But not an admirer. And he got it all right.

Aware of my protective gear, I knelt down beside the bin, Vic close behind, panning slowly around the area, establishing location, shooting the bin and its surrounds. I used a pair of medical tweezers to pick up the foil wrapping and place it on a clean sheet of white paper. Again, I held my breath with excitement, teasing it open a little. My excitement increased. This could be the wrapping paper I was looking for because, squashed as it was, I could still make out the impression of a curving shape embossed along one side. I took a powerful hand-glass out of my box of tricks, checking for any powdery residue.

A human egg is about one hundred micrometres in size and can just be discerned by the naked eye. What I was searching for was no more than one or two micrometres. What I was looking for was not visible. Not even with a powerful magnifying glass—but the medium surrounding it might be.

I moved out of the way so that Vic could record the screwed-up piece of red foil on the paper, its dimensions, colour and the fact that I was carefully transferring it to a container, then tightly sealing and labelling it.

If I was holding death in my hands, I intended to keep it well secured. I gave Vic the thumbs up and he came in close, recording the sealed container, my signature and the date, following me as I placed it in another larger outer container, prior to transferring it to the lab. I remembered to breathe again, protected by my respirator.

My plan was for Vic to take this straight down to my place of work, Forensic Services in Canberra, for examination. There's been a renaissance in microscopy in the last few years and I would take full advantage of this with a closer look at whatever might be found on the surprise gift wrapper.

It took nearly three-quarters of an hour before I was ready to go, hosed and sprayed and decontaminated by the HAZCHEM boys until they were satisfied that I was thoroughly sterilised. I looked around to see if the kookaburras had returned, but they'd missed their chance to laugh at me. Instead, the firies made their usual bad jokes as they worked me over. I put on my own clothes in the cramped quarters of the mobile police station, set up at the outer perimeter of the crime scene. Was this a one-off, I wondered, or were we in for more, as in the USA?

I saw the senior detective on the case, stooped Gavin Wales, his thinning hair stretched across his pate, having a cigarette out on the street and I remembered him from the briefing we'd had with other agencies after Tony Bonning's death.

'Get anything Jack?' he asked me, throwing the fag end onto the grass and crushing it.

Smokers. They use the world as their ashtray. I used to do exactly the same for years.

'I can't say until I examine it,' I said. 'I'll let you know if I find something.'

'Just keep me up to speed if you can. We've never had anything like this to deal with before.' He paused. 'That postal worker's just hanging on, the doctors say. The world's a bloody different place, mate, to how it used to be. But I'm not surprised. I've been waiting for something like this.'

'Like what?'

'We're in the front-line now. A terrorist attack.'

'It's far too early to be making that sort of assumption,' I told him. 'All we can be certain about is that it was an intentional contamination.' But I could see that his mind was made up.

I thought of the postal worker, Natalie Haynes, a young mother, who'd had the ill fortune to be in the wrong place at the wrong time, in a mail sorting section, doing what humans do all the time as she worked, breathing. Her place of work had tested positive. And despite thorough decontamination, the general public, including postal workers, was feeling nervous. And understandably so.

'I'll need tissue samples,' I told the detective, 'from the autopsy of Tony Bonning. Who did the autopsy? Was it Bradley Strachan?'

The detective nodded. 'I know Strawney well,' he said. 'I can send someone down with samples for you if you ring and ask for them.'

I nodded.